Sleepwalking with Ruby

THE MYSTERY OF THE THREE GEMS, BOOK TWO
A TWIN SPRINGS TRILOGY

DEE ARMSTRONG

SLEEPWALKING WITH RUBY
A Twin Springs Trilogy
The Mystery of the Three Gems

By Dee Armstrong

Published by: Big Dipper Publishing
Copyright © 2018 by Dee Armstrong, LLC
Cover design by Fiona Jayde Media
Author Photographs: Katie Lewis Photography
Print Edition ISBN-13: 978-1-949551-08-2

Dedicated to my mother, Sherlene,
who opened up a world of imagination for a little girl
by sharing her Nancy Drew books.

Part One

CHAPTER ONE

*2*8 September, 1928

Year after year, I watch the all mighty General preen before his public and those adoring sops that make an annual pilgrimage to Twin Springs just to bask in his glory. He wears the invisible uniform of widower proudly across his chest and the brainless women melt around him, for him. He holds everything that a man desires within his palm. Women, presence, recognition, power, family and wealth. Much more than he deserves. Much more than any man deserves. Anyone, except me.

I followed the General from the Great War to the backwoods of the Blue Ridge Mountains. Even after he left me behind for the mission that granted him so much glory. After my service, he turned away in distaste at the prospect of making me a partner and gave me kitchen servants to command. He thought that would put me in my place. Perhaps even placate me. His strategic move gave me my first advantage. It was in the kitchens that I discovered the secret passageway to the tunnels.

Within the cavern and tunnels under Twin Springs, I've created the greatest empire known to man. Bootlegging liquor is my own little pot of gold. Money is the answer, the great equalizer. No matter your birthright, if you have enough cash then Kings and Generals will bow down to you. Running moonshine is better than Greenbacks and I'm well on my way to becoming the next Rockefeller from selling it to the thirsty masses in D.C. and Richmond.

Next, I'll begin syphoning off the General's money, one mishap at a time. Once he hits rock bottom, I'll break him by seizing his most priceless possessions; Twin Springs and his three daughters, his Gems. With a little tutelage, Emma will become a proper wife. And Ruby, with her thick black hair, luscious body and sultry voice, I've decided to let her live. How I lust for her when she sings. I'll keep her high in Twin Springs' tower, my own little song bird. As for their older sister, Amethyst, I'm still going to kill her and her unborn babe. I have no choice, the powerful must rule.

Lt. Porter

CHAPTER TWO

PROLOGUE

"If Mommy's now an angel, do you think she's watching us?" Izzy mumbled the question around the thumb that she refused to remove from her mouth.

Ava Fairbanks wanted to pretend she didn't hear her sister. Her chest ached when they talked about Mom. But Izzy was only six and it was her job to take care of her. After all, she was a full two years older. Unsure what to say, she entwined her fingers between her sister's and squeezed. "Look up."

Both girls lay beneath the enormous Christmas tree that stood tall and proud in the middle of Twin Springs' Grand Lobby, the sprawling hotel their family owned and lived in. Boxes wrapped in bright holiday paper guarded the edges, keeping them safe inside their own little world. A few late night guests walked by chattering, utterly unaware of the hiding, PJ clad little girls.

The scent of freshly cut pine tickled Ava's nose, she breathed in deeply and pointed up to where hundreds of little white lights twinkled within the branches. "I think, that when our family goes to heaven, it's their job to watch over us." Quickly, she wiped away the tear that slipped from the corner of her eye. "Just like those lights shining down on us."

Izzy sucked hard on her thumb, her brows furrowed. She rubbed the seam of her pink flannel pajamas between her fingers like it was a blanket. "Do you think they'll tattle on us for playing here?" Her words sounded even more child-like around her thumb.

Ava's laughter flowed up through the branches and lit up their secluded world with its magical sound. "Naw, they have more important things to do."

Her little sister snuggled closer to her side and she wrapped her arms around her and stared up at the lights. "I wish one was Mommy, then we could talk to her anytime we wanted," she whispered. She picked out the brightest light, tucked high up in the branches and pretended it was her mother watching over them. Ava's lids grew heavy and the combination of her sister's warm body and the grand piano playing softly in the background lulled her into a helpless sleep.

A silver mist weaved a path down through the branches and hesitated over Izzy. Deep in sleep, her lashes lay upon her milky white skin and her long, blonde hair covered her shoulders like a thick blanket. Izzy's thumb sucking sounds were barely discernible within the late night quiet of the lobby. The haze encircled the little girl's arm and tugged until her thumb burst out of her mouth with a pop.

Moving on to Ava, the mist hovered over the length of her body and smoothed the wrinkles in her blue PJ's, covered with little white clouds. Raising and lowering in tune with her breathing, it reached out and swept her long, black hair away from her sleep, softened face. Leisurely, it lowered and melded with the slumbering girl.

. . .

Moving with a grace well above her tender age, Ava stepped onto the wooden stage of Twin Springs' Theatre. The clouds on her pajamas glowed brightly under the floodlights. She flipped her long hair over her shoulder and shook her head allowing it to flow down her back and shimmer under the sidelights' muted glow. Her body swayed in time with a tune playing in her head. From under her lashes, she stared sightlessly upon the empty seats of her audience and a low, jazz song flowed from her lips.

From the depths of her young soul, she belted out a tune of sadness, love and loss. Her juvenile frame rolled with the highs and lows of the melody until the crescendo where she flung her arms out, tipped her head back and hit a high note.

Angels wept when the magnificent clarity of the sound touched heaven.

Lowering her chin, Ava's eyes cleared and her arms dropped limply to her sides. Startled, she blinked and glanced around. The stage lights blinded her and she raised her arms to block the glare. "How?"

At the edge of the stage, her father and Izzy stared up. Her little sister's green eyes were huge in her face and her soggy thumb hung out of her slack mouth. Their father studied her through wet eyes. His normally tall, strong form was buckled as he held back emotions. Tears ran unchecked down his cheeks and dripped off his jawline. Sucking in a deep breath, he rubbed his hands over his face and wiped away the moisture.

Unsure of what had just happened, Ava's chin trembled and she swallowed hard. "Daddy?"

Silence stretched between them and a deep fear crept into her heart.

"I—." His eyes met hers and he scraped his fingers through his bright russet hair, searching for words. "I don't know where you heard that song, but you have a gift. A beautiful, one of a kind gift."

Relief flooded her thin frame. Everything would be alright. She had no idea how she'd ended up on the stage or knew the words to the song that she'd just sung. All she remembered was the heady scent of roses, golden eyes, and a desire so deep to sing again that it rocked her soul.

CHAPTER THREE

Sergeant First Class Jaxon Wolfe pushed his night vision goggles up onto his helmet, leaned into his sniper rifle and adjusted the thermal scope. Through the vision of the special scope, the darkened city below transformed from the night visions goggles' shades of grays and greens into a brilliant palette of oranges, yellows, purples and blacks. Zero white. White meant the shit was hitting the fan. Indicated fire.

He panned up and down the street, checking for heat signatures before zeroing in on the squatty, flat roofed, two-story building that his team had just entered. Things were quiet, just like he liked it.

Time ticked in his head and he checked the horizon. They were inching up on morning prayers, where the whole city would come alive with loudspeakers broadcasting the call to kneel. His Special Forces teammate crouched down at the door, rifle ready, protecting the back of their team inside. As a result of his thermal scope, Jaxon's view of Woody was just an orange outline with shades of bright yellow along the hottest points of his body. The sandy ground below his feet was a brilliant shade of purple and the building at his back a combination of muted tangerine walls and purple uprights.

Through one of the windows, he spotted his team's orange bodies filtering by, one after the other, in a silent dance. Tagging each other as they infiltrated the building searching for Tango one and Tango two. Get in, grab the bad guys, alive, if possible, sweep up any intel, and come home alive. That was the mission.

They were lucky for the intel. Not often did a member of the press give up information and expect nothing in return. His mind shifted to the gorgeous, tall blonde, who'd given them not only the names of the terrorists but the location and best time to hit the target. If he hadn't seen Doc pull his shoulder on the last drop, he would've thought he'd stayed behind just to cozy up to her.

The team paused before another window on the second floor and Jaxon frowned. "Bad spot," he murmured. "Keep moving, stay out of the kill zone." He suppressed the urge to break radio silence and tell them to move ass. They understood their jobs.

Below him, Woody's orange form moved. He stood and checked his wrist.

"Steady," Jaxon whispered, knowing full well his teammate couldn't hear him unless he clicked his mic on.

"Sixty seconds till exfil," Woody murmured into his throat mic.

"Damn it," grumbled Jaxon, annoyed with the break in protocol. Woody was such a surfer boy, all golden blonde, smiles and lots of action with the girls. "Thank God, my sister refused to date another guy from my team."

Adopted or not, JD was Jaxon's sister. Her childhood had been rough, jerked from orphanage to orphanage, her mother dead and never having known her father. He'd be damned if one of his teammates would jerk her feelings around too. Not even the good-hearted surfer boy, Woody. His heart picked up a beat when Woody's orange form checked the target pack on his wrist. If he didn't pull his shit together, they'd need to switch his nickname to surfer girl.

Woody's yellow head scanned the area around him and Jaxon shifted his position as an uneasy feeling joined the sweat beads rolling down his back. His instincts screamed. "Shit."

The orange blobs of his team mates scattered from the window and his headset went crazy. The team sounded off, breaking up and chopping each other's sentences into indiscernible nonsense. Woody jerked the door open to join the fight when the code word "Avalanche," was shouted. BOMB.

The floor under Jaxon's feet trembled and shades of white with black edges spread across the building's walls, casting out the oranges and purples with the heat of fire. Woody's orange form was dragged into the doorway, only to be expelled in a ball of bright white. One by one, his team stumbled from the building, their once orange forms consumed in a white haze, edged in black. Their screams pierced the desert air.

Men spilled from the surrounding buildings, flashes of white expelled from the barrels of their guns, peppering his team's burning forms with bullets. Automatically, Jaxon fired, taking out target after target as his team dropped, one after another, and rolled until they laid in white heaps on the purple ground. From the edges of his sight, their forms cooled from white to black, even as he killed the men running towards them. He took out eight more men. "Shit, there are too many of them."

Jaxon activated his Command Net by squeezing the pressel on the fore grip of his rifle. "Request Kinetic Strike on target," he shouted, as he dropped five more bad guys. "In thirty seconds."

Making a choice he'd forever doubt, Jaxon jerked down his night vision goggles, abandoned his perch, and thundered down the staircase. "Double time it, damn it. Your team needs you."

In the time it took him to get street side, only one team member remained alive. He sprinted across the street, his footfalls muted by death screams. The ground was hazy with smoke and the stench of burning flesh permeated the air.

His right side on fire, Woody gained his feet and staggered forward. Quickly, Jaxon took out two more men before he reached his friend. He rolled Woody in the dirt to extinguish the flames and a bullet pierced his thigh but Jaxon didn't even notice the sting, his adrenaline was running so hot. Grabbing Woody with by the collar with one hand, firing from the hip with his rifle, he pulled him to safety. Behind them, the Predator drone dropped fire, as the desert sun rose and the speakers spouted morning prayers.

CHAPTER FOUR

$\mathscr{A}$cres of rolling, emerald green hills were dotted with white gravestones, each denoting a fallen soldier. All equal in death, their wars blurred together, creating waves of white that expanded as far as the eye could see. Arlington National Cemetery, where America's heroes were laid to rest.

Each team of six horses pulled a fallen comrade, forming a long train of flag covered caskets, bringing not one, but eight soldiers to their final resting place. Their hooves clopped against the pavement, amid the suppressed sniffles of their loved ones, seated in rows before open graves.

Jaxon glanced over to where Woody stood rigid under a tree in his Army Service uniform. Just like all the soldiers present, his dark blue pants with their thick yellow stripe were bloused into the tops of his combat boots. On his black jacket, his medals gleamed in the morning sun. A green beret skimmed the top of his head and folded over towards his right ear.

That was where the similarities ended. The tree struggled to shade Woody's razed skin. Beneath his beret, a part of him still resembled the surfer boy the team had joked about but the other half was shriveled into a horrific mask of pain. Florid, biting scars enveloped the right side of his face and ate a path that flowed like molten lava down his neck and disappeared under his collar. More scars tacked the corner of his right eye into a half closed position. Only three fingers remained on his right hand and his right ear had melted into his head.

Failure roiled in Jaxon's gut, coating the lining with a black sickness. His disgust with himself was so great that he thought he might throw up and he adverted his eyes to the back to the crowd. If he hadn't trusted his shit instincts and believed the intel was prime, then his brother-in-arms wouldn't have been marked for life.

He spied the Geezers in the back row and groaned. Family. Always there, whether you wanted them or not. Out of respect, his father wore his stark Navy whites and Jaxon's uncle wore his Army dress greens. They were present not only for him, but also for the fallen. Once a soldier, always a soldier.

To cover the shame eating him alive, he grumbled under his breath, "Damn it." Now, they were witnesses to the pain and destruction caused by his bad judgment. "Why did they come?"

They glanced up, and the sympathy in their eyes almost brought him to his knees.

He searched the crowd for his adopted sister. Not seeing her, he breathed a sigh of relief and mumbled, "At least JD isn't present to witness the roll call of the dead. My friends. The ones that her worthless piece of shit brother couldn't protect when they needed him the most."

Their Company Commander stood and shouted out from the list of names to account for his men.

"Sergeant Gonzalez."

The call to report was met with dead air.

"Sergeant Jack Jose Gonzalez. Report!"

Pure silence. For one heartbeat. Two. Then a third. Not even the wind dared to answer for the missing as Gonzo's casket was lowered into the ground.

"Warrant Officer McCormick."

Muffled sniffles filled the silence.

"Warrant Officer Rodney Thomas McCormick. Report!"

The silence of the fallen cut away another jagged piece of Jaxon's soul and Roddie's casket also disappeared.

As the names of the dead were called, Jaxon waited for his name, bracing himself, hoping to be strong and not allow his voice to crack. To honor them with what little strength he had left.

"Staff Sergeant Borland."

His widow swayed with grief and her father grasped her around the waist before she collapsed.

"Staff Sergeant Oscar Borland. Report!"

Muted by death, silence coated the air as Stretch's casket descended.

"First Sergeant Wolfe."

"Here Sir!" He called out, his voice gravely but firm.

"Staff Sergeant Fitzgerald."

In the stillness, Fitz's widow did her best to hold back the tears and make her husband proud. Their two small girls stood at her side in their black dresses, with white bobby socks and shiny black patent leather shoes. Their blonde hair was pulled back into ponytails.

"Staff Sergeant Alan Liam Fitzgerald. Report."

Fitz's casket was lowered. His oldest reached up and clutched her mother's hand. Her small voice reached out to Jaxon, "Is that Daddy?"

Her mother's shoulders shook and all she could do was nod.

Jaxon stood tall and stared straight ahead, his jaw rock hard but inside he was crumbling into a heap and pushing back tears.

"Sergeant First Class Landon St. John."

"Here Sir!" The Doc called out from behind.

Jaxon turned. It was then that he noticed the shiny, blonde hair of the reporter. The beautiful bitch who'd given them the intel. She dared to stand among the grieving, right alongside Max's widow when his name was shouted next. Their fingers were laced together. Side by side, they swayed in the breeze like the thin branches of a willow tree. Both draped in black, one woman with shockingly flaming red hair spilling down her back, the other with hair the color of wheat, captured into a low ponytail at the nape of her neck. The reporter's cornflower blue eyes met his and he clenched his teeth to smother the snarl that begged to erupt from his throat.

His blood boiled and his hands flexed. He wanted to rip the traitor to shreds but he had to hold steady. He couldn't further disgrace his brothers by causing a ruckus at their funeral. On the open graves of his comrades, he swore to never trust a woman again. Especially a beautiful, lying bitch like the one before him.

"Sergeant First Class Oakes."

Woody refused to answer. Instead, he turned and limped away.

Bagpipes whined out the bars of Taps and Jaxon stayed until the bitter end. His heart wrenched when the gray smoke from the twenty-one gun salute back-dropped the row of widows clutching folded American flags to their chests. They flinched with each shot.

Like dominoes, one after another, their necks bent and they surrendered to their sorrow, weeping into the red, white and blue cloth. Only one widow refused to break. Max's wife. She stared sightlessly towards the horizon, the tips of her russet hair fluttering in the breeze.

It's my fault their husbands are dead. Their kids are fatherless. His brothers had believed in him. Trusted his damn instincts that the intel was good. *I failed them.*

Once all the other mourners had left, Jaxon placed a shiny, new quarter atop the curve of each headstone. In remembrance. In respect. Special Forces Green Berets, celebrated as the quiet professionals. "How could the country mourn for soldiers they didn't know, on a mission they'd never hear about?"

They're forgotten because of me.

Today, he'd shed his uniform for the last time. Fold up his green beret and shove it in the back of a drawer. He didn't deserve to wear either ever again.

CHAPTER FIVE

For a fleeting moment, Ava Fairbanks thought she was sleepwalking. Again. But even her dreams couldn't conjure the cliché of the man who lounged before her.

If only Director Terrence Hollingsworth realized what a laughable image he presented, draping himself against the proverbial casting couch. His tan pants left nothing to the imagination. In one hand, he brandished a cigar between stained fingers, while the fingertips of his other hand stroked his chest where the overly tanned skin was strategically revealed. As a Broadway star, Ava preferred to live in the dream world of the theatre. But Hollingsworth's office was a living nightmare.

Windowless, the room reeked with smoke. The illumination of a lone lamp and the glowing tip of his cigar hovered around him like a golden sickness.

The air glittered with her mocking laughter and she shook her head at the stage scene he presented. She tilted her head back and stared down at the little man. "Is this how you greet all your actors?"

"*The* AVA," the thick, sticky sap of his voice clung to her. Tainted her. The lamp's light lit up the delight on his thin face and he licked his lips. "Such a big night for you. I understand a movie producer has tucked himself into the back seats."

Her heart ticked up at the news. *Keep it together*, she ordered. *This is your big chance. You hold this production together and let it ride out its run. Don't let some self-important jerk ruin it for you, for everyone.*

"With your green eyes, and," he licked his lips, his stare penetrating, "that luxurious, jet-black hair, you'll go far in this business. That is, if you're the lead for tonight's opening."

Her stomach rolled with revulsion. She crossed her robe tighter over the costume for her first act, a simple cornflower blue, plaid dress with a white bow collar. Out of the corner of her eye, the gleam of a steel desk appeared to be the only safe haven. Refusing to allow him the pleasure of knowing he made her skin crawl, she skirted around his desk and gracefully draped herself in his chair. "Who else would be the lead?"

"Why, your understudy of course."

Her insides shook at the possibility. *Can't let it happen.* She spread her lips into a broad smile and hid her fear behind false bravado. "My understudy couldn't sing her way out of a wet paper sack. She wouldn't do the part of Charity Rae justice. With her as the lead, *The Rise of Rae* would fold and the crew would be out of work."

Leaning forward, Hollingsworth ground his cigar into the smiling face of a 1940s pin up girl that lounged in a tiny sailor suit at the bottom of his glass ashtray. He smacked his thin lips. "She and I came to an agreement just yesterday. It's my decision as the director."

Twisting the many silver rings on her fingers, her body's desperate demand to step out onto the stage built inside her. Like manna from Heaven, performing brought life, healing, and substance to her existence. On stage, reality faded to the background and was replaced by the warmth of bright lights and the heartbeat of the audience. Entrancing the audience with her acting was like sipping from the fountain of youth and she thirsted for one more drink. She couldn't, no wouldn't allow him to steal her dream. "I earned the lead for this production. You can't remove me."

Shaded an unusual color of blue by the contacts he wore, his eyes lowered and his gaze flowed over her body, making her feel cheap and dirty. Keeping his eye on her, he picked up a gold plated lighter from the table before him and clicked it open, closed, open. He snapped it shut, tossed it back on the table, and patted a spot on the couch beside him. "Ava. You and I need to come to an understanding before opening call. Don't you understand? I have final say. I'm the director." His voice descended to a sticky-sweet timbre. "I have all the power."

Across the expanse of his desk, she examined him. Anger bubbled within her, but she masked her emotions beneath a calm façade. She lifted the lid of a mahogany humidor box and selected a cigar at random. Acting as if she didn't have a care in the world, she unwrapped the cellophane wrapper, slid the cigar under her nostrils and inhaled its unique aroma. "Smells like crap. Just like what you're trying to sell me. "

His eyes narrowed and he bit out, "That's an eight hundred dollar cigar."

Picking up a pair of stainless steel cigar cutters, Ava observed how the sharp blades cut though the circular hole when squeezed. She palmed the clippers and rolled the cold metal over and over in her palm. "I'm a million dollar actor. Here to entertain the audience. Not you."

Hollingsworth surged to his feet and barked, "Who the hell do you think you are?" He slapped his palms on the leather blotter of his desk and leaned forward across the expanse. "You have a choice. Join me on the couch or, hell," he rapped the desk with his knuckles, "here on this desk, and you'll open tonight's performance. Otherwise, your understudy will replace you when the curtain goes up."

Her laughter cascaded off the walls of the little room.

Heat inched up his face.

"No man control's my destiny. No man has say over what I do. Not even the mighty Director Terrence Hollingsworth."

She rose and circled the desk until she stood in front of him. "The investors cast me as lead in this production, not you. They cut your check and mine. Besides—." Once again, she slid the cigar through the metal cutter and regarded him through her thick lashes. Her look was bitter cold. "Touch me and this will be your dick." She snipped the cigar in half and the pieces tumbled to the floor. "That should get through to both of your little brains."

She tossed the cutter on the desk and in one fluid movement turned to exit the room.

A rush of air behind her was the only warning.

Hollingsworth slammed into her and pinned her between his long body and the door.

The impact stole the breath from her chest and her forehead bounced off the wooden door. Dazed and unable to think, shock shuddered through her slender frame. Then rage. This was a part she'd never play. But her arms were trapped between her body and the hard door. She struggled to free herself. Fury scalded her cheeks and blood pounded in her ears. She ground out between clenched teeth, "Get off me. Now!"

He pressed his lips against her slender neck. She felt his hot, moist breath as he branded her with small, stinging bites along the unprotected length of her throat, until his lips lingered just above her earlobe. The stench of his cigar breath flowed over her. Slowly, he raised the back of her robe.

Then the hem of the blue dress beneath.

A chill snuck under the layers, followed by a shaking that started in her knees and trembled uncontrollably through her frame. Color washed from her face and an unbearable cold settled into her bones. She bucked but he held her firm, trapped against the door.

He slid his moist palm over her hip and down her flat stomach.

His other hand reached up and squeezed her around the throat, restricting her airway.

Her legs weakened. Fear so primal and primitive descended upon her, dug it's claws into her throat and stole her ability to speak.

His hand slipped into the front of her panties and he pulled hard, ripping them.

Her body jerked to cast him off and horror inked a black path into her heart and pumped it with a fist of terror. Lack of air caused the edges of her sight to darken.

Beneath her cheek, a light rap sounded on the door and a flicker of hope rooted within her frozen heart. She opened her mouth to call out.

But nothing happened.

From the other side of the door, a meek voice barely penetrated the thickness of the wood. "Terrence? Darling, are you in there?"

The Director stiffened and his hold loosened.

Seizing the moment, Ava shoved back with her arms and knocked him backward. She wrenched open the door. Light and fresh air flooded inside.

Whipping around, her mind rebelled and she struggled to cope with what had almost happened. Her breath was heavy and fast in her chest as she looked down at Hollingsworth, who'd landed on his ass.

Slack jawed, he stared past her at the person in the doorway.

Heat surged into her pale cheeks and rage vibrated within her. She swung her slender leg back and kicked him as hard as she could in the balls.

He writhed and rolled on the ground at her feet.

Satisfaction filled Ava and warmed her chilled body. "I'm calling the police and then the investors. One of us will be leaving. It won't be me."

She turned and faced her rescuer but the "thank you" froze on her lips. Ashlee Hollingsworth, the Director's timid wife, had saved her with a simple knock on a door. Her natural, flat, mouse brown hair had been curled and twisted up and now framed the horror on her tiny face.

Behind her stood Roger, the backstage hand. His mouth gaped open before he collected himself and mumbled, "Five minutes Miss Fairbanks. Five minutes 'till curtain call."

For the first time in her life, Ava wished she was sleepwalking and could wake up. But her nightmare had only just begun.

CHAPTER SIX

Director Hollingsworth hardly noticed Ava push past his wife. The look on Ashlee's face had stapled him to the floor. "Just a misunderstanding," he assured her. His laugh sounded stilted and false even in his own ears.

Placing his palm on the edge of his desk, he struggled to stand upright and choked back an agonizing groan. The pain in his crotch throbbed through his whole body and weakened his knees. The young stage hand still hovered in the doorway. Probably, hungry for gossip to use against him. "Get the hell out of here, Roger."

"Yes, sir." His Adam's apple bobbed high above the clipboard that he clutched to his chest, and he rushed away.

His dear, stupid, rich wife was frozen in place. Her pale skin was almost transparent. How he hated her pinched face. He grabbed her up by the arm, hobbled with her over to the couch and shoved her down.

"What—" As she gaped up at him, moisture welled up in her mud brown eyes, overflowed and rolled down her jutting cheeks. "Were you—" She bit at her lip, her rake thin frame jerking with suppressed sobs. "Terrence, were you going to rape her?"

"Don't be an idiot," he barked.

"It can't be true," she buried her face in her hands. "I'm married to a rapist."

His head jerked back as if she'd slapped him. "Hell no!" he shouted. He didn't rape women. He controlled them. Used them. And let them enjoy his attentions. "It was just a misunderstanding."

"A misunderstanding," she repeated. "I saw the awful fear in her eyes."

"No, we were acting out a part for the new spring play. Things got a little rough. She'll get over it." *If she knows what's good for her.* He rubbed at the ache in his crotch.

"And she's going to the police." She pressed her hands against her face and rocked back and forth. "It'll hit the papers. My family will find out. They'll know everything."

If his wife's family sniffed any impropriety, they'd cut him off. Actual panic set in, and he hated them for it. Time to sooth his wife's fears. Convince her to rally their cause with her family. Carefully, he sat beside her, clenching his teeth against the pain. "Nobody's going to the press." He placed his arm around her. "Don't worry, love. If anything reaches your parents, we'll stick together. Assure them nothing happened. I know you'll make this right."

His normally cowering wife, looked up at him and there was something other than fear in her eyes. Revulsion.

"Everyone will know the monster you really are," she scooted away from his touch. "It's all my fault. I should've spoken up before, gone to my father, something. But I thought it was only me." Her breathing hitched into panicked little gasps. "Now you're attacking other women. Because of me. Because I didn't stop you."

He couldn't believe what he was hearing. His wife was gaining a backbone? Contradicting him? Accusing him? Fury hazed his sight and he grabbed her up by the lapels of her rain coat. "Stupid bitch. What the hell do you know about monsters in your perfect, rich world?"

He tossed her back against the couch, fumbled with his belt, and unzipped his pants. "Somehow, you've forgotten who is in charge. Just like Ava." He jerked her dress up and shoved her knees apart. "I would've squashed that misunderstanding with her, if it wasn't for you. You always ruin everything. You're worthless. Only good for this and the money you bring. You're a fat, ugly cow." His harsh laughter flowed over her. "My cash cow."

He leaned forward to rut between her legs but instead of being massive and erect, his penis laid like a flat, dead worm. "The bitch has castrated me!" he roared. Shaking his head in denial, he wiggled and his penis just flopped around, unresponsive. With tender movements, he folded himself back into his pants. "That's it," he snapped. His lips pulled back, displaying perfect teeth. "She's done. Ava's career is over."

Disgusted, he shoved his wife aside and she curled up into a ball, crying into her arms. The bitch, Ava, had ruined everything. He rose up, righted his clothing and walked to the door. The sounds of the opening song reached him. It was too late to switch the lead actors but she'd pay for making him impotent, even though it was temporary. He'd make sure of it. He walked out of the room without a backward glance.

CHAPTER SEVEN

Seated before her gilded dressing room mirror, Ava doubled over and stuffed her long hair into a tight, gray, mesh stocking cap. She attempted to push the memories of more than an hour before out of her mind. More blood pulsed into her overturned head from her sickened heart and an involuntary shiver ran down the length of her spine.

She flipped her head upright. The tools of her trade lay scattered across the glass covered, plywood table. Fake eyelashes, cake makeup, and palette upon palette of shadows. A jumble of bright scarves and clipped newspaper reviews framed the edges of her mirror. Everything faded into the background as she stared into the eyes of a stranger.

Against her will, her mind replayed snippets of the scene with the Director. The stench of cigar. His hot breath. Stinging bites. Helpless. She shook her head. Denied the truth. But it hadn't been a role that she'd played. It had happened to her. Ava. A strong woman who usually wrapped men around her little finger.

Subconsciously, she reached past bottles and trays and selected the perfect foundation for the aging star that she would portray in the final scene. Tonight, she'd lost her naiveté in her own strength and power. She whispered to the victim in the mirror, "If the knock hadn't come when it did…"

Taking a deep breath, she squeezed foundation across a wedged sponge. Until closing call, she'd hide her pain with a woman's tools: makeup, a false smile and fake bravado. She'd wrap the role she played around her like a shield until the memories faded into the background.

Knuckles wrapped sharply against her dressing room door. Involuntarily, she jumped and pressed her trembling fist over the beating heart that threatened to leap out of her chest. "Yes?"

Instead of shouting through the door as he usually did, Roger cracked it open and poked his head inside, gripping his clipboard.

Unable to meet his eyes, she expertly patted the gray blue tinged stage makeup around her slender face. The makeup lay thick and heavy upon her delicate skin but she continued to pat the paste across the hollow of her cheekbones and her tapered jawline. Using the pad of her ring finger, she worked the greasy makeup closer to her normally ice green eyes. Now they were camouflaged with contacts that turned them into two deep blue sapphires. She picked up a thin tipped brush, scrunched her eyes and created the illusion of crows' feet by painting in her laugh lines with a darker foundation.

He stared fixedly at the floor, and finally, he spoke, "Five minutes, Miss Fairbanks."

The parroting of his words from before pierced her shield. A traitorous tear slipped from the corner of her eye and trailed a path through the thick grease. Using her sponge, she blended the tear, hoping to erase the weak wetness and memories that released it from her mind. "Thanks Roger."

She smiled at his reflection in the mirror, but his gaze had zeroed in on her neck and his lips formed a thin line. She smothered a gasp and used foundation to re-cover the red marks of Hollingsworth's teeth on her sensitive skin.

He shuffled further into her dressing room, but couldn't advert his eyes from the wounds. "Miss Fairbanks." He cleared his throat. "Is everything alright?"

"Of course. Don't worry." She cast a bright smile his way and straightened the padding around her midsection that thickened her waist. She rose and withdrew a sparkling black gown from the costume rack. "I'll be ready. The patrons will believe that Charity Rae has aged thirty years in the span of the last two scenes."

"I don't doubt it Miss Fairbanks. Pulling off transformations is your specialty. Second only to your voice." He tapped the brown clipboard against his scrawny chest. "I didn't see what happened but if you need me to," his eyes slid from her's, "I'll tell the police that I did."

Ava paused before stepping into the crystal laden evening dress. His words touched her heart and she wanted to grab him up and cry all over his young shoulders but she held herself firm. "All we need to do is focus on the next scene, play the role at hand and finish the show. The crew depends upon us to keep it together. The audience deserves our very best. If all goes well," she stepped into the dress, "our performances will bring down the house. Then, once the stage lights have cooled," and I've pulled off the most difficult performance of my life, she added to herself as she shed her robe and slipped her arms into the dress, "we'll have the power. Not Director Hollingsworth."

The gown coated her concealed curves and she quickly zipped the shimmering fabric into place. She slipped her feet into the impossibly high, black heels that captured the light reflecting off the dress. "One scene at a time, Roger." Fear gnawed at the lining of her stomach. "Then I'll face the beast again. Not you, me."

Roger nodded and glanced down at his watch. "Three minutes, Miss Fairbanks."

"Roger, Roger." For the first time that night, her twinkling laughter filled the air.

Finally, she donned the final touches of her transformation: a voluminous, platinum blonde wig and chandelier earrings that sparkled almost as brightly as her eyes. With one final examination of her refection, she tipped back her head slightly, softened her eyes into a sexy gaze and ran her palms down over her curvaceous but "delicately" aged body. Fully transformed, she allowed the part to rule her body, mind and voice. She dropped her voice by two octaves and projected it with a husky growl, "Here's looking at you, Charity."

Confidence seeped from her powdered pores. Framed by thick, long lashes, one of her sultry painted eyelids lowered into a mischievous wink towards Roger.

Blinded by the woman before him, the young man blinked rapidly. The words tickling the tip of his tongue rolled back and caught in his throat.

Unabashed, she strolled past him and exited her dressing room. No longer was she a slender woman who'd been almost raped by her boss. Now, she was a seductive superstar whose hip-rolling walk turned every man's head on the way to the stage. She paused in the wings, waited for her cue and entered the stage with the timing of a pro. Once the hot stage lights hit her face, the transformation was complete. She'd become Charity Rae and was no longer a victim.

The stage lit up with her presence. She gloried in the symbiotic rush of the live audience as it fed off her performance. The more the patrons loved her, the more she dug deep and gave back. Until, she'd emptied her soul for their enjoyment.

Gliding across the wooden floor with her male dance partner, they sung the final chorus together. She rolled her hips forward, parted from her fellow actor and moved center stage. Reaching down into the depths of her being, she belted out the crescendo of the melody and finished the high note with her arms spread and her head thrown back. Holding her position, her voice faded into the back of the auditorium and she waited for the audiences' love.

Instead, white silence filled the space. Stunned, her arms fell. She dipped her chin and squinted to see past the bright floor lights. Unable to scan the sea of faces, she slipped back into character and rested her hands on her waist, ready to save the closing scene. Suggestively, she rolled her hips towards the audience and opened her mouth to ad-lib a line.

Out of the corner of her eye, she caught a movement stage left. Turning her head slightly, the quip froze on her lips, for there, appearing out of place in the glare of the lights, stood Mrs. Hollingsworth. The woman who'd saved her with a knock.

Drenched, her brown hair plastered against her skull, Ashlee shook from head to toe in a raven black raincoat. The drip, drop of the water trickling from the hem of her coat and onto the floor was deafening in the silence.

The Director's wife stumbled forward and paused before her. Vast in her bloodless face, her gentle brown gaze searched Ava's features. Her lips moved and she mouthed out soundless words.

Ava leaned in to catch what she was saying but stopped short when the stage lights reflected off the metal of a large pistol that she'd tugged from her pocket.

Her lips still moving, Ashlee's tiny hand shook. She clutched the heavy weapon. Squeezing the handle until her knuckles whitened, she raised the barrel.

The audience gasped.

Ashlee laid the pistol against her own temple and pulled the trigger.

The sound of the shot ricocheted off the cheap seats and rang in Ava's ears. Bright red blood and gray brain matter splattered, muting the sparkles on Ava's evening gown and snuffing out all the light around the two women.

Instinctively, she caught and held Ashlee, watching as her doe eyes glassed over before turning blank and the life left her body. Ava buckled under the weight of the other woman, her feet slipped out from under her and she fell. Ashlee's dead body pinned her to the stage floor.

The world exploded around them. The audience flooded from the theater, while crew members and stage hands rushed to her aide. The flash of cameras blinded her and froze the moment in time for the world to witness in print and online.

Hollingsworth staggered back out of the wings and grasped one of the ropes hanging down from the ceiling props. "She killed her." His hands formed into tight fists. "Ava murdered my little cow. What the hell am I going to do now?" His mind raced and he pounded a fist against his leg. "She's ruined everything."

An idea struck. "She'll become my new cow. Ava Hollingsworth has a nice golden ring to it." He spotted a man with a camera and slid his features into despair, leaned his head against the rope and gave a loud wail of pain. "Ashlee. My little Ashlee. Why?"

CHAPTER EIGHT

Once again wrapped in her silk sarong, Ava slumped in front of her gilded mirror and methodically wiped the thick makeup and blood splatter from her face with tissues. The blonde wig and evening dress were now in the custody of the NYPD. With trembling hands, she removed every vestige of her on stage character until Charity Rae lay in a piled heap on the dressing room table and only Ava Fairbanks remained reflecting back at her. "Why?" She whispered to the woman in the mirror. "Why did Ashlee kill herself?"

Tears escaped and traced lines down her face. Lifting her leaden hands, she wiped them away with shaking fingertips. Her eyes widened in the mirror. Tiny droplets of red blood dotted the back of her hands. A whimper escaped from deep in her throat and her breath came hot and fast. She dipped tissues into the makeup remover and rubbed the white cream across the back of her hands and up her arms. Painstakingly, she scraped with the tissues until only pale, milky skin and freckles remained. "Why?" she chanted. "Why, why?"

Her cell phone buzzed on the table and she glanced at the caller ID. "Thank God! Isabella. Not the press this time."

Breathing a sigh of relief, she croaked her sister's name into the phone, "Izzy."

Her chin trembled. She bit her lip to keep from breaking down into a sobbing mess.

"You've already heard?" Isabella's quiet voice hitched in places.

Ava's forehead creased. Over the phone line, she could tell that her sister had also been crying. "What?"

Isabella didn't miss a beat. "Did Niles call you too? How long will it take you to get to Twin Springs?" She expelled a deep sigh of relief and kept talking into her ear. "I'm so glad I wasn't the one who had to tell you that Daddy passed away."

A roaring filled Ava's ears. "Almost like the roar of a crowded theater," she murmured and slid behind the black curtain and into unconsciousness.

CHAPTER NINE

The tall man emerged from the trees lining the immense driveway that curled and looped a path in front of Twin Springs Hotel and Spa. Brisk winds blew down from Virginia's Blue Ridge Mountains, darted around him and tugged the last of the gold and burnt orange leaves from the trees. Jaxon didn't resemble a man who frequented high-end properties, but rather his hardened body and broad shoulders still encompassed all the markings of a man ready for war.

Immune to the dipping temperature, his long gait consumed the pavement beneath his feet and his attention zeroed in on his target. Something about the property nudged at the recesses of his brain. The red brick hotel with its white columns and arching windows felt familiar. Where had he seen it? In the news? A photograph? He searched his memory for the connection. Maybe one of JD's sketches? Unsure, he gave a frustrated growl under his breath when he couldn't extract the data. He paused. Eyes narrowed, he studied Twin Springs. A tower with fresh, forest green awnings and bright new bricks stretched high above the sprawling hotel.

He muttered under his breath, "The owners clearly have cash for renovations."

Getting back to the job at hand, he rubbed at the black stubble littering his face and assessed the situation. A long covered veranda swept the length of the main body of the hotel. Two wings stretched out from the front entrance, four stories tall. The top story was peppered with tiny windows with peaked roofs. The main body of the hotel was broken up by a half circle portico supported by tall columns, already decked out with Christmas garland. "A little early," he muttered. "Not even Thanksgiving yet."

Expensive and sleek luxury cars zoomed around the circular drive, pausing only to expel the privileged owners. Bellmen in black and green monkey suits raced to open car doors and welcome guests to the hotel. The well dressed monkeys performed on cue, greeting the guests warmly before conducting the pass off of a concealed tip and driving away to park the guests' cars. The portico covered and protected the patrons' journey into the hotel. He glanced down at his faded blue jeans and the dark blue button up shirt under his leather jacket and grumbled, "Lord save me from monkey suits."

Evidently, his cousin didn't do enough background work for this job. He was going to stand out like a new recruit's freshly shaved, gleaming head. He mocked his cousin's words. "Quick job. Get in, get our intel and get out." He growled deep in his throat. "Dumb ass."

His cousin needed to get out into the field more and out from behind his large computer screen. *Perhaps the button up shirt will carry me through,* he considered.

Not a chance in hell, his mind rebelled and he dragged his cell phone from his back pocket and pushed speed dial.

A distracted voice answered on the other end. "Leeland here."

He grumbled hard and low, "What the hell, Lee? You sent me to some rich bitch mart."

"That's the job, Jax. Don't get your panties in a wad. Just get the information we need. It'll be easy. Pays well. You know we need to pull this one off without a hitch and prove our worth to the Geezers."

Jaxon's thoughts shifted to his father and uncle. Retired from the military, the brothers had decided to revive the family's long dead detective agency. After two decades of shooting off to one job or another, their wives had decided enough was enough. But, Lee's dad and his were looking for any excuse to get back into the game. Helping out the boys would be all they needed. The word "fine" ground out from between Jaxon's clenched jaw. "But I'm telling you, this had better not be a JOBB."

Lee laughed at JD's code word for a job that was Jacked Over Beyond Belief. "You know the deal," replied his cousin. "The insurance agency that hired us sent in some brainless fool who allowed one of the owners to wrap his fat ass around her pretty, little finger. Idiot returned in a daze, gushing about the stunning black haired part-owner who showed him around."

Jaxon muttered under his breath, "Useless excuse of a man."

Leeland ignored him and continued. "They want us to send in one of our top notch investigators. One who won't be swayed by a gorgeous face and can ferret out if the hotel's filing bogus insurance claims or not. They need results and quick because one of the owners is leaning heavily on them for payment. You're the only man I know who prefers his women butt ugly."

Jaxon snorted at his cousin's exaggeration and rubbed the short hair at the base of his neck. Butt ugly? Maybe not. But Lee was partially correct in his assessment. There was nothing he detested more than a beautiful woman. Give him a plain, average face any day over a conniving, lying, back stabbing, beautiful but evil bitch. "Screw you, Lee. You wouldn't know a good woman if she bit you in the ass and dragged you back to her bed." He ground his back teeth some more and surveyed the mission before him. "I'll get the job done. But no way in hell will I dress up in a god damn monkey suit to do it."

"Whatever, Jax. Besides, since you separated from the Army,

you've been driving me nuts under foot here at HQ. You needed some field time to get the debacle of your last mission out of your head. The Geezers got wind of you dragging ass around here and are making noise about coming back on the job if you don't stop. So, we both need this win. Report back with details. ASAP. I've got enough crap to deal with here."

Dismissed, Jaxon heard Lee yelling at someone else in the office before he disconnected. Pocketing his phone, he considered his options. He'd already memorized the floor plan that he'd downloaded from the Internet, surveyed the property from the road and stashed his jeep in the upper parking lot. Originally, he'd planned to walk in a side door and pretend to blend in with the guests. Blending in was a skill. All in how you carried yourself. Imitate the actions and attitudes of those around you, and all should be fine. He sneered at the men in the monkey suits. "Shouldn't be too hard."

Shrugging out of the black leather jacket that had accompanied him around the world, he unbuttoned his cuffs and folded each sleeve midway up his powerful forearms. He popped the collar on his shirt and loosened a few extra buttons before tossing his leather jacket over his shoulder and anchoring it there by the crook of his finger. As if he possessed all the time in the world, he strolled past the monkeys at the gate and in the front door of Twin Springs.

CHAPTER TEN

The grandness of the Twin Springs' lobby caught Jaxon by surprise. In his travels, he'd experienced the worst and best the world had to offer. There was something different about this hotel. Twin Springs jolted him. Rocked him to the core.

Covertly, he examined the massive height of the ceiling, crowned with intricate carvings and painted in an understated white. His feet sunk into the plush, flowered pattern of the carpet. A quick sweep of the room revealed families and couples cheerfully communing around antique tables, while lounging on cozy couches and chairs. Without a doubt, a unique property, even the air smelled faintly of roses, vanilla and the hint of another scent that reminded him of his sister. Was it lavender?

Unexpectedly, the setting before Jaxon seeped into him with a sense of peace, calmness and rightness that he hadn't realized he lacked in his life. Shaking off the unusual thoughts, he growled low in the back of his throat and grumbled, "Perhaps Lee was right. Roses and vanilla? Flowers? What the hell? Maybe my panties are in a wad. I'm becoming a pansy ass."

He zeroed in on three women running the hotel's Front Desk. The phones buzzing around them, together they efficiently handled a line of guests. *Business must be good.*

The morning sun streamed through the tiny cream and green square, stain glass windows high in the lobby's front wall and highlighted the three women's matching black hair. But the similarity stopped there. Any one of the women could be the part owner who dragged the insurance agent around by the nose. After all, beauty was in the eye of the beholder.

One of the women seemed less sure of herself. Her black hair was gathered back from her face in a simple ponytail. She also appeared a little young, but women's ages were always a mystery to him and none of his business.

One woman's hawkish gaze missed nothing happening inside the long lobby and studied him intently.

The last woman appeared to be in her teens, bubbly and vivacious with a youthful optimism that filled the air around her. A stunning girl with her dark chocolate ringlets falling around her face, but she couldn't be any older than sixteen, a mere baby. *Surely, the insurance agent wasn't referring to her as the beautiful owner who convinced him to change his wicked opinion. Unless the guy was a perv.* Jaxon made a mental note, and approached the Front Desk counter.

"Welcome to Twin Springs Hotel and…" The teenager's voice dwindled away and her smoky gray gaze fixed on Jaxon before filling with a dewy, vacant expression.

Perplexed by the change, he studied the girl. Since the colossal failure of his last mission, he no longer trusted his instincts. He'd learned first-hand to gain hard proof to back up your gut. Otherwise people died. And he wouldn't allow anyone else to be hurt by his bullshit instincts. *Perhaps she's older than I thought. She doesn't dress like a teenager. High end clothes. More like a fashion model. Could she be the part owner?*

"Ohh," the girl purred and covered her chest with her slender hand. "You must be here to interview for the job of Security Manager."

Perfect, he thought and cast her a lazy smile. Propping his lean form against the granite counter, he said, "Must be."

She held her slender hand out across the counter, "I'm Maddy and a co-owner here at Twin Springs Hotel and Spa."

Perv, fumed Jaxon as he ground his back teeth. Once the job was finished, he promised himself to track down the insurance agent and beat the shit out of him. Keeping his cover, he enveloped the teen's hand with his own and sunk into a relaxed position on the counter. His friendly gaze sparkled at the three women. "Quite the welcome crew you have here. I can see why business is booming." Cheesy, but all he could come up with on the fly. Schmoozing women wasn't his forte, but the line seemed to work.

Maddy's light black skin blushed bright crimson and she stared down to their linked hands. She didn't release his hand right away. Instead, she turned his arm over. His tattoo peeked out from under the cusp of his rolled up sleeve and he realized that it had caught the teen's attention. Frowning, she tilted her head and attempted to read the list of names upside down. "Fitz, Woody, Gonzo—"

He jerked. The black abyss of loss threatened to consume him but he evened out his breathing, nonchalantly released her hand and moved on to the other women standing beside her. *Flanked left, Caucasian, dyed hair, gorgeous turquoise eyes, young,* his mind noted. *Flanked right, Caucasian, late twenties, brown eyes, alert. Hair also dyed black due to the fact her eyebrows were a much lighter brown.* He filed the information away. Deciding to operate true name, he introduced himself to each of them and shook their hands, "Jaxon Wolfe."

"Sheela and Diana," said the plain faced, ordinary woman to Maddy's right.

"Excuse me," said Diana, the younger of the two. She ran off after a young boy separated from his parents.

Adding the women's names to his mental file, he focused in on Sheela and considered the possibilities of added benefits of this job. Plain Jane's, like Sheela, were always filled with wonderful surprises. Unlike his cousin, he understood there was no such thing as an ugly woman. All women were beautiful in unexpected ways.

He just hated women who used their beauty to lie and manipulate. Studying Sheela's caramel brown eyes, a niggling that something was off tingled in his long suppressed instincts. Mentally, he ground the uneasiness with the boot of his heel, killing it. Hard facts, that was how he survived now. No more gut instincts, feelings or hunches. Just cold hard facts. "It's a pleasure to meet both of you."

Sighing heavily, Maddy stared at Jaxon. "Your brown eyes have the prettiest green flecks."

Sheela elbowed the teen and broke her trance.

"Sorry." Maddy stood stock straight, adjusted her cream silk blouse, and pulled forth an older, more mature, facade. "I'll tell my brother that you're here to interview for the job." On crazy high spiked heels, she teetered back to an area blocked from his view.

Women. He turned his attention back to *plain—, er—, Sheela*, he corrected himself. "So, how long have you been without a Security Manager?"

Brow raised, Sheela answered, "A while. Mr. Beaumont didn't inform the Front Desk to expect you."

Smart woman. Even better. His smile deepened. "Heard about the job from a friend of mine. I was in the area. Decided to stop by and try my luck."

From behind Sheela, he detected movement. Unhurriedly, he straightened and took stock of the other part owner of the hotel. *Black hair, short. Six foot male, bi-racial ancestry. Dark gray suit, white shirt, no tie. Gray eyes.* Jaxon considered the eyes for a moment. *Eyes that matched little Maddy's. Brother and sister,* he mused.

A confident power exuded from the businessman. *Must be the owner pushing the insurance company to pay out. Gotta pay for that tower, after all.* Jaxon noticed that the man assessed him and waited for the verdict.

The steely stare gave nothing away and he offered his hand. "Theo Beaumont. I understand that you're applying for the job of Security Manager." He turned, motioning for Jaxon to follow.

"Come on back," he called over his shoulder. "Maddy, don't spend all day at the Front Desk. You have a test on Monday."

Crossing her arms, the teen shot back, "It's only Saturday and Isabella promised I could taste test a couple of her new creations for the bar menu. Plus Ava said I could go to the Aviary and try to teach her bird some new words."

Pausing, Theo turned and cast a look powerful enough to freeze a mere man alive, but it bounced ineffectively off his little sister. "School comes first. I want to check your homework and quiz you before Sunday at midnight. In fact, you'll meet me in my office on Sunday at 2:00 pm. Sharp, Maddy. 2:00 pm sharp," he reiterated, attempting to pin his sister with a look.

Jaxon preferred not to be on the shitty side of this man. But he would if need be. *After all,* he thought, *I'm here to do a job.*

Theo opened his office door and motioned for Jaxon to enter. He lowered himself behind a sturdy but aged oak desk.

Examining the room, Jaxon considered his choices. To the left, under the window, stretched an extremely comfortable brown leather couch. But the angle of that position wouldn't allow him to study Theo's face and reactions. Second option, sit directly in front of his desk, but in one of two girly chairs covered with large purple flowers. He resisted raising an eyebrow at the man across from him as he examined the chairs. *Just do the job,* he told himself. He squeezed his muscled frame into one of the feminine chairs and slung his leather jacket over his knee.

"Little sisters," muttered Theo under his breath.

One thing Jaxon understood was little sisters. His mind pictured his own little sister. All grown up but equally as gorgeous as Maddy. It didn't matter how old they became, the older brother still shouldered the responsibility to watch over them. "I under-stand, have one of my own. Older than yours, but no less of a pain in the ass. Beat up my share of hopeful suitors growing up."

Throwing back his head, Theo laughed. "I have the opposite problem. Have to protect others from my little sister."

Damn it, grumbled Jaxon. *I like this guy.* He crushed the weakness. The luxury of forming ties was no longer an option for him and especially not while on a job. No ties equaled no pain when things went to shit. "Been there, too."

Theo studied the serious man across from him. "Tell me about yourself. How did you hear about the position? Did you bring a resume?"

Any good operative understood the key in an undercover mission was to stick as close to the truth as possible without blowing your cover, or the job at hand. That way you don't have to juggle the lies. If he were successful, the payoff would be great intel. If he didn't sell his story well, then his face was blown and the agency would have to send in another detective. Or he'd need to come clean and state the real reason he came to Twin Springs. Neither of those scenarios worked for him.

No way in hell would he go back to the agency with his tail between his legs. The Geezers would laugh their asses off. They'd take great pleasure in smearing his failure in his face and ribbing him for years to come. "I can get you a resume. Heard about the job from an old Army buddy. I was in the area and thought I'd check to see if the post was still open. Security was my business in the military. Both personal security and property security. I've just separated after eight years of service."

"You decided not to reenlist?"

White flames of burning men played in the back of his mind. He settled on an easy half-truth. "Had enough of the politics, lies and death. Needed a new job, something without all the bullshit."

"Dale, the Head of Maintenance here at Twin Springs, his son left the Army a little ways back. He returned severely burned from serving. Right now, he is overseeing the completion of our new Lobby Bar and Tower. You two will have a great deal in common. He prefers to do most of his work at odd hours because of his burns. That, or he figured out ways to get around Twin Springs without being seen."

The sounds of an explosion and men screaming reverberated through Jaxon's brain. The memory of the searing flames licking their bodies danced in his vision and the pungent smell of burning flesh filled his nostrils. Their last breaths had branded him a failure. Their memories haunted him and gnawed at his soul. A part of him wanted to push their faces to the dark recesses of his mind but honor forced him to keep their sacrifices alive, breathing and in step with each breath he enjoyed at their expense.

The pain of their death stroked the constant reminder of his failure and ate him alive, consuming what was left of his soul one bite at time. He'd caused the brutal death of his brothers-in-arms. Like Judas, he stood beside their loved ones as their remains were lowered into the ground. He wanted more than anything to change places but it was too late. They were dead.

Swallowing hard and clearing his throat, he shuttered the pain behind his eyes along with the fetid odor of burning flesh. All he could do now was never allow his flawed instincts to cause another death. Maybe by accomplishing the mission at hand, he could prove to himself and the only family he had left that he was spared for a reason. Otherwise, he was worthless. He rolled his shoulders back, forcing himself to push the images to the edge of his consciousness and concentrate on the reality in front of him. *Computer, check for financials. High end RFID key card on Theo's hip. An unusual level of security, find out why.* His mind filed the information away and he felt a sense of relief at the simple task.

The images and screams blurred and faded into a mist that twirled and seeped into the deep dark regions. Determined to concentrate on the mission before him, he felt out the situation. "New Lobby Bar and Tower, sounds like things are going well."

Theo's eyes narrowed to slivers of ice and he twirled a silver pen through his fingers, contemplating.

Sensing the man was weighing his choices and coming to a decision about him, he waited.

Theo's voice contained a dangerous thread. "Let me ask you this, Jaxon. How far would you go to protect those you love? We're a family here at Twin Springs. For almost a century, my fiancées family has owned and operated Twin Springs. Isabella, my fiancée, is the Head Executive Chef. Her sister, Ava, is cutting her teeth as the new Group Sales and Special Events Coordinator. Generations back, my uncle was the Executive Chef in the Main Kitchen.

"This is our home. We live and work on property. You met my little sister. A few months ago, Niles, the old Security Manager went mad, sabotaged the hotel and attempted to kill both my fiancée and my sister. He tried to drown Isabella in an underground river that runs beneath a portion of the hotel. Wet and cold, both Isabella and Maddy almost froze to death before I could get to them. He was Isabella and Ava's childhood friend. Someone we all trusted. If Isabella hadn't fought him off, she would've been swept downstream instead of him."

Damn it what had the Geezers got him into? *Attempted murder? Sabotage?* He'd been assigned a damn JOBB. His mind scrambled to keep up with what Theo was saying.

"You see, they're all precious to me. Yes, I'm looking to hire a new Security Manager, but more than that, I'm hiring someone to watch over and protect my family as if they were his. So tell me, how far would you go to protect the ones you love? To protect your little sister? To ensure she was safe in her home?"

Picturing his tough, no nonsense adopted sister in his mind, Jaxon didn't believe anyone could take her. But he knew her softer side. The side she kept hidden from prying eyes. Her great heart and everything she'd overcome in her life. What would he do if someone harmed her or even threatened her life? His eyes darkened, the green flecks overshadowing the brown until his gaze glowed with a green sheen.

He transformed into a soldier right before Theo.

Jaxon gritted out between clenched teeth, "Whatever necessary."

Theo's lips spread into a satisfied smile. "You're hired. Get me your resume, plus a list of references and we'll be set."

CHAPTER ELEVEN

robing eyes tracked Jaxon, taking note of his easy manner, measured stride and constant awareness of his surroundings. Standing behind the Front Desk, Mackenzie Mill's reporter senses tingled. Deep in her bones, she felt a story brewing. The man exuded power and confidence. The type of self-assurance that came from steel being forged under great heat and pressure. She smoothed the black skirt of her front desk uniform and adjusted the badge with her fake name. Sheela.

Her fingers itched and flexed, begging to take out her small notebook and jot down notes. But, she pushed all thoughts of the dark stranger from her mind. She didn't secure a position at Twin Springs to get a scoop on Jaxon Wolfe. She showed up daily to find the justice denied to the weak. Perhaps to even the score and give a little payback.

A guest cleared his throat, drawing her attention. She reigned in her rampant thoughts and turned with a welcoming smile towards the newcomer. *Can't afford to lose my job now, not when I am so close.*

Swallowing a gasp, she took in the guest's tall, emaciated frame and brilliant blue eyes that sunk into his gaunt face. Short, white blonde hair lay close to his skull, smoothed back by a sheen of sweat, and his skin glowed a shade off tint, dampened with beads of perspiration. A dark blue suit hung from his rail thin frame as if it was made for a much larger man. The collar of his striped dress shirt gaped open at his neck and droplets of perspiration congregated in the divot at the base of his throat. It didn't take a world-class reporter to deduce the man was ill.

Many guests flocked to Twin Springs expecting the warm sulphur spring water to work magic on their illnesses. The hotel no longer advertised herself as a healing spring but the sick still converged on the Grand Dame, hoping and praying for a cure. Something about the guest's illness touched a cord inside her but the look in the back of his eyes sent a shiver down her spine. She sensed a hint of burning rage within the gaunt man, binding him inside a shroud of pungent smoke and brimstone.

Her cheeks burned. *The man's ill. He could be dying and here you're making up some type of insidious back story for him. First Jaxon and now this sick man. You must be losing it,* she admonished herself and pushed the sleeves of her white shirt up past the elbows. *Too much time high in the mountains. Your spidey senses are going off all over the place. Focus on the story you're pursuing. The one where Ava holds the leading role.*

The other media outlets were wrong on why Ashlee Hollingsworth, the wife of esteemed Broadway Director Terrence Hollingsworth, committed suicide. She wasn't a mad woman bent on self destruction. No, Ava was at the insidious center of Ashlee's suicide. She just knew it. Ava might as well have held the gun to Ashlee's head and pulled the trigger. She might not be able to pin her childhood friend's death on Ava, but she would expose her for the opportunistic, home wrecking slut she was.

That was the only way her friend's memory could be washed clean. People should remember Ashlee as the kind, soft spoken and giving woman she was. Sheltered by old money, her friend wasn't prepared for Ava to infiltrate her marriage. Mackenzie's brain was imprinted with the grainy black and white newspaper photo of Ashlee, laying on the stage in a pool of her own blood, and Ava striking a pose of shock.

Too busy chasing bylines, she'd abandoned her friend after college and wasn't available to protect, or help, her. During their phone calls, she'd sensed that something was off with Ashlee, but hadn't wanted to interrupt her own life, her own goals, to ferret out what. From the outskirts of the graveyard, she'd witnessed the heart wrenching grief of a mother and father consoling Ashlee's broken husband.

Where was Ava? She didn't even attend the funeral. Instead, she absconded to the mountains of Virginia. Untouchable. She glared over at the double doors leading to Ava's office. Once she figured out how all the pieces fit together, she would not only have the scoop of a lifetime, but she would also avenge her friend's death by destroying the woman responsible, *the* AVA.

Spreading her thin lips into a welcoming smile, she glanced up at the ill man, and began checking him in. "Welcome to Twin Springs Hotel and Spa. May I have the last name on the reservation?"

The man swayed on his feet and addressed her without needing to scan her name badge. "Yes, Sheela. My name is Ottoman. Clay Ottoman," he responded in a gravelly voice, barely above a whisper. "I have a suite booked."

CHAPTER TWELVE

A gentle tap, tap, tap, woke Ava. She was inside one of Twin Springs' old phone booths, curled up on a wooden bench. Sitting up straight, she smacked her shoulder on the little wooden shelf that ran below one of the old, gray, plastic phones.

Her sister, Isabella, was ready for work in her white chef jacket and skinny black jeans. Her blonde hair was pulled back into a bun. She rapped again on the glass bi-fold door, then opened it and poked her head in. The sounds of cups clinking signaled that morning tea and coffee were being served in the Presidents Hall outside. "Whatcha doing?"

Ava glanced down. She was still wearing her black slacks and silky emerald shirt from the night before. "I think I was sleep-walking."

She pressed her fingers against her eyelids, attempting to stem the flow of tears building up. "Izzy, the episodes are getting worse since Dad's death." She glanced around the booth, a quiet place where she'd hidden as a teen trying to soothe her teenage woes in peace. A tear slid down her cheek. "Do you think I'm having a mental breakdown?"

"No," her sister gasped. She stepped inside and pulled the bi-fold door closed, enveloping them in privacy. "You're as sane as I am." Isabella removed the kerchief from around the base of her blonde hair, kneeled and dabbed at the wetness on her sister's cheeks. "Sleepwalking can be unpredictable."

"That's just it. I remember joking with the Bellhop on duty, then, heading to the elevator. But I don't remember going to bed. Can you call it sleepwalking if you didn't actually sleep?"

"Do you remember anything this time?"

Ava closed her eyes and concentrated. "Just glimpses. Of the Nineteen Twenties. Music playing." She hummed a few bars. "That's jazz."

Her sister nodded, encouraging her. "Think back, try harder. It's the twenties. Jazz is playing. What do you see?"

Sensually, her body swayed to the music playing in her head. "I'm dancing with a man. I think we're in the Crystal Ballroom. He smells of leather and horse flesh. His thick, black hair is curling over the white collar of his shirt and I'm thinking, 'How improper.' A thrill shimmers through my body as his head lowers and his gaze meets mine." Her eyes flew open. "He has the most gorgeous brown eyes with little green flecks in them."

Sitting down, and criss-crossing her legs, Isabella hummed in the back of her throat, "What else?"

Ava gazed off into the distance, not seeing the small cubical before her, lost in her memories. "Roses. I smell roses. I remember twirling away from him. Daring him to take chase. I plucked a rose out of a vase and tucked it behind my ear."

Chuckling, Isabella reached up and pulled a pencil from behind her sister's ear. "Close."

Ava stared down at the thin pencil for a moment before placing it on the little shelf. "Why's this happening to me?"

"This is the first time you've actually recalled what happened." She scooted closer and grasped her hands. "You're ice cold." She rubbed them between her smaller ones. "Remember when I kept seeing my imaginary friend, Emma, as a child?"

Her brows furrowed, and she nodded.

"Then, we found out that she was really a ghost and our ancestor, Emerald Rockwell. I wonder if one of her sisters is haunting you. Maybe Ruby since you look so much alike. Unlike when Emma haunted me, Ruby's more intrusive."

"Are you saying she's taking over my body?" Ava felt sick. Like a puppet. A victim. A toy of someone else desires. "She's forcing me to act out scenes from her life?"

"I'm not sure."

Ava read concern in her sister's eyes. "Do you think she wants to show me how she died, like her sister Emma did with you?"

"Maybe," Isabella tugged her to her feet and gave her a hug. Her phone beeped a reminder, and she pulled back to check it. "I need to get the service together for your morning meeting. Do you want me to cancel it? We can sit and talk as long as you want."

Shaking her head, Ava cast her sister a huge smile. Time to act the part of Group Sales and Special Event Coordinator. Twin Springs was her new stage and she wanted nothing more than to leave the memories of the old stage behind. "No, I'll grab some coffee and be right in. Ruby's not going to hold us back in turning the hotel around and making it a success."

Opening the bi-fold doors, the sisters left the row of phone booths behind and entered the Presidents Hall. Isabella dashed off to the kitchens and Ava wandered over to the mahogany, claw foot table that dominated the middle of the hall.

A white linen table cloth covered the gleaming, polished wood and peeked out from under stacks of complementary newspapers. A huge crystal vase towered high in the middle of the table, bursting with draping purple, pink and white flowers that bent and bowed down towards passing guests. She scooped up a morning newspaper and tucked it under her arm.

She ignored the door to the Security Manager's office and crossed over to a long, mahogany buffet table with curved sides and claw feet. Large, silver chafer urns were lined up along the white table runner, and pumped out piping hot coffee paired with hot water for tea. Squatty, sterling silver decanters held low-fat and full octane creamer. Across from the coffee stood the tall double doors to the Crystal Ballroom, where her family's new business partner, Theo, had proposed to her sister. It also led to the hotel's theatre.

She swallowed hard. Even the thought of standing on that familiar stage made her feel ill. Would the events of her last night on stage ever fade from her memory? Pushing the thoughts aside, she paused at the hotel's complimentary beverage service for a quick dose of caffeine. Her hand hovered over the white porcelain cups around who's rims delicate flowers swirled, but she swept past them for a tall, tan, paper cup, stamped with a dark green Twin Springs logo. She tipped the cup under one of the silver chafer urns and filled it almost to the rim with freshly brewed, piping hot coffee. Inhaling the roasted aroma, her luxurious black lashes fluttered down over her light green eyes. "Caffeine. Sweet caffeine." She hummed in the back of throat. "My morning lover. Brightens my day as no man ever will."

Suddenly embraced from behind, Ava's eyes popped open as the momentum of the squeeze tilted her sideways and almost caused her to dump the steaming hot coffee onto herself. The Director never far from her mind, she panicked and her heart froze. The newspaper fell from her stiff limbs. She could feel the Director's hot breath on her neck and opened her mouth to scream but not a sound escaped.

Girlish laughter cascaded over her. Maddy released her and leaned against the table. "Morning."

Hands shaking, Ava placed her coffee on the white table cloth. She cleared her throat, swallowed hard and croaked, "Good morning, love."

"Are you coming down with something?"

She looped an arm around Maddy's shoulders and gave her a quick squeeze. "I'm fine. You're working early this morning."

The teenager returned the hug before releasing her to dance around, young exuberance gushing from her slender form. "I'm soooo happy that I showed up at the Front Desk early." She picked up one of the silver spoons from the white table cloth and scooped two heaping mounds of sugar into her porcelain cup. "I met my future husband today," she cooed.

"Well, they say the early bird gets the worm." One black eyebrow arched up, when Maddy dumped high octane creamer over the sugar and half way up the cup. "No wonder you like tea," she added dryly.

Maddy's glassy gaze flickered down at her cup and she shrugged before casting her a brilliant smile. "Aren't you listening? I met him. Him! My knight in shining armor, my prince." Clutching her slender arm with her hand, she leaned in closer. "The one," she whispered. The teen looked up, her eyes deep, gray pools of innocence. Just as swiftly, she turned and abandoned her tea before twirling away.

Smiling and enjoying the excitement encircling the teenager, Ava added a small dose of sugar and a drop of low-fat creamer to her cup. "One of the guests' sons?" She pressed a spill proof lid onto her coffee and leaned back against the edge of the oval table. "Don't let your brother find out. He's serious about the non-fraternization with the guests rule."

Maddy flipped about, her silky curls falling around her expressive face as she turned to face Ava. "A son? No way. He's a man. Tall, hair black as midnight, golden eyes, handsome with an unshaved look, a little mysterious." Her eyes twinkled, "A dash of bad beneath a black leather jacket." She trailed her fingertips up the inside of her arm. "He has the coolest tattoo running up his arm."

Alarm bells rang in Ava's head. She stiffened and placed her coffee back on the table. She glanced around. Theo was nowhere in sight. *Darn it.* She hated being cast in the part of the hard nose, grown up. All that grumpiness caused wrinkles. She was sure of it. But, it was up to her. *Time to play the adult.*

Ava adjusted her stance, pinned her shoulders back, and pursed her lips. Furrowing her brow, she addressed Maddy by glaring down her nose. Crossing her arms over her chest, she deepened her voice by one octave, and rattled off all the lines appropriate for the scene. "Who is this man? What do you know of him? Does your brother approve?"

For a moment, the teen gaped, before her mouth snapped shut and she giggled under her breath. "Please. Theo's way crabbier than that. Better luck next time."

The far off, mushy look once again flowed over Maddy's face. She plopped down into one of the cushy armchairs and sipped her tea. "Of course Theo knows him and he must approve. I'm sure he's going to hire him as the new Security Manager. Can you believe it? It's perfect! My husband will work at Twin Springs and I'll never have to leave. We can both work here, tending to the Grand Dame. Our children will grow up here, just like you and Isabella did."

Listening to Maddy prattle on, Ava loosened her stance and realized that the young girl had transformed into a real sister. Just like Isabella, she'd no longer be able to fool Maddy by playing a part. She relaxed and shed all pretense until all that remained was just her, Ava. "He sounds fantastic. But let's go a little slower and not start picking out wedding dresses quite yet. How about if we see how he treats the Grand Dame and then make the decision if he's future husband material from there."

Glancing up, Maddy's mind processed her words and the fog cleared from her eyes. "You're right. If he doesn't respect the Grand Dame, then he's toast."

Ava's full lips spread into a wide smile. "Great. Until then, how about if you help me get ready for the mother-of-the-bride from hell and her beautiful daughter. They're showing up to go over some of the finishing details for the daughter's wedding."

Maddy slumped a little in her chair, the excitement of a new found love seeping out from her.

Ava's cell phone beeped. She removed it from her slacks' pocket and glanced down at the text message feature Theo had installed on her phone for safety. "Office Door Open," she read. "Isabella must be setting up." For bonus encouragement, she added, "She's bringing petite cakes and hors d'oeuvres samples for the clients to taste test in my office."

Rallying, the teen nodded her agreement.

Ava scooped up her newspaper and tucked it under her arm. She grabbed her caffeine lover before extending a hand. "Let's go. Perhaps we can talk my sister out of some of the goodies before the bride and her mother come." Together they walked to Ava's office, many a male's head turning in their wake.

CHAPTER THIRTEEN

olding the door to her office open, Ava allowed the teenager to enter before her. In her heart, she marveled at the thrill of owning her own office. Some women might rebel at the masculine feel of the room with its paneled walls, dark leather furniture and the large manly desk. Not Ava. The room reminded her of a well-staged set and the power of it soaked into her bones and made her feel strong, in control and on par with any man, in any situation. Here with the General's strength surrounding her, she felt protected.

Unwilling to tamper with her safe zone, she'd left all the General's things untouched and in their rightful place. As a tribute, a mausoleum, to her ancestor, a great and powerful man. "Isabella," she called out entering. "We want some of your creations before the Wicked Witch of the West arrives with her beautiful princess daughter."

"Wicked Witch, huh?" asked Logan. "Where's a house when you need one?"

Surprised, Ava glanced further into the room. There stood Logan, her childhood friend-in-crime. Her heart wrenched at the still new sight of the scarlet and purple burn scars that swept across the right side of his face and down his neck. With his hands shoved into a ratty pair of washed out blue jeans, Logan stood in homage before an oil portrait of three sisters.

Almost one-hundred-years-old, the portrait brought Amethyst, Ava's great grandmother, and her two sisters, Emerald and Ruby, to life for all to behold. All three sisters had passed away generations ago. A leak in the guest room above had collapsed the floor and revealed not only the General's office but also the only portrait of his Gems, his three daughters. She pretended not to notice him staring up at the portrait. "Sorry, I wasn't expecting you this morning."

Maddy flopped down on the couch, perpendicular the portrait, and leaned her head back against the cushions so that she could also gaze up. "Don't bug him. He's busy courting. I think that he's in looove with the hundred-year-old red head. He likes older women." The teenager considered the idea for a moment and then bounced up. "Just like me. I like older men." Tilting her head, she examined the portrait. "Except, he likes his women ancient."

Logan whipped around towards the teenager, a purplish, red hue seeping up his neck and over his face, matching his unburnt side to the tragically scarred right side. "Maddy," he snarled under his breath. "I liked you much more when you were afraid of me. Do I need to rectify that situation?"

Snorting back a laugh, she sounded more and more like Isabella. "Yeah right," she replied and winked up at the angry man.

Tipping back her head, Ava contemplated the oil portrait. Her gaze skimmed over the ancestor who bore a remarkable resemblance to her sister and the red head who was her great grandmother. It was the third sister that captured her gaze. Her sparkling green eyes were framed by chin length, glossy black hair. Ruby Rockwell's blood red lips peaked and curled into an easy, sensual smile. Identical to her own. *Have you been haunting me since I was a child? When I thought I was sleepwalking?*

A squawk resonated through the tense atmosphere and her gaze honed in on the corner of the room, where a large cage was covered with black fabric. Clasping her hands together, she surged forward with excitement. "Logan! He's ready?"

Casting one last glare at the teen, Logan crossed the room with a crooked gait. His hand hovered over the black drape. "Yep, I believe living in the Aviary with the two falcons and the hawk did him good. He learned to respect the big boys. It's time for him to come out and join the rest of the living world." With the thumb and two fingers remaining on his mutilated hand, he removed the cover with a grand flourish.

The beautiful gray bird's golden eyes blinked at Ava and he released a welcoming caw. Just like the first time she'd heard about the bird, she realized that she'd found a soul mate in the African Gray Parrot. Another living being totally misunderstood and taken at first glance by others unwilling to delve below the surface. Trapped in a beautiful cage for people to admire and poke at, but never to understand.

The bird screeched loud and sharp, before dropping his caw into a sexy male voice and belting out a verse of jazz. Lowering her voice to a husky tenor, she blended her voice with his and he quieted. His gold eyes pinned her, while she finished the final chorus.

Involuntarily, Logan released a pent-up breath that had been trapped in his chest. "Wow, Ava. What the hell are you doing here? You belong on stage, sharing your voice with the world."

Gaping with awe, Maddy's mouth flapped open before she closed it with an audible snap. "I want to sing like you. Teach me. Please teach me."

A harsh snicker escaped the burned man. "You can't learn that. A talent of that magnitude is a gift. You have your own gifts. Be happy."

The teen continued to gaze up at Ava, her mouth slack.

Ava's laughter rang out like bells in the small room.

At once, the bird imitated her laugh with an uncanny exactness and he shook his bright red tail.

She waived off their compliments. There was no way in hell that she'd go back to the stage. "I love him, Logan. Thank you for nursing him back to health. He's so handsome with his feathers filling in."

The African Gray flapped his wings, moved over to his large stainless steel dish, and picked out an apple wedge. Holding the slice between one of his gray claws, he eyed the humans.

Studying the bird, Logan rubbed where his burnt ear melted into the side of his head. "He just needed some TLC. Getting him out of that underground cavern and small cage did wonders. I can't believe Niles, our illustrious Security Manager, kept him in those conditions. But, then, I didn't think Niles was capable of sabotaging the hotel or hurting Isabella and Maddy.

"I didn't need to clip his wings. He'll never fly; his wings are malformed from years of being confined in a tiny cage. It was sickening watching him struggle to stretch them out to their full width for the first time."

Finished with his apple, the parrot picked up a dried banana chunk with his strong black beak and tossed it through the bars of his cage. He barked out in a deep male voice, "Shitty grub."

Rubbing his mouth with the back of his hand to hide his smile, Logan's sea blue gaze focused in on Ava. "Are you sure you want him?" he asked. "He's a handful. Maybe I should keep him in the Aviary a little longer. You could visit him a little more until he stops being such an ass."

Again, Ava's laughter spilled from her lips and lit it up the room. "He'll mind his manners with me. Don't you worry. Thank you for taking care of him. I know Twin Springs pays your family to give hawking lessons to the guests since the Aviary is on your farm. But nursing him back to health was over and above. I really appreciate you and your brother taking care of him."

Kneeling on the couch cushions and leaning forward against

the back of the couch in order to watch the large gray bird, Maddy asked, "What are you going to name him?"

Shrugging her delicate shoulder, Ava responded, "He'll name himself."

Her phone buzzed and the office door opened to reveal Isabella. Her tiny frame backed in, wheeling a cart covered with a crisp white table cloth and piled with sweets and hors d'oeuvres on tiered silver serving trays.

Scrambling to her feet, Maddy rubbed her hands together. "Yum, I can't wait to taste some."

Isabella brought herself up to her full height, just a smidgen over five feet, and straightened her crisp white Executive Chef jacket. "No, you won't. These are for our bride and her mother."

Instantly deflated, the teen wailed, "But Ava promised."

Tucking a strand of blonde hair behind her ear, Isabella pinned her sister with her identical light green eyes. "Well, Ava will need to learn to not make promises she can't keep. If there are any left, I'll make sure to get them to you," she replied. "We barely have any time to prep before the bride arrives. Everybody needs to clear the room," she ordered.

Logan crossed the room, his slight limp eating up the distance. "Come with me, kid. You can help me with work on the Tower. Unless you're still needed at the Front Desk." He paused before he opened the double doors of the office. Tugging a dirty blue baseball cap from his back pocket, he slapped it on his thigh before placing it on his head and bringing the brim down low and tipping it to the right, covering the razed skin. Jerking open the door, he herded the young girl through before him. Quickly turning back, he snatched up a couple petite cakes. "Catch," he called out and tossed one to Maddy. With a wink at the sisters, he drew the office door firmly closed behind him.

Frowning, Isabella's nimble fingers rearranged the mini cakes on the tray and filled in the empty spots. "If Dale didn't love that man so much, I'd throttle him," she declared.

Ava sank into her place behind the massive mahogany desk.

Reaching into the bottom drawer, she removed a dark green folder, embossed in gold with the Twin Springs logo. A picture of a bride, tipped backwards by her groom's kiss, framed the front. The words, 'Imagine Your Ideal Wedding In A Timeless Setting,' swirled below. "You know his father has nothing to do with how you feel about him. You love Logan as much as I do."

Snorting under her breath, Isabella smoothed stray strands of her sunny blonde hair back into the folds of her top knot. Letting out a deep breath, she surveyed the General's room. "Where do you want to set up for the clients?"

Head down, Ava dug around in the top drawer and placed a pair of eye glasses, thickly rimmed in black, on the desk. She removed a thick gray hair tie from her wrist. Holding the band between her teeth, she tipped her head back and scraped back her long, glossy, ebony hair into a ponytail at the nape of her neck. She smoothed her hair until it flattened against her head and the light no longer reflected off of the gleaming, blue tinged highlights threaded through her black mane. Using the hair tie, she twirled and twisted her hair, capturing its long length in a tight bun.

After blotting the vibrant red lipstick from her lips with a tissue, Ava slipped the glasses on. The heavy black rims covered most of her upper face and the tinted lenses muted the green sparkle of her eyes. She removed the silver hoops dangling from her ears and tossed them into the top drawer. From the back of the chair, she cloaked herself in a dull, gray sweater. The mounds of fabric engulfed her trim figure and made her body appear sizes larger. She kicked her high heels under the desk and slipped on ballerina flats. Rolling her shoulders forward, Ava curved her spine and seamed to wilt right before Isabella's eyes.

She grabbed the folder, tucked it under her arm and rounded the desk towards her sister. Her usual graceful, confident stride had turned hesitant and slow. "I thought the couches and chairs would help the clients feel welcome."

Isabella evaluated her sister's transformation from the colorful, sexual and full of life woman who lived for the moment to a timid, mousy, woman, who appeared afraid of her own shadow. "Playing the school matron?"

Tipping her glasses forward, Ava peered over the black rims. "I found out that some mothers of the bride prefer to feel superior over the peons whom they employ. Whatever it takes to keep our client happy and excited about exchanging her vows at Twin Springs." She swung open the door and welcomed the bride and her mother with a demure smile.

CHAPTER FOURTEEN

Jaxon squeezed his body out of the girly chair and accompanied Theo out of his office. Now he understood why the Geezers had sent him on this job before they retired. Beautiful woman. Flawed intel. They were trying to help him right his last mission. Didn't they understand there was no way to bring back the dead?

It didn't matter. He'd complete his mission and prove to everyone that he could be one of their top investigators. Pushing his past failures to the back of his mind, he focused on the job. Sheela and Maddy were busy handling the phones and a line of guests. "Things are hopping here," he said, once again working on prying information out of Theo.

A proud grin spread over Theo's lips. "That's Isabella's doing. She turned around a terrible situation in the kitchens and impressed an influential food critic. His review of her menu increased sales by twenty-five percent over the past few months. We've been through a rough time. Our old Security Manager held a grudge against the hotel and the ownership team. He sabotaged Twin Springs and tried to destroy the family through the hotel. Niles might be out of our lives but he left us in one hell of a financial mess."

"How did you catch him?" asked Jaxon, slipping into his leather jacket.

"My fiancée stumbled upon his hidden stash of moonshine and his still. He was brewing in a secret underground cavern that lead from the back part of the hotel."

"A still? Moonshine? In this day and age?"

Theo shrugged. "I guess moonshine's having a comeback. I saved a couple jugs. Smooth. We'll have a drink after you get settled in with your new position. Anyway, this is the Grand Lobby of the hotel. The outlying property consists of a spa, stables, gun club and range, ski slope and lodge, golfing course, range and clubhouse and we lease an Aviary on a neighboring farm for hawking and falcon demonstrations. Of course, there is also the Hot Springs Pool for which the Grand Dame is renowned and an indoor spring fed pool. On property we have sixty-five thousand square feet of meeting space, a bowling alley, two ballrooms, a theatre, boutiques and three restaurants to include our famous Main Dining Room. Under construction, we have a new Lobby Bar and the Tower. Once finished, the bottom floor of the Tower will include a lounge, four luxurious suites on each of the next three floors and the top floor will be a ballroom with a restaurant that has a panoramic view of the surrounding area. I will introduce you to Dale."

"Head of Maintenance, right?"

"Yes. He'll show you all the ins and outs of the property." Theo withdrew a folded brochure from under the counter of the Front Desk. "We hand this map of the property out to the guests. It'll get you started. Are you staying in town?"

To keep his hands free, Jaxon slipped the map up under his jacket and into the crook of his back, an old habit from his Army days. "Nope, do you know of someplace cheap until I find a place?"

Theo turned to address Maddy. Jaxon felt uncomfortable as she stared at him with a weird look on her face and Theo let out an exasperated breath. "Doesn't Isabella need your help?"

"She's in a meeting with Ava, a bride and her mother." A long sigh trailed her statement. Her eyes soft and dewy, fluttered up at Jaxon. Without shifting her gaze, the teenager raised her arm and bonelessly pointed in the general direction of Ava's office. "Senator Whitcomb's daughter, Kennedy."

Shuffling his feet, Jaxon frowned down at the girl before his gaze followed to where she pointed, two thick double doors with a large stain glass window above. Even with his untrained eye, he noticed the doors resembled the quality of an era gone by. They were painted to match the rest of the doors within the Grand Lobby but they seemed grander, larger.

As he appraised the workmanship, one of the doors flung open. A platinum blonde woman flew from the room, dragging her grown daughter out by the hand. Color high in the young woman's cheeks, she rushed to keep up with her mother. Both women matched in navy blue cardigans with white pencil skirts. They appeared ready for a summer jaunt on a yacht, instead of a trip to the mountains in the fall. A loud screech called out to the pair, then, a gruff male voice shouted, "Get the fuck out."

"Now what's going on?" muttered Theo, his long strides carrying him towards the two women.

Taking his time, Jaxon trailed behind Theo, assessing the women. *Daughter, blonde. Low twenties. Mom, platinum blonde, mid forty's. Stinking rich, lots of sparkly crap at her throat, ears and hands. Pissed. Obviously Senator Whitcomb's wife and his daughter.*

He watched Theo expertly guide the women back into the room. Bringing up the rear, Jaxon entered the room and left the door ajar. He positioned himself so that he could evaluate the situation while still keeping the door within his vision. Scanning the room, he honed in on a young girl. *No, woman,* he decided, *in a white chef's jacket.* She soothed the future bride and her mother, who sat straight as a poker in one of the twin leather chairs facing her from the couch. *Must be one of the part owners and the savior of Twin Springs.*

He studied Twin Springs' Executive Chef with her fresh, clean face, bare of makeup. Gorgeous pale green eyes and handfuls of blonde hair piled high on her head. *Theo's woman,* he reminded himself.

Another woman worked to cover a massive bird cage with a black cloth. Jaxon caught a glimpse of a huge gray parrot, his head hanging low as he tried to eye the humans from within the cage before the dark cloth obstructed his view.

The parrot actually growled from within his prison and shouted out, "Fucking bitch."

The woman hushed him.

Jaxon pushed the hysterical mother and the foul mouth parrot from his mind and focused in on the woman with the dull black hair standing next to the bird cage. Something about her caught his attention. There was a subtle grace beneath her slow, measured movements. She turned towards him and froze. Her eyes blinked at him from behind her thick glasses.

Unknowingly, he stepped forward and the room around him blurred. More than anything, he wanted to protect this plain bird trapped in the oversized drab sweater. Checking his actions, he studied the hidden jewel before him. It took everything within him to remain where he was and not rush over and safeguard her from the platinum blonde mother now screeching louder than the bird in the cage. She moved to sit beside her sister on the couch and across from the hysterical mother, attempting to calm the bride's mother in a shy, quiet voice.

After only one look at the quiet woman, Jaxon knew he wanted her more than anything he'd wanted for a long, long time. The heady smell of roses filled his nostrils and flooded his subconscious. His inner voice gave a relieved sigh and a great weight he hadn't realized he carried lifted from his shoulders. *You found her.*

CHAPTER FIFTEEN

The woman was a gentle dove and he was entranced by her. The desire to protect this vulnerable creature rocked Jaxon to the core. He itched to contact his cousin for information on her past and how he could help her.

"I've never been so offended in my life," gasped the mother of the bride, patting her perfect hair into place.

Jaxon dragged his eyes away from the dove and watched Mrs. Whitcomb fan herself with her hand.

The sunlight from the stain glass window over the door caught the diamond facets of her jumble of rings and scattered a reflection of vibrant sparkles around the room. Briefly distracted by the rainbow of colors her actions caused, the mother stopped fanning herself and wiggled her fingers in a slow wave like motion, admiring the results.

Jaxon growled deep in his throat. *What a dimwitted, self-absorbed woman.* She reminded him of a Second Lieutenant, sporting his shiny new academy ring for the first time.

"Suck it up, bitch," screeched the bird from inside his darkened cell.

His growls were covered by the parrot's outburst, and Jaxon

raised an eyebrow towards the cage. *I couldn't have said it better myself,* he mused. *This bird has possibilities.*

The wealthy mother exclaimed her displeasure and again furiously fanned herself. She turned and addressed her daughter. "I don't understand your fascination with this horrid old hotel. How are you going to feel if that—" she pointed towards the cage. Searching for the right word, her mouth flapped open and closed. "Bird, starts yelling? And so obscene!" Her hand increased its waiving movement and she made little tut-tutting noises. "The Senator will not be happy."

Secretly, Jaxon enjoyed the scene before him. Theo's woman leaned in and placed cups of tea in front of the mother and the bride.

"Mrs. Whitcomb I apologize for the bird," she soothed. She slid a sweet cake under the mother's twitching nose before placing the tempting morsel on the antique table in front of her.

Isabella continued in a gentle tone. "The bird's new to Twin Springs. He was abused and we only recently rescued him. Ava took him in."

Mrs. Whitcomb scoffed at the comment and brushed imaginary lint from her skirt. "Some animals and people cannot be saved. I suggest you cut your losses with that monstrosity."

The daughter, battened down tighter than a sub on maneuvers in her sweater with little pearl buttons, stiffened. Jaxon would bet money that the Senator and Mrs. Whitcomb held their prized possession on a tight leash and that the young girl's fiancé had yet to breach that hull.

Kennedy's voice was hesitant at first but built with steam as she spoke up. "Dad would laugh and declare, 'If the bird can talk, then he should have the right to vote.'" She winked at Jaxon.

It was always the shy ones, he mused and his gaze bounced back to the dove.

Mrs. Whitcomb seemed to relax a little in her chair. "I should never have married below my station. Even if your father will someday be President." She picked up another sweet cake from the tray and bit a minuscule piece from the white, square pastry. Pausing half chew, her eyes flew to her daughter's. "Your father better fulfill his duty and become President. Only then will he be able to make everything up to me."

Keeping tabs on his gentle dove, Jaxon watched her lean in towards the mother of the bride, while simultaneously squeezing Kennedy's hand.

"Mrs. Whitcomb, I'll keep the bird far away from your daughter's wedding," she promised. "Holding Kennedy's wedding at Twin Springs will be everything you've imagined and more."

Her voice was just above a whisper and Jaxon caught himself unconsciously leaning in to catch her words.

On the other hand, the Senator's wife had no difficulty hearing his dove. "For some reason my daughter adores your hotel. I don't know why. Anyone who's anyone in DC holds their wedding at the Mayflower Hotel. But she says the chandelier in your Crystal Ballroom reminds her of Gone With The Wind. Personally, I don't see it."

"Burn it down!" cackled the bird.

His dove rushed over to the cage and gently sang to the bird under the black sheet. The bird calmed and joined his voice with hers. The sweet tune barely reached the corner of the room where Jaxon stood and he strained to hear the melody.

"No way!" gasped Kennedy jumping to her feet and holding her fingers to her lips. "You're AVA! The glasses threw me off but you're *the* AVA. I saw you sing on stage last summer. I love your voice. What are you doing here?"

Amazed, he watched Kennedy's eyes bulge and almost fall out of her head with her excitement. An uneasy feeling rumbled in his stomach. Even he'd heard of AVA. His sister had browbeat him to take her to one of her Broadway plays but a case had come up that needed JD's special skills and he'd given the tickets away and prepped for his next mission.

"Do you sing here at Twin Springs?" The bride clasped her

hand over the pounding of her heart. "Will you sing for my wedding? I'd be deeply honored."

Settling back into her seat, Mrs. Whitcomb assessed Ava. She brandished another piece of cake in the air. "Darling, of course she'll sing at your wedding. What an honor for her."

Gathering her bulky sweater closer around her, Ava rose from before the cage. "I'm sorry, Mrs. Whitcomb. The last thing I want to do is disappoint your daughter, you, or the Senator. Regrettably, I don't sing on stage anymore."

With a flick of her free hand, the Senator's wife waived off her protests and scattered shimmering rays around the room. "I heard about that unfortunate incident on stage. It was a grisly scene. All that blood." She raised a tea cup and sipped. "Don't worry about it. We can't help the mental stability of others." Her manicured nail tapped the brim of her cup. "Of course you can sing for my Kennedy."

A tremor vibrated through Ava.

Jaxon stepped forward to protect her from the Senator's privileged wife. Unsure what the hell she was talking about, he made a mental note to contact Lee.

"Mrs. Whitcomb, I no longer sing on stage. I—I'm unable to." From behind the thick glasses Ava's eyes flitted to her sister's.

Rising to her feet, the Senator's wife addressed the room. Tipping her head back she looked down her long nose at the inhabitants. Her high and tight voice rang with the authority of a woman who was used to getting what she wanted. "My daughter desires for you to sing at her wedding. Is that too much of a request after what happened today? Don't sing from the stage, if it is a burden for you. Stand in the back of the room. I don't care, but you'll sing."

Squeezing the fabric from the cage tight in her fist, Ava breathed in deeply. She held the breath for a moment before squaring her shoulders, replying with a firm, "No."

The atmosphere in the room thickened. The Senator's wife pursed her lips at Ava's abrupt refusal. She tossed her unfinished petite cake back onto her plate. With her linen napkin, she wiped her hands and tightly clasped lips.

Theo strode forward, offering the mother of the bride an easy smile. "Mrs. Whitcomb. Singing's not part of Ava's job description. Perhaps we can offer you a different incentive to keep Twin Springs as the venue for your daughter's wedding. Not only will you enjoy our Executive Chef's outstanding services but, may I offer you an added bonus? Our Lobby Bar will be finished prior to the wedding. I'd like to offer you an open bar, compliments of Twin Springs. Your party will be the first to enjoy this new addition to our historic hotel."

Kennedy caught her mother's sleeve between her fingers and gently tugged in a futile attempt to turn her attention. "The Senator will love that. Won't he?" The bride's cheeks flushed and she peeked up at Ava from under her lashes. Under her breath, she murmured, "Mother, please."

Mrs. Whitcomb's chin lowered and she relaxed her stance, but she refused to regain her seat. Instead, she gathered up her purse and placed the strap in the crook of her arm. "That will suffice." She tilted her head towards Jaxon. "You may have my car brought around. We'll wait in the lobby. Come, Kennedy."

The bride glanced apologetically at Ava. "Yes, Mother."

Looking down at himself, Jaxon inspected his clothes. He wasn't wearing a monkey suit. What made the woman think he'd bring her car around?

The Senator's wife marched across the room and paused momentarily before the double doors, waiting. With a flick of her lashes and nose high in the air, she cast an expectant look at Jaxon and then back towards the door.

Just do the job, he reminded himself. Reaching forward, he pulled the slightly ajar door open.

He entertained the idea of releasing the handle and permitting the door to smack the pompous woman in the ass. But he resisted and slowly allowed the door to latch.

After the click of the door, Theo tugged a walkie talkie out of an inner pocket of his jacket. "Mrs. Whitcomb would like her car brought around. Please meet the Senator's wife in the Grand Lobby and escort her and her daughter to their vehicle." He waited, listening for a moment, then said, "Thanks."

Crossing his arms, Jaxon leaned back against the massive double doors. He noticed Ava's shoulders shudder slightly before she jerked the black fabric off the bird's cage with a grand flourish. The gray parrot flapped his wings and shook his body from the tip of his beak down to his red tipped tail. "Fuck you," his deep voice rumbled.

Theo shook his head. "What was Logan thinking giving you that bird? This is a high 'visibility' wedding. The positive press will ensure future bookings. Logan needs to take that bird back to the Aviary until his vocabulary improves."

She bristled at his words. "Never! He's mine and he remains here with me. Don't worry. I'll pull Kennedy's wedding together. I've already contacted *Today's Bride* Magazine. The wedding of Senator Whitcomb's daughter will grace the cover of their February edition. Anyway, teaching my bird to behave isn't one of Logan's duties."

Her full lips canted into a sideways smile that made Jaxon's heart slam against his chest.

She added, "I appreciate any help Logan can give me with my bird, but I'll teach him new words. Besides, the idea of owning a male that will repeat what I tell him to say? Amazing." The air filled with the bells of her laughter.

Jaxon's body hardened. He wanted her. No, he needed her.

Transfixed, he watched Ava slide off the black glasses. His brow furrowed and he examined the face revealed from behind the thick frames. Shrugging his shoulders, he noted, *So, she's not a complete plain Jane.*

Tucking her glasses into the pocket of her gray sweater, Ava shrugged her way out from under its bulk. She rolled the jacket into a ball and tossed it on the couch, revealing a stunning body. The green shirt clung to her curves and dipped into the valley created by the high peaks of her breasts. Slipping out of her shoes, she bent and extracted tall, strappy shoes from under the desk and stepped into them. Her black pants skimmed the long length of her legs, kissed the rounded curve of her bottom and nipped in at her trim ankles.

A tight fist squeezed his heart and trapped the air within his chest. An uneasy feeling slithered down his spine and he broke out into a fine sweat. Swallowing hard, he thought, *Holy shit.*

Dragging the gray band from her hair, Ava shook out her glorious ebony mane. It came alive and caught the light as it cascaded down her back.

Dumb shit, his mind taunted him.

Stunned, he stood hypnotized by the luminescent twin pools of her light green eyes. Ava wasn't beautiful. The word didn't do her justice. Ava Fairbanks was a breathtaking woman. Gorgeous. Magnificent. Jaxon fumed. *Gentle dove my ass.*

Betrayal sucker punched him in the gut. Just like before, his instincts were crap. She wasn't a plain Jane but a stunning, conniving bitch. One who manipulated her looks for her own personal gain. He focused in on her and hatred poured from his eyes. He watched her adorn her ears with silver hoops. *Well, not this time. No one will be hurt by my failures.*

But someone would get hurt, possibly him, if he didn't watch it. He gritted his back teeth and hardened his heart. *Keep your distance,* he reminded himself. *Finish the job you were sent to do and get out of this crazy hotel.*

Theo motioned with his hand for Jaxon to enter further into the room. "Come in and meet everyone."

Jaxon noticed his new bosses lips moving but the words never reached his brain. Shaking his head, he cleared the fog created by Ava and focused.

"Isabella, Ava, may I introduce you to Twin Springs' new Security Manager, Jaxon Wolfe. He'll live on site until he finds a place in town. Jaxon, this is my fiancée Isabella Fairbanks and her sister

Ava. Their family has owned Twin Springs for over a hundred years."

Dragging his thoughts back to the job at hand, he reached forward and shook Isabella's tiny hand. *Better and better*, considered Jaxon. Living at the hotel gave him the opportunity to explore even off duty and at odd hours. Turning towards Ava, he attempted to mask the contempt he felt for her kind and gave a curt nod.

The welcoming smile on Ava's face froze, just for a moment, before being covered by a polite nod. Stiffening, she toyed with the rings on her fingers and replied, "Welcome to Twin Springs Hotel and Spa. If you'll excuse me gentlemen, I must sketch out the placement of the tables that we discussed with the bride."

Stunned, Jaxon watched her depart. Gone was the shy woman who'd meekly made her way through the world. She flipped her silky hair over her shoulder and her rolling walk mocked the mere mortal women who graced the red carpet.

"It's a pleasure to meet you," said Isabella. She removed a checkered kerchief from her pocket and worried the cloth between her fingers. "But if you'll excuse me, I need to get back to work," she added, before popping a quick kiss on Theo's lips and hurrying out the double doors.

Jaxon ground his teeth and tried to block out the image of Ava's stunning body walking. If you could categorize the swaying of her hips as mere walking. Mortals walked, not goddesses. Relieved to be released from the powers of her splendor, he combated the pull to rush after her, throw himself at her feet and beg for any scraps she offered. *Close call.* Another woman's face flickered across his memory. *I would've made a fool out of myself. Again.*

His conscience piped up, *You're a dumb ass.*

Alone with Theo and his thoughts, he fully examined the room for the first time. Angry at himself for once again allowing a beautiful woman to distract him from his mission, he reigned himself in. *A man's office, yet it belonged to a woman. No feminine touches. Almost gave the impression of stepping back in time.*

His gaze swept up to an immense portrait hanging above the fireplace. His heart stopped beating. The world around him stilled and white noise filled his ears.

In the portrait stood three women. One subject blonde, one black haired, one redhead. All three Caucasian. All three from the 1920's. All three obviously sisters.

One woman similar in every detail to Isabella. From her blonde hair coiled up high on top of her head, to her child sized form. One woman resembled the bitch Ava. No, hair chin length, instead of the long, flowing hair she'd released earlier. Third subject, long red hair, with her high cheekbones sprinkled with freckles, and a wide sweeping smile that he knew all too well. She was a carbon copy of his sister JD.

CHAPTER SIXTEEN

hile the bird sang some wacko song in the background, the world around Jaxon sped up. The room spun crazily, circling him, increasing in speed and sound until it thundered in his ears. The bird's catchy tune faded off into the background.

"Jaxon. Jaxon. Jaxon," Theo repeated, snapping his fingers in front of the new Security Manager's eyes.

He shook his head and focused in on his new boss but his mind was reeling. *Attempted murder? Sabotage? Moonshine? A crazy parrot?* He was in a damn looney bin. *And now his sister's face.*

But the last point cancelled out all the others. His sister's face. Painted over a hundred years ago. His thoughts raced and he used his training to sort through the facts presented and pushed his faulty instincts aside. He must find the connection. How had JD's face ended up in an old portrait in the mountains of Virginia? He didn't know, but it twisted him in knots. And he'd make it his mission to figure it out.

Hiding a smile behind his raised hand, Theo offered, "Ava has that effect on men. I should've warned you."

He ground his teeth so hard he thought they might turn to dust. "It's not her. It's the painting."

"Excuse me." Theo wiped the smile from his face. "I've become accustomed to picking up men in Ava's wake." He focused in on the painting. "Eerie isn't it. I was thrown too the first time I saw the resemblance to Isabella and Ava. Those are the General's three daughters. The red head was nicknamed Ame. She was Isabella and Ava's great grandmother, Amethyst Fairbanks. The black haired woman was her sister Ruby and the blonde was her other sister, Emerald. The family and the community thought all three sisters died in the fire that had destroyed Twin Springs' tower, part of the kitchens and stables on New Years Eve 1928. That is, until a few months ago, when Isabella discovered that Emerald, or "Emma" as family referred to her, was murdered in a tunnel running under the grounds of Twin Springs."

Only half listening, Jaxon's muscles hardened. His hands flexed, ready to rip Theo's throat out and demand to know how his sister's face ended up in an one-hundred-year-old portrait. Suppressing the anger by breathing through his nose, he smoothed his face into a friendly smile. Inside he seethed and realized the simple investigation was no longer just a regular case. Now, the mission was personal. "You say the redhead is their great grandmother?"

Theo glanced up at the portrait. "Yes. Funny, isn't it, that neither Isabella nor Ava resemble her. She gave birth on New Year's Eve, right before the Great Fire. Dale told me that if her husband hadn't scooped up his newly born son to show off to the General, then the baby would've perished in the fire too. The General's whole line would've died out in one night."

Flexing his hands to relieve the anger burning within him, Jaxon asked, "What caused the fire?"

"Everyone assumed it was sparked by the faulty installation of a row of gas Monarch stoves in the main kitchen. We now suspect an employee of Twin Springs set off a chain reaction of fires by compromising a secret still under the kitchens. We think the explosion traveled through the gas lines and caused the fires in the stables, kitchens and the Tower."

The office door flung open. With a rush of air, Maddy bounded into the room, skidded to a stop and stared slack jawed at Jaxon.

Theo groaned under his breath and shared a look with him as if to say, "sisters". "Do you need something?"

Melting against the open door frame, she continued to gaze dewy eyed up at Jaxon and gave a long sigh.

Theo threw his hands up and moved towards the teen, grabbed her up by the arm, and whispered, "Snap out of it. You're embarrassing yourself." He added, "And me."

Maddy's mouth clicked shut and she glared at her older brother.

Taking pity on the teenager, Jaxon tried to diffuse the situation. "I was just discussing the portrait with your brother." He moved further into the room and farther away from the teen's adoring looks. He studied the features of Amethyst Fairbanks. Up close, there were minute differences between her and JD. For one, his sister's eyes were a little more almond shaped and guarded. Amethyst's lips appeared fuller, but that could be because his sister's lips were usually in a tight line. The woman in the portrait had led a pampered life, where everything was handed to her. While his sister had scraped her way up from meager beginnings, earned anything she received and would beat you into a bloody pulp to keep the things she possessed. Plus, his sister didn't sport a long necklace spaced with amethyst gems and little balls of diamonds. Jaxon shoved his hands into his jean pockets and moved closer to the portrait. "That's one heck of a sparkler hanging around her neck."

Theo laughed. "Sure is. From what I understand, the General presented each of the girls with a present. Ruby with a headband made of roses shaped by rubies, with diamond leaves. Amethyst, with the amethyst and diamond necklace. And Emma, sorry I mean Emerald, with an emerald necklace."

Jaxon whistled under his breath. "Some gifts."

"We thought all the jewels burned in the fire with the sisters.

But Emma's emerald was discovered the night we found her body."

Not wanting to be left out of the conversation, Maddy moved towards Jaxon. She draped herself over the couch, inched her skirt up above her knee and pretended to look up at the portrait while trying to strike a pose between sexy and sophisticated. She inhaled a mighty gulp of air, sucking her stomach in, and trapped her breath behind an awkwardly alluring smile, thrusting her petite breasts towards Jaxon as she lounged backwards.

Theo eyed his little sister's actions, "Do you have a kink in your back or something?"

The teenager's shoulders slumped and she let out the breath with a mighty rush. Attempting a different pose, she elongated her neck and pushed her curly hair back over her shoulder to bare the delicate skin on her neck.

Ignoring the siblings' banter, Jaxon said, "I'll bet that bought a lot of improvements."

Shooting glares at his sister, Theo answered, "We couldn't sell an heirloom like that. It's on Isabella's finger. Her engagement ring. But, she wears it mostly on a chain around her neck when she is working in the kitchen. We're waiting for the insurance claim funds to come through. They'll help offset the improvements and repairs from the sabotage."

His mind switched back to the case at hand. "What's the hold up?"

The teenager sighed and fluttered her lashes at him.

Theo rubbed the hair on the back of his neck and frowned at his sister. "Not sure. I thought Ava had addressed the concerns and questions the insurance investigator had raised but apparently not."

His suspicions confirmed, Jaxon mumbled, "Of course she did."

Shifting her pose on the couch, the teenager undid the top trio of buttons on her shirt and pulled the fabric apart, exposing more of her chest. She cleared her throat and wet her lips with the tip of her tongue.

Theo seemed to realize he needed to put a stop to Maddy before she melted into a pool of drool at the poor man's feet because he rushed forward to redirect his sister and his arm hit the bird cage, almost knocking the parrot off of his perch.

Dropping the walnut he munched on, the African Gray's eyes pinned Theo and he called out in a gravelly voice, "Stupid bitch."

Clearly exasperated with the entire situation, Theo's back went ramrod straight and his eyes turned to chips of coal. "Maddy, go find someone else to bug. Or study for your test. Just get away from Jaxon and give him space. Now!"

Her face beet red, she glared at her brother. "You're such a jerk." She twirled and stomped from the room.

Theo mocked, "Well, now that you've enjoyed an introduction to the Twin Springs' family, let me show you to your new office."

Jaxon tore his eyes from the painting. This might just be a damn JOBB, but he'd examine the facts and find the truth. And protect his sister from this crazy family. "Great, I'm ready."

CHAPTER SEVENTEEN

After escaping her office, Ava slipped inside one of the telephone booths in the Presidents Hall. She drew the etched glass, bi-fold door closed behind her. Perched upon the tiny bench seat, she kicked off her high heels and pressed her bare feet against the wall opposite the telephone. Hugging her legs, she bent her head and laid her hot forehead against her knees. Her heart pounded within her chest. Gulping deep breaths of air, she attempted to calm her breathing by slowly releasing each breath. "He can't be," she murmured, trying to recall the face from her dreams. But in her heart, she knew. There was no mistaking those eyes.

The bi-fold door folded back with a snap and Ava's head whipped towards the sound only to discover her sister's face lined with worry. "I'm sorry. We should've realized that Mrs. Whitcomb might bring up your last time on stage."

Shaking her head, she rubbed the palms of her hands on her pants. Ava studied the peeling gold and cream wallpaper inside the booth. "The stage no longer holds magic for me."

Not after holding Ashlee's dead body against hers on the cold stage floor.

Isabella closed the glass door. "Are you sure?" She crouched down, twisting her red and white bandana into a knot between her hands. "You're too young to give up on such a successful career. Too good. You were born to sing. Besides, you once told me singing was the only time you felt truly alive."

"Not anymore. The stage only holds death for me. All I can see is Mrs. Hollingsworth, soaking wet. Shaking." Her body jolted as if a shot rang out. "The roar of her gun. And her warm blood spurting over me. Sticking to my skin."

Squeezing her eyes shut, Ava tried to forget. Ashlee's knock had prevented her from being raped but she'd failed to prevent the woman from killing herself. She hadn't uttered one sound. Just stared at the Director's wife and watched her lips moving. Guilt spilled over her. A traitorous tear escaped and rolled down her cheek. "The thought of standing on stage makes me feel physically ill."

Isabella shoved the scarf into the pocket of her chef jacket and grasped her sister's hands within her own. "You don't have to do anything, if you don't want to." She switched topics, trying to soothe her sister. "What did you think of the new Security Manager?"

How could she tell her sister that when Jaxon Wolfe had entered the General's office, it wasn't just the strong planes of his face, or his golden eyes flecked with green that had attracted her. A powerful pull had tugged at her and drawn her towards him. Greater than anything she'd ever experienced. Her chest had almost burst from the feverish tempo of her beating heart. In those brief moments, she was sure that her soul had touched his.

She hadn't needed to draw on any acting ability to stay in character and not further upset Mrs. Whitcomb. Jaxon had stolen her breath and managed to turn her into all thumbs and jerky movements during her small performance.

But hope was a mirage for the weak and foolish. The true Ava wasn't worthy of being liked, or even loved. The proof had flashed back at her from the pure hatred that had emanated from his eyes when Theo had introduced her. She'd experienced such intense hatred many times before. From women who despised her for how she looked. And from the Director who thought he could use her for his own pleasure and success.

The now familiar rush of emotions pelted Ava and over-whelmed her with their power. Humiliation. Fear. Helplessness. All the feelings twisted and clawed within the black, decaying space left deep inside her after being attacked, growing in fervor until she choked on the putrid stench of their power. "Why did Theo hire him? Twin Springs was supposed to be my safe haven. The one place for me to hide from the outside world. The one place where people like Jaxon Wolfe couldn't follow and torment me."

Her sister's brow furrowed. "What do you mean?"

Shame poured over Ava. Her mind screamed the words she couldn't voice. *The Director almost raped me. I wasn't strong enough to push him off. Couldn't even scream. And because of my weakness a woman killed herself.* She opted for another less terrifying secret to reveal. "He's the man from my sleepwalking dream."

"What?" Isabella plopped onto her butt. "Are you sure?"

Ava twisted the rings on her finger. "Positive."

The bi-fold door clattered open again and Maddy popped her head in, the long ringlets of her hair springing around her young face. "What's going on? Are we having a meeting? Did you see him? Isn't he awesome?"

Isabella jumped to her feet and attempted to force the teen from the booth. "Not now."

In the blink of an eye, Ava transformed herself. Lighting her face with a smile, she addressed the love struck teenager. "Of course I saw him. Yummy. Are you sure he isn't a little old for you?"

Maddy's eyes narrowed and she studied Ava with her head tilted to the side.

Ava's breath caught and held within her chest. *Please Maddy, please don't see past my facade. Don't ask. Not now. Please.*

Shrugging her shoulders, the teen's attention shifted and she bounced up and down on her slender heels. Her words surged forward and tumbled out of her mouth, one after the other. "He's perfect. Theo's showing him around. I wanted to help but for some reason that irritated my jerk-o-la of a brother and he told me to hit the bricks. And guess what?"

Joy seeped into her heart with Maddy's enthusiasm. Even if it was about the one man her heart desired more than anything but could never have. "What?"

"Theo put him in a guest room between ours."

Ava's heart froze. Not only would she need to steer clear of him at work but, now, she must avoid him in the mornings and nights around her bedroom? *How could jerk-o-la Theo do that to me?*

Suddenly distracted by her surroundings, Maddy paused and inspected the tiny booth. She picked up the gray, plastic phone receiver and tugged on its long, looped cord. Mesmerized, she watched the loops expand and then spring back to their original length as she tugged and released the cord. Taking her time, she pushed the tiny square buttons numbered zero through nine, before placing the receiver back in its cradle on the wall. "Wow, this is like a time machine. What did you do if you misdialed? Where's the back button?"

Isabella snorted. "You actually hung up and started over again."

The young girl's eyes widened. "No kidding," she breathed.

The corner of Ava's mouth rose with a tiny smile. "This space is relatively unchanged since the General installed the booths. Yes, the phones are different, but the rest of the cubby stayed true."

Maddy's brow arched up. "Looks it."

Chuckling, Isabella added, "Only the General would've had enough foresight to come home from War, purchase a grand hotel and install a row of phone booths. In a time when most homes across America didn't own phones and the few homes lucky enough to gain access to a phone were usually on a party line."

Ava nodded. She couldn't see into the future like her ancestor had. Couldn't see past her sleepwalking and memories. Now all she wanted to do was hide and play the role of Group Sales and

Special Events Coordinator for Twin Springs, for her family, for herself. "He was amazing."

The teen contemplated the small booth. "You know—"

Ava loved watching her mind work. For a young girl, or even for an adult for that matter, her mind was astounding. The moment inspiration struck, the fine features on her face lit up, and her eyes sparkled.

"We should update these booths. Take out the phones. No one needs them anymore. Put in cell phone charger cords and adapters. Thin computer screens with cameras for the guests to video chat, surf the web and work. With little effort and cost, these booths could be transformed into a useful space." Warming up to the idea, she rubbed her hands together. "Can I borrow your phone?"

Isabella dug her cell phone out the front pocket of her chef jacket and handed it over to her future sister-in-law. "Sure, did you lose yours?"

"Nope." Maddy pressed speed dial and lifted the phone to her ear. "Dale won't answer my calls but he'll answer if he thinks it's you." Spinning around, she sped away from the door of the phone booth and called back over her shoulder, "I hope you saved some cake for me. Or you're not getting your phone back."

Rushing from the booth, Isabella's short legs attempted to keep up with the teen's long stride. "You give me my phone or I'll tell Theo." Her voice rose to a high pitch that Ava remembered from when they were kids. "Right now!"

Leaning her head back against the wall, Ava's eyelids fluttered closed and she listened as their voices faded into the distance. The past moments reinforced how much she loved being home at Twin Springs with her family. If there was any chance of her healing, she needed to be here. Sitting up, she squared her shoulders. "This is my home and no man will force me from Twin Springs. Not even yummy Jaxon Wolfe with his stubbled face and strong shoulders."

She pulled her phone from her pocket, clicked the camera function, and reversed the camera view so that her face stared back at her. Powdering her nose, she examined her face for weakness. "All you need to do is stick to your plan and immerse yourself in your new role as the Group Sales and Special Events Coordinator. Play the part of disinterested and indifferent part owner towards Jaxon and then move on to rude socialite bitch till he goes away."

A tear escaped, and she blotted it with the powder. "Maybe if you immerse yourself in the new roles deep enough, you'll forget the roar of the pistol vibrating through your skull. Or in time, you won't round a corner and associate the smell of cigarette smoke to the acrid smell of gun powder, or cigar smoke to the Director. Perhaps, as the years pass, when you close your eyes, you won't feel the warm, wet splatter of blood across your face and arms. Or the weight of Ashlee Hollingsworth pressing you into floorboards as the life drains from her body."

She clicked the phone off and her chin trembled. "Just pretend to be anyone else but Broadway Star AVA. A victim who wasn't strong enough to save a woman's life."

CHAPTER EIGHTEEN

*J*axon suppressed a smile when Theo gave the bird one last glare before leading him out. They made a right before reaching the Bell Stand and passed through open double doors with a sign above that said, Presidents Hall. Immediately on the right was a window, with curtains drawn, and a white door with a black Security Office sign.

"Here's your office." Theo opened the door and gestured for him to enter.

Jaxon surveyed the cubby hole of an office. The desk was pushed up under the window. A flat screen computer, mouse, cup of pencils and walkie talkies sat on the table. Above the desk four monitors flashed different scenes of Twin Springs.

A bright red and rectangular console with flashing lights hung on the wall to the left of the desk and a full-length mirror hung on the opposite wall. Framed pictures lined the back wall, above a short bookcase. A rat hole of a space, but he wouldn't be here long, so it didn't matter. His mind made a snapshot of the office for him to disseminate at a later time. "Looks good."

Theo shrugged and rubbed the back of his neck. "We haven't moved or rearranged anything since Niles held it. Take your time and acquaint yourself with this office and the rest of Twin Springs.

I'll check back with you tomorrow and find out how everything is going. Pick up the key to your room from the Front Desk."

Jaxon nodded. He was ready to complete the insurance job and his new mission; find out how his sister's face ended up in a one-hundred-year-old painting. He waited a few moments after Theo departed and shut the door, then shrugged out of his leather jacket and dropped it on the back of the chair. Pulling his cell phone from his pocket, he rang his cousin. "So much for getting in and out."

Not waiting for his cousin to say hello, he immediately started talking once Lee picked up. "It's me. I need you to work your computer magic. Do a background investigation on a subject; female, name: Ava Fairbanks."

"Sure," responded his cousin. "A new girlfriend?"

Picturing Ava's fine features in his head, his gut clenched with desire. Casting the treacherous feeling aside, he settled into the rolling chair in front of the desk and growled. "Hell no."

"Give me a minute."

Jaxon heard the clicks of a keyboard and he picked up one of the walkie talkies lined up along the desk.

Lee gave a low whistle, "You lucky son of a bitch. She's AVA! From the Broadway show you gave me the tickets to see. Wanna trade places?"

He tossed the walkie back and forth between his hands. "Kiss my ass. Just give me the particulars."

"Someone's a little cranky," muttered Lee before rattling off. "Ava Fairbanks, Broadway actor, early thirties. Has a butt load of awards for a budding star."

Nodding his head, he listened as Lee listed the names of the plays she'd featured in and the awards she'd earned.

The clicking paused, "Wait! Here we go. Career cut short when the Director's wife came on stage during the closing scene and blew her brains out in front of Ava, the entire cast and the audience. Has not returned to the play since. According to this article, her understudy is doing a piss poor job of filling her shoes.

"Wait, there's another article." Lee's fingers tapped away. "An article by a guy called, Mac Mills. He insinuates that Ava was sleeping with the Director."

Jaxon knew it. Beautiful, powerful women. Who used their position and looks to manipulate men. "I wouldn't doubt it."

"What does she have to do with our insurance job?"

"Not sure yet. But she's part owner of the hotel. Just don't trust her."

"Of course you don't." Snickering under his breath, Lee added, "She's one hell of a looker. You've got to move past it, Jax. Not all beautiful women are. . ." he paused, running through the database in his brain. "What's your new favorite phrase? Oh yeah, lying, evil, conniving bitches."

He compared Ava to the blonde who'd changed his life and the lives of his comrades forever. Unwilling to trust his gut instinct that there was no comparison, he threw the walkie back on the desk. "Whatever Lee. We've got another problem." He rubbed his temples, knowing his next actions would poke at a hornet's nest best left alone. Taking a deep breath for courage, he added, "I need you to pull JD's file."

Silence stretched between the two men and Lee whistled low and long. "Your sister's adoption file? Are you nuts? Why? What does she have to do with the insurance job?"

With his knuckles, he rubbed the black stubble along his jawline. "Don't know. Yet. But this is important. Find her file and any ground work the Geezers did about her childhood and get it to me fast. But don't let her or the Geezers know I want it. Keep this quiet. I don't want them showing up here."

"Yeah right, Jax. The Geezers find out everything. Besides, the file isn't at HQ. One of the Geezers keeps it secured. It's hard copy, not in the computers."

"Just get it." Leaning back, Jaxon's golden gaze followed the action on the security monitors. "I think we have a lead on her past. Don't let anyone know. Particularly, not JD. I don't want to get her hopes up." He waited. There was a long pause from his cousin.

"No shit? Roger that, I'll get you the file. But she's going to be pissed if she discovers that you've been hiding things from her. Especially, any clues about her past."

Jaxon hesitated. Since his last mission, his credibility was shot with his family. But he needed to tell Lee. "There's a picture of JD here."

"What are you talking about? A mug shot?" He snickered, "Like from a wanted poster. Has she been on the lamb since she was a kid?"

"I'm serious. Cut the shit. It's a painting." He didn't have the nerve to add the portrait's age. Lee would laugh his ass off and discount anything else he said.

"Are you sure it's not one of her paintings? A self-portrait?"

"No. It's not. I promise." Frowning, Jaxon leaned forward and studied the monitor, noting a man who didn't fit the environment, wearing a pair of rag-tag jeans and a filthy shirt. He tracked the man's limping movements from screen to screen till he disappeared. Tapping his fingers on the desk, he leaned back and mentally filed the man's description. Something about the stranger made his instincts sit up and take notice. He'd almost seemed familiar. "Just get the file Lee and report back to me. ASAP."

Switching back to the mission on hand, his cousin responded, "Got it. What's your cover for staying at the hotel in order to get long term intel? Did you check in?"

Jaxon grunted and his satisfied smile gleamed in the tiny office. "I guess you could say that. You're talking to the new Security Manager for Twin Springs Hotel and Spa."

CHAPTER NINETEEN

...Wrapped in her wide collared mink coat, that covered her body down to the hem of her skirt, Ruby caught sight of the row of tiny windows running the peaked roofline of the stables. The General had slapped aside her dreams of becoming an actress as foolish and unbecoming of a Rockwell. Her ears still rang from the tenor of his ire.

She intended to ride her speckled horse, Freckles, till her problems pounded away beneath the horse's hooves. She cared not that she wasn't dressed properly for riding. She wanted to feel the power of the horse under her, the wind against her face and pretend she possessed the power to make her own choices. Anything to escape her father's smothering rules.

The wide, wooden doors were already pushed aside and she walked underneath the towering opening. The smells of horse manure, gasoline and leather greeted her. Rows of stalls, once filled with the guests' horses, were now peppered with automobiles. Modern, streamlined automobiles. She trailed the tips of her fingers over the long nose of a gun mettle grey Duesenberg and she changed her mind about riding Freckles. Even though the automobiles were made in America, they were built by German born brothers and her father would never own one. Halting, she eyed the tan and black Cadillac. Its great big eyes stared back at her.

American through and through, just like her father. His baby and now hers.

"Don't think your father would approve of you taking her for a drive, Miss Ruby." Guy's voice coursed through her like a forbidden whiskey, scalding her throat and leaving a fire burning in her gut.

She paused next to the Cadillac. Turning on her heel, she reclined back against the wide fender and gave a welcoming smile to her father's new chauffeur. God he was delicious. The sleeves of his white shirt were folded back to reveal his tanned, muscled forearms and a sprinkling of black hair. The rounded collar of his work shirt was spread wide and the buttons strained against the pull of his wide shoulders, but his suspenders held the fabric in place. She itched to pop a few more buttons and discover if his chest was also covered with a mat of silky hair. Who'd want to ride a horse when she could dally with him? She only just stopped herself from purring deep in the back of her throat. "Just what I need. A chauffeur. Take me for a spin."

His lips slid into a knowing, crooked smile and he leaned back against one of the stable's wooden supports. With his hat tipped low, the golden glow from his gaze pierced hers from the shadows under the brim. "I didn't receive word from Twin Springs about anyone requiring my assistance today."

Burning with the need to be free from her father's world and out from under the rule of his thumb, she used her womanly wiles to attain her goal. Freedom. If only for a few hours.

Leisurely, she unpinned the scarf from around her head and shook her long hair free. Taking her compact out of her pocket, she painted her lips. Slowly. Daringly. Knowing he watched as the lipstick slid against her full lips. Finished, she pocketed her tool and pressed her lips out into a full pout. Her eyes devoured the length of him. His lean body was clad in long wool trousers. He held a grimy cloth between his hands. "Don't be such a flat tire. Just need to borrow you and the Cadi for the afternoon." A wide, sensual smile spread across her lips, daring him to accept. "I promise to bring you both back in one piece."

Chuckling under his breath, Guy finished wiping his hands on the cloth and tucked it into his back pocket. "If you want to go for a ride, I'll take you. But we're not going to, as you say, 'borrow your father's car'. We'll take mine."

Her eyes lit up, and the fire in her belly boiled, warming her. "You have an automobile?" She gave a throaty chuckle. "Perfect."

Guy shook his head and crooked his finger, "Come with me."

She trailed behind him, out the back of the stables and towards the tack room.

Wrinkling her nose, she asked, "Why isn't your automobile in the stables with everyone else's?"

"My automobile? In with all those fine autos and prime horse flesh?" Guy's golden eyes twinkled and he poked fun at her, "You're so fresh."

Feeling like a child put in her place, the hair rose on the back of her neck. "I'm not," she declared awkwardly, plodding after him as the heels of her garden shoes sunk into the mushy ground behind the stables.

"Before we go, let me grab my jacket." He eyed her up and down. "And something to keep your legs warm, from my room." His boots rang out hollow against the inclined wooden walkway and he disappeared behind the wide plank door on the side of the tack room.

Unsure of what to do with herself without an audience, she called after him. "You live in the tack room?"

From within the darkened interior, he shouted, "Yep. Benefit from the job. Free room and board, plus left-over meals from the kitchens."

Carrying a thick plaid blanket, Guy came back out and motioned for her to follow him around back, behind the building he called home. Shaded under a young oak tree stood a Ford Roadster Pickup. Shiny black with its soft, tan top removed. Opening the door, he held her hand as she stepped up on the running board and slid into the passenger seat.

He settled the blanket in around her legs and her breath caught. She watched him through her lowered lashes. He smelled slightly of horse flesh, gasoline and man. She leaned in further, enjoying the unique and forbidden mixture. "I'm amazed that the General's chauffeur owns a Breezer," she whispered.

Quickly, stepping back, he raised a brow at her actions. "Now, now, Miss Ruby. If you don't behave, Breezer or not, I'll have to tactfully decline taking you for a ride. I received instructions from the Lieutenant about fraternizing with the upstanding ladies of Twin Springs."

Giving a roguish grin, she laughed and her green eyes twinkled with merriment. "What a waste of your time." She re-secured her ebony hair in place by wrapping her long silk scarf around it. "I'm no lady."

Admiring her spunk, he closed the door, cranked the engine and slid in beside her. He tipped his cap towards her before placing it back on his head, cocked to the side. Over the tick, tock of the motor, Guy shouted, "I like your lipstick."

Her heart skipped a beat. No judgment. No sneers like the Lieutenant. He'd accepted her just the way she was. His words touched her heart. Admiring the strong line of his jaw, she felt a tug towards him.

He revved the engine. Excitement tingled through her body and her laughter flowed behind them as they sped down the hill and toward the entrance of Twin Springs. Grasping the metal windshield frame in her hands, she stood up and waived to the shocked faces of the guests lounging on the veranda.

A shining star on her own stage, Ruby blew kisses and thanked her audience for attending the opening scene of her future life away from Twin Springs. Not her father, nor society, would tether her to their antiquated opinions. Relieved from the tedium of denying her true self, joy flooded her soul. "Stick that in your pipe and smoke it, General!"

Speeding away from the curved drive with the crisp, December wind on her face, she leaned forward against the windshield with her arms akimbo, the long tail of her scarf flapping like a red flag behind her. "Faster, faster!" she shouted out. "I want to fly!" Happiness bubbled within her and burst out of her lips in song. At the top of her lungs, she sang loud and clear. . .

CHAPTER TWENTY

*D*riving back from an early morning meeting with the Sheriff, Jaxon slowed his jeep. Just ahead, he could make out the slender form of a woman on the side of the road. As the distance narrowed, the clear tones of her voice reached his ears before his eyes discovered her shapely form. Ava. "What the hell's she doing?"

Arms spread wide, she ran down the road. And she was— "Singing. Damn me, the woman's belting out jazz."

She seemed oblivious to the dipping temperatures in wide-legged, yoga pants and a matching black cotton shirt. Her thick black hair was loose and wild down her back in an unbrushed mess. "She looks like she's just tumbled out of bed." He gave a disgusted grunt when lust rolled in his gut. "How does the woman manage to look so damn good, no matter what she wears?"

Following his first instinct, he pressed the gas pedal to zoom past. "Let someone else deal with the beautiful, crazy bitch."

But his mama's upbringing had him decreasing his speed and matching the jeep's pace to hers. Grumbling under his breath, he pressed a button to lower the passenger window and shouted out over her singing. "Need a lift?"

She broke off mid chorus. Her arms dropped, she stumbled to a stop and stared sightlessly ahead.

"What the hell?" He brought the jeep to a halt beside her.

Her chin dropped to her chest and she stood there like a broken robot with hunched shoulders and arms hanging at her sides. The lushness of her hair curtained her face.

"Ava?" Concern furrowed his brow but he thrust it aside and shouted, "Hey! Ava!"

When she still didn't respond, he climbed out. Zipping his leather jacket closed against the biting wind, he stuck his hands into the pockets of his tan, tactical pants. As if finding women singing on the side of the road was an everyday occurrence, he ambled over and stood in front of her. "Ava?"

She swayed lightly in the breeze but didn't reply.

"What the hell kind of game are you playing?" He lifted her chin and her milky, pale skin felt cold to the touch. He stared down into her exquisite face, parted and full, ruby-red lips, finely cut cheekbones, and green eyes. The kind of green of newly born grass in the spring. The kind that was velvety soft and fresh to lay down upon. Damn, she was spectacular.

Sightless, she stared ahead and her gaze reflected blankly back at him. His instincts screamed that something wasn't right but he ignored it. He grasped her by the shoulders and gave her a little shake. "Are you alright?"

She jolted and her legs collapsed under her.

He tightened his hold and reluctantly pulled her against his chest to keep her from falling.

Her eyes came alive and met his.

A disloyal huskiness coated his voice. "Careful," he whispered, unable to pry his eyes away.

Her eyes darted from side to side and she stiffened. She opened her mouth, almost as if to scream, but nothing emerged. Then, the woman went wild. Slapped at his arms, his chest. Pushed, bucked against his embrace. Instantly, he released her and stepped back. "Whoa, relax. I wasn't going to hurt you."

Ava stumbled towards the jeep and leaned against it. Chest heaving, she glanced around, down the length of her body and then at him. She wasn't in the Director's office. It wasn't slimy Hollingsworth clutching at her. She was on the side of the road with Jaxon. And she hadn't the faintest clue on how she'd ended up there in her pajamas. "Don't," she gasped to catch her breath. She couldn't, couldn't have any man's hands on her. Not after *him.* "Don't touch me."

Crazy bitch. Jaxon narrowed his eyes, considering her. "Look, I'd rather hold a porcupine than you. I thought you needed help. You didn't respond when I said your name."

How long had she stood there? Sleeping but not sleeping? "Sorry." Her cheeks flushed scarlet. "I was lost in another world. Thinking." She shivered and hugged herself. She needed to say something to throw him off the scent or he'd discover her secrets. "You scared me."

"Thinking, huh? Do you always sing when you're thinking?"

She opened her mouth, at a loss for words. "Of course." She added through chattering teeth, "Clears the mind."

Liar. His suspicions were confirmed. She was a lying, evil, conniving bitch. Just like all other beautiful women. "Where did you come from?"

She glanced around. She had no idea. But somewhere in her subconscious hay, barn wood and horses rang true. "The stables." She stared into his golden eyes, hoping for confirmation.

Lie number two. "The stables are in the opposite direction."

Embarrassed, she tipped her head down and tried to figure out where she could've been. Twin Springs was in front of her. It wasn't the stables to her right. Inspiration struck. She smiled and peeked up at him. "Well…"

God, she had a sexy smile. Her eyes glittered as she looked up at him from behind thick black lashes and his thoughts rolled into an erotic fantasy with her as the leading lady. His heart shuddered and he gnashed his teeth. He wouldn't succumb to her beauty.

Trade what was left of his tattered dignity by slathering all over her like a lonely, lost puppy.

"You're right, I was heading to the Aviary."

Lie number three. Thankfully, her deceptive mouth shoved his wanton visions aside. He couldn't stand listening to her anymore and stomped his way back to the driver's side. "I'll let you get on with it then."

She couldn't believe it. He was abandoning her? On the side of the road? The wind blew straight through her PJ's. "Wait!" She rubbed the goosebumps blooming along her arms. "I've changed my mind. Could you give me a lift back to the hotel?"

His eyes met hers over the hood and he calculated the distance to the hotel against his self-discipline. He had to be honest with himself. Even though she was a lying bitch, he wanted her. "Fine. Get in."

They both climbed in and he immediately regretted his decision. She smelled like roses. He rolled the window down and pulled out, sucking cool air into his lungs to purge her sweet scent.

"Thanks." She blew into her hands, rubbed them together. "What are you doing out this early?"

He met her lie with one of his own. "Just driving around. Getting the lay of the land."

She shivered beside him.

He bit back an angry retort about mountain temperatures and stupid women, closed the window and jacked up the heat. "I've heard that people think the old Security Manager must've froze to death after being swept downstream and here you are, traipsing about on a bone-chilling, fall morning. Without even a coat." He glanced at the dashboard. "It's a few clicks below freezing."

What could she say to that? When you're sleepwalking you don't feel anything but your dreams. Or maybe, Ruby decided to take a walk. She settled on something that she hoped wouldn't push her into the crazy woman column. "Um. It didn't feel that cold when I first left." She lifted a delicate shoulder. "The temperature must have dropped. Besides, Niles couldn't have frozen to death. It was summer. He must've drowned."

"Haven't you been in a mountain river? Even in the summer, they're ice cold. Hypothermia is a killer." He grunted and breathed through his mouth. "Do you always wear so much damn perfume?"

Had Ruby doused her with perfume? She pulled the front of her shirt up to her nose and sniffed. No. "I'm not wearing any."

He scowled and squeezed the steering wheel. *Could the woman open her mouth without a lie slipping out?* "Then why do you reek of roses?"

Oh my God. Ava finally understood. She only smelled roses when Ruby was near and he must be able to smell her too. Was she in the car? An invisible passenger tagging along behind them? She stiffened in her seat and stared straight ahead, afraid to glance behind her, in case her own face stared back at her. "I do not."

"You sure as hell do," he grumbled. If he had to put up with her damn smell and lies, then he'd pump her for intel. "That's quite the portrait in your office. One of the women looks a lot like you. Some would say identical."

Did he guess? Her heart thundered in her chest and she refused to meet his eyes. "She's a relative, so I suppose she should."

She was holding something back. He felt it and pressed harder. "I understand the redhead's one of your relatives too."

No. He was just making conversation. A little of the stiffness in her shoulders left her and she leaned her head back against the headrest. "Yes, my great grandmother."

He rubbed the stubble on his chin and asked the question burning a hole in his head. "Do you have any cousins or anyone that resembles her? She's quite the beauty. Do you have any missing cousins with red hair?"

Missing cousins? Did he think they kept people locked away or something? "What? What kind of a question is that?"

Realizing he'd pushed too hard, too fast, he switched topics. "How long was Niles sabotaging the hotel?"

Her eyes narrowed. What was his sudden interest in Niles? In the painting? A horrible thought struck her. Was he a reporter? "What's with all the questions?"

"As the new Security Manager, it's part of my job to know what's going on. Even what happened in the past. Especially, something as important as someone undermining the success of the hotel."

Her cute little nose wrinkled as she considered his question and he averted his eyes back to the road, but all he could see was her beautiful face. He squeezed the wheel. Even her scent clung to him.

"I'm not really sure. I wasn't here when it started."

He'd almost forgotten how self-absorbed powerful women were. Women who'd reached the pinnacle of success in their profession. Just like the blonde correspondent who'd transformed from America's sweetheart into a traitor. "That's right. You're a big Broadway star," he sneered. "The AVA." He couldn't help himself, he had to twist the knife. Cause her pain as he was sure she did to the men that must flock around her. Just like his team had flocked around the blonde news reporter. "Didn't have time to check in on your father?"

Ava averted her head and looked out the window, twisting the rings on her finger. He was a soothsayer. A modern-day psychic that could smell and see the past. How else could he know that she'd abandoned her family and Twin Springs for her career? For her needs. Tears welled up in her throat, choking her. What could she say?

He could've sworn she sniffled but he pushed it off, due to the cold.

"You're right."

He could barely hear her words above the blast of the heater and leaned in closer.

"I focused on my career, my needs. Not what my family needed."

She turned and her eyes shimmered, green as a deep sea.

"If I could take all that back I would. But I can't."

The first truth out her mouth. He felt like an asshole and ground his teeth together. But she was an actress. *Couldn't they turn tears on and off like a faucet? Damn JOBB.* "How will you pay for all the incidents?"

She blinked back the moisture at the switch in topic. "Theo fronted funds for the damages. We hope to pay him back with the insurance claims."

Just using the guy for his cash, he mused. "And if the claims don't come through?"

"We could lose Twin Springs."

Her phone buzzed and Ava pulled it out of a pocket hidden in the side of her PJ pants. "This is Ava. What do you mean the Christmas tree isn't paid for? It's supposed to be delivered in a couple days. How much?" She rubbed the bridge of her nose between her thumb and forefinger. "I'll take care of this myself. Today. Thank you for letting me know."

She clicked the phone off and stared out the window, figuring out what the twenty-thousand-dollar tree would do to her savings. *Wipe it out.* But she couldn't burden Theo with more financial problems. Not after the sabotages and their previous Executive Chef's embezzlement of funds. She'd just have to pretend everything was all right.

"Problems?"

"Nope." She turned towards him and her lips spread into a full, wide smile that stole his breath. "Everything's just fine."

And another lie.

Rage boiled under his skin. Every time the woman spoke, lies tumbled out of her beautiful mouth. He pulled around the front of Twin Springs and screeched to a jarring halt. Leaning over her, ignoring the brush of her soft body against his, he pushed the door open. "You can lie to other men all you want. But don't sling your bullshit my way. Get out."

She gasped. Slid out of the car and slammed the door behind her.

Jaxon couldn't help himself, his gaze trailed her as she walked away and climbed the front steps. Even mad, Ava had a grace all her own. "Damn it, where the hell are her shoes?"

CHAPTER TWENTY-ONE

"He found you, on the side of the road, singing?" Isabella paused in staking the outline of a rocking horse into the ground. "That's so embarrassing. What did you say?"

On the expansive lawn, flanked on four sides by Twin Springs, the Casino, the Spa and the Hot Springs pool, the two sisters laid out a fairyland of light-up Christmas decorations.

"I lied through my teeth." Ava plugged a gingerbread man into the extension cord. "Told him I was out," she paused for dramatic affect. "Thinking."

Isabella snorted back a laugh and shoved the stake in with her foot. "Even with your acting ability, there's no way he believed that."

"He didn't seem to. But, what should I have said?" She dragged over a toy soldier, propped him up and her sister staked him down. "Sorry, I'm sleepwalking. Or, excuse me, I'm being haunted by a hundred-year-old ghost who uses me as her own personal Barbie doll."

"As the new Security Manager, he's going to find out." Isabella plugged the light up decoration into the next extension cord in the chain. "Are you sure he's the man from your sleepwalking dreams?"

"Resembles him in looks but not manners." Ava's voice rose, "He scolded me about lying to him and kicked me out of his jeep. Right at the entrance of the hotel. In front of everyone."

"Well, you did lie." Isabella stared past her sister and up to the dual, brick staircases that led down from the east entrance to the hotel. "Speaking of the handsome devil. Here he comes now."

Ava whipped around. Even at a distance, strength emanated from the man and permeated the air around him. Her traitorous heart thundered in her chest at the sight of his dark hair and broad shoulders. His tan pants had a tactical look to them that she'd never see before, with the special pockets and loops. His black leather jacket was scuffed and worldly, just like him.

Trotting along beside him, Maddy's excited voice reached them. "This building is called the Casino. It has a small restaurant and golf shop. During the holiday season, the shop's transformed into Santa's Workshop and offers Christmas decorations and gifts for purchase."

Lacing her arm through Jaxon's, she leaned her head against his shoulder. "Over there, next to the pool, is our ice rink. It becomes a Victorian village with ice skaters dressed as nineteenth century carolers."

The man frowned down at her and untangled their arms.

Oblivious to his discouragement, the teen's face glowed with excitement. "The lawn between the Casino and the hotel becomes Candy Cane Lane, with oversized, light-up gingerbread figures, toy soldiers, toys, eleven-foot candy canes and huge lolly pops and gum drops." Spotting the two sisters, she waved, and called out, "Hi Ava, Isabella."

Immediately, Jaxon's intense stare zeroed in on her. He was still pissed. Her heart leapt into her throat. "Well, let him be," she murmured and bent down for a gigantic candy cane. "Let's finish up and get out of the cold."

"What's the rush?" Isabella tugged on the string that would anchor the thin frame down.

Ava searched her mind for something to justify escaping Jaxon's impending arrival. She couldn't explain that she ached for the man yet hated him for how he made her feel when she was around him. "I need to finalize arrangements for the Christmas tree's grand entrance."

Jaxon ignored the blabbering of the teen beside him. He'd already pumped her for intel on the portrait and the insurance claims. It had been an exasperating experience. She couldn't stay on topic and kept giving him the heebie-jeebies when she stared at him.

Instead, he studied Ava. Since their short morning drive, peaceful thoughts were a luxury of the past. She'd penetrated his mind, his thoughts. And even his dreams. He studied the two sisters. Exact opposites. Isabella was short, sporting comfortable jeans and a green hoodie, while Ava's long legs were encased in navy blue slacks that skimmed her firm butt. The rest of her curves were hidden by a billowy, white coat with fur at the collar. But at least she was wearing shoes.

He couldn't get it out of his mind that something was seriously wrong yesterday. That he'd been so tangled up in her beauty that he'd missed something. Was she taking drugs? Could she be on something that made her so out of it that she had no idea of where she was or what she'd been doing? In her intoxicated state, could she really be responsible for some of the so-called accidents around the hotel? And conveniently blamed the ex-security manager who'd tried to hurt Isabella and Maddy?

The teenager grabbed him by the hand and pulled him over to the sisters. "I'm just showing Jaxon around."

"Hmm," murmured Isabella. "I'm sure he's a big boy who can wander around on his own."

Again, he pried himself from the teen's grasp.

Isabella shook her head and glanced over to her right. "Maddy, why don't you go over to the pit and light a fire for those two teenage boys. Take them into the Casino and set them up with s'mores."

"Awe," whined Maddy.

"Guests first," murmured Ava.

"Got it." The teen sighed deeply and rubbed Jaxon's arm. "I'll be right back." She called out to the boys. "Let me help you with that."

Isabella's phone beeped and she pulled it out of her back pocket. "I have to go prep for dinner service." She shoved a giant candy cane into Jaxon's hands. "You help finish up with Ava."

Ava's head shot up and panic glazed her eyes.

So she didn't want to be around him. Jaxon growled deep in his chest and spoke over her. "Decorating's not part of my job."

Isabella's brow rose. "Making Twin Springs successful is in everyone's job description."

What the hell was he supposed to say to that? "Fine," he snapped.

"I need to prepare for the Christmas tree arrival."

Even as the words tumbled from Ava's beautiful lips, he knew she was lying. Again.

A smile spread across her face and everything around him stopped.

Then, she added, "Maddy can help him."

"No," Isabella and he shouted together, and he felt compelled say, "She's a little clingy."

Isabella laughed. "I think she has a crush on you." A sly look came over her face. "Now, my sister's closer to your age."

A shocked gasp parted Ava's lips and she licked them. "Stop match making. Besides, we're not compatible."

"You look pretty compatible to me." Isabella winked at her sister. "Do try not to cling to him. Even though he's tall, dark and handsome. Hold yourself back." She spun around, her laughter following her as she bounded up the stairs to Twin Springs two at a time.

"And I thought my sister was embarrassing." Understanding her pain, he patted on her back.

Ava cringed and moved away. "She can't help herself. She's turned into a hopeless romantic since her and Theo got together."

"Not compatible, huh?" The words slipped from his brain and out of his mouth before he could stop them.

Ava stiffened. "You're rude. Abrasive and a real jerk. Yes. Not my type." She reached down for the extension cord.

It irked him that she didn't want him. He didn't know why. He sure as hell didn't want her. *Not want her? What a load of crap*, his mind mocked. "Well, you're a liar and a nut case. Damn JOBB." He jammed the metal candy-cane frame into the ground. "There. Now, plug it in."

"I'm not crazy." She retorted icily and shoved the cord into the extension.

He stood before her but she refused to look up. Instead her thick, silky hair shielded her from his gaze.

"You wouldn't understand," she murmured.

Damn it, she was an addict. He squatted down to her level. Her eyes lifted to his and their faces were inches apart. She still smelled faintly of roses. Some of the perfume had worn off and he found her natural scent even more intoxicating. "When I was in the Army, there were men on the team who couldn't deal with what they saw during war. Couldn't take what they sometimes needed to do."

She blinked rapidly, reached out and touched his hand. "I'm so sorry. It must've been terrible."

He looked down at her finely sculpted hand on top of his large one. His skin burned where she'd touched him and he swallowed hard. "They turned to drugs, too."

"Drugs?" Her arched brows squished together.

He lowered his voice into what he hoped was a calming tone. "There are places you can go for addiction. Confidential places. No one needs to know." He paused. "Not even your sister."

She leaned back and pressed her hand against her chest. "I'm not a drug addict!"

"If you're not on drugs then you're mentally unstable. You need help." Even though the stories his sister had told him about the loony bin from when she'd been committed as a child circled around in his head, he knew she needed a qualified psychologist and added, "There are places for that too."

She shoved him back and out of instinct he grabbed her arms and rolled until he landed on top of her.

The long length of him pressed down into her softness and she froze. Her lips moved and he leaned in to hear her but she only gasped in jerky puffs of air. His heart wrenched. She needed help. He cupped her exquisite face in his palm and electricity shot up his arm. "It will be alright, Ava. I want—" She went wild, bucking, and shoving at his shoulders, thrashing around beneath him.

The 'to help' part of his sentence caught in his throat.

Animal sounds emitted from her body as she struggled for release.

Immediately, he leveraged himself off of her and rolled up onto the balls of his feet.

She crawled away, shoulders hunched, her chest hitching as if she was about to throw up.

"Ava," he held his hands out, palms up and realization socked him in the gut. He understood why she cringed when touched. Why she distanced herself with lies. Why she couldn't stand to be touched. Knowledge and regret curled into a cold ball in the pit of his stomach. "I apologize. I didn't mean to scare you. To insult you."

She looked up at him, tears streaming down her face and finally words squeaked from her throat. "Don't," she panted, "touch me." Her emotions back under control, she swiped at the tears. "Stay away from me."

He reached out to help her up but she smacked his hands away. "Didn't you hear me?"

She gained her feet and swayed.

His first urge was to grab her up, comfort her. Instead, he shoved his hands into his pockets. "Sorry."

She backed away, never taking her frightened eyes off of him, and when she reached a safe distance, she turned and sprinted for the stairs.

His gaze never left her. She was right. He was a jerk. More than that, he was the stupid asshole who couldn't read the signs right before him. Prior to his last mission, his instincts would have set off warning bells in his head. Instead, he'd read her completely wrong. Insulted her. And, even worse, scared the hell out of her.

The charcoal smell from the fire pit snuck into his nostrils and his gaze hazed, blending today's vision of Ava's body clad in a white jacket with his memories of Woody's burning body consumed within a white blaze. He shook his head and shoved the painful memories aside. "Maybe I need the loony bin," he grumbled.

He tugged his phone out of his pocket and speed dialed JD. When she answered, he asked, "What are the usual indicators that a woman has been attacked or," his mind revolted at the thought but he ground the word out, "raped?"

CHAPTER TWENTY-TWO

*E*ntering the elevator, Ava pressed her floor number and leaned her forehead against the paneled wall. She'd prepped the lobby with stacks of wrapped presents to go under the tree. Given out orders on how the fifteen-foot-wide tree would fit through the double door opening into Twin Springs' lobby. Everyone knew their roles, whether it was Santa, Mrs. Claus or even the elves who would set up and trim the tree at seven the next morning. Everything was in place, but even the exhaustion couldn't erase the embarrassment of how she'd acted with Jaxon.

Moisture welled up in her eyes. Even though she yearned for Jaxon, when he touched her, she was transported back to Hollingsworth's office. With his sticky breath against her neck and his teeth nipping at her throat. Wiping her tears away, she rubbed her forehead against the cool wood of the elevator. Fatigue overwhelmed her. "I should've asked Isabella to help me wrap those presents. Then it wouldn't be six in the morning and I'm just now escaping for a quick shower before my day begins." She allowed her eyes to close. "Rest here. Just for a moment."

With her eyes closed, exhaustion slowed her heart and she didn't notice the shimmering mist rolling under the crack at the bottom of the elevator door. The silver fog glimmered, hovering for moment around her ankles, before weaving a path up and around her legs. Filling the elevator with its presence, it melded with Ava.

. . . A skip in her step, Ruby exited the elevator. Glancing down, she admired the slimming effect of her new wide legged slacks on her long legs. The silky white fabric nipped in around her buttocks before flowing loosely around her legs. Free from restraint, her breasts jiggled beneath the fabric as she walked.

A low whistle from the Bellhop confirmed the knowledge she gloried in. The pants hugged her body in a luscious way and in all the right places. She'd purposely picked a white, flannel Middy top to wear for her appointment with the General. Perhaps the sailor shirt with its gold stripes, navy blue piping and bright red scarf tied underneath the low cut v-neck, would soften her father and remind him of his golden war days. Besides, it was all the rage and she felt on top the world and ready to strut her new feathers.

Unfortunately, she needed to deal with the General again before she commenced with her day. She prepared herself for another round with her father and a sigh escaped between her painted lips. "This time it'll be different," she announced to the Bellhop. "I will make the General feel my passion for the stage."

The young man winked back, with a smile and a nod. "Stand your ground!"

Spying her sister, Ame, exiting the General's office, Ruby paused. Even in the bowels of winter and her body heavy with child, Amethyst Fairbanks was as lovely as a spring breeze in her pink, silk jersey dress.

Pacing in front of the General's door, Ame unconsciously rubbed the Gingham checkered fabric at the base of the huge mound that stuck out a good three feet in front of her. Even though the dress was low waisted, the white satin trim belt was barely able to buckle under her baby belly.

"Ruby," Ame said, her voice hushed. "Father dear is in a rage and he wants to see you. Rumors reached him about you and the chauffeur driving around Twin Springs with you singing. What were you thinking?"

Popping out her silver compact, Ruby powdered her chin, nose and forehead, before rubbing her lips together and blowing a kiss at her reflection. "The General's such a bore."

She snapped her silver compact closed and slipped it in the pocket of her slacks. Pants, such a wonderful invention that men had kept all for themselves. Her green eyes met Ame's, "Thinking? I wasn't. I was living for the moment. Feeling the passion of my song. I felt free!"

Her sister's gigantic bosom rose and fell with a great sigh. "Ruby, you have responsibilities to your family, to Twin Springs. People are talking. You were seen not only by guests and the staff, but also by the Lieutenant. Didn't Everett explain the importance of your situation?"

"Your husband? What do men really know about women? Besides, don't judge me. I can't live by the rules you prescribed in those etiquette pamphlets you write. The one's the General's so proud of." She cast a shrug towards her sister and laid her hands palms down, fingers splayed on each side of her sister's stomach and gently rubbed. Bending down she placed her lips close to the high curve and shouted, "How's my nephew?" Pressing her ear, where her lips had just hovered, she waited for a response. Rewarded with a swift kick against her ear, she whispered, "That a boy. When you're born, we're going to give the General hell."

Chuckling at the high-spirited response from her baby, Ame ran her hand lovingly down her sister's long hair and tugged a strand. "What are we going to do with you?" Her gaze brushed over Ruby's attire. "You know Father feels service stripes should be earned and not worn for fashion." Shaking her head, a bright red lock of hair escaped and she tucked it back up into the intricate twist of her hair rolled at the base of her neck. "Nothing we can do now. He's waiting for you. For once in your life, try to be demure." She held her fingers up, showing an inch between them. "Just a little."

Ruby straightened, rubbing the roots at the base of her scalp. "Careful Ame, my hair is one of my greatest assets."

Laughter trailing behind her, Ruby approached her father's inner sanctum. "Sure, I can play demure," she muttered. Untying the crimson red scarf from under her collar, she draped the wide scarf over her hair and tucked the ends around the front of her shirt, hiding the exposed curves of her breasts and the offensive service stripes on her sleeves. She wiped the ox blood red lipstick from her mouth with the back of her hand. Eyes downcast and shoulders lightly rounded forward, she entered the General's inner sanctum and sat. Teetering on the edge of the leather chair, she crossed her long legs at the ankle, tucked them up and behind her and clasped her slender hands lightly in her lap. "Father dear, you requested to see me?" she murmured, mimicking her sister's gentle voice.

The General glanced up from his paperwork and assessed his greatest challenge. His second daughter. The air hung quiet about Ruby and her dark lashes lay against her creamy white skin. Stunned, a pent-up breath expelled from his lips in one fail swoop. "Yes, my dear." His big, bushy eyebrows furrowed. "Ruby, are you ill?"

Allowing her lips to curve gently, she said, "No, Father dear," she mimicked her sister's endearment. "Did you need to see me? May I be of assistance?"

The General was taken back a smidgen at the change within his daughter. His chest puffed out and the reason he called for her drained away with his anger. "Apparently, my talk brought some sense to you."

Tilting her head, she murmured. "Yes, Father. I understand my duties to the family and to Twin Springs."

A great sigh exuded from the General and he rustled his papers. "Good girl. You're dismissed."

The General's dismissal bristled against her nerves. Her back straightened and her shoulders popped back to their normally proud position. "Dismissed?" Her demure facade slipped.

Studying his papers, he waived his hand at her. "Yes. Yes. Knew you would come around. You're smart for a woman."

Slowly, Ruby unwound her scarf and shook her glorious mane free. She yanked her boobs up so they were displayed proudly and retied the crimson fabric into a tie just below the v-opening of the shirt, so it would draw the eye downward to her smooth flesh. "'For a woman?'" she asked faintly, a sharp edge entering her voice.

Engrossed, the General gave a non-communicative grunt under his breath.

Surging to her feet, Ruby shouted, "I'll show you a woman."

The General sighed heavily, but refused to shift his attention from his work. "Calm yourself."

Not done, she roared. "I'm sick of men running my life! Why can't you just leave me alone?"

Gradually, he lifted his gaze, starting from the fabric swirling around her legs, up to her sailor stripes and over to the cleavage spilling out of her shirt. A rumble built within his chest, gaining in speed and volume until it spewed from his lips. "Are those trousers? No daughter of mine struts about in trousers!"

The stain glass palladium shook with his anger but Ruby weathered the storm. She raised her compact and painted her lips blood red. Jutting her chin in the air, she shot back, "Yes, they are and I like them."

The man who defeated the German Army rose before her and he slammed his fist down on his desk. "Quiff, prostitute, hussy. That is what people will say. If you dress like a woman of the streets, people will treat you like one. Do you want to end up in the family way like your maid?"

Feeling like a peacock trapped in a gilded tower, Ruby fought to spread her beautiful wings and soar through the open skies. "No, I want to sing on stage. Become an actress. I want to be free."

The General's brows grooved a trench across his forehead and his face flushed scarlet, matching the shade of his hair from his youth. "I've had enough of your foolish ideas and insolent ways. Ruby, you will fall in ranks. You will do as I say. Tonight I'll announce your engagement to Widower Henderson. You will not embarrass him or myself further. Do I make myself clear?"

She gasped. There was no way she would exchange her father for the binds of a husband. Another man controlling her actions. Her future. "He's twice my age," she sputtered.

The General pulled at the cusps of his tweed jacket and smoothed the gold buttons down the front with the palm of his hand. "You ruined yourself, girl, with your actions in front of Twin Springs. Only Henderson and my Lieutenant asked for your hand. The matter is settled. Go change into something befitting of your station and the future wife of a respected widower." Dismissing her, the General returned to his papers.

"Says you!" shouted Ruby. The desire to control her own destiny vibrated through her slender frame and her fingers curved around her compact, suppressing the urge to throw the metal disc at her father's head. . .

CHAPTER TWENTY-THREE

reaking the stillness of the crisp fall morning with a rumble of thunder, a Jaguar Coupe honked impatiently at a semi-truck that pulled a massive tree around the front of Twin Springs. Swerving around the truck bed, the Jag skidded to a stop at the circular drive of the hotel. The racing red vehicle reflected how the driver liked his women, long, lean and sexy. Unfolding himself from behind the wheel, his short blonde hair glinted in the morning sun and his wide toothpaste white smile blinded the valet who rushed down to open his door.

The gentleman adjusted the collar of his polo shirt and tucked a rolled up newspaper under one arm before tossing his keys to the expectant youth. Immediately dismissing the servant from his mind, Director Terrence Hollingsworth looked up at the hotel through tinted lenses. Licking his lips with anticipation, he muttered, "The hiding place of the one who got away, AVA." Then, he bounded up the stairs to find his prey.

Slinging his leather satchel over his shoulder, he entered the hotel, paused on the threshold and surveyed the lobby. Appraising the dated backdrop with a slight sneer, he slipped his sunglasses into the v neck opening of his shirt and made a beeline for the Front Desk.

Cutting to the head of the line, he snapped his fingers at the desk clerk and demanded her attention. "Terrence Hollingsworth. You have a suite held for me."

He surveyed his surroundings instead of paying attention to the staff. Only for Ava, would he leave the upscale glamour and fast pace of New York City. Impatient, he tapped his newspaper on the counter and waited for the clerk, who'd suddenly turned into a complete waste of space. He thrust out his chest. "Obviously, you recognize me. It's okay. I'm sure you don't get many celebrities in these hillbilly mountains." He glanced down at her name tag and added, "Sheela. What an unusual spelling."

Usually, he wouldn't give a woman like her the time of day in her unattractive white-collar shirt and boxy black pants. But, something about the clerk reminded him of someone he knew. Terrence pumped his memory for when the black haired woman with brown eyes and funny looking eyebrows had crossed his path.

Unable to place her, he quickly signed in two spots as instructed. He pocketed the card key to his room and rolled the map of the hotel up in his newspaper. Turning his attention to the task at hand, he asked, "Where would I find Ava Fairbanks?"

The hotel clerk blinked at him, then pointed across the Grand Lobby. "Those double doors are her office, but I don't think she's on the floor yet."

He digested the information, studying the doors for a moment. *How dare she hide?*

He squeezed the newspaper in his fist. Time to teach Ava a lesson. No one abandoned one of his plays and got away with it. Damn it, no one abandoned *him*. Without her *The Rise Of Rae* was on the verge of folding. It would be his first failure as a director. Bit by bit, he relaxed his stranglehold on the paper. Time to dole out a little payback and let her know just how much she cost him.

"Sir, would you like to set up an appointment with her?" asked the Front Desk clerk, breaking his train of thought.

Prepared to bide his time, for the right moment, he shared a cocky smile with the clerk. "No, I'd rather surprise her."

Turning away, he dismissed the woman from his mind. Removing a cigar from the pocket of his satchel, he rolled it between his thumb and forefinger and considered his game plan.

"Oh my God, you are Terrence Hollingsworth, the Broadway director?" gushed a well-dressed woman, blocking his path.

Terrence studied the older woman, in her skin-tight skirt and silk shirt unbuttoned to display her wares. He dealt with women like her every day. Women who attempted to cheat Father Time with their injections, creams and surgeries. Dismissing her from his mind, he tilted his head in a slight affirmative nod. "Yes, if you will excuse me."

The platinum blonde placed a well-manicured hand, sparkling with diamonds, on his sleeve, "I am Lilith, Senator Whitcomb's wife. I adore your plays." She moved closer, her rich perfume entwining the two of them within a private, scented circle. "My condolences on the unforeseen death of your wife." She lowered her voice to a sensual whisper. "Some wives are unable to handle a strong and powerful man."

Rolling his tongue over his teeth, Terrence perused the woman before him. *Hmmm,* he mused. *Never sampled a Senator's wife before. Might be worth my time. Even if she is well past her closing call.* "Perhaps you could show me around."

CHAPTER TWENTY-FOUR

While her reporter senses tingled on another story at the hotel, Mackenzie quietly and efficiently checked in a line of guests. Stories swarmed among the staff of a saboteur. Rumors of embezzlement, an illegal brewing operation, and hidden jewels wetted her journalistic taste buds. Something hinky was going on at Twin Springs.

Her heart leapt out of her chest when Ashlee's husband snapped his fingers and commanded her attention. For a moment, she was unable to process his words over the sudden ringing in her ears. Frozen stupid, she wondered at first if her friend's husband would recognize her from photographs, even with her hair dyed and her eyebrows darkened. He'd always been too busy to accompany his wife on one of their joint vacations, so she'd never had the pleasure of meeting him. Otherwise, she would've grabbed Ashlee and told her to run.

When he glanced down at her name tag, she thought he might just be clever enough to realize that her alias, Sheela, was really an anagram of his dead wife's name.

But, the great Terrence Hollingsworth couldn't see past the ego on the end of his nose. His breath, rancid from the cigars he smoked, wafted over Mackenzie. Her stomach rolled and propelled her into action.

She'd noticed the newspaper he carried. Obviously, he'd read her article on Ava and came to conspire with her on how to cover up their affair. Her fingers stumbled across the keyboard as she checked him in. Wanting to gouge out his fake blue eyes, she bit her lip and the metallic taste of blood reminded her of her friend lying in her own blood on stage and her mission. Ashlee deserved justice. Mackenzie believed in fair play. After all, as a reporter, it was her duty to discover the truth and fight for those unable to protect themselves.

Firmly under control, she observed the puffed up jerk in his nauseating bright orange shirt and anger coursed through her. She'd never understood why Ashlee had married him. Where were his tears now?

Even so, she couldn't allow him to blow her cover before she finished the last story, or nail in the coffin of Broadway star, AVA. Mackenzie couldn't believe her luck. This was perfect. Now, she could bury them both with the same series of stories.

Under her lashes, she watched him stroll away with Mrs. Whitcomb. Her blood boiled. Obviously, he enjoyed women fawning over him, while Ashlee rotted in her grave. She jotted down mental notes about the sabotage at Twin Springs. Add the sordid sex with the murder from her current story, and she'd definitely found the headline of the year. She'd be just the reporter to break both stories wide open and ruin the two people responsible for her friend's suicide.

CHAPTER TWENTY-FIVE

Strolling out of his office with his hands tucked in his pockets, Jaxon turned into the Grand Lobby. From his security monitors, he'd watched a semi-truck, with a gigantic fir tree on its flat bed, pull up in front of Twin Springs and he wanted to see how they were going to get that big ass tree through the front doors. He leaned against the Bell Stand and waited for the morning show to begin.

"I'll show you a woman," bellowed a feminine voice from behind the double doors of Ava's office.

Jaxon's head pivoted towards the sound and his eyes narrowed. "Maybe it's the bird," he muttered.

"I'm sick of men running my life! Why can't you just leave me alone?"

"Ava." With quick strides, he crossed to the doors and jerked one open. The odor of roses socked him in the nose. "Damn it, someone needs to throw her perfume bottle in the trash."

In the corner of the room, the bird cage was covered with a black sheet and he could hear the fluttering of wings. His gaze shifted. There stood Ava, still dressed in the same blue pants and white shirt from the day before. Except, her shirt was unbuttoned and the mounds of her soft breast almost spilled free.

She stood there, facing the desk and going through the motions of applying lipstick with her phone held in her hand as if it was some sort of compact. But there wasn't any lipstick in her other hand, just air. He couldn't help himself, his mouth fell open at the eerie sight.

She'd finished painting her lips, clenched her phone in her fist and shouted. "Yes, they are and I like them."

Jaxon snapped his mouth closed. Her actions reminded him of his sister. Of when JD was in one of her fits and spoke to thin air. Did Ava have the same condition? Did she also refuse to seek treatment? Did she deal with stares and people talking behind her back? Was Ava's condition brought on by her being attacked, as he thought his sister's was brought on by the tragic death of her mother? Whatever the reason, it didn't matter. Damn it. Beautiful or not, Ava needed him, just like his sister needed him growing up.

Ava flung her arms out and addressed the desk as if someone invisible was seated there. "No, I want to sing on stage. Become an actress. I want to be free."

Glancing behind him to make sure no one else had witnessed her episode, Jaxon entered the room and gently closed the door.

Ava gasped, and sputtered, "He's twice my age."

Moving closer, Jaxon examined the gorgeous, confused woman. She didn't realize he was there. His brows furrowed. That was different. JD was always aware of the situation around her. Even in a fit. "Ava," he kept his voice calm, measured, placing himself between her and the desk. "Let me help you."

"Say's you!"

He hesitated, afraid to touch her but unsure what else to do. Grasping her by the shoulders, he gently shook her. "Ava."

Her green gaze focused on him, and a sultry smile spread across her lips. "My Guy."

The seduction in her voice flowed through him and desire pierced him. "Sure sugar, I can be your guy. If you want."

Suddenly, her eyes rolled back and her legs gave out. Before she collapsed, he scooped her up and carried her over to the couch.

Carefully, he settled her onto the cushions and bundled up a pile of red fabric with white, fuzzy trim as a makeshift pillow for under her head. He crouched down beside her and categorized the worry eating away at the lining of his stomach as natural concern for any human being. He pressed the backs of his fingers against her forehead, and muttered, "Cold. Ice cold."

Her glossy, ebony hair spilled across her shoulder and with a mind of its own, his hand reached out and rubbed it between his thumb and forefinger. "Silk. Pure silk."

Pulling his hand away before he was caught, he scanned her for any injuries. Her dark lashes laid softly against her creamy skin and his gaze traveled down her slender neck, past the divot in her throat where he felt the urge to place a kiss, and down to the swell of her silky breasts. He rolled back on his heels and rubbed his hands hard against his face. "Reign it in. Get control. The last thing she needs is you drooling all over her."

Her phone buzzed from the floor where she'd dropped it, and he leaned over and grabbed it. Turning back to her, he was relieved that her eyes were open. Confused, but open.

"I—" she began, then, covered her face with her hands. She composed herself and sat up. The motion popped another button on her shirt and her breasts broke free. "Oh, my god. Did you?"

He splayed his empty hand out, "I didn't touch you."

"Right." She glared at him, buttoning up her shirt. "Who's lying now?"

He rose to his feet and shoved his hands and her phone into his pockets. He paced the small space between the couch and the coffee table. "After you collapsed, I just carried you to the couch." He paused. "I swear that I didn't—" He waived his hand at her shirt and felt his face heat up under her intense gaze. How could he help her if she didn't trust him? "Pop your buttons." He growled at the suggestive images that entered his head with his poor choice of words. "Un-do you?" Damn it, he was botching everything and grumbled, "Where the hell's your bra anyway?"

She gasped. She had no idea what had happened to her bra. Last she remembered, she was in the elevator and heading to her room for a shower. "I'm not sure." She glanced around the room. "It hadn't occurred to me that with the monitors in the Security Manager office, you could see all over Twin Springs. I suppose you saw me acting strange and followed me."

"I'm not spying on you." He shook his head and rubbed the back of his neck. "I heard you yelling from the lobby."

"I was yelling?" Mortified, she averted her head. "Did anyone else hear me?"

The phone buzzed and he pulled it out of his pocket and handed it to her. His high cheekbones glowed red above the manly stubble covering his face. "You dropped it."

"Hmm." She took the phone from him. Ignoring the insistent buzzing, she asked, "What did I say?" All she remembered was the feeling of being trapped. Needing to escape.

"Something about wanting to be an actress and sing on stage. To be free."

"Well, the free part is correct," she replied, thinking of how she was haunted. Not only by Ruby, but by the Director's touch, and Ashlee's fraught, doe-like eyes. And, finally, haunted by the fact she'd failed her father when he needed her most. "But, I never want to be on stage ever again."

"Why the hell not?"

The phone buzzed again and she lifted it to her ear. "Yes." She listened. "What do you mean she can't make it? Why not?" Her gaze traveled up the long length of the man before her. His kaki pants, black t-shirt that covered, but couldn't conceal, the rock hard ab muscles beneath. Swallowing, she averted her eyes and attempted to focus in on what Sheela at the Front Desk was telling her. "Baby?" Her mind raced to catch up. "Isn't she too old for a baby?" Her gaze flickered back to Jaxon and how his biceps bulged when he crossed his arms. "Of course, her granddaughter had a baby. I suppose she can't help that. Don't worry. I'll take care of it." She ended the call and sat there for a moment.

"What's going on?" he asked.

She hesitated.

"It's alright, I understand that you owners keep issues amongst yourselves, in your tight group."

Is that how he saw it? Maybe they did. She bit her lip. But after the Director, the long time deception of Niles and the Executive Chef stealing money, it'd become harder and harder to trust. But if you couldn't trust your Security Manager then who was left? Taking a deep breath, she explained. "Mrs. Claus can't make the grand reveal of our Christmas Tree."

"Does that really matter?" He scratched at the stubble on his jaw with the back of his knuckles. "As long as the big guy is there?"

"You don't understand. Santa sits with the kids for pictures. Mrs. Claus runs the show. Tells the elves what to do on the tree." She shrugged. "I'll just have to play Santa's wife this year."

Relief flooded her frame. As Mrs. Claus, she could push all the emotions aside and hide. If only for an hour or two. By then, she'd have her feelings back under control. She'd make it through one more hour, one more day. She rose, circled the desk, and pulled her makeup case out of a bottom drawer. She settled herself into the chair and opened the lid to reveal a mirror and the bottles of her trade. Patting the thick, gray tinged foundation onto her skin with a sponge she glanced over the box and watched him. He'd settled onto the couch and was holding the red and white fabric lying there.

"That's for Mrs. Claus. Her costume." She felt like she owed him something. An explanation. After all, she'd made a fool of herself three days in a row. First, she'd sung and run barefoot along the side the road. Yesterday, furious with him accusing her of taking drugs, she'd pushed him, causing the momentum that rolled them, until he'd lain on top of her. Then she'd freaked on him. Finally, today, sleepwalking and shouting in her office. "I'm sorry for how I've been acting. I can't explain the reasons. But I apologize."

"Please, don't." Agitated, he swept his fingers through is coal black hair. "I already know what's going on."

"You do?" The sponge fell from her fingertips. Obviously, he'd figured out she was sleepwalking. Did he also know she was being haunted? Had Isabella told him?

His eyes darkened and the green flecks overshadowed the brown until they glowed with a greenish sheen. "I know that something happened to you."

"Uh—" He was talking about Ashlee. She squeezed her eyes shut. Deep in her soul, Ava knew she'd never forget the events that had brought about the death of a young woman. Guilt had placed a great weight on her slender shoulders that refused to fade. A sick sensation coated her gut. Maybe, just maybe, she could've said something to Ashlee Hollingsworth before she'd escaped the Director's office. Something, anything, to make a difference with how the final scene had played out. "It's my fault that she killed herself."

"What are you talking about?"

"Ashlee Hollingsworth. About the fact that she killed herself on stage beside me, because I—" She cleared her throat. "Her husband—."

"Was it her husband who…" He paused and studied the portrait above the fireplace. He sat stiff on the sofa as if he was keeping the emotions within himself caged. "You don't have to tell me. I figured out that you've been raped."

"Raped?" She shuddered and felt cold all over. "He didn't. I mean. Almost." Disgust, fear, helplessness swelled over her. Engulfed her. Her acting abilities abandoned her and moisture welled up in her eyes, and swelled her throat. Hoarsely, she added, "I couldn't push him off. Ashlee saved me. Knocked on the door and he loosened his hold."

"Let me help you." His gaze swung to hers. So intense that she gasped.

She blinked back the tears and twisted the rings on her hands. "How? It's too late. She's already dead. All I could think about was myself and getting out of his office. I didn't pause to see if she needed help. To consider what he might do to her. Something terrible happened in that room after I left. Something that caused her to shoot herself in front of me. Me. She wanted *me* to see her die."

"We don't know what happened to cause her to kill herself. And we can't go back in time to fix our errors in judgment." In his minds eye, he saw his team spilling from a building. Their bodies consumed by white flames because he trusted his instincts and not facts. Didn't verify the reporter's intel before the op. "But I can help you now."

"How?"

"I can teach you how to defend yourself. So that no man can ever hurt you again."

"He was too powerful." She shook her head and dug her fingers into her pant legs, smearing foundation over the blue fabric. "I never could've stopped him."

"I don't believe that." His resolve was so strong, she almost believed his lie.

She attempted to swallow away the clog in her throat. *Hide, just hide,* her mind chanted. She layered the sponge with additional foundation and spread it across her face.

"Think about it." Silence filled the space and Jaxon studied the sexy woman before him. Desperately, changing her face to erase herself. Pretending to be anyone but her own drop dead, gorgeous self. Her face was moist with tears but she tapped the foundation over them. Dried them with her new facade. Her chin trembled but she clenched her jaw and used a pencil to fill in her lips. "I'll be in the hotel's gym tomorrow morning at five. Show up, if you never want to be a victim again."

CHAPTER TWENTY-SIX

*L*eaning against a column in the Grand Lobby with his hands buried deep in his front pockets, Jaxon observed the holiday production.

Even aged into a Mrs. Claus, he couldn't take his eyes off of Ava. Her curves were concealed under a long, red, velvet dress with fake white fur tipping the collar, hem and cuffs. An apron accented her small waist and a lacy, white bonnet covered her thick hair. Her milky skin was now tinged with gray, and makeup prematurely aged in lines around her eyes, forehead and mouth. Even the back of her hands showed age with tiny brown spots.

Gingerly, she moved through the room, her body slightly curved with age. She stopped only for kids' questions and to pose for a quick selfie.

The base of the fir tree poking through the four-foot front door distracted Jaxon. His eyes widened at the sight of the Maintenance Crew. Bundled up in tan work coats and jeans they supported the tree. But, on top of their heads were felt green elf hats, trimmed in red and little bells. "Monkey suits." With a wry twist of his lips, he grumbled, "At least they aren't trussed up fully into little green outfits."

The branches of the tree were bonded tight with rope and a

long rope was tied to the base. Her voice hitching with age, Ava called out orders like a general. Together the elves pulled, dragging the tree forward inch by inch. A limb snagged up on something within the door way and she rushed over.

"Wait! It's caught on the handle." She pushed in on the branches, releasing the tree. "Now pull, Elves. Pull."

The Maintenance Crew struggled to drag the gigantic tree through the opening. With each jerk of their movements the bells on their hats jiggled and rang out through the room.

The smell of fresh pine tree permeated the air, bringing a holiday feel to it. Guests gathered around, clicking pictures. Children clambered over the furniture for a better view, their faces alight with delight. Santa's lap all but forgotten for the spectacle before them. His phone buzzed and he pulled it out. At the sight of Lee's caller-ID, he clicked it on. "What's up?"

The tree broke through the opening and spontaneous applause broke out.

"What's all that racket? Are you on the job or lounging there?"

The crew of elves split, half going to the East wing balcony and strapping on climbing gear. "I'm working," he grumbled, pushing aside the guilt of hanging out in the Grand Lobby.

The other half of elves hooked up pulleys and ropes to the tree. Carefully, they lifted the massive tree into place.

"I've figured out where JD's file is. Let me tell you, it wasn't easy to get the Geezers to spill without letting them know why. She just left on a new case—missing little boy. The details are still fuzzy on what happened. But, I'll distract the Geezers with something and grab the file while they're all away."

Jaxon's brows furrowed. "Shit, a lost boy? Do you need me back there?"

"No. You know JD will find him."

Hopefully not too late, he thought, but left the words unsaid.

Elves snipped the twine binding the tree and the limbs of the evergreen opened and nimbly fell into place. He had to tip his head back to fully view the easily fifteen-foot-wide and twenty-five-foot tall tree. He whistled low under his breath.

All the while, a sick feeling of dread coated his stomach, hoping that JD could find the missing little boy. He vowed that when his job was done and JD'd found him, he'd pay for the boy and his family to experience the holidays at Twin Springs. "Thanks for digging up her file."

"There's something else. I checked into the financials of all the owners. Beaumont's been pumping in money like we discussed. But Ava Fairbanks recently drained her savings. To the tune of twenty thousand."

Jaxon glanced over at Ava, her hands on her hips directing the men, the kids trailing behind her, shouting out orders right alongside of her. She glanced up at him and the circular, wire rimmed glasses couldn't mute her glimmering, green eyes. Even as Mrs. Claus, Ava was spectacular. And she'd emptied her savings to bring this joy to others. She broke his gaze and tended to the kids. "She used it to buy a tree."

"A tree?" Lee choked on the other end of the line. "What the hell kind of a tree costs twenty thousand? Is it covered with gold? Damn me, you are on a JOBB."

He chuckled. "Don't worry about it. I'm getting things worked out here. Thanks for the intel. I'll report in when I have more."

He ended the call, slipped his phone into a side pocket and got back to the show. Hanging by ropes off the balcony across the Grand Lobby from the Front Desk, the crew wound lights around the tree's massive girth, followed by ornaments, while Ava and the rest of the crew pushed pre-wrapped gifts around the base. Despite himself, Jaxon felt the holiday spirit creeping into his soul. He couldn't remember the last Christmas he'd experienced out of a war zone.

He wandered over to Ava and looked up at the tree. "Mrs. Claus that was quite the feat."

She laughed and it sounded like hundreds of silver bells.

Goosebumps broke out on his arms and his heart jerked to a stop, then slammed against his ribs.

"Santa and I are only too glad to bring one of our trees down for everyone at Twin Springs to enjoy."

He leaned in, whispering close to her, his gaze attempting to penetrate the only piece of her not concealed by a façade—her eyes. "Meet me in the morning. Let me help you."

Panic glazed her eyes and he backed off.

"It's up to you. But I can help you take back what was stolen from you. Your power." He walked away, having said what needed to be said. He hoped she'd show up. With a lot of work, she'd be on track to experience some of this holiday joy for herself.

CHAPTER TWENTY-SEVEN

*A*va stumbled to a stop in the doorway of Twin Springs' fitness center. Due to the ungodly hour, the row of treadmills stood still. No one spun on the stationary bikes, hunched on the elliptical or even pumped the exercise machines. The room was empty except for Jaxon.

Clad only in baggy shorts, his tanned body glistened with sweat under the overhead lights. From a steel crossbar in the blackened out ceiling, hung a long white bag. On the balls of his bare feet, he circled the bag, pausing only to deliver a series of blindingly fast kicks and punches against the aged leather.

His breathing thickened with his movements. Tattoo's flowed and melded to the muscles of his forearms. Thick, fingerless gloves protected his hands as he delivered punishing blows. A dense layer of black hair covered his muscled chest and dusted the ripples of his abs, before disappearing under his shorts. One long tattoo ran the inner length of his right forearm. The power within the room was palatable. Breathing hard with him, she backed out of the room and whispered, "I can't do this."

"Ava!" His face lit up with a boyish grin and her heart wobbled.

He jogged over to her. "I'm glad you came."

Averting her eyes, she focused in on the water cooler and spoke to it instead of the hard planes of his hairy, muscled chest. Imagining her fingers running through the thick mass of chest hair, her knees weakened. His musky scent and rugged body filled all her senses and her mind screamed for her to escape while her heart begged for her to stay, reach out and touch. She searched for a reason to leave and glanced down at her black yoga pants and white t-shirt. "I'm not wearing the proper clothing," she lied.

He reached out, grasped her fingertips within his gloved hand and tugged. "Come on. It doesn't matter what you're wearing."

"Obviously not," she grumbled, allowing herself to be pulled further into the room. "I'm wearing a shirt and shoes. Did you forget yours?" She tilted her head and let her brow wrinkle with fake concern. "Are you taking drugs?"

His laugh was quick, true and dimples flashed at her from his cheeks, softening the strong lines of his face. "I guess I deserved that."

Her lips tilted up in response but she pressed them into a firm line. Unsure of the feelings swirling through her, she fell back on acting and picked the part of an old-fashioned school matron. Seamlessly, she slipped into her new role. "It's not decent to traipse around half dressed."

He shot her a knowing wink. "Sugar, you're going to have to do better than that."

She stumbled and he tightened his grip. For some reason the endearment felt warm, familiar. Comforting. Her heart swelled and he pulled her over to the bag.

Releasing her hand, he reached down into a black backpack and pulled out a small, white towel. Quickly, he ran it over his body, drying the sweat.

She attempted to moisten her dry mouth as her gaze greedily consumed each of his movements.

He tossed the towel out of the way and pulled two, long strips of red fabric from the backpack. "I've ordered some gloves for you, but until they come in, we can wrap your hands with these. Go ahead, hold your hands up."

She held her hands out, fingers spread, and he laced the cotton fabric across her palm, around her fingers and back again, securing at the wrist. Finished with one hand, he began with the other. With his focus on her hands, she took the opportunity to examine his face. Black hairs stubbled his face below his high cheekbone and across his jaw line. His lips were firm and full. A bump wrinkled his straight nose. "Did you get the crooked nose from a fight?"

"Yep." He glanced up at her, his eyes twinkling with amusement. "A rip, roaring fight."

"Did you lose?"

"Hell, yes."

"He must've been a huge man." Her eyes bounced away from his intense stare and back again. "To best you."

"Naw, tall and slim. My sister broke my nose."

She gave him an incredulous look. "Your sister?"

"Yep." Back was the Cheshire grin, full of straight white teeth. His dimples flashed and her heart sighed.

"My little sister."

Speechless, she gazed into his incredibly handsome face.

"Don't worry. I taught her everything she knows."

Her brow arched up but her mind raced. If his sister had bested him, then there might be hope. Maybe he did have something to teach her that would help her defend herself. He'd promised to give her, her power back. And she wanted that more than anything. To stop being afraid. To stop feeling like a victim.

"Almost everything." He amended, giving her a sheepish grin. "Otherwise, she couldn't have kicked my butt. Okay, wiggle your fingers. Make a fist. We want the wraps to be tight but not restrictive."

She squeezed her hands into fists and attempted to look tough.

He opened her fist and repositioned her thumb. "Let your thumb lay along the base of your knuckles. Like this. Don't tuck it. Or you'll break it when you punch."

"Awe." She pressed her thumb into the correct position. "I'll remember that."

"Alright, this is the proper stance." He faced the bag, legs apart, left side of his body slightly forward.

She attempted to mimic his stance.

"That's good. Just shift forward a little." He came around behind her, grabbed her by the hips and shifted her.

She dropped her arms, flipped around and slapped him away.

He held up his hands, fingers splayed. "Sorry. I was adjusting you. Let's start again."

There was something in the back of his eyes. Anger? Disgust? Ava wanted the ground to open up and consume her. Before the Director, she would've given a cute offhand comment and not embarrassed herself by freaking at his touch. She raised her fists. "I'm ready."

He pulled her fist up higher. "Protect your face. Now reach out with your left fist and tag the bag." He demonstrated and she mimicked his movements perfectly.

"Great!" His smile warmed her heart. "Again."

Ava punched the bag. A little harder this time.

"Now a back punch. Pivot on your back foot almost like you are squashing a bug with your toes. This allows your punch to reach further." He demonstrated and she mimicked his movements.

"Good, if you use your hips with your back punch it'll have more power. Imagine power coming up from your hips and through your fist." As he spoke, he swiveled with his punch.

She copied.

But he shook his head. "May I?"

Clearing her throat, she replied, "Yes."

He placed his hands on each side of her hips. "Now punch." He swiveled her hips with the force of her punch and her knuckles smacked the bag with a thwack.

"I did it!" Excitement coursed through her.

"Yes, you did." He nodded with encouragement. "Keep hitting the bag."

Timidly, she tapped the leather surface.

"Pretend you're a prize fighter. Circle it, wait for your opening and strike. You're good at acting."

She did as he suggested and felt the difference. She felt lighter. Her punches were stronger. "You make it sound like acting is a bad thing."

He stood back evaluating her. "Well, isn't acting another word for lying?"

Her arms dropped slightly.

"Keep your guard up," he ordered.

"What?"

"Keep your hands up, protect your head."

"Oh." She raised her fists. "Haven't you ever wanted to be someone you weren't?"

"Nope. Alright, you've got the stance. The form. Now hit harder. Imagine my face. Smack me in the nose."

Another face floated in her imagination. Bright blue eyes that glowed with a sick desire. Deeply tanned skin. She thunked the bag.

"That's it! Show me what you think about me. Give a yell with each punch. A kihup."

She gave a loud yah, with each hit, punching Hollingsworth in his imaginary eyes, nose and mouth. She felt his breath on her neck and slammed her fist into the bag. His teeth nipping her skin. Her punches grew frantic and her breathing began to hitch with built up emotions. One of his hands on her throat, the other slipping under her skirt. She was crying, hitting the bag over and over. Gone was the power in her punches. She leaned her forehead against the bag, pummeling it with her fists. "Stop. Stop." She cried. "No!"

Jaxon reached out for her, "Okay, okay. That's good." His voice was soothing, coaxing.

But she couldn't stop. The emotions flooded out of her.

"Sugar," he turned her towards him and she pounded his chest, tears running down her face and dripping off of her chin. "I've got you. You're safe."

He gathered her up into his strong arms. "Shush." He stroked her down her back. "You're alright. Shush."

Awash with emotions, Ava cried into the crook of his neck. For the first time since the Director's office she felt safe.

Her emotions spent, she pried herself from his arms and wiped her face. "Forgive me. I didn't intend to blubber all over you."

"Anytime." His deep voice held a question that she wasn't ready to answer.

Using her teeth, she pried the end of the wraps loose and unwound them. She wouldn't meet his gaze. Couldn't. He must've been sickened by her disgusting display of weakness. "Do you mind if I join you again?"

"I'll be here every morning. Come as often as you want."

CHAPTER TWENTY-EIGHT

Late that night, Ava slipped into a long white nightgown and collapsed onto her bed, the satin nighty silky against her skin. She adjusted the lace halter top and stared up at the coffered ceiling. Past eleven o'clock and she'd just finished addressing Mrs. Whitcomb's latest concerns and requests. "All her concerns for today."

The day was a trial. The emotions that she'd held back for so long, kept bubbling back up to the surface and she'd have to excuse herself to cry. Her bird seemed to understand that something was wrong and kept screeching curses at the top of his lungs.

Fatigue weighing her body down, she stretched her long, limber frame to its fullest extent and tried to ease the tension and tightness in her muscles. Her ears still rang from the squawking bird. "Tomorrow I'll track down Logan and ask for his assistance with teaching my parrot a more appropriate vocabulary. Right now, I need a full night's sleep." Her eyelids drifted down and blanketed the room in complete darkness.

Tossing in her bed, Ava slept unaware of the silver mist that seeped through the crack under her bedroom door. Foaming silver waves rolled across the floor and stormed against the edges of her bed. Rising into the air, the pale fog swirled around her dormant form. Infusing the room with its rose scent, the mist wafted over her. Her upper body rose and fell in tune with the sparkling rolling waves. Rising within her chest, the fog lifted her off the mattress. Her arms fell lifelessly back and her knuckles barely brushed the bed's downy comforter. Lovingly, it lowered her, turning her and lifting her body up to a standing position. Her head cocked to the side and hung limply from her slender neck. The mist played with her, twirling her around, lifting one of her limbs after the other in a marionette dance. Unsatisfied with the results, the mist seeped into her pores. Filled her. And they became one.

She gracefully walked with her bare feet inches above the carpeted floor. As she moved, the room around her shimmered, brimming with the afterglow of the shining mist, fogged with glittering stars of light. As each of her steps brought her closer and closer to her makeup table, the fog dissipated and the room around her changed into a luxurious suite. Gradually, her walking form descended in concert with the transformation, until her bare feet sunk into a thick, Persian rug. The windows before her no longer opened to the rolling lawns of Twin Springs, spotted by fall leaves. Instead, thin paned windows, with rope rollers, framed the tips of the mountains in the distance. Darkness rested upon the Blue Ridge Mountain tops and flakes of snow fluttered down and huddled within the peaks and valleys.

Her fingertips stroked the mirrored surfaces of the dressing table. She settled herself down in front of a large, oval mirror that hung from the wall and was etched around the edges with silver inlay. Accidentally brushing the colored beads dangling from the wall scones to each side of the mirror, she flicked the switch for each. Warm light flooded her face.

Picking up a silver backed brush, she stroked her long, ebony hair. Her right eyebrow arched and scrutinized the results. Tossing the brush on the table, she opened the mirror-fronted top drawer and removed a long pair of sheers. Lifting a portion of her hair, she smoothed the silky strands between her two fingers and pulled tight and taut. The light glimmered and reflected off the metal sheers as she snipped off her long hair at her chin. She worked her way around her head, clipping her luxurious mane into a tight bob that curved around the base of her neck and dipped forward into a sharp line. . .

. . ."*What are you doing?*" *cried out Emma. She stared at her sister Ruby with strands of her beautiful ebony hair scattered about the floor around her feet.*

Sitting in her pink satin teddy, Ruby's throaty chuckle filled the air and she shook her head side to side. "I'm free you ninny. The weight of the world just fell from my shoulders." She spun around on a frilly, satin and lace stool. Slanting her head to the side, she fluffed her hair with her long fingers. "Do you want me to cut yours too? It's liberating."

A gasp escaped Emma's lips and her fingers flew up to protect the long blonde locks piled high on her head. "Goodness no."

Already turning back to the large, oval mirror of her vanity, she withdrew her ox blood red lipstick and shaped her lips into a fashionable cupids bow. "I didn't think so. Look Emma, you need to get with the times. Women have more power than ever before. Power over their lives, over their future, over their appearance. Rebel a little, be reckless."

"Rebelling got you engaged to old Mr. Henderson," muttered her sister.

"Don't worry, I'm going to fix that." Rubbing her lips together, she thought of Guy. She lifted her chin, puckered her lips and blew a kiss to her reflection.

Opening a long, red tin box, she pressed the bristles of a short, stubby brush into a pat of black mixed ash and India ink. Expertly, she worked the dark color into the base of her lashes, until they darkened and lengthened giving her a smokey eye. Carefully, she painted and filled in long, arching brows over her eyes. "Do I look like Louise Brooks?" she asked.

Emma rolled her eyes and dropped onto her sister's feather bed. She adjusted the pleated skirt of her dress, so that the kelly-green fabric covered her knees. "You look gorgeous as always. Stop asking. It's vain. Father wants to see you in his office. He said it's," she deepened her voice by two octaves and attempted to imitate their father. "A private matter."

Ignoring her sister's statement, Ruby hummed under her breath. She placed her toes into the tips of her stockings and rolled the beige stocking up her long legs along with a garter, before folding the top of the rayon stocking over the garter and rolling the material, garter and all, back down to just below her knee. She powdered the shiny stockings until she was happy with the illusion of a shapely bare leg.

She slipped into her ebony, satin under-sheath and drew the gauzy, silver beaded outer layer over her head, until it shimmered down her body. Then, adorned her earlobes with tear drop rubies that dangled from silver. Since her arms and neckline were bare, Ruby clasped a ruby and pearl studded bracelet on her wrist and looped a long, matching necklace around her neck. After puffing a delicate rose scent around her body from her crystal perfume bottle, she struck a pose and asked, "Do I look like a film star? Ready to meet my public?"

"I'm surprised you didn't lace down your breasts and flatten your chest, if you wanted to look like a film star."

Ruby cupped each of her breasts in the palms of her hands and lifted their fullness. She bent over until they almost spilled from the top of her gown. "Now why would I do that? These are my secret weapons." Her flirtatious laughter filled the air.

Eyeing her sister's efforts, Emma grimaced and shook her head. "The General will cast a kitten when he see's you showing so much exposed skin. Put a shawl over your bare arms or something. He'll shove a hankie down the front of your dress and cover those weapons for you."

Winking at her younger sister, she retorted, "Emma, if you ever want me to help you to discover the power of your own secret weapons just let me know." Her light green eyes twinkled with mischief. "For a certain Chef, we both know."

Emma's eyes widened with horror and she looked away, unable to meet her sister's gaze. "I don't know what you are talking about."

"You're so transparent. Let me give you some sisterly advice. Before you leave the kitchens, be sure to dust all the flour from the back of your neck and from the front of your dress. Unless you have a habit of holding your breasts with flour covered hands while you cook."

Drawing out the fabric of her blouse, Emma's attention honed in on the front of her dress. Open mouthed, she stared in dismay at two distinc-

tive flour hand prints that covered the mounds of her breasts. She gasped and patted herself until the evidence disappeared.

Gathering her sister up into her arms, Ruby squeezed her tight and whispered in her ear, "Keep your secrets, darling. Just live life to the fullest." Leaning back, she held her petite sibling at arm's length. "Next Monday will be New Year's Eve. I'll dress you up for your beau and keep Father away so the two of you can dance and enjoy yourselves. Then, Tuesday morning we celebrate the glory of 1929. The world will be new and full of possibilities for you, your Chef, and for me on stage."

With a loud smacking noise, she pressed a kiss on her sister's cheek. Laughing at the mark her lips left, she wiped the red lipstick off with the swipe of her thumb. "Now go chase yourself, while I go see what our staunch, bluenose General wants."

Taking her time, Ruby fussed with her hair a little more. She wrapped a satin scarf around her shortened locks, turban style, allowing for wisps of her ebony hair to escape out from under the silver satin in a sharp line at her jaw. She flattened her glossy hair at the crown of her head and dropped her lipstick and compact into a beaded purse that matched her dress perfectly. She pulled the drawstring closed and looped the purse string over her wrist before she left her tower room to meet with her father.

Standing outside the double doors to his office, she smoothed her hands down over her sparkling dress, tugging a little at the fabric as if her efforts would lengthen the material. Scoffing at the worthless action under her breath, she rapped her knuckles against the wooden door.

The General's booming voice penetrated the thick door. "Come in."

Rolling her shoulders back, she entered. "General Rockwell, you wanted to see me?"

In his signature tan sports coat with circular brass buttons down the front, her father's gigantic frame bent over the paper he was writing. The pen appeared tiny and out of place within his massive fist. Signing the letter with a flourish of movement, the General pushed his work aside on the polished mahogany surface of his desk. With a sigh, he scratched at the gray tipping the sideburns of his flaming red hair and lifted his eyes. "I told you to stop calling me that." Her father's gaze froze into chips of green ice as he appraised his daughter. "Ruby, what happened to your hair?" Taking in the sight of her before him, the pen snapped within his hand and black ink oozed over his thick fingers. "Put on some god damn clothes, woman!"

Laughing with delight, she perched herself on the corner of her father's desk. "General, you're such a fuddy-duddy." She fiddled with the pencils on his desk. "Emma said you wanted to speak with me?"

Jerking a white handkerchief from the inside pocket of his tweed jacket, the General wiped the ink before it stained his fingers. "This is not acceptable. Thank God your mother isn't alive to see you gallivanting around in this manner."

Stiffening, her gaze bounced off her mother's face in the wedding picture behind her father's huge form. She gathered herself up and cast a jaunty salute towards him. "General, Private Ruby Rockwell reporting for duty."

Surging up from his chair, the General extended to his full height. He placed his hands on the desk, his face just inches from hers. "This is exactly why I wanted to see you—your saucy attitude. The time has come for you to grow up and stop acting like a petulant child."

He slammed his fist on the mahogany surface of the desk. "Damn it! You're a Rockwell. Put away your silly dreams of being an actress on stage and start acting like a good, pure, decent woman."

He attempted to stay his anger. "Ruby, it is time for you to set a date and marry Widower Henderson. He's an upstanding man, a man worthy of a woman of your station. If you keep following the path you're on, then he'll cry off."

Her chest tightened, squeezing her heart, and an uneasy feeling crept into her stomach, churning it and planting a seed of doubt. Perhaps, the plan she had was a step too far. No, she decided, rallying against his heavy handed approach. "General, I'm not one of your soldiers that you can order around. I will be an actress. I will sing on stage and one day in the talkies on the silver screen. You can't stop me."

Power radiating from his body, the General towered over his daughter." You don't think I can stop you?"

Picking up a clean corner of the handkerchief, he grabbed Ruby by the back of her neck and rubbed the shocking lipstick from her mouth until her naked lips were revealed. "I'm your father and you'll do as I say. But if you prefer to refer to me as the General, then you'll do as I command. I order you to go up to your room and change into something tasteful. I order you to do something with your hair to make it acceptable to an eligible man."

The General's eyes narrowed into slits and he released his daughter. "Perhaps I gave you too much time to dream. To fill your head with foolish, silly thoughts. Duty, courage and honor make a good soldier. You, Ruby Rockwell, are now in charge of hosting the Tea Dances here at Twin Springs. Plus, you are in charge of managing the Ladies Retiring Room for Tea Time and in the evenings. That should keep you busy."

The General settled himself back in his chair. "You're dismissed to change and report to the Crystal Ballroom where our employees are busy setting up for tonight's Tea Dance." Finished with his tirade, he ignored his daughter's presence and resumed working.

Lips pursed and tender from mistreatment, she stormed from the room and slammed the door behind her. Who was he to tell her what to do? She was a grown woman and she wouldn't cower to any man. Releasing the drawstring and reaching into her purse, she removed her shiny compact and lipstick. Leaning back against her father's door, she attempted to steady her breathing. The compact shook in her trembling hands and anger coursed through her body. "Perhaps, I haven't gone far enough."

In front of God and everyone, she powdered her face in the tiny, circular mirror before reapplying her red lipstick. Snapping the lid shut, she muttered, "General, we'll see who will win this war. Nothing is going to keep me from my dreams and I have only begun to fight. I'll use every weapon at my disposal: my face, my body, your wealth. Even if it means embarrassing myself and you, Father dear."

In order to enter the Crystal Ballroom through the ladies entrance, Ruby stalked away from the General's office towards the Ladies Retiring Room. Who was the General to decide her future? She couldn't permit a man to control her future, not even her father. "I'll do what I want and act the way I want," she decided and paused between the Front Desk and the Bellhop Stand. "Otherwise, I'll continue to be trapped at Twin Springs and inside my velvet cage."

Determined to gain her freedom, she made an about face and detoured around the Bellhop Stand, rounding the corner to cut through the Officers Hall. With the palms of her hands, she thrust the double doors apart and stepped into gentlemen's territory.

Immediately, the smell of cigar smoke overwhelmed her senses. Men lounged in deep leather chairs, with newspapers propped open before them. They exclaimed out loud when she entered their private sanctum. She twirled her purse in a wide circle by the drawstring and winked at a shocked older gentleman sporting a thin mustache. "What a sap," she muttered under her breath. "You don't look anything like John Gilbert."

She paused at the Telephone Exchange and Broker's Office on her right. Peering through the large window of the Brokers Office, she gaped at the domed ticker tape machine available to the rich men in order to check their portfolios. In the reflection of the window, she caught sight of a row of telephone booths. "You men have private areas with telephones?"

Anger coursed through her veins at the unfairness of her world. The Ladies Retiring Room was comprised of long settees, wicker chairs and a piano. "Well thank you General, for giving me the authority to change some things. Bet he didn't think about that," she grumbled. Skirting past the balding heads and outraged faces, she swung open the towering doors and strutted to the Crystal Ballroom.

Commanding a grand entrance to the occupants within, she paused on the threshold and surveyed the ballroom floor. Windows arched high above a wall of French doors that led out to a patio. Green ferns and small, sputtering fountains lined the room. Rattan chairs were pushed tight against circular tables and dotted the perimeter of the waxed dance floor.

Two tall ladders were piled high with men disassembling the magnificent, large chandelier from which the room earned its name. Crystal fobs sparkled and shimmered, casting a rainbow of colors throughout the room. Ruby's arched brows furrowed and she sauntered over to the workers and drew their gazes from their task. She called up to the men high in the air, "Who ordered you to take down the chandelier?"

"The Lieutenant, Miss Ruby," one thin man called down. "He said we're to replace it with a smaller, less gaudy one."

Nibbling her lip, she placed her hands on her hips and surveyed the smaller chandelier where it laid upon the floor. Mostly black iron and bulbs, it resembled a dead octopus with its arms and legs splayed out in all directions. She yelled up, "Did the General approve of this change?"

The man shrugged his bony shoulders and resumed working.

Ruby was torn. She loved the brilliance of the old chandelier but didn't want to face her father again this morning. Especially, since she'd disobeyed his orders.

Her gaze honed in on a gaggle of employees arranging red roses and white carnations in huge glass vases that stood three feet tall. Other servants placed roses into squatty, silver plated vases for the tables. Two women, in their black uniforms with starched white linen cuffs and collars, faced Ruby. Their faces were dipped downward, but she could tell their cheeks were unusually rosy. They giggled and talked to a tall gentleman with midnight black hair. "Guy," she purred.

The sound of Ruby's garden shoes rang out against the wooden dance floor. The women hushed, their movements stiffened, then, they burst into a frantic rush.

Thick with child, her personal maid, Betty, stood beside her sister Ame's personal maid, Gabby. Both refused to meet her eyes. "What's going on in here?"

Her maid, Betty, rubbed a spot between her breast bone and the roundness of her large stomach with her finger tips. Her eyes darted in every direction except towards Ruby.

"M-m-miss Ruby," Betty stuttered. Her lips struggled to form the words that her throat refused to release. "M-m-miss Ruby," she expelled, tucking a curly strand of chestnut brown hair behind her ear. "The L-L-Lieutenant, told us to help you with the Te-Te-Tea Dance."

Ruby studied the extended belly of her personal maid and the fatigue that wrinkled the corners of her tawny brown eyes. Stupid man, she thought. Inconsiderate bastard.

Just like her sister, Betty was imminent to giving birth. Even without her stuttering impairment, the maid was no match for the Lieutenant.

Anger surged through Ruby and green sparks shot out her eyes. "Isn't that just ducky." Sarcasm dripped from her lips.

Turning, she noticed Gabby clutching the large, wooden cross that hung from a leather string around her neck. The maid judged her appearance and pursed her lips. Releasing a frustrated sigh, Ruby said, "Gabby, you should be monitoring my sister. Her time could come any moment now."

She couldn't help but wonder why she needed to deal with these ninnies when all she wanted was to sing. "And you," Ruby pivoted towards her personal maid, "should not be here playing with flowers."

Taken aback by Miss Ruby's reaction, Betty stumbled backwards, one hand splayed across her bosom and one protecting the mound of her unborn child.

"Miss Ruby," said Gabby. "Betty's just a lost sheep. As our Lord's book preaches, 'But when he saw the multitudes, he was moved with compassion on them, because they fainted, and were scattered abroad, as sheep having no shepherd.' So sayeth the Lord, Matthew 9:36."

Ruby looked up towards the ceiling and frowned at the ugly chandelier being hoisted into place. She attempted to school her face. An actress must have full control over her features, she reminded herself. "Betty," she soothed, "you should be resting. You're my personal maid, not the Lieutenant's. And I—," she stressed the last word as her eyes lowered from the ceiling, "want you to rest. Unless I call for you." Her words hung in the air, when Guy's husky laughter spread between them.

"You tell them. Go rest!"

Entrapped by his hazel eyes, her breath caught in her throat. Today, he wasn't dressed as a chauffeur but in light brown slacks with a white shirt that glowed against his tanned throat. A tingling started in her fingertips and toes and coursed through her limbs, until the electricity sparking from him to her cascaded into a jumble of waves within her core.

Except while singing on stage, Ruby never felt this magnitude of excitement. This alive. She soaked in the sight of his wide shoulders in his white collared shirt. His black suspenders made the width of his frame appear even broader. Her gaze flitted over the smooth planes of his face and the strength of his long tapered fingers, gently holding one of the roses. "Perhaps when Betty's time comes, I'll shift your duties to fulfill hers."

The maids gasped at her brazen words.

But Guy's eyes twinkled and he held the rose out to her. "It'd be my pleasure to serve you, Miss Ruby."

The cat becoming the mouse, Ruby's heart lurched as she accepted his gift and raised it to her nose.

Only the disapproval of Gabby's humming shook her from her daze and she flushed a deep crimson, her cheeks almost matching her lipstick. She dipped her head, expecting the long curtain of her hair to hide her embarrassment, only to remember she had chopped it all off.

Mentally, Ruby shook herself. *You're going to be a world famous singer and an actress, you're above all this dribble. You don't have time for a husband. There is no place for love when one is treading the boards.* Gathering herself up, she tipped her head to the side. *She just might be in love.*

The rose fell from her grasp as she stared into his eyes. Her mouth curved into a sensual smile. "I look forward to your attentions."

Betty pitched into a fit of giggles. "Miss Ruby, you're so fresh."

Guy scooped up the rose and brought it over. "Even this rose pales to your beauty," he murmured, his voice low and husky.

Up close she could see the green flecks in his golden eyes and a slight bump breaking up the straight line of his nose.

Trailing the rose's velvety petals across her cheek, he tucked the flower behind her ear.

Sparks shot through her body. She felt as if he'd caressed her, and her knees quivered. Softly under her breath, Ruby whispered, "My Guy."

His eyes deepened. The green flecks emitted a greenish glow through the gold and he cast her a roguish grin. He tipped his head in a courtesy nod. "At your service, ma'am."

Embarrassment surged through Ruby, that her thought actually left her mouth and he heard her. This wouldn't do. Wouldn't do at all. Worse yet, this impertinent man enjoyed her discomfort. "Betty, go rest. Gabby, sit with my sister. And you, go do whatever chauffeurs do when not driving. I'm sure it's not playing with flowers."

She pivoted on her heel and quickly walked towards the double doors of the Theatre. Her escape. The one place where she was free to feel and be who and what she wanted.

"I like y-y-your hair Miss Ruby," called out Betty.

Ignoring her comment, Ruby jerked on the rounded knob in the middle of the mirrored doors and plowed into the darkened Theatre. She stood within the pitch black room and allowed it to surround her. She breathed in deeply and filled her lungs with the smell of the crushed velvet seats, the linseed oiled stage and the remnants of the patrons' expensive perfumes and cigars.

In her mind's eye, she felt the grandness of the curved, towering ceiling, inlaid along the borders with arches of intricately pressed silver tin to reverberate the sound from the stage down towards the audience. Moving forward, she reached out a hand and flipped on the stage lights. She left the house lights off so that the stage illuminated like a beacon in the dark. She didn't need to feel her way down the aisles between the wrought iron rows of seats. Her heart knew the way.

She climbed the wooden stairs, to center stage, to home. Her purse slipped from her wrist, her chest swelled and she leaned back her head. She spread her arms open and released the song within her soul. Holding nothing back, her voice rose and fell in a crescendo of waves, rolling across the Theatre. Until, it peaked in a tsunami of raw emotion.

Gradually, her arms fell to her side, her head lowered and her lashes lifted, opening to the world around her. There he stood before her. Her Guy, with a red rose in his hand. He vaulted up onto the stage beside her with a deft movement. Gathering her up into his arms, he tucked the rose behind her ear and his firm lips branded hers, releasing the suppressed waves of desire to course through her body. . .

CHAPTER TWENTY-NINE

eet up, Jaxon drummed his fingers on his desk and stared at the monitors. Instead of seeing the different parts of the sleeping hotel filtering by before his eyes, his mind's eye saw Ava. Her creamy white skin wet with tears. Her green gaze hazed with fear. Her words, well, her words had wrenched his soul.

Something on the monitor caught his attention and his boots scraped against wood as they dropped to the floor. Eyes narrowing, he leaned in and studied the scene before him. He mumbled under his breath, "Man. Mid thirties. Blue cap. Grungy clothing. Who the hell are you?"

He shrugged and ignored the vagrant. But his gaze flickered back to the screen that had shifted to another part of the hotel. He thought about his promise to keep innocent, little Maddy safe. He thought about Ava.

The screen filtered back to the homeless man and Jaxon recognized the double doors that swung closed behind him. "Damn it, you've just exited the Presidents Hall right outside my office."

He bounded to his feet and charged from the room, intent on snagging the man before he disappeared out one of the exits within the Crystal Ballroom. "I'm going to escort him out of Twin Springs. Just like a real Security Manager would."

He circled the large table in the Presidents Hall and made a beeline for the Crystal Ballroom where he'd last seen the man exit. There, he thrust open the double doors. "Hold it right there."

But an empty room greeted him. "Shit, where the hell did he go?"

A heart piercing melody reached his ears and searching for the homeless man was wiped from his brain, replaced by a siren's call that reached down into the depths of his being, until he had no choice but to answer.

He followed the call through the mirrored doors and into the darkened Theatre, mesmerized by the sound coming from the lit stage. A woman shone like a beacon, her curves hugged by a tight white dress that shimmered, almost translucent in places, and left nothing to the imagination below mid-thigh. A sparkling white fabric was wrapped around the crown of her head and framed her face.

He bounded up on the stage as the siren's sensuous body swayed with the emotion exuding form her song. She turned towards him, her green eyes twinkling brighter than any star. His siren was Ava.

"Ava, are you all right?" He was unsure if she was having an episode or singing on stage. But that wasn't right? Ava despised the thought of returning to the stage. *Maybe after her training she felt stronger,* he thought. "Do you need my help?"

Ava glided towards him, her hips swiveling to the beat of the music in her head. She wound her arms around his neck and pulled his lips down to her's. Just inches from her parted lips, he paused and resisted. "Are you sure?"

"Sugar," she tossed his pet name for her back at him. "You're my Guy."

He sunk into the kiss. It felt right. She felt right. Ava tugged his shirt out of the waistline of his trousers. She ran her hands up under his shirt, kneaded the hair on his chest like a kitten making biscuits. Then she purred.

Mind blown, Jaxon answered his siren's call.

CHAPTER THIRTY

*A*va felt branded, the kiss searing her lips. This was one of the most intense dreams she'd ever had. Releasing herself to the innocent pleasure of a fantasy, she murmured beneath the assault, "My Guy, my Guy, my Guy," until the phrase became an insistent chant. "Please. Love me."

Her dream guy's strong arms held her tight against his hardened frame. His lips branded a trail across her neck. Tugging at the fabric on her shoulders, he lowered her to the stage floor and released her breasts to the hot lights of the stage.

Instinctively, she moved to cover herself but she squashed the action. After all, it was just a dream. Harmless. The outline of his head blocked the glare and shadowed his features. His tongue flickered over her nipple, tasting and teasing it to a furrowed peak. The gritty stubble of his face was a sharp contrast to the velvet softness of his tongue. Ava's arched brows furrowed. *Guy's face was smooth.*

Arching with pleasure, the smell of roses tickled her nose. She reached up for the rose tucked behind her ear and grasped thin air. The flower wasn't there. The sleepwalking dream began unraveling at the edges of her mind.

Her dream lover's strong hands tugged at her dress, lifting the material, sliding his hands along her silky, hose clad legs, past the expanse of bare skin where her garters began, until resting at the juncture between her thighs. Her eyes popped open and it was as if someone had thrown a bucket of water over her head, freezing her and bringing her back to her own reality. Memories slammed against her consciousness of the last man who'd dared to touch her there. *The Director.*

Free of the dream, she realized the man above her was solid. Strong and real. Frantically, she pushed against his shoulders. Her voice raised to a thunderous pitch, "No, No, NO!"

Tears gathered at the corners of her eyes. She felt trapped under his weight. Just like with the Director. Frantic to free herself, she bit down hard on his shoulder.

"Holy crap," Jaxon roared and thrust her away. "I'm sorry, Ava. I should've backed way. I shouldn't have permitted my emotions to let it go that far." He gained his footing and towered above her, rolling his shoulder where she bit him. "I didn't teach you that move but it was a good one. Let me help you up."

After his warm body abandoned hers, cool air rushed in. Ava drug deep, cleansing breaths into her lungs and attempted to purge her mind and body from his presence. She lifted herself up to her knees with her shaking arms, her head bent, and gazed down at the wooden floor.

The smells of the room and the bright lights filled her senses. She was not in the Director's office. She focused in on the cracks between the boards of the stage and remembered. She was safe at Twin Springs. "I'm on stage. I'm on the stage in the Theatre at Twin Springs."

Blood thundered to her ears and roared as bile worked its way up her throat. In her mind's eye, she saw the wood underneath her hands splattered with blood. Ashlee's body weighing her down. Trapping her. Her stomach revolted and she threw up on his boots. Horrified with her reaction, she wiped the bile from her lips with the back of her hand.

Jaxon stumbled back from her and they stared at each other in shock, before speaking simultaneously.

"How did I get here?" asked Ava.

"What the hell did you do to your hair?" roared Jaxon.

CHAPTER THIRTY-ONE

*J*axon felt like a stupid fool and shoved his hands into the pockets of his pants. What did he care if she cut her hair? So what if the shortened length gave her slender neck the appearance of being impossibly long and smooth.

The nauseating smell of her bile reached his nose. *Awesome,* he thought, inhaling deeply. Anything to replace the constant, heavy, sticky smell of roses that permeated his senses since arriving in this forsaken hotel.

If he would've stuck to his job of searching Twin Springs for clues and not attempted to find the homeless man, he'd be in his office right now and not making an ass of himself. Why did he have to think about Maddy and Ava's safety? When all he needed to do was keep his nose to the ground and search for leads.

His gaze swept over the gorgeous woman before him, imprinting her image on his soul. A part of him still begged to answer her call, to feel her silky skin beneath his hands. Her essence whispered to him and dared him to come closer.

He ground his teeth with frustration and rebelled against his instincts. *Push her away,* he told himself. Wipe away the memory of her sweet lips and silky skin. Even though the taste of her was still fresh on his tongue. *It was too soon. She's not ready. She needs time and healing to move past her attack.*

He extended a hand and helped her to her feet.

"Are you alright?" he questioned, his voice hard even to his own ears. He couldn't help it. He wanted her even though his mind said no.

Her cheeks flushed a rosy red, causing the unwelcome desire building within him to surge and course through his body. Silently, deliberately, he crushed his body's betrayal.

Shuffling and straitening her dress, she replied "Yes. I guess I was sleepwalking. Again."

Disgust left a vile taste in his mouth. Sleepwalking? His brow furrowed. Damn it. She called her mental breaks sleepwalking. She'd been in one of her fits and he'd taken advantage of her. How could he have not realized that she wasn't present? She felt present. Spoke straight to him.

He grasped at straws to make her feel comfortable with him again. "Sugar, if that was you sleepwalking, then you can sleep-walk with me anytime you want." The words slipped easily from his lips.

Her cheeks flamed red hot and he wanted to bite the sentence back, word by word, but it was too late.

Begrudgingly, he looked down at Ava and admired the gentle swell of her breasts visible above her dress. A shiny disc with the Twin Springs logo nestled between the soft mounds. Hooking his finger under the chain, he lifted the necklace from its hiding place. "What's this?" he asked, noticing as the circular pendant twirled that it had shiny black glass on the reverse side. But he knew. RFID, Radio Frequency Identification. High grade. Just like Theo's.

"That's my Twin Springs medallion. A gift from Theo and my key to open all the doors within Twin Springs." She tugged the necklace from his grip. "I'm sorry I bit you. I was disoriented and didn't know what was going on when I came to."

Was she not having mental breaks? Was she really just a heavy sleeper that walked in her sleep, acting out her dreams? Appalled,

Jaxon ground out, "Are you saying that you weren't in control of your actions? That you had no idea we were—umm—kissing, until you started screaming no?"

Unwilling to meet his eyes, she looked out over the dark Theatre. "I thought I was dreaming in my bed. Dreaming of," her voice dipped to a whisper, "my Guy."

He didn't know who her guy was but he was one lucky bastard. The fire she'd ignited still burned within him. Jealousy bit a chunk out of his heart. Despite himself, he leaned in, aching to hear her siren's call again.

A fire alarm screeched through the air, piercing their private world and pulling them apart. Propelled into action by the sound, Jaxon's military instincts immediately kicked into gear and he swept the area for danger. He'd witnessed first hand, the life shattering destruction that fire caused. Not seeing any immediate threat he jumped from the stage, turned to grab Ava about the waist and lowered her down. He shouted over the ear piercing sound, "Where's it coming from?"

"The alarm panel is in your office. We must hurry. The fire doors will slam shut within five minutes and cordon off sections of the hotel until the fire department comes."

Horrified, visions of men trapped in a burning building filled his mind. Their remembered screams brought goosebumps to his arms and his strong body shuddered. "What? You block off sections of the hotel? What about the guests? Will they be trapped?"

Ava shook her head. "No, there're multiple exits between each section. The fire doors just keep the fire from spreading throughout the hotel. The General installed them after the Great Fire in 1928."

He rushed from the Theatre, pulling Ava along with him by the hand. He needed to find the fire, to fight it. He'd failed before and refused to let another person burn to death on his watch. Jerking open the door to his office he searched for the fire panel. Zeroing in on the bright red box, he realized he didn't understand how to read it. Frustration churned in his gut.

Ava pushed past him and opened the red door with a glass insert that covered rows of blinking lights. With the tip of her finger, she trailed the blinking lights over to the identification tag. "It's in one of the shops on the Promenade." She grabbed one of the walkie talkies stacked up along the desk and hit send all, "Fire on the Promenade! Fire on the Promenade!"

Ava set off in a full sprint through the Presidents Hall and turned right to rush up the stairs between the Front Desk and the Bell Stand.

Grabbing her by the arm, he shouted over the noise, "Isn't the Promenade to the left down here?"

She tugged her arm free without pausing her forward movement and yelled over her shoulder. "Yes, but the fire doors would've closed by now. We must take a different route."

She leaped up the stairs, past frantic guests being moved along by Sheela and Diana. She ran down a long hall that paralleled the length of the Grand Lobby, before turning left down another long hall. Frightened guests in their night gowns stuck their heads out of their rooms, unsure how to proceed.

Loosing precious time, she addressed the guests. "Please everyone, exit your rooms and proceed down the hall to the right," she pointed back to where they'd come from. "There will be Twin Springs employees there to assist you. Everything will be fine."

Working beside Ava, Jaxon verified that all the guest rooms along the hallway were cleared. Once finished, they raced to the end of the hall and opened a metal door to another flight of stairs. Dark smoke twirled up the stairwell and greeted them.

Jaxon removed his button up over-shirt and balled it up to hold against his nose and mouth. He looked down at her pristine white dress and heels and compared her attire to his jeans and black t-shirt. "Stay here," he commanded.

Ava unwound the scarf from around her hair and held it over her face. "No. This is my home." She pushed past him, delved down into the stairwell and disappeared within the black smoke.

Growling in the back of his throat, he followed and pushed

past her at the last moment. Holding up his hand, he prevented her from opening the door at the landing. "Wait."

Smoke swirled around them, causing moisture to drip from their red rimmed eyes. He placed his palms close to the metal door and tested for heat. "Feels cool," he shouted. "Stand back."

He leaned out of the way and cracked open the door. Relieved that flames didn't lick their way around the door frame, Jaxon pulled the door wider and exited on to the back end of Twin Springs' row of shops.

More thick, black smoke filled the long Promenade. Through his blurry, wet gaze, he discerned two people, covered in soot and battling the blaze.

Jaxon froze. His heart thudded in his chest. Two figures from his memories replaced the forms before his eyes. Now, Woody stood before him, flames consuming his flesh, the twisted features of his face, as horrific screams were wrenched from his body. Then, Roddie tumbled from the doorway. Engulfed in flames, he collapsed to his knees and submitted to the hunger of the fire.

"Don't let the flames get to the Christmas Tree!" shouted Ava. "Or the fire will reach the second floor!"

She rushed past him and snapped him from the nightmare within his memories. Shaking his head, the figures shifted within the smoke and transformed back into Theo and Isabella. He snatched a fire extinguisher from the wall and joined the fight as flames licked their way out of the shattered window of Twin Springs' Body & Spa Boutique.

In the distance, a fire truck's sirens wailed. While Theo and Jaxon concentrated their extinguishers on the blaze, Ava joined her sister and pulled one of the now soot blackened bathrobes from a shelf and used it to beat at the flames. Together, the two couples battled the fire. Firemen with their heavy suits rushed down the hall, dragging hoses. The two couples stood back as firemen turned on their hoses and flooded the area with water.

Another fireman herded them out of Twin Springs and to a safe area marked off with yellow tape reading "Fire Line—Do Not

Cross." In a surreal scene with the stars above twinkling over the mountains, Twin Springs' employees sprung to life.

White folding chairs appeared on the frost covered lawn. Employees guided guests in various states of dress into the chairs and provided blankets as needed until the all clear was given. Two Oakes Casino and Club, adjoining the lawn, opened its doors to pipe out hot chocolate for the families huddled together in the cool, fall night. Lighted soldiers and gingerbread men glimmered in the background.

Wrapped in a blanket and relieved that no one had died or was seriously injured, Jaxon leaned back against a bank of grass and scanned the crowd for the homeless man or anyone else who didn't seem to belong. He muttered under his breath, "Damn it, once again I let a beautiful woman impair my judgment. I should've tracked the homeless man. Then, I could've prevented this fire."

Walkie in hand, Theo shouted out commands as an EMT treated him for a small burn on his arm. The EMT moved on to place oxygen masks over Isabella and Ava's faces. Grimy and smoke stained, Ava's sexy white dress was muted below the starry sky.

When the EMT attempted to place an oxygen mask on Jaxon's face, he refused. "I'm fine, thanks." Besides, the burning in his throat would be a welcome reminder to keep his wits about him.

"It's a hell of a thing," muttered the EMT.

"What do you mean?"

"Chief said that someone lit a bra on fire. Stretched it between a display of pamphlets and books." The EMT shook his head and walked away.

Jaxon thought about the fire. The unique placement, in a closed shop, only opened by a few employees and those lucky enough to own a special charm with an RFID. Maybe the homeless man had nothing to do with the fire. Perhaps they'd found Ava's missing bra.

Could she have lit the fire while she was sleepwalking? Was

she sabotaging the hotel and not even knowing it? Or was she aware of her actions and lying to him and everyone else?

Even though the fire alarm was finally silenced, it still rang out in his brain, a reminder to him of the consequences of dealing with a beautiful woman. Nothing good came of it. Someone would always get hurt. Some even burned. At least this time, no one died.

Part Two

CHAPTER THIRTY-TWO

*1*7 December 1928.

I know there's an undercover revenuer sniffing about, trying to find my hidden stash. But I have my sources. My own little army of servants. Provided to me by the Great General Rockwell.

This Noble Experiment has made me wealthy. I'm about to finish my largest batch of shine ever. Soon I'll be richer than even the General. Making gobs of green cash with my secret still. In public, I speak up on the side of the Dry's, pushing to keep the Eighteenth Amendment strong and squash the evil power of liquor over our upstanding citizens.

I shout right along with them, "Keep America a Dry Country!" All the while, my shine pumps from Twin Springs' heart. Shipped out of the Blue Ridge Mountains by boat, automobile, horseback and, hell, even by foot. Slowly winding a slippery path down to the thirsty masses.

What if my still is found? God, the irony. How easy it will be to shift the blame. I revel in the paradox I've created. If found, my still will bring down the great and powerful General Rockwell. He'll crumble before his peers and I'll roll with laughter as he is dragged away in chains. Then, I'll become the saving grace for his daughters, for the community.

Just in case the revenuer gets too close, I have avenues of escape. I might take one of the General's Gems with me. Perhaps the song bird. Let her sing. Sing just for me.

Lt. Porter

CHAPTER THIRTY-THREE

After the previous night's adrenaline rush of fighting the fire, Ava needed a dose of morning courage and strength from her caffeine lover. She donned a business suit, a feminine version of a man's power suit in an admiral blue, and added her own touch of style by layering a white, ruffled silk shirt beneath. High heels augmented her height and gave her a feeling of control that she desperately needed.

Slipping into the Presidents Hall, she surveyed the room before her. For the first time, she remembered so much from her sleep-walking dream. The room looked different from when it was named the Officers Hall but eerily the same in some places.

The bones of the room remained constant, long in length, surrounded by pillars, the phone booths tucked into the left corner and an office space on the right. But in place of a Western Union and Telephone Exchange was the Security Office. Gone were the thick carpets and lighted sconces of naked bronze women holding globes of light. Clean, elegant crystal light fixtures stood in their place.

Groaning under her breath, Ava rushed past Jaxon's office. Lack of sleep from last night and running low on caffeine, she was in no condition to face him. He asked too many probing questions and his hazel gaze bared her soul.

A shiver rolled down her spine. He seemed to possess an uncanny ability to see past any character she hid behind and identify the real her. Besides, how could she explain her behavior from last night?

Countless times growing up, Ava had woken to find herself in different locations within Twin Springs, never understanding how she'd ended up there during her sleep.

Last night was different. Last night, she remembered every-thing. Every thought, touch and caress experienced by her ancestor Ruby. She felt akin to her as never before. Ava ran her fingers through her short hair. Visible proof that it was all more than just a dream. *Was this how Isabella felt? Were Isabella's dreams this real?*

She speculated about what it was like to be loved, to be desired like her ancestor, Ruby. But Ruby and her Guy's budding love was a farce. True love wasn't real. But what about Isabella and Theo? Their love seemed true, strong. Maybe some people were lucky enough to find love.

Like all human beings, she had a need deep inside of her to be whole, to search for and to find her other half. But she understood love was a myth, a dream, and unattainable for her. Women like her didn't find true love. Men saw her as a plaything without feel-ings. She thought of Jaxon and knew his rejection would hurt too much, would devastate her. She had no choice but to avoid Twin Springs' new Security Manager. Hide behind her duties to the Grand Dame and to her family.

Snagging a tall paper cup, she tipped the lever of the coffee urn. Closing her eyes, she inhaled the nutty aroma of her morning lover, absorbing his strong, heady presence within her. Adding her sugar and cream, she briefly blew on the hot surface and surveyed the room. Unusually quiet, even for this early in the morning, she assumed most of the guests had slept in after their late night fire drill. Pressing the lid firmly on her cup, she mused, "How will Theo soothe the ruffled feathers of the guests this time?"

Glancing around she muttered, "Something's off." Her eyes searched the room. Unable to put her finger on the problem, she headed towards the large, round table for her morning paper and stopped short. Under the huge flower arrangement, the white linen table cloth was empty. Not a paper in sight. Stunned, Ava's jaw dropped. "Where are the newspapers?" Twin Springs always provided a morning paper for their guests. "Theo's going to have a coronary over this."

The faint sound of rustling drew her attention. Slowly, she skirted the table and barely glimpsed an elegant, expensive, high heel shoe before it disappeared under the long tablecloth. Grasping the edge of the white linen in her hand, she bent down and lifted the fabric. Within the darkened space, Maddy sat with her legs crossed and her silver eyes blinking back at her. Piles of newspapers surrounded her. Concern lacing her voice, Ava asked, "What are you doing?"

A smile spread across the teen's innocent face, "Umm, counting the newspapers." She tapped the stacks beside her. "Yeah, Theo and I are trying to work out a cost-benefit ratio to providing papers for the guests. Very detailed process, you wouldn't be interested. I love your hair."

Ava's elegant brows rose with the statement. "Thanks, but I do understand what a cost-benefit ratio is. May I have a newspaper?"

"No!" shouted the teenager. Quickly, she covered her mouth with her hand. Stared at Ava. Then, lowered her hand. "It's just that I'm not finished counting and it would throw me off."

Swiftly, Ava reached under the table and scooped up a newspaper. "I'm sure one will not hurt."

Maddy lunged out from under the table and attempted to snatch it. "Don't!" she shouted. "Give that back to me."

Surprised by the teenager's actions, Ava held the newspaper away from her quick hands. "What's gotten into you?"

Turning away, she held open the folds and read out loud the huge headline across the front page. "Broadway star Ava Fairbanks responsible for suicide death of Director's wife."

The newspaper shook within Ava's grasp and a deep coldness filled her, freezing her from the outside world as she attempted to focus in on the blurring black words before her.

Snippets of the article floated before her eyes. She whispered, "'Broadway actress, Ava Fairbanks, found in a compromising position before show...Discovered by Directors wife...Secret love affair...Intimate interlude...Her marriage at an end, devastated wife shoots herself in the head on stage beside the other woman... Curtain falls and actress never seen again...Found hiding out in her family's hotel, Twin Springs Hotel and Spa.'"

Ava's caffeine lover fell from her numb fingers and splattered hot liquid around her feet.

CHAPTER THIRTY-FOUR

The smell of the fire hung within the Grand Lobby. Ropes portioned off the area in front of what was once Twin Springs' Body & Spa Boutique. Trying to erase traces of the fire from the night before, cleaning crews buzzed about, scrubbing walls and spraying surfaces with lemon fragranced cleaners.

Even the fresh scent of pine sap, from the huge tree at the end of the hall, couldn't combat the offending smoke smell.

Jaxon rolled his shoulders and leaned against a pillar. He was ready for this JOBB to end. To get back to women who didn't sleepwalk and confuse him at every turn.

Isabella smiled up at him as she rolled a miniature version of Twin Springs, made entirely out of sugar and gingerbread, down the hall. He shook his head. The amount of coordination it took to keep the hotel running was amazing. Like fighting a war with many different fronts. He continued down the lobby to grab a cup of joe before he went to his new office.

He turned into the Presidents Hall and there was Ava. Desire slammed a velvet fist into his gut. Even after last night's ordeal, she was gorgeous. Her sexy body was fluid and graceful as she walked. The curtain of her hair caressed her face and swayed with her gait. The midnight black color of her hair framed her face and contrasted against her light green eyes.

Immediately, his eyes zeroed in on her full, red lips. He remembered them swollen and soft from his kisses. *Get a grip*, Jaxon admonished himself. *You know the rules. Get in, get out, get the job done. Help her learn to defend herself if you want but be analytical. A tough, hard ass.*

Jerking himself up by his boot straps, he reassessed the mission before him. *Subject, female.*

Yep jackass, his inner voice responded. *She's all woman.*

Jaxon pushed the thought away and continued his analysis. *5 foot 9 inches.*

Of long lean legs, his mind rebelled.

He groaned under his breath and tried again. *Black hair.*

Silky, smooth hair that glides through your fingers, his mind added.

Unwillingly, his eyes once again focused in on her soft, full mouth. *Caucasian, currently talking to thin air.*

"Shit, is she sleepwalking again?" he muttered under his breath. He lengthened his stride. Who knows what she'll do in her sleep and with whom. One thought vibrated through his mind as he rounded the large table, *Damn it, that's my sleepwalker!*

Up close he noted her face was unusually pale with a greenish hue. *She's gonna blow chunks.*

A trembling started with her sexy legs and traveled up her body. Swaying on her feet, Ava's coffee cup slid from her fingers and poured its hot contents all over his boots.

"I'll be damned." He stared down and shook his head. "Do you have something against my shoes?"

Dazed, Ava looked up from the paper and focused in on Jaxon's golden eyes. "W-w-what?" she stuttered.

He gave a pointed look down at the black leather of his boots then back at her. "My boots," he repeated. "I take it you don't like them."

At a loss, she glanced down at his shoes. They were covered with the hot contents of her caffeine lover.

"Did I burn you? I'm so sorry!" She bent down and used the disgusting newspaper as a towel, in a vain attempt to soak up her spill. Smashing the paper against his boots, she chanted, "Horrid, stupid, paper." Her efforts splashed the liquid around more than it absorbed the coffee. "My coffee. Stupid piece of trash came between me and my morning lover."

Morning lover? wondered Jaxon. *The woman's gone over the edge.* He reached out and grasped Ava's elbow, dragging her up and against his strong frame. "You don't have to beat me to death. They're just shoes. Are you alright?"

Maddy scrambled out from under the table. She bounced into the couple and knocked them apart with her abundant energy.

Steadying Ava, to keep her from toppling over, he scowled down at the teenager. "Careful," burst from his lips.

"Good morning, Jaxon," Maddy purred, batting her lashes up at him.

The teen stood uncomfortably close to him, staring up with her innocent gray eyes. She looked the closest to her age as he'd ever seen her with black leggings and a long shirt. Except for those stilts she called shoes. Mindful of her tender age, he immediately took a large step back and placed an appropriate distance between them. *This is a crazy bin*, he thought, before asking, "Why were you hiding under the table?"

Reaching out, the teenager ran the tips of her fingers down his arm, "Umm, working on a cost-benefit analysis. Of course." She made a slight humming noise in the back of her throat.

Ava tossed the newspaper into a trash bin, "Maddy, the game is up. You might as well put all those newspapers back on the table. Unless you stopped all deliveries for the town, for the world, it's over."

The teen's shoulders slumped but she rallied quickly. "It doesn't matter what that paper reports. My brother will discover the truth. I overheard him yelling at someone at the newspaper this morning. That's how I knew to start hiding the papers."

Turning back to Jaxon, Maddy slipped her arm through his and pressed her young body up against him. "I also heard that you helped put out the fire last night." She fluttered her long lashes, and squeezed his arm.

Feeling uncomfortable, he noticed her rapidly blinking up at him. "Did the smoke from the fire hurt your eyes? If they're dry, eye drops would help."

Hugging his trapped arm, the teen leaned her head against his shoulder. "That's so kind. I knew you'd be awesome."

Alarm bells rang in his brain. Firmly, he unwound the teenager from his arm. Grasping her by the shoulders, he placed her two feet away from him. "Stay," he growled. "Your brother needs to talk with you about boundaries. Until then," he waived his hand between their two bodies, "this space is my boundary. Don't cross it."

Was his sister like this growing up? Thank God the Geezer's kept her on a tight leash. Getting back to the task at hand, he bent down and threw back the tablecloth. Hundreds of newspapers were stacked below. Keeping one eye on the teen, he snagged a newspaper and scanned the headline. Shocked more than he wanted to admit at the damning words, he turned to Ava, only to find only Maddy's feline eyes blinking back at him. *Shit.* "Where did Ava go?"

CHAPTER THIRTY-FIVE

Standing under the portrait, Ava stared up at her ancestors. The article weighed heavily on her shoulders. It was just as she'd thought. Everyone, including Ashlee, assumed that she was having an affair with Hollingsworth. Ava hung her head in shame and rubbed her temples with her fingertips. All it would've taken was one moment. Just a minute of her time to explain, to mend. Then she could've changed Ashlee's destiny, could've saved her.

Now the newspaper had revealed her ugly secret to the whole world. Told all that she was responsible for a woman's death. Jaxon entered her office, with Maddy trailing not far behind. She couldn't meet his eyes. He must think the worst of her. A harlot and a crazy woman. Soon, he'd discover just how weak she really was.

Jaxon tucked the newspaper into the crook of his back, leaned his hip against one of the bookcases that lined the back wall, and buried his hands deep within his pockets. "With your hair cut, the resemblance between the two of you is uncanny."

Ava rubbed her lips together and drew in a deep breath, "I suppose you think I'm insane."

Unwillingly, he chuckled. "The thought did cross my mind."

Maddy's head pivoted between the two. "Why?"

"I had an unfortunate incident with Ruby Rockwell last night and Jaxon witnessed my embarrassment. I was sleepwalking."

"Ruby Rockwell?" Jaxon rubbed his stubbled chin. "What does a dead woman have to do with what happened on stage last night?"

"Is that all?" asked the teenager, twirling a ringlet of her dark hair around her finger. "The General's daughter, Emma, haunted Isabella. It makes sense that Ruby would haunt Ava." She looked up at the portrait, "I wonder if Amethyst will haunt me. Even though I don't look like her, I'm the only woman left in our family."

"You're being haunted? Now, wait just a minute." He rubbed the back of his neck. "I could understand that your episodes might be caused by sleepwalking but ghosts?" He shook his head. "Maybe we need to see someone. Talk with a professional."

"I told you, I'm not crazy."

"Yeah," added Maddy, her arms folded across her chest. "She's not crazy. Isabella dreamed about Emerald's life in the twenties. That's how we found the secret room and passage way that lead to the still." The teen shot him a disgruntled look and plopped down on the couch. "That's how we found out that Niles had been sabotaging the hotel. That's how we found Emerald's bones. So, there!"

"No way in hell am I believing that there are ghosts."

Fury consumed Ava. She marched over to Jaxon and tapped him on the chest with the tip of her finger. "It's easy for you to not believe. You're not the one who's waking up and finding yourself in embarrassing situations. Finding yourself a mile away from home, barefoot and wearing your nightgown." She punctuated each sentence with a tap on his chest. "It's easy to mock when you aren't the one who's a living, breathing doll for a dead woman. Where she dresses you up, cuts your hair and puts you on stage for anyone to see!"

The door swung violently open and slammed against the glass side panels.

Brandishing a newspaper before him, Theo walked into the room with Isabella double timing it behind him to keep up. Rolling the newspaper up, he smacked it against the dark gray fabric of his pant leg. He stalked the small area in front of the General's desk. "They can't do this to you, Ava." He punctuated each word with a thrust of the newspaper. "We'll sue. I have a friend at this paper. I've already left a message with his secretary."

A squawk emitted from the corner of the room. "Fuck the bastards," screamed Ava's new bird.

All eyes swiveled to the angry parrot pacing within his cage. Ava rushed over to calm him, making gentle hushing sounds under her breath. Reaching in, she rubbed the feathers at the base of his head between two of her fingers. His golden eyes closed and he hummed with satisfaction. "He hasn't had any food yet. Probably just cranky." Finishing the rub, she reached down to collect his stainless steel bowl. Surprised, she stared down into a full bowl of fresh fruit and nuts. "Did one of you feed him?" she questioned, looking from one person to another for confirmation.

At their denial, she shrugged and replaced the bowl within the cage. "I didn't either, must've been Logan."

"Well, for once I agree with your bird," stated Theo. "I swear, I'll take care of this. You know I keep my promises."

"I'm sure you'll try. But this is one promise you might not be able to fulfill. Just let it go." She stared at him beseechingly before adding, "For me."

Theo glanced down at his fiancée. After receiving her slight confirming nod, he threw the offending newspaper on the desk and continued. "Has the world gone crazy? Last night, a guest complained about two people getting it on in the Theatre. On stage no less. Then, the fire and now, this. What the hell is going on?" He paused for a moment and his steel gaze narrowed. "What the hell happened to your hair?"

"Burn it down," squawked the gray bird, and he munched on a walnut seed held within the grasp of his claw.

"I like her hair," interjected Maddy. "I might cut mine too."

Everyone in the room gave a resounding, "No!"

Sinking further into her seat, the teen muttered, "Fun suckers."

Ava's face burned bright red and Jaxon growled under his breath. Both cast their gaze anywhere but in Theo's direction.

Theo's head swiveled between the couple. "You two? On the stage?" He reached to tighten his tie, only to grasp the thin air of his open collar. Instead, he threw his hands up in disgust. "You know we have rooms here at Twin Springs for that sort of thing."

Maddy shot to her feet. Her eyes were huge in her young face. She stared at Ava and Jaxon. "You two were on the stage last night, doing it?"

Turning to Ava, her gray eyes filled up with tears that pooled at the rim of her eyelashes. "I trusted you. I confided in you. I thought we were sisters," she whispered, her voice raw. Unable to hold back the flow, a stream of tears dripped from her eyelashes.

Horrified at the pain she'd caused, Ava covered her mouth with her hand. She stepped forward, wanting to repair the young girl's broken heart but knew she'd fail just like she did with the Director's wife. She searched for a part, for a persona to smooth the pain and to hide within. But all she found was herself.

"You—you went behind my back and stole him." Maddy wiped the tears aside with the back of her hands. "I hate you! I hate your guts!" She fled the room in a mass of curls and tears.

Unable to deal with the pain, Ava turned away from everyone. Hugging herself, she leaned her forehead against the cool metal of the parrot's cage.

Rubbing the short hair on the back of his head, Theo gave a great sigh. "She'll get over it. I can't tell you how many shirts my little sister has soaked over the years with tears about boys. But you," he swiveled to address Jaxon. His hands balled into fists. "I didn't hire you to sleep with Ava and I sure as hell didn't hire you to romance my teenage sister."

Isabella laid a restraining hand on her fiancés sleeve. "You're not being fair and that's not like you. You told me that Maddy was throwing herself at him and that you planned to have a talk with her."

Theo's steely eyes pierced his new Security Manager. "I don't like the women under my responsibility being hurt. Do it again and I'll kick your ass, your fault or not. Got it?"

Jaxon tilted his head. "Completely understood."

Turning back to the room, Ava wiped her face and took a steadying breath. "We didn't have sex and it's not his fault. I was sleepwalking. He found me on the stage and things just progressed out of control from there. He immediately stopped when he realized something was wrong."

"You sleepwalk?" asked Theo, amazed.

"Oh, Ava." Isabella ignored him and replied, "Why can't Ruby give you a break."

"Ava's sleepwalking because of Ruby?" Giving up, Theo sunk down into one of the leather chairs and rubbed his brow with the tips of his fingers. "Of course, she's sleepwalking because of Ruby," he muttered under his breath. "Why not?"

Ignoring him, Isabella straightened her chef jacket and addressed her sister, "Perhaps it is just like Emma and me. Once I found Emma and discovered the true way she died, she stopped haunting me. Maybe that is what Ava needs to do, find Ruby."

"Are you all crazy?" Jaxon addressed Theo. "You can't seriously believe in ghosts."

Theo's eyes narrowed at Jaxon's tone. "Yes, I do. If it weren't for Emma entering my dreams and showing me her world, I wouldn't have found Isabella until it was too late. Hell, I might never have found her."

Jaxon snapped his mouth closed and glared.

Isabella studied her sister, "What made you decide to cut your hair?"

Embarrassed, she tucked her shortened hair behind her ears. "I don't remember doing it. I went to sleep and dreamt about Ruby." She explained her dream. "And I woke up on stage. Umm, kissing Jaxon, and discovered I'd cut my hair."

Picking up the discarded newspaper, Theo asked, "Is this why you don't want to step on stage ever again?"

Refusing to meet his eyes, she nodded. "Before, when I stepped from behind the curtain, excitement and possibilities flooded my body. I felt the energy of the audience. I felt alive. Now, all I see is her face looking at me. Her big brown eyes were sad, defeated. And all I feel is the splatter of her blood across my face and arms. I can't do it. I can't deal with that."

Isabella rushed to her sister and hugged her. "Do you know why the Director's wife committed suicide? Why she chose to kill herself on stage in front of you and the audience."

Tears pooled in Ava's eyes. Her throat raw from the smoke of last night and bags from her sleepless night swelling under her eyes, she felt miles away from the Broadway star she'd once been. She swallowed hard and pulled away. She wanted to hide. She couldn't face her past. Her lack of action. She needed to bury the pain, erase the shame and conceal the guilt beneath a mask. "I killed her. I abandoned her when she needed me most."

CHAPTER THIRTY-SIX

*S*hutting the door of the Security Office, Jaxon threw himself down into the swivel chair. The two sides of his brain battled in a silent war. A part of him believed in Ava. His damn instincts buzzed, telling him to protect her, to ease her pain. But experience muted out those instincts and screamed about conniving bitches, fire, and death. What the hell was he doing? His MO was plain Janes. Safe, secure, sweet, plain Janes.

He slammed his fist down on the desk and the line of walkie talkie soldiers wobbled before toppling over like dominoes. "A guest had observed us on the stage. Where the hell's my situational awareness? Out the damn window!"

Once he'd heard Ava singing, had felt her passion and tasted her sweetness, he was blinded to everything around him. He growled in the back of his throat and wanted to smash something with his fist. Anything. "Lock it down," he muttered. "Drill down to what's important."

He removed a small ball from his pocket and squeezed it between his fingers before tossing it against the wall and catching it. He muttered under his breath, "First, who's sabotaging Twin Springs?" The ball hit the wall. "Second, is this a nut house or is something deeper, more sinister going on? Third, how's my sister connected?"

He caught the ball and squeezed it tight in his fist. "And, oh yeah! If I have time," he thought about the biggest ball buster of them all, "I need to figure out my feelings for one black haired wench with a drop dead body, gorgeous face and voice that pierces my damn soul."

Tossing the ball on the desk, he rubbed his face with his palms before tilting back in his chair. He laced his fingers behind his head and stared up at the ceiling. "Break down the objectives. Develop your plan of action and execute your mission, Soldier. Do the job and get home alive."

Right, his experience chimed in, *whatever 'alive' means after your soul is torn to shreds by a woman who doesn't know who the hell she is from one moment to the next and molests innocent men in her sleep.*

"Yeah," he muttered. "I was just an innocent bystander. She attacked me."

Jaxon squeezed his eyes shut. "Who the hell am I fooling? I'm doing everything I can to keep myself from groveling at her feet and begging for scraps of her affection. Jeez, what would Ava be like if she was actually awake?"

He moaned as a different type of frustration coursed through his body. Leaning further back, his knuckles scraped against the buttery, soft leather of his jacket. Instantly, his body went deadly still, and he was on guard. He'd left his jacket in his room, not on the back of his chair.

Not moving a muscle, Jaxon's senses went on full alert. He examined his surroundings. *Five walkie talkies, one missing. Could be the one Ava used last night.*

Above him, the security screens filtered through different images of Twin Springs. The desk was clear, except for the walkies, the pencils in a cup and the computer. *Something was off. Something was missing.*

He searched his memory of the room. Mental images flashed

through his brain in time to the images on the screens before him. The image of the darkened Theatre flashed before him at the same time the image of the wall behind him flashed in his mind. *A picture was gone. A picture of Ava, Isabella and a hairy mountain of a man.*

A knock on the door interrupted Jaxon's thoughts. His muscles tensed, ready to spring if needed. "Come in."

His new boss entered the room and closed the door behind him. "I received your resume and references. Very impressive."

Jaxon kept his face blank. *What the hell did Lee include in the packet he'd emailed?* "Thanks."

"All the excitement last night reminded me that I forgot one important thing, to hand over your key to our facility." From his pocket, Theo pulled out a circular disc that hung off a key chain. The disc matched the one hanging around Ava's neck. "This opens all the doors within Twin Springs, to include the back offices." He dropped the disc into Jaxon's outstretched hand. "I figure, with your background, you know how this type of a key works."

"Sure." Jaxon rolled the disc over in his hand. "Who all has one of these passes for Twin Springs?"

"The owners, Dale, his son, and now you." Theo paused for a moment, choosing his words. "I understand that you haven't been here long but did you notice anything unusual before the fire last night? I just spoke with the Fire Marshal and he's keeping his findings close to his chest."

Surprised, Jaxon leaned further back in his chair and thought about the bra that was strung up and used to light the fire. Maybe it wasn't Ava's missing bra. Perhaps it was from one of the other shops. "The Marshal won't release his findings?"

Theo nodded. "Not yet. Did you notice anything to make you think differently? Or notice anything unusual last night?"

"Other than Ava sleepwalking you mean?"

Theo flushed. "Other than Ava."

Jaxon debated mentioning the homeless man who reminded him of an old friend. A comrade who'd barely escaped another fire alive. Or was that was just his guilty conscious seeing things? "Well, we have a guest pocketing silverware from the Main Dining Room." He paused, then, added, "But I did see a man who looked homeless. I shadowed him until I heard Ava singing in the Theatre."

Momentarily distracted, Theo digested this new information. "She was singing in her sleep?"

Jaxon's chair squeaked under his weight, "Among other things."

Removing a silver pen from his pocket, Theo tapped it against his thigh. "Keep an eye on her. She's not only my future sister-in-law, but she is a special woman. A one of a kind. As for the homeless man, did he have blonde hair, darkened by dirt? Jeans needing a wash? A rock and roll band shirt?"

"Yep. A known vagrant?"

Theo chuckled, "No, that's just Dale's son, the one in charge of the bar renovations and rebuilding the Tower. He's working through some things, but he's harmless. As for the guest pocketing the silverware, alert the staff. Not that we'd embarrass one of our guests for a random teaspoon. But if the guest gets up to pilfering a full set of dining ware, then let me know and I'll address the situation."

"Will do."

"I asked Dale to show you the ins and outs of Twin Springs. He knows the property better than anyone. The cleanup of the damaged portion of the Promenade has already started, but the restoration of Twin Springs' Body & Spa Boutique will start this afternoon. Take Dale and evaluate the place where the fire started before the cleaning team starts in the Boutique and give me your feedback." Theo picked up a walkie talkie, "You'll need to carry one of these too."

Jaxon glared at the walkie as Theo departed. In his view, it was one step closer to one of the monkey suits out front. "Bullshit, if I'll be around long enough to be fully assimilated."

Filtering through the eventful last twenty-four hours, Jaxon pulled out his cell phone and pressed speed dial. *So much for in and out,* he thought. *It was an asinine saying anyway.*

Sure, it ticked him off that someone was messing with him, gaining access to his room, and moving his coat. But it pissed the shit out of him that someone had set a fire. Fire destroyed people's lives.

Another fire at Twin Springs but, this time, on his watch. Even though being Security Manager was his cover, he'd be damned if the claims would continue. Not while he was on the job. It was a matter of pride. A matter of honor.

He examined the screens and tossed the ball against the wall. The Promenade was closed off for repairs. Begrudgingly, he admitted how efficient Theo was. Right after the Fire Marshal had left, Theo had a team on cleanup. "No findings, my ass," he fumed as his cousin answered the phone.

"Jax, good timing. I've got intel on Ava Fairbanks. There's been another article by Mac Mills, now saying that's she caused the suicide death of the Director's wife."

He growled deep in his chest, "You're a day late and a dollar short. The whole world found out that intel from this morning's newspapers." The tattoo on the inside of his arm burned and he rubbed it. "Find out what you can on the reporter who just schooled you on intelligence gathering. See if he knows anything else."

Jaxon paused, picked up the ball and squeezing it. It was too late. Ava was under his skin. He couldn't remain detached and focus on the mission. Deep down he knew he'd failed. Again. And once he spoke the words that were lodged in his throat, the Geezer's would have proof that his instincts were shit. He cleared his throat, time to admit it and deal with the consequences. "I'm compromised."

Lee's voice exploded over the line. "What? Less than a week and you blew your cover?"

Squeezing hard, the ball disappeared within his fist and his nails bit into the palm of his hand. "No. Damn it. My judgment is compromised. I let her get under my skin."

"Who? The lying, evil, conniving bitch?"

He threw the ball and it ricocheted through the tiny room. "Don't call her that," he roared.

Dead silence stretched across the phone line.

Lee let out a long, low whistle. "Damn, Jax. I'll contact the Geezers and see what they want to do. Perhaps we need to send a woman. All you pansy ass men are dropping like flies around Ava Fairbanks' honey pot."

"Screw you," responded Jaxon, but he knew it was true. "There was a fire last night. So Twin Springs will be filing another claim."

"Holy shit, the Geezers are going to come unglued. So much for them staying in retirement. Aren't you a ninety day wonder."

"If it makes any difference, I don't think the claims are fraudulent. Someone has it out for the owners of Twin Springs and they're willing to destroy the hotel to get to them. The fire last night showed they don't care who gets hurt during the process."

"Great," replied Lee. "Perhaps we need to send two investigators. Our reputation is on the line now."

Failure seeped over him and proved his instincts were shit. "Whatever you want to do. But, I'm not leaving till I figure out what is going on here and how it relates to my sister. Did you get JD's file?"

"Yeah, mailed it to you yesterday. Busted my ass to keep the Geezers from finding out. Not that it matters now. They'll be hip deep in this investigation within hours."

Guilt gnawed on his ass but he knew there was no stopping the Geezers now that he was compromised and someone had torched Twin Springs on his watch. "Roger that. Tell whoever you send to replace me on the investigation not to blow my cover completely, and let me know what the Geezer's decide to do." A knock sounded at his door. "Out," Jaxon pressed end call and looked up to see an older, gray haired man in his doorway.

His eyes were faded blue just like his jeans. The man held out his hand, "Dale, Maintenance." His southern drawl flowed over Jaxon like a warm, soothing bath.

Standing, Jaxon shook his hand and felt the hard calluses of a man who worked for a living. He didn't appear to fit in with the rest of the uniformed employees at Twin Springs, with his well-worn, thick blue work shirt over a plain white t-shirt. "Jaxon Wolfe, new Security Manager."

Assessing the younger man, Dale rolled a toothpick around in his mouth. He made a humming sound in the back of his throat, "Hmmm, we'll see. Supposed to show ya around. Let's get a move on. Time's a wasting."

Maddy skidded into the room, slipping in around Dale. "Good. I didn't miss you guys. I wanted to look at the damage from the fire. If we're going to be tearing out and repairing stuff, I have some ideas on making the space more useable."

Unhurriedly, Dale removed the toothpick from his mouth and placed it in the small front pocket of his jeans. "Now, Miss Maddy, let's not get all excited here."

Jaxon shrank back in horror. The last thing he wanted to see was Maddy breaking down into tears again. He lowered his voice into a calm, measuring tone, "I'm not sure if you coming is—" he cleared his throat and tried again. "I don't want to hurt your, er, feelings."

Dale lifted an eyebrow at the young man. "Good God son, her feelins?" Shaking his head from side to side, he patted the younger man on the shoulder. "Stick with me, or this lil' girl will eat ya alive." He placed a new toothpick in his mouth. "First lesson, approve anythin' Miss Maddy says through her brother. And a word to the wise, don't give her your," he paused searching for the right word, "digits."

Tapping her toe, the teen shushed the older man. "Don't listen to him. He's going senile." She raised her voice, speaking overly loud. "You have to talk to him in a loud voice so he understands your words."

Again shaking his head, Dale focused his clear blue gaze on Jaxon. "Learn from me son, or suffer the consequences."

Maddy harrumphed and rolled her eyes. She ignored Dale's comments and addressed Jaxon. "Don't worry about my feelings. I'm over you. You were too old anyway." She unfolded and held out a dark green polo shirt in front of her. Twin Springs was embroidered on the breast, with the words Security Manager below. She tossed the shirt to Jaxon. "This is for you."

Greatly relieved that the teenager had moved on, he caught the shirt and stared down at it.

Grabbing a walkie, Maddy attempted to slip it into her pocket, but Dale snatched it from her hand and placed it back on the desk. Glaring at the older man, she added, "Theo sent it over. It's part of your uniform, and he said to wear the shirt with a pair of Dockers, tan."

Jaxon tossed it back. "No. Way. In. Hell. I'm not wearing a monkey suit. What I have on will do just fine. In fact," he paused, and unbuttoned his shirt. Jaxon shrugged out of the confining dress shirt and threw it on top of his jacket, revealing his black t-shirt. He rolled his shoulders and felt as if he could once again breathe freely.

Her jaw dropped. "You're saying no to my brother?"

"Yep, and not just no." Jaxon's face hardened to steel. "But, hell no."

Dale doubled over, laughter rumbling in his chest. He straightened and pounded Jaxon on the back with his large hand. "I like ya, son. You're gonna do just fine."

CHAPTER THIRTY-SEVEN

Relieved to be alone in her office for at least an hour, Ava tossed her suit jacket over the back of the couch. She ripped up Theo's copy of the newspaper and stuffed it in the bottom of her bird's cage. The parrot canted his head, watching her efforts. "Look bud," she instructed. "I need you to watch your language. No more cussing."

Flapping his wings, the bird opened and closed his mouth before letting out a loud wolf whistle.

Her laughter rang out, filling the room, and a glimmer of joy seeped into her heart. "Flirt. If you want to be my guy, then you need to stop dropping 'F' bombs."

"Bombs away!" screeched the bird, scooting backwards on his perch and pooping off the side.

Understanding how much work she had ahead of her, Ava shook her head. "You're a sick little man but I love you." She reached in and stroked the bird on the head with the tip of her finger. Pressing her finger lengthwise against the bird's chest, she ordered, "Step up." The bird willingly climbed onto her finger. She brought him out of his cage and held him up high. Excited, the bird flapped his great wings, fanning her with puffs of air.

Ava's cell phone beeped. Reluctantly, she placed her bird on top of the cage and answered.

"Ava," said Sheela. "Senator Whitcomb's wife is waiting for you in the Crystal Ballroom. She'd like to go over the final seating plans for the wedding."

What a wonderful topper to my morning, thought Ava. "Thanks Sheela, I'll be right there." She grabbed up her file for the Whitcomb wedding party and blew a kiss to her bird. "Momma's got to work. We need to talk later about naming you, buddy. Be a good boy till I return."

Rushing from her office, she gave a thumbs up to Sheela at the Front Desk. A male guest stepped out in front of her and she bumped into him. The guest grabbed her by the arm and stepped in close.

Laughing under her breath, she glanced down at him, "Sorry, I shouldn't be rushing."

The tree stump of a man appraised her. His eyes raking her body, he ran his hands up and down along her bare arms. "So, you're one of Hollingsworth's beauties. He speaks highly of your talents." He winked.

"Hollingsworth?" Shocked, Ava froze and the file slipped from her fingers. Her mind blanked. A deep cold soaked into her limbs and she couldn't remember one thing that she'd learned from Jaxon.

He took her silence as compliance, pulled her behind a column and drew her closer. "Even prettier than your picture. Hollingsworth and I go way back. College buddies."

His words jumbled in her head but Jaxon's voice roared through. *Guard up!* Her fists shot up to protect her face, jarring the man's hold and tagging him in the bottom of the jaw.

His head jerked back with a snap and he backed off rubbing his chin.

"Don't touch me again." Her right thumb burned with pain because she'd forgotten and tucked it into her fist but she quickly backed out of his reach. She noticed a newspaper on the table beside them. It was opened up to the front page and her own face stared back at her.

"Sorry, I just want you to know that I'm available if you're lonely since our Director friend is not here. My mistake."

Her legs shook and she glanced around. It had all happened so fast, that no one had even noticed. "Don't come near me again," she replied through clenched teeth.

Keeping the guest within her eyesight, Ava gave him a wide birth. She'd learned a hard lesson from the Director. Never turn your back.

The distance between the General's Office and the Crystal Ballroom never seemed so far. Her gaze flitted from guest to guest. All seemed to be talking behind raised hands with newspapers close by. She felt like every man leered at her.

The female guests averted their eyes and whispered together. Her home was transformed into a maze of terror. Out of the corner of her eye, she swore that she saw the Director's bright blonde hair.

A good looking young man stepped in front of her and she thrust her guard up.

He adjusted his gaze from over her shoulder, gave her a quizzical look and mumbled, "Excuse me." He skirted past her and called out, "Honey, wait up."

She dropped her guard and her cheeks burned. She muttered under her breath, "Get a grip, Ava. Not every man is out to attack you."

But she kept her hands balled into fists as she made her way through the Presidents Hall. Finally within the Crystal Ballroom, Ava leaned back against the doors, and realized she'd left Kennedy's bridal file on the floor of the Grand Lobby.

"It's about time," declared Mrs. Whitcomb, standing beside her daughter with her arms crossed against her chest. Her gaze pinned Ava, and her jaw dropped. "Where are your glasses? You look, you look." She snapped her mouth shut and glared.

"Mom," admonished Kennedy. Stepping forward she asked,

"Miss Fairbanks, what happened? Do you need to sit down for a moment?"

Slapping a professional facade on her face, Ava settled into the role of Group Sales and Special Events Coordinator. She waived Kennedy off with a bright smile. "Of course not. Just a new haircut." She turned to the Senator's wife. "Don't you look lovely, Mrs. Whitcomb, and your shirt is such a beautiful shade of sky blue."

"Yes." Mrs. Whitcomb fluffed her bangs back with the tips of her painted fingers. "Raw silk from one of my husband's many travels to Asia."

Ava's full lips spread into a smile, "Just lovely. Shall we discuss the details for your ceremony and reception dinner?" From memory she described the layout of chairs, tables and flowers. She spent an hour bending and scraping before the Senator's wife until the woman was finally satisfied.

Kennedy clasped her hands before her. "I'm so excited. Your team is wonderful and I appreciate your efforts in making my wedding perfect."

Sniffing and tilting her nose upward, Mrs. Whitcomb huffed. "It will do."

Ava's laughter sprinkled the air, "High praise from both of you. Thank you. I'll pass your compliments on to the rest of the Twin Springs employees. Ladies, will you be staying for Tea Time?"

Considering the idea, the Senator's wife tipped her head. "Yes, I think we will."

Leading the mother-daughter team through the Presidents Hall, Ava stuttered to a stop when Jaxon rushed passed them in a full sprint. "I'm sure everything's all right," she said, trailing behind him.

The trio rounded the corner into the Grand Lobby and into bedlam. Standing beside Jaxon, just within the Grand Lobby, Ava stared up in shock. A huge, gray bird with a red tail soared over the heads of the guests.

Her bird.

Having the time of his life, the parrot circled the star at the top of the sparkling Christmas tree. The African Gray flew free through the Grand Lobby, his wings flapping, singing his happiness.

Circling over a trio of young boys, he screeched, "Bombs away!" before releasing a poop bomb on the unsuspecting youths.

The boys scattered, knocking over tea cups and rushing for cover. Unsure what to do, the wait staff froze in place. Another large dropping splattered onto the piano player, dribbling a mixture of white, green and yellow poop down the back of his black tux. The bird dove down between the guests and rounded the lobby for another pass.

"I count three guests hit," said Jaxon. "Plus the piano man, four."

The bird turned and flew their way. Grabbing Ava about the waist, Jaxon dodged to the side.

Shouting, "Bombs away," the parrot sailed over their heads and dropped another bomb, which spattered down the front of Mrs. Whitcomb's silk shirt.

The Senator's wife held her arms out to the side and shrieked high and loud.

The bird answered with his own call.

"Oh, no," gasped Kennedy, her hand covering her mouth.

Within the protection of Jaxon's arms, Ava watched her bird. He flapped his wings, came in for a landing and crashed into the huge evergreen. The impact shook the ornaments. "Burn it down," he screeched.

Her eyes wide with wonder, Ava gasped, "But, he can't fly." Unsure what to do, she twisted her rings and gaped in horror at Mrs. Whitcomb. "But, he can't fly," she repeated.

Chuckling under his breath, Jaxon straightened before releasing Ava. "Make that five. You should name him 'Ace'!"

CHAPTER THIRTY-EIGHT

*E*arly the next morning, Jaxon pounded the bag. With each punch, he attempted to expel the anger boiling within him. He'd stayed up all night, pouring over the security monitors in case Ruby decided to take Ava for a midnight walk.

Sweat poured down his bare chest and created damp spots on the black mat. He inflicted an elbow strike into the bag. "A ghost."

Pivoting on the heel of his foot, he delivered a punishing spinning back-fist on the bag. "How the hell am I supposed to protect her from a damn ghost?"

Grabbing the top of the bag, he slammed his knee into its length. "Screw you Ruby Rockwell," he muttered.

He'd pushed-kicked the bag with his bare foot when it occurred to him. Ava's episodes, his sister's fits. The portrait. All three women replicas of dead women. Was Amethyst Fairbanks haunting his sister?

The bag swung back from the force of his kick, delivering its own body blow. Jaxon flew back and landed on his ass.

Ava's sensual voice reached him from the doorway. "I'm not sure if there's much you can teach me if a bag can kick your butt." Her full red lips were tilted up into a sultry smile. She cocked her head to the side and her glossy, black hair kissed her jawline. He didn't think it was possible but he wanted her more than ever.

Her eyes twinkled and she laughed low and sexy.

Jaxon's hesitated, then, scrambled to his feet. "Ruby?"

"I thought you didn't believe in ghosts." She walked towards him, never breaking his gaze.

Even in black yoga pants and a black t-shirt, her hips swayed provocatively and his mouth went dry. "Look Ruby, we've got to come to an understanding."

She kept coming. The glint in her eyes spoke of hunger.

He held up his hands and backed away. "You need to leave Ava alone. No more unscheduled walks with her body."

The sultry woman before him laughed and the world around him lit with stars. *Damn it. I think I'm in love with a hundred-year-old ghost.*

Ava paused just inches from him, their lips almost touching.

He firmed his resolve. "No way in hell am I kissing you while you're in Ava's body." He pressed his lips into a firm line.

"Is that so," she purred, her slender hands sliding up his chest and around his neck, her fingers entwining themselves in his hair. She tilted her head and parted her full lips. "Not even a little kiss?"

Her warm breath bathed his skin and he growled deep in his throat. "No."

"Such a shame." Her lips puckered and she placed a small kiss on the right corner of his lips. "Not even here?" Her supple lips trailed a blaze of fire across his lips to the other corner. "Or here?"

How he wished that the alluring woman before him really was his Ava. He dreamed of the day that she'd burn for him like he did for her. She'd want him as much as he wanted her.

Driving the wishful thoughts aside, he placed his hands on her hips, and braced himself to push her away. "I'm impervious to your feminine wiles, Ruby Rockwell. Go back to the ghost world or where ever you belong. Leave Ava alone."

She hummed, deep in her throat. "How about…"

He swallowed the moan that almost escaped and she answered with a smile against his lips. *Damn it, could ghost read minds?*

"How about, here," and she leaned back and tweaked his nose with her finger.

He froze and his stunned mind attempted to unscramble what had just occurred. "What?"

"It's me, Ava." Laughter erupted from her lips. "You should've seen your face." Arms wrapped around her waist, she bent over and shook with mirth. "Like I was a snake charmer or something."

Realizing she'd just played a joke on him, Jaxon folded his arms across his bare chest and waited for her to gain control. "Funny, Ava. Real Funny."

But satisfaction coursed through him. A week ago, she wouldn't let any man within ten feet of her. Now, she could joke with him. Laugh. She was gaining her power back. Perhaps one day, she'd let him hold her and kiss her for real.

She glanced back up at him. Belly laughter shook her from head to toe and happy tears filled her eyes.

Her beauty socked him in the gut. She was gorgeous before but happy Ava was mesmerizing.

You don't have a chance in hell with a woman like her, he scolded himself. *When she's strong enough, she'll go back to the stage where she belongs and forget all about your mangy ass. So, lock it down. Besides, the Geezers will laugh their asses off if you come home, head down, tail between your legs like a love sick puppy.* He cleared his throat. "Are you done?"

"Yes." Ava wiped her eyes, composed herself. "Sorry."

He kept his gruff attitude, stomped over to his backpack and wiped himself down with a towel. "What can I help you with?"

Suddenly, unsure of herself, Ava twisted her rings. "I," she began. "Um, I was wondering if I could get a few more lessons from you."

He threw the towel on top of his backpack. "You bet. Let's begin where we left off."

She smiled and moved over to the bag. "Thank you."

"No thanks needed." He pulled gloves out of his backpack. "Your gloves came in." He showed her how to put them on. "Alright, circle the bag."

After a half hour of punching the bag at his direction, she asked, "How do you keep from freezing during a fight?"

He nodded. "Repetition. Practice. The more you work out and punch the bag, the more it becomes instinct."

Through her lashes, her gaze flowed over him. "Looks like you work out a lot." She reached out and pushed on his bicep. "Rock hard."

Was Ava Fairbanks flirting with him? "Yeah. If I have time, twice a day."

"Thanks for telling Ruby to leave me alone." She unwrapped her gloves and placed them on the bag. "You could've taken advantage of the situation if I was really sleepwalking."

"It was tempting," he joked. "Ruby is one hell of a kisser."

"Really," she murmured.

He walked over and tossed their gloves onto his backpack. "Oh, yeah. Rocked my world."

Her eyes twinkled. "She's that good, huh."

He nodded and slapped his hand against his chest as if shot. "I don't think a woman alive could compete with her."

She hummed deep in her throat. "Not even me?"

His attention shifted to her. Her face was soft, seductive, and desire shot through him. "Naw, she was too good."

She sauntered over, her hips swaying in a sexy, rhythmic roll and the game shifted. Now she played with him.

"Ava," his voice was husky. Deep.

"That's right, Ava, not Ruby," she purred and slid her hands up his chest until her fingers tangled within the hair on his chest. Digging in, she tugged and then kneaded the taut muscles, before sliding her hands up behind his neck and pulling his head down. Her lips parted beneath his and she poured her soul into the kiss. Her breasts pressed against his chest, and she leaned in giving as much as she was taking.

Blood roared in his ears and he crushed her to him, bending her back and cradling her head within one of his palms.

She pulled away from the kiss and he straightened, released her, still fighting the swirling waves of passion that threatened to drown him. His eyes focused in on her clear, green gaze. He was at a loss for words and drew himself in before he dissolved into a puddle of blubbering desire at her feet.

"Sugar," she whispered, turning away.

He leaned in to catch her words.

Over her shoulder she added, "There's no woman alive or dead who could hold a candle to me."

Jaxon admired the sway of her hips as she strolled away. Ruby's kiss had rocked his world, but Ava's... Her's devastated him. She'd delivered the knockout punch. Left him bare, vulnerable and wanting. Realization hit and a grin spread across his face. Ava wanted him too.

CHAPTER THIRTY-NINE

uttering to a stop within the doors of the stables, Ruby tumbled from Guy's automobile. She loved escaping the confines of Twin Springs and spending time with him.

"That was glorious. The rumble of the motor. Wind against my face and the trees rushing past." She whipped around and focused in on Guy. "Teach me how to drive."

He rounded the automobile and leaned against the rough, wooden door frame. He folded his arms. "Get permission from your father, and I will."

Ruby threw the blanket, that had covered her legs in the car, over a pile of hay and laid back against the softness. She looked up at her Guy through her thick, dark lashes. "Are you afraid of the Great General Rockwell? Did you get in trouble for kissing me on stage?"

He flashed her a lazy smile. "Nope. They blamed the lure of your beauty. But if I step out of line again, I'll lose my position."

Crossing her ankles and lacing her fingers behind her head as a pillow, she watched the man before her. A strange mixture of concealed power and confidence for a servant. She was amazed that he wasn't intimidated by her father. Plus, he accepted her for who she was. A new feeling fluttered in her chest and she realized that by using him to escape her father's binds, she just might lose her heart and her dream of singing on stage. Could she turn her back on her dreams for Guy?

"I understand you're now running the ladies tea parties. Do you run a wet or dry party?"

"Wet?" Delicious laughter rolled from her lips at the thought of liquor being served within Twin Springs. "Like the General would allow a wet tea party."

"Since he gives you the freedom of wearing trousers, I was wondering if he also permitted women the same liberties at their parties as the men."

"The General has no say over what I wear. If there's liquor being served within Twin Springs then my father doesn't know about it. A good soldier follows orders." She saluted him. "General Rockwell would never break the law by serving liquor."

Guy rolled and lit a cigarette, watching Ruby preen in front of her tiny compact. "Perhaps if he doesn't know about your trousers, he doesn't know about the moonshine flowing within Twin Springs."

Leaning forward and snagging the cigarette from him, she lifted it and pulled on it from between her red lips. Her smoky gaze assessed him. "The General knows about everything. Even what I wear."

Frustration rolled through Ruby that the men had even more privi-leges than was legal while the women didn't possess any. If men were drinking spirits then she'd make sure golden Champaign flowed to the women at the tea parties. "What do you care if liquor's served here? Even the farmers keep a barrel of hard cider by their doors."

Kicking hay with the toe of his boot, he looked out through the massive doorway and noticed large flakes of snow falling. He followed the path of the snowflakes, before answering in a low voice. "My wife was murdered by a runner transporting liquor from these mountains. My family cares for my infant son as I work here to support him. The illegal trade of liquor ruins lives. I know. I live with the daily regret of not being there for my wife. The festering pain that if I'd left work a minute sooner, she'd still be alive. At night, I can hear the sounds of my son calling out for his mother. And when she doesn't answer, can't answer, he cries himself to sleep. So, I do what I can to make sure that doesn't happen to another family. As my dad used to say, when duty calls we answer and keep the innocent safe. No matter the cost."

His wife was dead? His son left without a mother and now a father with him working so far away. The cigarette fell from her limp fingers. "That's terrible. No wonder you're one of those drys against liquor." She clasped her scarf against her chest. "Don't worry, the General would never bend the rules. For my father, everything is black and white. Right and wrong. He doesn't recognize a gray area."

Leaping forward, Guy stamped out the budding flame caused by her errant cigarette. "Careful, you wouldn't want Twin Springs to burn down around you and your family."

Enjoying his closeness, her gaze devoured the muscles rippling underneath his thick, cotton shirt. An idea glimmered in the back of her mind. What if she gave into the constant craving he'd created within her? Certainly she could guard her heart.

She worried her bottom lip between her teeth. She'd seduce him, by using her body and her beauty, to help her escape. Perhaps he'd escape with her. Desire boiled within her at the thought of him being her first and her breath caught.

She mulled over the idea. Her actions would embarrass and hurt her father. Could even tarnish Ame and Emma. She tossed her head back. Losing her virginity might cause a scandal but at least Widow Henderson wouldn't want her anymore. A tainted woman would be free to pursue a singing and acting career. And the one thing she wanted more than anything was to be free.

She reached up and drew him down beside her. Ran her fingertips down the planes of his clean shaven face, the muscles of his throat and into the open collar of his shirt. Pulling the buttons apart with her movements, she laid the palm of her hand over his thudding heart. "The General wouldn't let his baby burn down."

Lifting Ruby's hands above her head, Guy pressed his body against hers. His hand cupped the back of her neck and his mouth plundered the sweetness of her lips. A horse neighed in the background and slowly he raised his head. His face was inches from hers. "Are you sure?"

Daring to sing the lead in a new song, she whispered, "Yes, I've never been more sure of anything in my life."

The air twirled around them and drew the snowflakes in through the open stable doors to flutter around them . . .

CHAPTER FORTY

"Do you sleep outside in the snow a lot?"

Jaxon's deep voice penetrated Ava's consciousness. Her lashes fluttered, before opening up to a night sky above her. Disoriented, she glanced around at her surroundings. Moonlight kissed the bushes lining the pathway she laid upon. A light, wet snow had sprinkled around them and trees leaned in guarding them. The intimate atmosphere dotted her skin with goosebumps and she felt bare before Jaxon's gaze. Bewildered about where she was and how she'd ended up there, she attempted to redirect his attention. "What, no kisses?" she flippantly replied.

Visually, he assessed her. She was dressed in a white silk shirt, thin dress pants, and heels. No coat. No gloves. No hat. The need to protect her from others swelled within his chest. Noting her clothes, he searched for signs that she was hurt or, worse, attacked.

At her words, the corner of his lips lifted, self-mocking his early failed exploit with her. "Sugar, I could never get enough of your sweetness."

She blushed and her eyes darted away from his piercing gaze. She licked her lips.

Kneeling beside her, he brushed strands of her hair away from where it caught in the delicate corners of her luscious lips. He grazed her hot cheeks with the back of his knuckles. Not noticing any signs of an attack, he asked, "Did you slip and fall after dropping off Ace?"

"Ace?" questioned Ava. Then she remembered. Ace had bombed everyone in the Grand Lobby. For an hour, the parrot had flown free. It wasn't until Maddy had suggested that she sing a jazz song that she'd finally coaxed the freshly christened bird down. Theo had oscillated between soothing guests and letting her know, in no uncertain terms, that Twin Springs wasn't a place for a bird. Especially, an African Gray parrot named Ace.

Raising herself up on her elbows, she focused in on her surroundings and realized she was a short distance from Twin Springs' Aviary. "I—I don't know. Last I remember, I was in my office."

Brushing the dirt from her shoulders, he paused. In his mind, he started going through the checklist taught to him by the Medic on his old team during cross training. Her hands were blue with cold and he rubbed them before replying, "You don't remember how you ended up here."

Feeling like a fool, she rubbed her temples and attempted to remember. Tilting her head away to curtain her face with her hair, she squeezed her eyes closed to keep tears from escaping. "I left Ace with Logan at the Aviary and headed back to my office, sat down on the couch. I leaned my head back and closed my eyes for a second." Her eyes met his. "Just a second. I couldn't have fallen asleep in such a short time."

His mind roared at what could have happened to her sleepwalking this far up into the mountains. *Damn you, Ruby,* he thought, grinding his teeth with frustration. But Ruby was a ghost. Not someone he could grab with his hands and pound into the ground for leaving Ava unprotected in the middle of a dirt path. He breathed in deeply through his nose to control his anger before gently asking, "You came all the way here sleepwalking? Ava, that's dangerous."

Uncomfortable with the attention she received, she retreated within herself and covered her uneasiness with a flirtatious attitude. "Why Jaxon, are you offering to monitor me in my sleep and keep me from wandering about?"

His eyebrows rose and the tempo of his heart picked up. "If you ever need a bed buddy or sleepwalking partner, then I'm your guy."

At a loss for words, she stared into his molten gaze. The heat he emitted warmed her. Entranced by the golden green glow his eyes cast in the darkened night, her body involuntarily leaned up towards his.

A gigantic, wet snowflake plopped down on her nose, spraying both of them. More freezing droplets splattered craters into the dirt walkway and the nighttime sky opened up, pelting the couple with sleet. With a swift movement, Jaxon helped Ava to her feet and they rushed towards the safety of the Aviary.

Bounding up the slanted board walkway, he held open the large, plank door and followed her inside to where nice, warm heat greeted them. She flipped a light switch and rows of long, florescent bulbs lit the room.

With a shake of his head, he shook the droplets of sleet from his dark hair and examined the room. He noted the room's details and began filing them away. Rectangular room. Approximately ten feet by twenty. Clean, extremely clean. "Whoever cares for the birds, takes their job seriously."

To his right, the shiny, white walls were lined with a quartet of thick, wooden doors. A stainless steel sink and counter lined the opposite wall, only broken up by a large fridge and freezer combo. The cement floor contained two drains and a hammock fashioned out of a blanket and ropes hung from the wooden rafters.

Ava glanced at Jaxon, noticing him examining the hammock. "Dale's son sleeps in here sometimes." She avoided his gaze and lied to protect her childhood friend. "Probably to care for the birds."

"Nice set up." He turned towards Ava. Under the stark light, her wet, white shirt had become transparent, outlining the swells off her high, firm breasts in one of the tiniest lace bras he'd ever seen. He swallowed hard, trying to moisten his suddenly dry mouth and attempted to look anywhere but at her gorgeous body.

The voice in the back of his mind mocked him, *Good luck, asshole.*

"Damn it," he muttered under his breath at the futility of ignoring her stunning curves. He shrugged out of his leather jacket and draped it over her shoulders. *There,* he thought, *out of sight, out of mind.*

His inner voice whispered, *Fool. She's a thirst you'll never be able to quench. No matter how many times you kneel at her spring.*

Ignoring the gnawing ache eating away at his gut and his instincts to pull her into his arms and worship her body with his, Jaxon covered up his lame actions by clearing his throat and mumbling, "You're soaking wet. Theo would kick my butt if you got sick."

Knowing he wasn't fooling anyone, even himself, he continued his assessment. Four roughly shod doors faced him, each with a glassless window, lined with silver bars. Below each window hung a name placard from two tiny hooks. To the left of each door a clipboard was nailed to the wall. Above three of the doors' clipboards hung tiny leather hoods, each no bigger than his palm, with their leather strings swinging below. "D'Artagnan, Aramis, Porthos," he read out loud. "The Three Musketeers."

The last door was bare and he looked inward to the cellmate. Fresh straw covered the floor and moonlight shone through the wire mesh wall opposite. Standing on a t-perch was Ace.

Ava joined Jaxon, resting her forehead against the cool, metal bars, feeling like a part of her family was locked away. She sang a couple bars of the parrot's favorite jazz song. One of the hawks in an adjoining pen cried out with a loud careening call.

Perching on one foot, Ace's gold eyes pinned her before he turned and flew to another perch extending from the wall. Ignoring her, Ace turned his head away and faced the wall.

Her song faded away and a sad moan escaped her lips. Curving her fingers around the bars, she closed her eyes against the heartache and murmured, "He hates me. I didn't know he could fly, or I would've locked him back in his cage. I've failed him. Just as I fail everyone."

Jaxon hesitated. His experiences chanted, *Don't do it Jax. Keep your distance. Beautiful women are lying, evil, conniving bitches.*

With the words pounding away in his brain, he turned Ava towards him. But the mantra no longer held truth for him.

His fingers curved under his jacket and around her shoulders. The jacket fell to the ground and he drew her towards his warmth. His inner voice whispered, *Finally.*

He pressed his cheek against her damp hair. Inhaling deeply, he breathed in her scent and the smell of roses seeped into his soul. "You put up a strong front, but underneath you're scared just like the rest of us. Fail, Ava? You couldn't fail. Even if the part you landed was of a woman lying in the gutter without a dime to her name. You are too vivacious, too giving, too loving," he whispered in her ear.

Trailing light kisses, his lips blazed a path from her ear and stopped just shy of her lips. Pausing, he placed a finger under her chin and raised her face up towards his. He admired her thick lashes lying against the paleness of her skin and the small gasps escaping her parted lips.

Moistening her lips with the tip of her tongue, Ava sighed. "Heal me, Jaxon. Help me forget."

He felt something within himself pop. Freedom to live and to act was suddenly within his reach. Ripped from deep within his soul, a sound torn between a battle cry and a groan was released.

He cupped the nape of her neck and devoured the sweetness before him. Intoxicated by her, he tasted the melted snow on her salty skin. His shaking fingers worked the tiny buttons on the back of her shirt. Leaning back, he watched the wet fabric release its hold on her silky skin, before he drew the shirt down and away from her body.

Need swelled up inside Ava, a longing for him, to be with him. Making a humming noise in the back of her throat, she fumbled with his t-shirt and drew it over his head, before letting the black fabric fall from her fingertips. "Faster," she chanted. "Faster. I don't want to think. Just feel. Please, Jaxon. Faster."

"Let me savor you." He kissed and licked the cool droplets from the curve of her neck. Working his way down to the strap of her bra, he pulled the fabric away and kissed the silky skin on her rounded shoulder. Chuckling under his breath, he kissed the skin on her shoulder again before reaching behind her and releasing the lacy bra. The tiny fabric fluttered to the floor between them.

Her full breasts rose and fell before him, the pink nipples tightening into small peaks. "My God Ava, you're exquisite," he breathed, before bowing his head before her.

Cupping one succulent mound with the palm of his hand, he lifted the hard nub to the warmth of his mouth. He sucked and teased her nipple with his lips and tongue, before he blazed a trail down her body.

Kneeling before her and undoing her pants, Jaxon peeled the wet fabric from her body and tossed it away. Holding her by the hips, his thumbs brought shivers down her body as they caressed the delicate skin of her inner thighs. His lips and tongue explored every inch of her flat stomach and inner thighs as he removed her panties, before teasing their way back up the delicate skin inside her legs to her soft mound. Pressing kisses against her belly button, Jaxon's strong fingers played and twirled within the wet lips behind Ava's curtain. Replacing his fingers with his warm mouth, he licked and sucked until her back arched with pleasure and her fingers wound themselves in his hair, tugging with urgency.

His heart raced to the melody Ava's moans played. The heat from their breaths made the room feel heavy and moist. Glancing up and enjoying Ava's pleasure, he suddenly realized that he'd pinned her up against the cold bars and hard planks of the door. Rising to his feet, he released the hammock and laid the blanket on the floor. Grabbing his leather jacket, he draped his jacket over the hammock and lowered her quivering body down upon the makeshift bed.

"Sorry, Ava," he whispered.

Catching her breath, she reached up and pulled his firm body down upon her. "You're killing me. Ever so slowly." She reached down and tugged at his pants.

Swiftly, he removed the rest of his clothes, before resting himself between her silky thighs. The tip of his hardened manhood paused at the warm, moist opening of her core. "I want to make love to you. Not some role you are playing. Just you."

A tear escaped from the corner of her eye. She held back, afraid to bare her real self before him. Did she dare? If he rejected a role she played, then she could pretend the pain wasn't real. But if he rejected the real her, there'd be no place left to hide. She nibbled on her bottom lip, contemplating, before deciding it was time for her to step out beneath the bright stage lights and sing. A sensual smile spread across her lip and she welcomed him. "This is me. For better or worse, you have me."

Jaxon surged forward, her name upon his lips.

Magnificent feelings rose up her body with his movements and she hummed in the back of her throat. The song of their love-making beat against her ribs, bursting to be set free. His strokes built in momentum until she released a high note of pleasure that put the efforts of any world famous opera singer to shame.

CHAPTER FORTY-ONE

Stretching, Ava lingered in the afterglow of lovemaking. Curling and releasing her toes, she enjoyed the delicious feelings within her. She felt yummy and didn't want the sensation to end. She wanted a relationship with Jaxon more than any role or star on Broadway. In his arms, she was free to be herself. Something she hadn't felt since the night under the Christmas tree with Isabella.

With one arm, Jaxon rolled her into the crook of his shoulder and held her tightly against his body.

Trailing her fingers along the passion moistened skin on his chest, she gazed up at his usually hardened chin before she rested her head upon his chest. Her mind wandered over the past few days and shifted to the male guests who'd read the newspaper review. *Did Jaxon believe the lies too?* she wondered. *Did he think she was easy and for the taking?* Suddenly, their lovemaking felt cheap and dirty. "You don't think I'm easy do you?"

His chest rumbled under her ear with his laughter. "Ava, there's nothing easy about you."

Relieved, she snuggled in and pulled the hair on his chest in response.

He wrapped her tighter within his arms. "I do think I'm one lucky son of a bitch."

She relaxed, trying not to think about the paper, the forward male guest or about her sleepwalking. She'd give anything to live in the moment and forget the world outside. Her mind raced over with the day's events and the necessity to tell him everything bubbled up inside her and pressed for release. She didn't want any roles or lies between them. Breathing in deep, she expelled the sentence in one breath, "I didn't tell you everything."

"Hmmm," replied Jaxon, his eyes closed, his hands caressing her satiny skin.

The sounds of the birds rustling filtered through the room. "When you found me outside, I didn't tell you everything. I haven't been completely honest with you."

His body stiffened beside her. He rolled away and pulled on his briefs. His expression was guarded. He looked down at her and asked, "What didn't you tell me?"

The gap of air created between them caused a chill to roll down her naked body. Sitting up, she wrapped her arms around her legs. "I closed my eyes in my office and I don't remember how I ended up in the dirt outside Twin Springs' Aviary. But I do remember something else. A dream, of Ruby and her guy at the stables."

As she told Jaxon about her dream, he knelt beside her and pulled her back into his arms. As her story continued, he stretched out beside her and his body once again warmed hers.

Enjoying the safety of his arms, she added, "I felt so sorry for Ruby. All she wanted to do was be the person inside her, screaming to get out. But her father couldn't see past his own ideals and expectations. He perceived her as a commodity to be traded and used for the good of Twin Springs and his legacy. But she was effervescent and lived for the moment. She didn't let anyone or any fears hold her back from living." Feeling like she shared too much, she peeked up at Jaxon. "I suppose you think I'm crazy."

He squeezed her and shook his head. "I've learned that there are a lot of things I don't understand. Especially, here at Twin Springs."

Ava hummed in the back of her throat and snuggled into his warmth. His lack of judgment caused a great weight to lift from her shoulders. She enjoyed the feeling of the rise and fall of his chest. How he lifted his free arm and smoothed the skin down her arm with his fingertips, brushing her hair aside, placing a kiss upon the crown of her head. *Perhaps, he's my guy,* she thought. She glanced up and noticed the tattoo on the inside of his arm.

Distracted by the unusual tattoo, she reached up and held his right arm out for her to examine. At the top of the tattoo, an eagle held a dagger within his beak. Wings spread, the eagle grasped an arrow in one talon, crossed over what appeared to be a pick axe in the other, the words 'E Tenebris Erutum, Induravique Ferrum' over a list of names. The tattoo was definitely a list of some type with strange names all ending with the same date. "What does your tattoo mean? And who are Fitz, Woody, Gonzo, Roddie—"

Jaxon pulled his arm away and prevented her from calling out the roll-call of the dead. He held his forearm tight against his chest. The tattoo burned the skin on his arm and his lips parted with pain. "That's my team. Most of them are dead and the ones who survived might as well be."

Ava sat up. Curling her fingertips around his wrist, she lightly tugged. "May I see?"

Looking at the ceiling, he let Ava lift his arm and study his tattoo. "What does, 'E Tenebris Erutum, Induravique Ferrum' mean?" she asked, stumbling a little over the strange words.

Gritting his teeth, he paused before answering. "It's Latin for 'Mined From Shadows, Forged By Steel'. Just my old Unit's motto. Nothing important."

She rubbed the tattoo of the eagle with her thumb. "Jaxon, what happened to your team?"

Jumping to his feet, he slipped into his jeans before raking his fingers through his jet black hair. "I should get you back to Twin Springs."

Naked, Ava sat back on her heels and stared at her guy's back. "Tell me what happened."

His haunted gaze swept over her, taking in her staggering beauty. Her long legs bent underneath her, the pocket of curls at her apex, her full breasts and her striking face. Averting his head from her alluring beauty, he tried to speak over the lump blocking his throat. "I believed in the wrong person and I killed them."

The door to the Aviary swung open and surprised both of them. She scrambled to her feet and held her damp shirt in front of her body.

Immediately, Jaxon stepped in front of Ava's nude body and blocked her from the view of the intruder. Ready to protect her, his hands curved into raised fists.

Inch by painful inch, his gaze swept over the intruder. His mutilated face was illuminated by the bright lights of the room. Stumbling backward from the sight before him, Jaxon's fists dropped. Out of the darkness before him rose a ghostly figure, the cold night air blowing in around him. The half his face that was melted by fire was forever scorched into his memory banks. "Woody?"

CHAPTER FORTY-TWO

*L*ogan halted in the open doorway. "Wolfeman?" His features flowed from surprised to pleasure. "Jaxon G. Wolfe. What the hell are you doing here?"

When Jaxon didn't reply, a deep crimson rose up Logan's neck and spread across his face, causing the florid purple scars on the right side of his face to darken. A scowl crossed over his features. "Look. I don't need you here. I told you at the V.A. hospital, I'd be fine on my own. Why are you checking up on me?"

Rocked to his core, Jaxon stared at his old team member, taking in his filthy clothes and greasy hair. The jeans and rock band shirt jiggled his memory. Disoriented between two worlds, he felt dizzy and then sick. The homeless man he'd seen at Twin Springs. Theo had told him it was Dale's son, working through some stuff. *Damn it*, he brooded. How did he not recognize his friend? "I'm not checking up on you. I'm the new Security Manager for Twin Springs. Didn't realize you worked here until just now."

Rubbing his scars with the knuckles of the two remaining fingers on his mutilated hand, Logan studied his Army buddy and weighed his words.

Jaxon winced at the sight of his disfigured comrade. His fault. It was his fault that this man was almost burned alive. His fault that the rest of his team that day had perished in the explosion or the fire caused by the explosion.

A lopsided grin split Logan's face, stretching the taut, burned skin into a bizarre mask. "No shit?" He extended his hand. "I thought you were back working for your family's detective agency. Hunting down cheating wives and deadbeat dads. Doc said you were working a case about fraudulent insurance claims?"

A rustle of fabric behind Jaxon drew Logan's attention. "Who's that behind you?"

Having donned Jaxon's black t-shirt and her high heels, Ava emerged from behind him.

"Good morning, Logan." She reached up and kissed her childhood friend on his razed cheek.

Stunned, Logan's jaw dropped and he glanced from Jaxon to Ava and back. "You and Ava?" Then, switching to Ava, "You and Wolfeman? No shit."

Bending down, she scooped up her lingerie, shirt and pants. "So, Wolfeman is it?" She waited for his confirming nod. "You work for a detective agency? Fighting insurance claims?" Her voice was deceptively soft.

Jaxon's breath froze in his chest and his stomach rolled with an uneasy feeling. He sensed rather than saw her sliding into a new role and slipping away from him. "Yes. It's my family's detective agency."

Her voice as smooth as silk, she whispered, "Does Theo know?"

Guilt churned in his gut. He'd lied to her. Connived behind her back, and then slept with her. He was a bastard. "No, no one knew. Until now."

"Holy crap," muttered Logan. "You're undercover as Twin Springs' Security Manager to find out if we are filing fraudulent claims? Theo's going to bust a gasket when he finds out."

Feeling like the bitch he'd hated, Jaxon replied, "Yes." He ground his back teeth before adding, "That's the current JOBB."

Ava moved closer to Jaxon. So close that he could smell her

scent and his from his shirt mingling around her. Her lips inches from his, she stopped. "We're the current job?"

Drawn in by her honey, he moved his lips closer to hers. Internally, he struggled to find a way to keep her. To fix the hurt he'd just caused. Caught between his need to fulfill the mission and his need for Ava in his life, he answered, "Yes. My assignment was to discover if Twin Springs is filing fraudulent claims or not."

Ava drew back her arm and slugged him hard in the solar plexus.

A whoosh of air expelled from his lungs. He fought to keep from throwing up from the unexpected punch. Hands on his knees, sucking in deep breaths, he watched as Ava flipped her wet clothes over her shoulder. She exited the Aviary, wearing nothing but her high heels and his black t-shirt barely covering the rounded curve of her bottom.

Logan whistled long and low, causing an immediate reply from the wild birds. "Damn." He shook his head at his comrade before standing taller and thumping himself on the chest with his hand. "I taught her that move in the fifth grade. When Bobby Johnson teased her about wearing a bra for the first time." He scratched at the scars on his face. "I hope she didn't tuck her thumb in her fist though. Had a bad habit of doing that. You're lucky she didn't go for the nose. Or a swift kick to your balls. That was one of her favorites."

"Good punch. Solid hit," growled Jaxon. The voice inside him roared, *Fight boy. Tell her everything. Tell her how you feel.* He frowned, squashing his instincts. "I don't know what part she's playing now."

"That's no part. That's Ava." Logan placed his earbuds back into his ears. "You don't really know her at all. Do you?"

CHAPTER FORTY-THREE

For a whole day, Ava did her best to avoid all men. Especially Jaxon. The next morning, she deliberately tried to defuse her recurring hot dreams of Jaxon by showering in freezing water. She couldn't get past the fact that he'd lied to her. "At least the sleazy Director was honest and upfront about what he wanted," she muttered to herself.

Purposely, she'd dressed in a cute little dress that graduated in color from white at the tip of her shoulders to black from the waist down. The dress spoke to her. The sleeveless shell with little red rose buds dotting the bust line, growing to fully bloomed roses at the midline and ending with spent petals along the flared ebony hem. The beginning, middle and end in one full swoop. How her life felt. How her career had ended and the mockery of true love.

Moving quickly through the Presidents Hall, her high, black heels elongated her legs and gave her a sense of power. She grabbed her caffeine lover and staked out Twin Springs as hers. Sniffing smoke in the air, her nose wrinkled. "Cigar smoke? Twin Springs is a smoke free hotel. Who'd be smoking a cigar?"

The smell drudged up other bad memories. Pushing the ugly thoughts to the back of her mind, she entered the General's Office and tossed her cell phone onto the desk. Ace's empty cage drew her gaze. She missed his welcoming call. Turning and placing her coffee on her desk, she was surprised by a long stem rose laying on the polished, mahogany surface. *Jaxon. No, Wolfeman,* she corrected herself. *Did he think he could sway her with a rose?* Picking up the flower, she held the unopened red bud to her nose. "What a stupid name for a stupid, stupid man," she grumbled under her breath.

She wanted to throw the rose in the trash but couldn't bear to take her anger out on the beautiful flower. Instead, she snipped it and placed the stem behind her ear. She sniffed, the smell of cigar still in her nose.

She glanced down at the desk and noticed a snubbed out cigar, drowning in the dredges of coffee inside a Twin Springs tea cup.

Twirling around, her gaze searched the room. One of her armchairs was turned and faced the fireplace. A crown of blonde hair showed above the high back. Acting as if the world belonged to him, Director Terrence Hollingsworth rose from the high back chair and turned to face her.

A shaking began in Ava's legs and worked its way up her torso. She leaned back and braced herself against the desk. She realized there wouldn't be a knock to save her this time. "How did you get in here?"

Moving closer, he flicked cigar ashes from the front of his turtleneck. The deep, dark wine color of the shirt clashed with his bronzer-browned skin and made his face appear sallow. Mindless of the conflicting color combination he wore, he snapped the front of his indigo blue sport coat into place. His tight, tangerine pants showed every bulge as he stalked her. The deadly look glinting in his blue eyes was in stark contrast against the fake smile he flashed. "Why Ava, is that any way to greet me? I just came to see my best girl."

Her face ashen, she held one hand out in front of herself as if it would stop him. Her heart thundered in her ears and she fumbled behind herself, searching across the surface of the desk for her cell phone. Her chin quivered. "Get the hell out of here and off my property." Even to her own ears, her voice sounded weak and thready.

Stepping closer, so her hand was only inches from his chest, the Director's lips pursed into a hard line. "Now, now, Ava. Get control of yourself." He pulled a folded up newspaper from inside his jacket. "See here," he tapped the black print. "We're long lost lovers."

Her mind ordered her limbs to stop shaking but her traitorous body refused. Finally locating her phone, she pressed speed dial with her thumb. She clutched the phone and the rose fell from her ear, but she didn't notice. She lifted the phone to call for help. Each movement felt as if she swam in molasses. She forced words from her throat, and her teeth chattered between them. "We are not and never will be lovers."

The Director leaned in and snatched her outstretched hand within his and bent it back at the wrist.

She cried out in pain and her knees buckled.

He pressed his lips against her ear. "Listen to me carefully, or you'll never grace any stage again. According to this newspaper, you and I are in this together. You're going to play one last part. One where you are head over heels in love with me. You'll tell the press how unstable my wife was. That we have an undying love and her death ripped us apart. Until now. You got that?" He squeezed her fingers within his fist and she winced with pain.

"You will keep your mouth shut about the other ugly business. Or I'll tell the press that you set a scene for my wife to walk in on. You pushed her delicate mind over the edge and broke my heart. No need for a casting call, my dear. I'll grant your greatest wish of once again being my starring lady. You wanted the part so badly before." With on last squeeze to her hand, he pecked her on the cheek and was gone.

Flinching at the sound of the door clicking shut, Ava froze in place and her mind blanked. Still as a statue. Time ceased to move. Her mind ticked forward and attempted to grasp the past scene. The Director. At Twin Springs. Not safe. Hide! Her daze was broken by the constant call of her name through the phone and Ava's mind fast forwarded to her present reality.

"Ava? Ava?" her sister shouted.

The phone pressed against her ear, Ava's mouth repeatedly opened and closed. No sound came out. Her vocal cords had iced over with fear. He was here. In her home. She was no longer safe at Twin Springs. What if he returned? Her gaze darted around the room and her breath came hot and fast in her chest. She closed her mouth and swallowed hard, moistening her throat before gasping out, "I need you, Izzy. I need you now."

CHAPTER FORTY-FOUR

errence let the heavy doors of Ava's office close. His blue eyes sparkled with excitement and met the gaze of the Front Desk clerk across the lobby. Something about her continued to pluck at the back of his brain. Perhaps she'd auditioned for him once.

A sly smile twisted his face. Maybe if he grew bored in these backward mountains, she would again. Pushing all thoughts of the servant aside, he concentrated on developing his and Ava's lines in their little play for the press.

She'd fall in line. Women always did. All it took was a little, okay a lot, of brute force. Women really were such simple creatures. Threats went a long way but pain was their real motivator.

Pain for themselves or someone they loved. He just needed to find Ava's sweet spot and then apply a little pressure until she was under his thumb. Fear and fuck, his two favorite four letter words. If she didn't fall in line, then he'd use both on her. He considered the idea for a moment and then chuckled low in his chest. Perhaps even if she did.

Amused by his cleverness, he strolled out onto the veranda. He removed his lucky gold lighter from his pocket and lit a cigar. The door swung shut behind him and he missed the pounding of feet coming to Ava's aid. Reclining in a cushioned lounger, he flicked the lighter open and closed before setting it on the glass table beside him.

The dusting of snow from two evenings before had already melted and the day promised to be warmer than usual for November in the mountains. Despite himself, he enjoyed the crisp, fall air mingling with the heat from one of the tall, propane heaters dotting the veranda. Cars slid to a stop and he granted a bright smile to three women as their bags were gathered by the help. The covered roofline of the veranda shaded his eyes, as he lazily watched them and cast them into roles of his choosing. "Perhaps Twin Springs was worth the drive."

He leaned back and closed his eyes and relaxed. Ava would play the part he'd chosen for her. He was sure of it. Gripping the cigar between his teeth, a satisfied grin spread across his face and adrenaline revitalized his body. With the star power of AVA by his side, he'd once again be unstoppable on Broadway. The press and patrons would once more fawn over him.

Daydreaming, he permitted his mind to play scene after scene about his future success. Perhaps once the sun warmed the earth, he'd play a round of golf. Then warm his body in the Hot Springs Pool before his next visit with Ava. "After all, I deserve it. I deserve it all. Fame, money and AVA."

CHAPTER FORTY-FIVE

Ava sunk onto the leather couch. The rose was crushed under her feet. Sightless, she stared off into the distance.

Removing her chef jacket, Isabella draped it around her older sister's shoulders. Not satisfied, she pushed Ava's coffee cup into her hands. "Drink. It will help."

Shaking worse than any opening night jitters, Ava sipped the coffee. "He was here." Her teeth chattered. "Here in my office."

Her brows furrowing over concerned eyes, Isabella rubbed her sister's free hand and asked, "Who was here?"

Ava didn't want to say his name out loud. As if when she uttered his name, the sound would call him back. But she needed help from the one person she trusted most. Her sister. "The Director from my last play, Terrence Hollingsworth."

Sucking in her breath with surprise, Isabella leaned forward to see Ava's face. "The one whose wife shot herself on stage in front of you?"

Like when they played hide and seek as children, Ava squeezed her eyes shut. Acting that if she couldn't see anything, then the memory couldn't find her. But the horrible scene lit up behind her lids. She felt the weight of Ashlee's body dragging her to the floor, the stickiness of her blood spraying across her face.

"Yes," she breathed, the smell of remembered blood and cigar filling her nostrils and choking her.

Sitting on the couch beside her, Isabella rubbed her sister's arm. "Will you share with me what happened?"

Shaking her head, Ava refused to open her eyes. "You can't tell anyone," she whispered. "Not even Theo. I couldn't stand it if he knew."

"Tell me. I want to help."

Her watery eyes met her sister's. "I was stupid. So full of myself. So foolish." She explained to her sister about meeting the Director in his office. As her story progressed, her sister's eyes widened and also filled with tears.

Shaking her head, Ava said, "Don't cry for me. I'm alive. His wife, she deserves our tears. If it wasn't for me and my stupidity, then she'd still be alive."

Isabella leaned into her sister, encircling her within the arms of her childlike frame. "No. None of it's your fault. He's a disgusting man, who probably destroyed his wife's mind long before you met her. We'll call the police."

Throwing her hands in the air, Ava scoffed, "And say what? That I went to his office in my robe? The police and the public don't understand theater life. I know how this story ends. I'll be heralded as a harlot. Just like that piece of trash column stated. The jury of public opinion will try me and find me guilty of taunting him. I'll be accused of leading him on and the public will blame me for her suicide. Yesterday's newspaper article was only the beginning. Others will follow." Her head turned towards Izzy. "After that article was published, a male guest started touching me, propositioning me. I believed I'd be safe here at Twin Springs and his vileness couldn't touch me. But it did."

Jaxon and Theo entered and heard that last statement. "What happened?" asked Theo.

Jaxon stood sentry at Ava's desk, where he could monitor the door and keep all the occupants in the room within his sight. All Theo had shared was that Isabella said her sister needed help. Legs braced slightly apart in his tan tactical pants and hands free, he was ready to protect her. The tattoo on the inside of his arm burned and he rubbed it against his black t-shirt.

Examining the room, he took in the dead cigar, crushed rose and the pallor of Ava's skin. His body stilled, the hair tingled on the back of his neck and his inner voice hummed. *Danger. Ava and danger.*

Immediately, he thrust the notion aside. He wouldn't place Ava's life in further danger by listening to his bullshit instincts. He prepared his mind to deal only with the facts at hand. He crushed the worry and played back what Ava had said when he and Theo entered the room. Touching her. Not safe at Twin Springs. Something about his vileness?

Was she accusing him of raping her? Perhaps, he'd read her all wrong from the beginning. Maybe she'd never been attacked. Just acted the part. Liked the attention.

Isabella turned towards the men, with her arm encircling Ava's shoulders. "A male guest hid in Ava's office. He threatened her and scared her. After the newspaper article, male guests have been approaching her and acting overly forward with her."

"What the hell are you talking about?" shouted Theo. "Why didn't you come to me?"

He swung around towards Jaxon. "Where the hell were you? What am I paying you for, but to protect my family?"

Disgust coursed through Jaxon's body. He was so far off base with the beautiful woman before him. How could he think she'd accuse him of rape? He needed to get a grip on the situation unraveling before him.

Ava canted her head away from Jaxon and wiped the tears from her face. Her mocking laughter filled the room. "Don't ask him. He fooled all of us. He knows Logan. In fact, they were on the same team in the Army."

Rising to her feet, Ava cast her sister's jacket aside and she dramatically waived her hand towards Jaxon. "Let me introduce you. Isabella, Theo, this is Jaxon G. Wolfe. The Wolfeman, as he's called by his Army buddies. He left the military to become a private investigator within his family's detective agency. His current JOBB, as he calls it, is to go undercover at Twin Springs. He's investigating us for filing fraudulent insurance claims."

Silence filled the room and her accusation hung in the air.

Each of her words chewed a bite out of his ass and he had no choice but to take it. He surveyed the family in front of him. In his suit, the color of an overcast sky on the verge of delivering torrential rains and thunder, Theo's body stilled and his steel gaze razed the ground where Jaxon stood. No wonder the man was a legend in business. Who'd want to cross him?

He glanced over to Isabella. With her small hand covering her gaping mouth, she appeared childlike in her white tank top without her chef's jacket. Jaxon felt like he'd stolen a little girl's favorite candy.

His attention shifted to Ava, covered with roses, with her chin raised and shoulders thrown back. She resembled a queen ordering for his head on a pike. For once he wished the crazy bird was still at Twin Springs to blurt out something outrageous and shift their betrayal filled gazes.

"What's the name of your detective agency?" asked Theo, his voice deadly calm.

"White Wolfe Investigations. Why?"

Teeth clenched, Theo bit out in no uncertain terms, "Because when I'm finished, I'll financially destroy your agency, your family and you. You all won't have a pot left to piss in."

Isabella pulled a white kerchief from her pocket and began wringing it between her hands. "Is Wolfe even your real last name? What does the G stand for?"

A great loss filled him, as if he had tasted something wonderful only to have it stolen from his grasp. Shame poured into the hole left inside him. In the field, there was no wondering if you were doing right or wrong. You followed orders, believing that your Country and superiors thought through all the consequences. You fought for God, Honor and Country.

There was no honor in deceiving this family, working hard to retain their home and bring the Grand Dame, as they called the hotel, back to her former glory.

He let this job become personal. Perhaps completely shutting out his instincts was a mistake. Without his instincts to guide him, his actions embarrassed himself and his own family. He shoved his hands into his pockets and addressed the people he'd wronged. "Yes, Wolfe is my last name. The G stands for Guy, my middle name."

"What did you say?" Ava blanched. "Did you say Guy was your middle name?" She searched Jaxon's face, taking in the width of his strong jaw and the color of his eyes. The same color as Ruby's Guy. "I knew they looked alike but could they be related?" she murmured under her breath. She turned to stare up at Ruby's face in the oil portrait. Keeping her voice monotone, she asked, "Where did your family get the name Guy from? It's unusual."

"It was my great grandfather's name. He founded our agency."

Blood roared in Ava's ears and she swung around to face Jaxon. "I knew it! You must be a descendent of Ruby's Guy. The man from my dreams."

Isabella gasped with shock. "Ruby's guy is related to Jaxon?" Her gaze pivoted from the portrait to Jaxon.

Theo sunk down on the couch, pulled his fiancée down beside him and placed his arm around her. He glanced up at the door when Logan entered the room. "Of course Jaxon is. And I'm sure Logan is the direct descendant of Amethyst's husband. Why not? Then all the chess pieces will fit into a convenient little line."

His body rocking with his limp, Logan maneuvered his way across the room and took up a strategic position. He glanced up at the portrait and kept his inhuman side from everyone's gaze. Removing his baseball cap, he rolled the hat before shoving it into his back pocket alongside a rolled up newspaper. "As much as I wouldn't mind cozying up to this century's version of that red headed beauty, I'm not the descendant of Amethyst Fairbanks' husband. Who's Wolfeman the direct descendant of anyway?"

Isabella chimed up. "Ruby's lost love, Guy."

Scratching the scars below the patches of stubble on his right cheek, Logan replied, "No shit. How did you figure that out?"

Ava filled him in. "I started sleepwalking again but this time, during my late night wandering, I've been dreaming of Ruby and her guy. I guess that's not real proof. We should do some investigating."

All eyes pivoted towards Jaxon.

"Isn't that what you do? Investigate?" asked Isabella.

Theo lightly squeezed Isabella's shoulder. "Wait. Don't start pulling him under your wing, when I'm getting ready to throw his butt off property. Besides, there's no way in hell we are hiring him to investigate his own family tree."

"Why are you throwing Jax out of Twin Springs?" questioned Logan. "He's an outstanding investigator. He was in charge of security on our team. We dubbed him the human lie detector. The man could smell bullshit a mile off. Saved my ass, more than once. I'd trust him with my life, and I have."

Jaxon felt as if a grenade exploded within his brain. How could Logan still trust him after his intel had almost killed him and left him maimed for life? He opened his mouth to ask, no, to beg, for Logan's forgiveness but glanced up into Ava's clear green eyes instead. Unwilling to reveal to her that he had almost killed her childhood friend, that he was the one responsible for Logan reeking of body odor and walking around in filthy clothes, he snapped his mouth shut.

"Besides," Logan added, "he was just doing a job. He didn't choose the mission. He was assigned it and was just following orders. Like a good soldier."

Jaxon wanted to stay at Twin Springs. But the facts were stacked against him; he'd lied, he'd wronged Ava, he'd failed to protect Ava. What could he say to sway their opinions back in his direction? How could he prove he was the man to protect Ava and the Grand Dame with his life? His hands in his pockets, Jaxon said quietly, "You don't need to hire me. I'll have my cousin dig up any information you want."

Desperate to stay at Twin Springs and remain close to Ava, to have the chance to repair their relationship and remove the pain from her eyes, he continued. "My family has a motto, 'When duty calls we answer and keep the innocent safe, no matter the cost.' You all were innocent and I didn't keep you safe." He looked directly at Ava.

An involuntary gasp escaped Ava, breaking his train of thought. He paused, unsure if she'd allow him the opportunity to state his case. When she refused to even glance at him, he continued, "I broke that oath with all of you during this investigation. Let myself, and my family, make it right. Permit me to continue in the position of Security Manager at Twin Springs and I'll help you discover why Twin Springs is plagued by the recent accidents, to include the Promenade fire. Let me help clear your name, by finishing the investigation for my family's agency."

Theo's gaze pierced the man before him. "Logan, what do you think? Should we trust him again?" he asked. "Should we trust him with our greatest treasures?"

Logan snorted, "Yeah, he can be an ass. But he'll find the truth. Sooner or later. He always does."

The room remained silent, all eyes on Theo as he studied Jaxon, weighing the options and coming to a decision. "Alright, finish your investigation and stay as Security Manager. But you'll work for free and I'm billing your agency for your hotel stay," he stated. "Just keeping it business. Understand?"

Realizing he'd dodged a bullet, Jaxon replied, "Of course, I'll start immediately." He pulled his cell phone out of the side pocket of his tactical pants and pushed quick dial. "Lee, I need you to contact the Geezers. I'm completely compromised and so is the agency." He paused and held the phone away from his ear. Everyone listened intently to the extensive variety of profanity emitting from Jaxon's phone.

"Roger that, I understand you're pissed." He paused again to listen, hanging his head. "Shit, JD's back from her last job?" His voice lowered, "I've got to ask. Did she find him? Was he alive?" Listening he rubbed the stubble on his face with the back of his knuckles. "Okay, keep an eye on her and do your best to keep her and the Geezers in the dark. I need time to pull all the pieces together. Them in the middle of all this is the last thing we need."

He looked up, his gaze surveying the other occupants in the room. "Look, contact the Geezers and ask them about Guy Wolfe. What's his story and how he's connected to Twin Springs. Yes, the hotel. Thanks, out." Jaxon removed a small ball from his side pocket and squeezed it within his hand.

Logan's gaze pivoted from the portrait to his Army buddy. "Shame to not get to meet your dad and uncle. Like to know if those tales you told were really true."

Jaxon slipped his phone back into his pocket, while squeezing the small ball with his other hand. "Believe me, the Geezer's would just complicate things further."

"And JD? Who's she?" asked Ava in a quiet voice.

Jaxon tossed the ball between his hands, studying the portrait before answering. "My sister."

Logan scoffed. "You think Maddy's a handful to raise. The stories I've heard about Wolfeman's little sister. Believe me, you don't want her and Maddy comparing notes." He pulled the newspaper out from his back pocket.

"Speaking of Maddy, found her at the loading dock arguing with the truck driver delivering the daily newspapers. From what I understand, she refused delivery of this morning's newspapers due to the article on the front page. Quite a clear photo of Ava and Jaxon kissing on stage."

Ava snatched the paper from Logan's hand. "Let me see that." Scanning the article, her hands shook. "'Leading lady finds new love. Broadway star grants a special midnight performance. Is anyone safe from her charms?'" Ripping the paper into little pieces, she shoved it in the bottom of Ace's cage. "How are they getting their information? And this picture?"

Theo watched Ava take her anger out on the newspaper. "Looks like we have a spy here at Twin Springs. Other than Jaxon, that is."

Once again the voice within Jaxon's head hummed. He wanted Ava to trust him again. To experience the passion that she'd kept welled up inside herself. To make love to her again and bathe in her warmth. He wanted to be her guy and right the wrongs he'd committed against her. Never would he silence his instincts again. Especially, since her safety depended on it.

He watched her. Noticed her barely looking at him. She'd shut herself off from him. Once again hiding her true self behind a facade. She'd closed off her heat, her heart and her warmth. He understood what he needed to do. Fight and lay siege to her heart. Prove to her that he was her guy. Prove he wanted her just the way she was. No fabricated lines, backdrops or special effects required. Receiving his orders loud and clear, Jaxon prepared himself to move out. "I'm on it," he vowed.

The lights within the room flickered and went out, leaving the room pitch black except for the sunlight shining through the stain glass window.

Jaxon's voice rang out in the darkness. "I'm on that, too."

CHAPTER FORTY-SIX

His hair still darkened by the water from his earlier swim at the Hot Springs Pool, the Director slipped his cellphone back into his pocket. Clad in black from head to toe, he dressed purposefully for the upcoming scene. From his cashmere crew neck shirt that molded to his body, to his leather trim jeans, down to his matching black belt and loafers. He gave an approving glance at the broken phone within the tiny phone booth, setting the stage nicely for the arrival of his leading lady. There were few places in Twin Springs without prying eyes. The phone booths were the perfect, secluded spot to get Ava alone for her first lesson in pain, so she could learn from her mistakes.

Her first mistake was denying him in New York. If she'd behaved in the beginning, he wouldn't have to resort to these measures. But she was difficult and wasn't as easy to mold as the others. She required a stronger hand.

His world had changed after Ava left his office. His meek little wife, afraid of her own shadow, crossed him. Threatened to contact her family and leave him. Ashlee did as she'd promised. After all, she'd left him, just not the way he expected. Instead, she'd made a spectacle out of herself and him. She'd forced him to take the stage and play the part of the grieving widower.

He wanted his comfortable life back. Where he was king of those he directed and commanded about the stage. Where he was admired and people revered him. In the Theatre, he held power. Ava was the key to getting that power back. She was his new lucky charm. He needed her and he didn't like needing any woman.

Holding the most recent edition of the newspaper open in front of his face, he stepped out the booth and leaned against a wall in the Presidents Hall. "It will only take a moment for the clerk to call Ava," he mused out loud.

Sure enough, Ava's long legs carried her right to him. For a moment, he admired the way she moved towards him, grace flowing through every step. He was just coming back from a rather enjoyable round of golf and his dip in the pool for Tea Time, when he'd spotted the front page article. Anger had surged through him, causing his fingers to crush the edges of the newspaper. Damn her, she almost ruined his plan by being photographed onstage, with some nobody. Time to teach her a painful little lesson. The first of many if he didn't get her buy-in on his vision of their future.

CHAPTER FORTY-SEVEN

Quickening her step, Ava cut through the Presidents Hall towards the Crystal Ballroom. Sheela's call that one of the guests wished to speak with her about a future wedding ceremony at Twin Springs was the one bright spot in her day. Everyone now trusted Jaxon to find out who was habitually sabotaging Twin Springs, but his betrayal had cut her deep.

Thank goodness, Dale and Logan found the issue with the lights. They were keeping disgustingly quiet about the cause, which Ava found extremely frustrating. Suddenly, the men of Twin Springs decided to form ranks and protect the poor, unsuspecting and weak women. She skirted around the male guests within the Presidents Hall and kept to the left of the huge table. She muttered to herself under her breath, "Damn it, I'm not weak."

Something gripped her, winding its way into the hair at the base of her scalp and pulling. Taken off guard, it took a moment for her brain to switch from surprise, to shock, to panic. The pain of her hair ripping from her scalp sped up the process. She opened her mouth to scream but a hand covered her mouth. Dragged backwards by her hair, she scrambled to maintain her footing and scratched desperately at the hand attached to her hair and the one covering her mouth. Thrown back against the wall of one of the small phone booths, the weight of her assailant pressed against her.

Her eyes broadened into green pools above the hand covering her mouth, when Director Hollingsworth's face came into focus just inches from hers. Flashing his white teeth, Terrence panted from his efforts and leaned his sweaty forehead against hers. His shoulders shook with amusement and he rubbed his face along her cheek. "Ava, you're so much fun. All my other leading ladies fell quickly into line. But you, no, you enjoy adventure. Enjoy pain."

A mad sheen gleamed in his blue eyes and she knew the depth of evil within the Director. *Escape!* her mind screamed.

Trembling with fear, her mind searched its limited arsenal on how to get away. Quickly lifting her knee, she aimed for his soft crotch.

Reaching down with one hand, the Director shoved her leg to the side before it met its mark and settled within her spread limbs. He rubbed his hardened crotch against her. "Tsk, tsk, Ava. Responding to violence with violence is not the answer." He chuckled at his own joke while slowly lifting the hem of her skirt. "Perhaps we have a little time for pleasure before we get down to business."

Bucking her body, Ava fought for release, knocking the telephone receiver from the wall with her efforts.

He reached down with one hand, grabbed the telephone cord and wrapped it around her throat, pulling until she wheezed for air and stopped moving, understanding the uselessness of her actions. He was stronger and he held the power.

Terrence grunted with satisfaction. "There, now that you are acting like a civilized human being we can talk." The Director placed a small bite in the curve of her neck. "Just enough air for you to enjoy this as much as I will." He moaned and bit an inch higher before giggling excitedly. "If you continue to struggle, then you'll black out and miss all our fun."

He bit harder and Ava whimpered. Licking with the tip of his tongue, he lapped up the tiny drops of blood caused by his teeth.

"Salty and sweet Ava, with a little metallic after taste. You're always such a contradiction." The planes of his face hardened and he pulled the cord higher. "Here are your lines. Are you listening?"

Her sight darkened at the edges and she nodded. The movement of her head caused his sweaty palm to slide back and forth against her lips.

He reached under the volume of her skirt, grabbed ahold of her panties and ripped them down the side so they were no longer in the way. Digging his fingers into her thigh, he jerked her leg up around his hip. With one hand he fumbled with his belt. "You'll tell the reporter of that rag that you lost your way after the tragedy of my wife's death. Desperately, you tried to forget our great love with others. But once you were reunited with me, you knew our love could not be denied. Only now, that we are both free to love, could we—"

A flash of bright light blinded Ava. She blinked for a moment, trying to regain her sight, before pain exploded in her skull. Released, she crumpled onto the little white seat with the phone cord tightening a noose around her throat.

CHAPTER FORTY-EIGHT

Blinded by the flash, the Director blinked rapidly and searched for the source. As the world moved into focus, he saw the light brown eyes of the Front Desk clerk and he thought of his wife Ashlee. His confused mind churned and stumbled, limping along the road of comprehension.

Triumphantly, the clerk smiled over her phone camera and winked at him.

Realization flooded his consciousness. A photograph. The woman was much younger when she stood beside his errant, dead wife. His wife's old friend, the reporter.

"Gotcha," she mouthed to him and disappeared from the folding glass door.

His face grew hot and loathing welled up within him. He'd known something was off about the Front Desk clerk and, as a director, he should've seen through her costume of long black hair to the scum below. Damn it, how dare she go off script and ruin his plans. He was in control. He held the power. His fingers entwined themselves into the hair on the top of Ava's scalp. Time to bring the women around him back under control and beneath his thumb where they belonged.

Consumed by rage, he grasped the crown of Ava's silky hair

within his fist and slammed her head against the wall, grunting with satisfaction when she crumbled in the seat. Her lesson could wait till later.

A plan clicked into place. For now, he needed to get that phone. If the reporter published the picture in that rag she wrote for, then the public would know his secrets. His heart pounded in his chest at the ramifications. He'd search every inch of this hotel and find her. Then, he'd destroy not only the camera but also the photographer. Otherwise, his illustrious career would be ruined.

CHAPTER FORTY-NINE

*E*xcitement pumped Mackenzie's heart. She scurried up the stairs two at a time to the attic space above the Front Desk. She glanced over her shoulder, for the blonde head of Ashlee's husband. If he caught her, he might prevent her from avenging her friend.

She rushed past the sign stating "Employees Only" and down a crooked hallway with faded, threadbare carpet. Nearing one of the doors at the end of the hall, she twisted the knob of the tall, skinny door open. Turning, she slowly closed the door behind her and held the knob tight until it silently latched. She pressed her ear against the door and listened for movement signaling that he'd followed her. Hearing none, she leaned back against the door and smiled. "Success."

A musty odor permeated the room. Light filtered in through a dingy window above a long, padded window seat. Age yellowed drapes whispered in a breeze that snuck through a winding crack in the window. The attic storage room was more than enough for her purposes.

Working her way around an old sewing machine and a table surrounded with boxes, Sheela sat on the faded and threadbare carpet covered by decades of dirt. In her service uniform of black pants, white shirt and black jacket, she didn't care how much dirt there was. Her uniform would wash, but the story couldn't wait.

From under an empty box, she dragged out her dark blue backpack, monogrammed with two intertwined M's in red stitching, and leaned back against the black iron frame of an old bed, stacked against the wall. Taking her laptop out of her backpack, she opened her small notebook and stared down at her notes. The corner of a picture poked out of the back of her notebook. Removing the picture, she leaned her head back against the cold iron and stared at the photo of herself and Ashlee. Eighteen and sixteen, bundled for a day of skiing. Her gaze swept over her friend's face. Even now, she heard her infectious laughter and saw the excitement sparkling in her eyes. Her loss stole her breath, and she rubbed at the pain in her chest, realizing no matter what she did, she would never see her smile again or hear her voice. She missed her, desperately.

The urge to strike out against those who stole her friend burned within her. They caused the suicide of a woman on the cusp of life. They needed to feel her pain. They, too, must suffer. Why should Ava and Terrence be able to laugh and love when Ashlee never would again? Her fingers flew across the keyboard and Mackenzie wrote her story. Once completed, she let out a relieved sigh.

Feeling something poking her in the back, she leaned sideways and pulled a Batman action figure out from behind her. "The things one finds in the attics at Twins Springs," she muttered.

She threw the toy across the room and watched Batman skid under a half dressed Christmas tree. Quickly, she connected her phone to the back of her computer, downloaded the picture and attached the photo with her story to her email.

When she'd found them having sex within the phone booth, she couldn't believe her luck, or their stupidity. Finally, evidence that Ava and Terrence were having an affair. With the combination of the photo and her behind the scenes story, she could finally destroy them. After all, a photo was worth a thousand words. Added proof that Ava was a slut, willing to spread her legs for all men. That would be her title, 'Broadway Star Performs For All'.

CHAPTER FIFTY

With care, Jaxon unwrapped the phone cord from around Ava's slender neck. The skin above the phone cord line was already shading into purples and swollen.

His chest clenched with fear. Now that he'd found Ava, he couldn't bear losing her. Placing the tips of two fingers along the artery at the side of her neck, he held his breath and waited to feel a pulse. He swallowed hard, "Thank God."

He expelled a huge breath and bowed his head, laying his forehead lightly against hers. He didn't lose her.

You love her, you asshole, his inner voice chastised. *You love this mad woman of many faces.*

On her knees beside him, Maddy clutched Ava's limp hand to her cheek. "Is she dead?" she whispered, her voice hitching with suppressed sobs. "She can't be dead. I didn't have a chance to tell her that I don't hate her anymore."

Not trusting his voice to work, he took a moment to collect himself, unsure at first if he could speak. "She's alive. Go find Theo and Logan." Noticing the teenager's crumpled form didn't move, he hardened his voice. "Now, Maddy! Go find them. We need their help and a doctor."

Huge tears streaming down her face, Maddy nodded and scrambled from the booth.

Tamping down his own anger and guilt for not protecting the woman he loved, he surveyed the tiny booth. He reached down and picked up a small bit of torn lace. Ava's underwear. An uncontrollable, blinding rage filled him, shaking him and propelling him to kill the man responsible. Before others could see it, he stuffed her ripped panties into the side pocket of his pants, choked back the building anger and focused in on Ava. His lips curled back, baring his teeth. Later, he would find the bastard and rip him apart limb from limb.

He searched the tiny booth for something, anything, that would lead him to the bastard. He couldn't stand seeing her hurt. Her graceful neck swollen and marred by a crooked bruised line. Glancing up, he noted a crimson streak of blood smeared head height on the wall. Delicately, he turned her and painstakingly searched through her silky hair on the back of her head. Wetness. Pulling back his hand, bright red blood coated his fingertips. Ava's blood. Meticulously, he felt along her body and limbs for broken bones and other injuries. A rank smell reached his nostrils. Leaning in, he sniffed her clothes. "Smoke. She smells like cigarettes. No, cigars."

The green flecks in his eyes glowed with purpose. On the hunt, his hackles rose and the beast within him howled to be released; to hunt, to follow the scent and track down the bastard who dared touch what was his.

Ava moaned, her long eyelashes fluttered and she lifted her hand to her temple.

His voice husky with suppressed emotions, he whispered, "Hold still, sugar. We don't know how badly you're hurt till a medic checks you out."

"My head's killing me," her voice cracked with the effort of speaking. She lifted her hands to rub her throat. "And my neck hurts."

He halted the upward journey of her hands. "I know." Her hands felt cool to the touch and he rubbed them gently between his. "Ava, who attacked you?"

"Attacked me?" she repeated, thinking hard. Her chin trembled. She looked over Jaxon's shoulder, her frightened gaze searching the area around her.

"Did he rape you?" His voice was low and deep within his chest. He cupped her beautiful face within his hands. "I'll find out who the bastard is. Just give me a description and I'll hunt him down."

She shook her head, then, winced with pain. "No, he didn't. He—"

Maddy's wail filled the booth. "Your alive!" She squeezed in, bumping Jaxon to the side and knelt in front of her. "I love you. I could never hate you. I'm sorry. You can have Jaxon. I don't want him. Anyway he's soooo old." She rubbed the back of Ava's fingers against her cheek. "You're just like a sister to me."

"Move Maddy," roared Theo. "And stop going on." Taking the situation into his own hands, he picked up his little sister, heels and all, and placed her behind him. Then he crouched down behind Jaxon, hovering. "I called an ambulance. They should be here in minutes. What the hell happened?"

Closing her eyes to the bright light and noise around her, she waived Theo's suggestions off. "No ambulance. No sirens. No attention. Please. Just get me to my room as quietly as possible. I don't want the guests to see me or the press to find out." She squeezed her eyes, attempting to keep the tears at bay. "Please."

"Okay." Jaxon kept his tone soft, soothing. "You need to remain calm." He spoke over his shoulder to Theo. "You and Maddy clear a path to her office. We can lay her on the couch there until the doc sees her. Later, when the Grand Lobby's empty, we'll get her to her room."

"Thank you," she whispered, squeezing his hand.

Jaxon lifted her into his arms and held her close to his heart, protecting her. Leaning down he kissed her on the forehead before whispering in her ear, "You'll get your way for now. But you will tell me who did this to you. So that I can kill the bastard."

CHAPTER FIFTY-ONE

*E*arly the next morning, Jaxon left Ava sleeping in her bed, under doctor's orders, for rest. She'd received a hard crack on the head, but the doc felt she was in the clear. Some jackass Sheriff showed up to take statements. Jaxon had marveled at Theo's calm demeanor when the Sheriff started throwing around innuendoes and half brained ideas about what had happened.

At Ava's request, they towed the company line of 'slipped in the phone booth and hit her head against the wall'. Pitiful excuse. He didn't blame the Sheriff for not buying it. But Ava batted her eyes and soothed his feathers before sending him on his way.

It disgusted him to admit it, but Ava's skills in handling people did come in handy. *Other men. Only once in a while,* he decided.

He exited the Promenade elevator and worked his way down the Grand Lobby towards his office. With the hotel quiet, now was the time to examine the security footage for information on her attacker. He noticed that Dale and Logan were removing the giant, white paneled barriers blocking the construction on the new Lobby Bar. He paused, "Need some help?"

Logan grunted, "What?" He pulled a panel away and placed it length wise on a cart. "You don't think I can handle a couple slabs of wood? Get lost Wolfeman. Let the real men do the hard work."

In his usual work shirt and jeans, Dale looked up and winked at Jaxon. "Don't worry about 'em son. We've got it."

Guilt filled Jaxon as he watched Logan struggle to grasp the edges of the panel between his two fingers and thumb. Unable to take it anymore, he stepped forward to help, halting when Logan's blue eyes pinned him to the spot.

Bending his knees, Logan wedged the edge of the panel in his armpit and pinned it by applying pressure with his bent arm. His good hand grasped along the top and he lifted the long panel, balancing its weight. He placed the panel on the cart with the others. The great, big, dirty tongue of his Rolling Stones band shirt stuck out at Jaxon, mocking him.

Unsure of what to say but unwilling to leave in case he was needed, he asked, "How's the Promenade store clean up going from the fire?"

Logan shot him a glare.

But Dale answered good naturedly, his drawl easy on the ears. "We've got the space gutted. Waitin' on drawings from Maddy. She wants to turn the space into a confectioners shop. Where the guests can watch candy being made by hand through a big, awning covered window. Then guests can purchase boxes of freshly made candy inside. She wants to knock out the wall between that store and the one next door and place in a counter where sandwiches and milkshakes can also be served. Waitin' on the big guy to approve her ideas." He paused, his faded eyes penetrating Jaxon's. "And the insurance checks to come in of course."

Jaxon blushed like a school girl. Rubbing the tension from the back of his neck, he mumbled, "Yes, sir. I'll get right on that."

Hoisting another panel easily between his work aged hands, Dale paused before replying. "I'm sure ya will, son. Sure ya will."

The last board loaded, Jaxon continued to his office. Leaving his door open, he slid into the rolling chair and moved the mouse, bringing the computer alive. He just needed to search through the day's earlier footage. See if Ava's attack was burned to the hard drive. He seized on the opportunity to find the bastard before the local Sheriff. No worries, he'd leave a little bit of the man for the police to find. Just a little. Maybe.

It ticked him off that Ava refused to tell him who attacked her. "How the hell would she handle this herself?" he growled under his breath.

Determined not to let Ava down like he'd let down his team and his family, he studied the footage as it streamed before him. The way the system rotated through the different feeds, only recording bits and pieces from each area in the hotel, frustrated him. He'd need to talk with Theo about putting in a different system. What if the system rotated right past the attack and he missed his chance to find the asshole?

What the hell are you doing? he admonished himself. *Thinking you belong. Like you're going to stay and become a part of the Twin Springs family, a part of Ava's life. Do you really believe these people will accept you after you betrayed them, after you scarred one of them for life? You're a traitor to them.* But damn it, he liked these people. Most of all, he loved Ava.

Spotting something, his hand snaked out and paused the frame before backing up the footage and playing it again. His instincts buzzed, telling him there was something wrong with the footage in front of him. Leaning in, he squinted his eyes to make out the blonde haired man. Something about the way he acted made the hackles rise on the back of his neck. His back to the camera, the man climbed up a stairway leading to the attics. His head began to turn and Jaxon leaned in further, with his finger on the mouse to freeze the frame. Then the picture switched to footage of the pool. Jaxon slammed the palm of his hand down on the desk, rattling the cup of pencils and pens, but he caught the walkies before they toppled over.

"What's the matter?"

He glanced up. "Hey Sheela. Looking at today's security footage. I'm sure you heard. Apparently, there are no secrets in Twin Springs."

Chuckling, Mackenzie propped herself on the edge of Jaxon's desk. "Secrets don't make friends. Didn't you know that?"

He made a non-committal grunt. "Guess only the Grand Dame gets to keep her secrets."

Clasping her hands innocently in front of her, Mackenzie asked, "So, what happened?"

Clearing his throat, Jaxon released the words that burned in his gut. "Ava was attacked in the phone booth."

Mackenzie snickered, "Yeah, right."

Jaxon's eyes pierced her to the spot. "What are you implying?"

Immediately, the Front Desk clerk leaned back from the fury of his gaze and splayed her hands in front of her. "What I mean is, who'd dare attack Ava?"

He forced his shoulders to relax. Sheela had a point. No one messed with Ava. "Since those newspaper articles came out, the male guests started making unwanted advances on her. Pawing her, grabbing at her and propositioning her."

Turning a little green, Mackenzie squeaked, "They have?"

Feeling sorry for the girl, he patted her on the arm and focused back on the footage. "Yeah, you couldn't have known. I guess Ava's almost as good at keeping her secrets as the Grand Dame is. Today, a male guest dragged her into one of the phone booths, wound a phone cord around her neck and tried to rape her."

The blood flooded from Mackenzie's face and she gasped, "No!"

Not paying attention to the woman, he inspected the footage. A satisfied grunt escaped his lips. "Here's the bastard. See?" His finger pointed to the screen. "There's Ava. Keep your eye on the man holding the paper. Tell me if you recognize him."

A foul sensation churned in his gut as he watched Ava grabbed from behind and pulled into the alcove of the telephone booths. He could tell she fought for her life, kicking and scratching at the bastard, but he jerked her around like a puppet on a string. "Christ." His breath expelled in a whoosh.

Even though he was a war-hardened soldier, the violence on

the screen shocked him. Seeing Ava dragged back, the newspaper shoved into her face. "Shit, shit, shit." Jaxon's fist pounded the table. Leaning forward he rested his head in his hands. "All we can see is that he's taller than her and has light hair, perhaps blonde. Damn it."

"Oh God," Mackenzie said, pressing the heels of her hands into her eye sockets. "Oh, no."

Jaxon's instincts screamed. *Sheela knows him. She recognized who Ava's attacker was.*

He grabbed her by the arm, squeezing hard and pulled her closer. "Do you recognize him? Do you know who the bastard is?"

Vehemently shaking her head she tugged on Jaxon's grasp to free her arm. "No, that was horrible. I can't believe it." She wrenched her arm away. "I have to go."

He watched her run from the room. His gut knew she lied. Or at least was hiding something. Whatever it was, he'd hunt down the truth.

Slamming the Ladies Room door aside, Mackenzie sprinted for a stall door. She bent over the toilet just in time to release her evening meal. Dry heaving, her mind raced. *Ava was being raped.*

Her fingers shook and she dragged toilet paper from the roll and wiped her mouth. She rubbed at the corner of her eyelid, over and over. "How did I get it wrong?" she whispered.

The Director raped her. "I took a picture and left her there. What kind of a monster am I?" Realization hit that she'd not only snapped a picture of a woman being raped, but had also printed the picture with a scathing column. Lightheaded, she bent over and emptied the rest of her stomach's contents. "I didn't even stop the crime."

Her dry heaves turned into sobs and she moved away from the toilet. Leaning against the stall wall, she wiped her eyes and mouth before sliding down and landing hard on her butt. Weeping uncontrollably, she moaned, "She was innocent, just like Ashlee. Innocent." Another victim of the Director, same as her best friend.

Breath hitching, she wiped her nose with the sopping tissues. Her cheeks burned, she'd wronged Ava. Made her a victim not only of a disgusting creep but also of the press. She knew that, even now, the papers were being delivered to the hotel. "I must fix this. How?"

Resting her head on her knees, she wrapped her arms around her legs and rocked herself. "Do your damn homework. That's how," she muttered.

She thought back on how she'd run with this story. Her own emotions ruled. There were no facts. She'd shaded her article with her own pain and accusations.

She used to pride herself on the validity of her stories. But she'd sunk to his level, using her power with the written word to destroy a woman. Now she needed to prove to herself that she could once again be impartial and report the facts without emotion clouding her, tainting her story. How could she fix the pain she'd caused Ava? She needed to find the truth. There was one thing she knew as a reporter—how to dig. And she would dig. Dig and find out all the dirt on Ashlee's husband. He was the monster.

She must inform the world that he was a rapist, a murderer and a pariah feeding on women. She'd need to hide until she obtained the whole story. Since she was a witness, he'd try to stop her. After her new story was printed, she would come forward and stand by Ava's side. Terrence, on the other hand, could rot in jail. Where he couldn't hurt another woman.

She pulled out her notebook and jotted down ideas. There must be other victims. She just needed to find them and convince them to speak with her and coax them into telling her their stories. She'd start with the Director's other leading ladies, then his crew. Hopefully, with a computer and phone, she could obtain enough information to bury the bastard, clear Ava's name and finally find justice for her friend.

CHAPTER FIFTY-THREE

*L*ater that morning, Ava fiddled with the edges of a long, sea green, silk scarf, ensuring it concealed the wobbly black and blue line on her neck. Her sea foam blue and green blouse reflected the confusion and crashing thoughts within her mind. A black waist coat, skinny pants and pumps completed her attire. Not ready to brave the Presidents Hall, she grabbed a cup of coffee at Independence Place, a little gourmet shop on the Promenade.

Taking her caffeine lover by the hand, she rushed to be the first to view the new Lobby Bar. She skirted around the red velvet ropes looped between brass poles and tapped on the smoked glass and richly polished, mahogany sliding doors. Receiving no answer and eager to view Logan's makeover, she tapped again.

"Alright, aright," grumbled Logan from behind the glass. He cracked the doors open and glared through the small space. "Should've known it would be you. Always wanting to see behind the scenes. Besides, Maddy and Isabella came by to judge my finished product just after dawn."

Ava's face fell, "Why didn't they get me?"

"Something about you needing to rest from being attacked yesterday." He opened the door further and searched her features, noting the scarf tied high around her neck. "Do you know which male guest it was?"

Tipping her chin down, she looked down at her hands and shook her head. "We can't focus on that today. This afternoon I host my first wedding at Twin Springs. No time to rest now, need to show the Senator and his influential friends that Twin Springs is the ideal spot for a wedding. Come on Logan," she urged. "Let me in."

Smoothly, the glass doors parted, granting a large, open walkway, before folding back on themselves and disappearing into the side walls. A long, curved, mahogany bar was topped by granite lined with veins of fool's gold and silver and protected down the front by a brass kickstand. Multiple, white marble pulls lined the lower half of the bar's back wall. Seemingly hanging in midair above the pulls, a large, brass still protruded from the black, glassed wall. To each side hung glass cabinets. Inside, various types of glassware were backlit so they sparkled and shined. To the right of the still, in bold letters curved in brass, read the words, 'Still Waters Bar & Grill'. Dark leather seating curved intimately around tables and filled the rest of the long room.

Noting a doorway tucked in the back corner, Ava walked through an arched opening and was greeted by a shot of modern entertainment with three, large, flat screen T.V.s and two expansive gaming tables. She met Logan back by the bar. "Was that the still from the cavern under Twin Springs?"

"Yep." He scratched the giant tongue on the front of the Rolling Stone's t-shirt that he hadn't changed for two days. "Dad and I had a hell of a time slicing it into a facade for the back wall. We polished her until she shined."

"She makes a statement when you enter. I love it." She hugged him and placed a kiss on his cheek, wrinkling her nose at his body odor. "You're amazing, but you smell."

"Doesn't stop you from molesting me." Logan rubbed off her kiss and glared at her. "Damn it, did I get all the lip lacquer guck off? Ava, you have a way of marking a man without him even knowing it."

Immediately, her mind shifted to another man and she put her coffee on the bar. "Sorry." Her laughter was light and quick. "Just not the one I really want."

His head swiveled side to side searching for an avenue of escape. Seeing none, he let out a long sigh and tucked his thumbs in the openings of his back pockets. "Ava," he groaned. "I'm not good at the mushy crap. You know that. Go talk to Izzy. That's what sisters are for."

Enjoying his sudden discomfort, she grinned and hugged his arm tight. "It's alright. I so enjoy seeing you squirm. Don't worry, I'll muddle through."

Glancing down, he admired his childhood friend. This was a new avenue for them. They used to only connive on how to torment Izzy and Niles. "Give Jax time."

Leaning back, her green eyes pierced the blue of his. "He has a tattoo of the names of the men from the team on his inner arm, with a date. Your name is there."

"Mine?" Only Logan's left eye widened with surprise, his other remained partly shut by the scars and unmoved by the new information. "I guess he didn't escape the full effect of the explosion after all. It might not show on the outside but, if that is the case, then he took a heavy hit from our last mission." He looked off into the distance, his eyes glazed. "It was a terrible day. My ears still ring with the screams of the dying." He rubbed where his ear melted into the side of his head.

Shaken, Ava sipped from her cup. The hot coffee scalded her tongue but she didn't care. "I think he blames himself for the explosion."

"No way." Logan shook his head with denial and cleared the fog of war. "We all looked at Wolfeman as an incredible asset. Fully trained in all the different MOS's." He paused to explain himself. "Military Occupational Specialties of the team. When in doubt, we turned to Jax for guidance. He always knew how to proceed, who could be trusted and who to watch out for. He had this crazy inner compass. Always pointed us towards completing our mission."

Trying to understand, Ava abandoned her caffeine lover and asked, "What was different with your last mission? What went wrong?"

"Hell if I know. The intel was solid. An American source. A woman. A drop dead, gorgeous, woman. We pushed it through Jax and it was a go. Suddenly, the whole thing went to shit and all hell broke loose. Don't know what Wolfeman could have done different."

Pain misted her eyes with unshed tears. "He said he believed the wrong person. He said he killed his team."

Logan laid his mutilated hand on her shoulder, "Jaxon's a good man. He didn't kill anyone on our team. The enemy did."

She leaned back against the bar. "When I'm with him, I feel the same tingling and excitement running through my veins as I do when I'm opening for a new play. A rush of excitement. I feel alive."

A pained expression crossed Logan's face and he rubbed his face with the palms of his hands. "Good God Ava. Go find a girl to share your feelings with." His face flushed purple, with embarrassment. "I feel like I need to go shoot or hit something so I can feel like a man again." Beseechingly, he held his hands up in front of him. "I love you, but please, no more. First, Maddy, sharing all day long, now you. You women really need to learn operational security."

Delighted, she laughed, hugged Logan tight and again kissed his cheek.

Growling in the back of his throat he again rubbed the offending kiss off. "That's it! Get moving. Don't you have a wedding to finish? Let me pound my hammer and screw something to get my man card revalidated."

She waggled her fingers bye and her lips curved into a mischievous smile as Logan pushed her through the doorway and slid the doors closed behind her with a snap. She heard him muttering under his breath behind the fogged glass.

Not even the fact she'd left her caffeine lover behind could break her good mood. Logan was right about Jaxon. She picked up her pace and headed to the Crystal Ballroom to check on the wedding set up. Determined to bring her world back under control, she braved the Presidents Hall's entrance. Her gaze flickered towards the booths and she doubted she would ever find solace again behind their bi-fold doors. Giving the booths wide birth, she scrutinized each male guest before she passed. Her hands balled up into fists and anger replaced her joy. The Director had ruined her safe place. She promised herself that she'd not let him win. After the wedding, she'd confront him. "I'll take great pleasure in kicking his ass out of Twin Springs and out of my…" She repeated to herself, "my home."

CHAPTER FIFTY-FOUR

Tugging open the towering doors to the Crystal Ballroom, Ava marched through and assessed the proceedings. Eight hours till the curtain went up. The local florist's strawberry blonde head peeped above a mountain of red and white flowers.

Quickening her pace, Ava approached the woman. "June, how are we doing?"

Dressed in a shapely pantsuit in pale lavender with a cute little white canvas tool belt synched around her waist, June was ready with the tools of her trade at hand. "Everything is almost in place."

Slipping shears and a coil of thin, green wire into the pockets of her belt, together they stood back to take in the floral arrangements. A small stage stretched in front of the long line of white paned French doors. A shiny, black, baby grand piano was tucked into a corner to the left of the stage. White chairs, ready to be swept away for dancing, created an aisle for the bride and her party to approach the steps to the stage. A delicate arch in black iron laced a canopy for the couple to say their vows beneath. Kissing balls, in the bride's chosen flowers of red roses and white lilies, dangled from the ceiling by white satin ribbons and strings of pearls. The edges of the stage and the arched windows above the French doors were also dripping with blooms. Reflected by the sparkling chandelier, the soft twinkling of lights glimmered around the room.

Admiring the results, Ava said, "Beautiful as always. Oakton and Twin Springs are lucky to have you."

"Thanks, I think the bride will appreciate our efforts." June lifted a brow. "Her mother on the other hand."

"There's always a critic." Ava glanced over, noticing Jaxon entering through the side entrance. Brows furrowing, he approached them. Clad in a black t-shirt and tan pants, his long legs ate up the distance between them.

June gave a low wolf whistle under her breath, loud enough for only the two of them to hear. "Goodness, nice addition to the Twin Springs staff."

Ava's lips curved appreciatively and her heart leapt. "Our new Security Manager."

"Does the man come with handcuffs?" joked June.

"I don't think cuffs are part of his uniform. In fact, he doesn't seem to conform to our standard uniform."

Admiring the muscles bulging out from under his black t-shirt, June made an appreciative sound. "Who wants standard issue?"

Thinking about the florist's comment, she had to agree. Why settle for standard, when you can have exceptional. Jaxon definitely was exceptional and he was her guy. Her pert mouth slid into a roguish grin. "If you'll excuse me, I will see what he needs."

Slowing her pace, Ava waited for Jaxon to reach her. With each of his steps, her heart beat faster. Displeasure crossed across his face. Never one to miss a cue, she slid up to him, entwining her long fingers into the dark black hair at the nape of his neck and guiding his lips down to meet hers. Leisurely, she took pleasure within his firm lips, delving between them to taste his power. Nibbling on his full bottom lip, she whispered, "My guy."

His arms swung up and encased her in a world of security and protection. Impatient with her teasing, he dragged her firmly against his hard body and deepened the kiss.

Scattered applause penetrated their bubble and the couple broke apart.

Holding an imaginary skirt out to the side, Ava curtsied for the spectators.

Jaxon frowned at their impromptu audience, his scowl causing heads to lower and workers to scurry. Turning his attention back to the unpredictable woman before him, he asked, "What was that for?"

Running her hand down his arm, she intertwined her fingers within his. He was like a drug. She couldn't help but touch, help but taste. Her mind searched for any excuse for her unusual actions. "Just a thank you. A thank you for keeping an eye on me during the night. For not pushing on what happened yesterday. For understanding my need for time."

"You can thank me any time, sugar." His eyes studied her red lips, swollen and moist from their shared kiss. His eyes traveled down to the bruises peeking out from under the green scarf. A reminder of how he'd failed her. "You should be in bed," he growled, adjusting the strap of silk. "And time is running out for you to tell me all you know about yesterday."

Ava bristled. "I'll take care of him, Jaxon."

His hands balled into fists and his stance hardened. "You know the bastard. Don't you? Tell me who it was."

She shook her head and tucked a glossy strand of ebony hair behind her ear. Putting on her best stage smile she side stepped his question, "After the wedding. We have a job to do and the Grand Dame's needs come first. Don't you understand? The success of this wedding will propel Twin Springs to the top of the charts as one of the premier venues for weddings. It'll help save Twin Springs. Prove that I am more than just a pretty face. That I can hold my own in business. That Theo's faith in placing me in the position of Group Sales and Special Events Coordinator was valid and give me back a stage where I belong and can shine."

Her passion flowed over Jaxon. He'd never considered that she needed to prove herself and searched for a place to belong, a place to perform. How could she? Any floor Ava walked upon became her stage. She glittered in any setting. He was stunned that she felt her beauty wasn't an asset.

Guilt rumbled in his stomach. At first, he'd assessed her only by her beauty. Never looking past her gorgeous face and body. If the success of this wedding proved to her how spectacular she was, then by damn he'd help her make it a success. "Alright. I'll give you time." He paused, his gold eyes glinting with a green sheen. Growling in his throat, he added, "Until after the wedding. Then you'll let me hunt the bastard down."

Imploringly, Ava gazed up at her guy, sensing his desire for action. "Don't you understand? I have to confront him myself. He sees me as weak, as something he can control. He can own. I have to show him that I'm not his pawn to manipulate. I must be the one who handles him."

Removing the ball from his pocket, he squeezed it. "He needs to learn a lesson. He has to go to jail for what he did."

"Let me prove to myself that I'm not his victim. Let me show him that he can't mess with Ava Fairbanks and get away with it. Then you and the police can have him. Give me my piece of justice first by letting him know he'll never be able to abuse me again. Let me find him and kick him out of my home."

Jaxon ground his back teeth, understanding her demands, wanting to help her but needing to protect her. Shoving the little ball back into his pocket, he asked, "No way am I allowing you to place yourself in danger."

He softened his voice. The results from yesterday were evident for the world to see across her neck. "Let me show you how to break away if someone is holding you by the neck."

Ava thought of everything she still needed to finish for the wedding and clicked off the list in her mind and shook her head. "I don't have time. Show me in the morning."

He crossed his arms over his chest and broadened his stance. "I'm not leaving unless you take the time. Your safety is important."

She glanced around, everyone busily working around her. Perhaps things were progressing nicely. The more she thought about it, June was ahead of schedule. "Alright, just a couple minutes."

Jaxon's white teeth gleamed against his stubbled face, "That's my girl."

At his words, she felt her legs go weak at the knees.

"First," he grasped her hands within his. "These fingers are weapons. Powerful weapons. Especially your thumbs. A thumb in the eye will stun him. Keep pressing and his eye will pop out."

Ava gasped, snatching her hands back. "Gross! I'll not 'pop' anyone's eyes out!"

Narrowing his eyes, his voice lowered to a growl, "If you aren't prepared to go the distance, then give me his name and I will."

Thinking for a moment, she twisted the rings on her fingers, before holding her hands back out for him to demonstrate.

He grunted with approval and continued. "His throat is a soft spot." He flattened her hand and brought it to his throat. Jab anywhere in the soft front part of his throat, his Adam's apple and the fleshy divot above his collar bone." He curled her fingers so her knuckles protruded out. "Your knuckles are strong too. Hit with your knuckles, palm, fingers, or fist. It doesn't matter which. Don't think, just do."

He wanted to teach her so much but he knew his time was limited. "Also, where his nose goes, he goes." Jaxon pushed the heel of her palm up against his nose and showed her how to force his head away by applying pressure to the soft tissue at the base.

"And your voice, your glorious voice is another one of your tools. Scream, yell, let people know you need help. If cornered, your aim is to hurt him enough to get away, to get to safety. If you can't get away, keep hitting him until you can. Until he is down, and staying down." He paused and his eyes met hers. Squeezing her hands gently within his, he said, "Remember, Ava, the most committed wins. Don't just poke him, gouge him. Hurt him. It is you or him. Remember that."

Listening intently, Ava swallowed hard before asking, "What if," she moistened her suddenly dry lips. "What if, he has you from behind? Pressed up against a wall and you can't use your fingers or your fists?"

Understanding her question came from experience, black rage burned in Jaxon's eyes. Silently, he vowed to never let her deal with this bastard alone. No matter what. "You still have weapons." He pulled her into an alcove of the Crystal Ballroom. "Stomp on his feet with your heels. Slam your head back against his."

"But what if you are pressed tight against the wall and his head is to the side and not behind you? And his feet are spread apart, or my feet are."

He trembled with fury. Taking deep breaths he calmed himself and focused on how to help her. "Let me show you."

He turned Ava and pressed her against the wall, in the position she described. "Now squirm, move your body, head and legs to loosen my hold. Your goal is to get an arm loose enough to slide it up your body towards your ear. Once your hand is close to your ear, push your arm up and swing your elbow back."

Feeling trapped, Ava began to shake. An uncontrollable shiver that trembled throughout her body and weakened her limbs with remembered fear. "I can't," she whispered.

He squeezed harder. "Yes, you can. Remember, the most committed wins. You must be prepared to fight to the finish. Don't let him win. Reach deep within yourself, be strong." It broke his heart but he compressed her arms and pinned her against the wall.

She struggled, kicked and flung her head around. Until, her arm shot up and her elbow swung around cracking him hard in the side of his face. "I did it! I did it!" Ava jumped up and down. Shooting her fists in the air she imitated a Rocky pose.

Grinning, he rubbed his bruised cheek. "Yes, you did, sugar. Indeed, you did."

Realizing she might've hurt him, she grasped his head between her palms and pulled his face down to hers. "Goodness Jaxon, are you okay? Did I hurt you?" She placed little healing kisses across his cheek, until her lips found his.

Smiling against her sweet lips, he whispered, "Sugar, you can whack me anytime." His mouth slid over hers and he gathered her tight.

CHAPTER FIFTY-FIVE

*E*ngrossed in the softness of his lips, bringing a need within her that only he could quench, at first Ava didn't hear the gasp behind her. She only felt loss when Jaxon raised his head.

"What the hell do you want?" he growled over her head.

For a moment she wondered whom he spoke with, but decided she didn't care. Instead, she squeezed him around the waist and laid her head down upon his chest, listening to the thundering beat of his heart. *Must be Logan,* she thought. He'd never talk to a guest in that tone. At the thought of staying in his arms for a few more stolen moments, she hummed in the back of her throat.

"Don't you dare speak to me like that!" Mrs. Whitcomb's voice rang out high and loud through the ballroom.

Thrusting away from his warm arms, Ava turned to meet the icy glare of the Senator's wife. "Mrs. Whitcomb," she gasped. Her panicked gaze fluttered to the Senator's wife, already dressed in a long, red satin dress for her daughter's wedding. She elbowed Jaxon in the ribs, whispering to him, "Apologize."

He crossed his arms. "Hell, no. I'm not her monkey to order around."

Mrs. Whitcomb thrust a newspaper in front of Ava. She tapped the front page with the tip of her manicured claw. "This is disgusting. You're disgusting. The Senator can't associate with people of your ilk. He has a reputation and a daughter to protect. If the wedding wasn't today and all our guests weren't already at Twin Springs, I'd rip our contract to shreds."

Ava saw her family's future crashing down before her. In one fell swoop, she'd destroyed all the positive press Isabella had generated with the food critic. She must find a way to calm the enraged woman before her. She searched her mind for what to say, to do. Then her mind lit on an idea.

Immediately, she pushed the thought away. Fear buried the idea, choking and freezing her vocal cords. But, her family needed her, the Grand Dame needed her. Pushing back the bile creeping its way up her throat at the thought of what she must do, Ava replied loud and strong, "I'll do it."

Mrs. Whitcomb's face scrunched up in anger. "Do what? There's nothing you can say or do to change what you did. Who you are."

Desperate, she inched forward. "I'll sing. Sing for your daughter's wedding."

"Old bitty," Jaxon growled under his breath. "Let me see that." He grabbed the newspaper from Mrs. Whitcomb's hands.

She gasped with outrage and smoothed her platinum blonde hair back. "How dare you?"

Ignoring her, he opened the newspaper to the front page. There, in black and white, was a fuzzy but blown up picture of Ava pressed against the phone booth wall. A short, stocky, light haired man held her there. Out of context, the embrace appeared to be a lover's tryst. The corner of the newspaper balled in Jaxon's fists and he scanned the column.

Ava pulled on Jaxon's forearm, attempting to see what was featured on the front page.

Rolling the newspaper up, he honed in on the Senator's wife. "You believe this piece of trash? Miss Fairbanks was attacked. We have proof on our security tapes that she was dragged into the booth and assaulted."

He held the paper up and away from her prying hands as she tried to gain hold of it. "You don't want to see it, Ava. You don't want to read this filthy trash." His eyes hardened and focused on Mrs. Whitcomb. "Some people believe everything they read."

Her hands on his forearm, Ava looked deep into Jaxon's eyes and read the truth. She nodded, accepting his decision. Turning, she didn't realize the scarf around her neck had slipped and the bruises across her delicate throat showed.

At the sight, Mrs. Whitcomb's diamond laden hand covered her own throat, and she stuttered. "I had no idea. I just assumed that because it was in print…" her voice trailed off.

Gathering herself up, she addressed the Senator's wife, noting the woman's pale face now blended in with her light hair and her painted lips appeared garish in contrast. Ava felt for the woman. She laced her arm with hers, patted her arm reassuringly and guided her away from Jaxon's anger, for a detour around the ballroom. "How could you know? A simple misunderstanding."

"Yes," murmured Mrs. Whitcomb. "I—I, um, are you alright?"

"Of course, my dear." Ava dazzled her with a stage smile. "The show must go on, you know. Let me show you how everything's coming together."

Mrs. Whitcomb's eyes touched everywhere except the violence reflected on Ava's throat. "Thank you. You don't have to do it you know. I just feel terrible."

Realizing her bruises were visible, her normally smooth steps fumbled and she adjusted the scarf with her free hand. "Do what?"

Her eyes refused to meet Ava's. "Sing, sing for my daughter's wedding."

Ava's stomach fluttered and flipped, knowing what was expected of her. But to save her family's home, to save Twin Springs, to prove Director Terrence Hollingsworth had no power over her, she must sing. "Mrs. Whitcomb," said Ava, understanding it was time to return to the stage and face all her fears. Her chin lifted and she tossed her glorious hair. "It would be my pleasure."

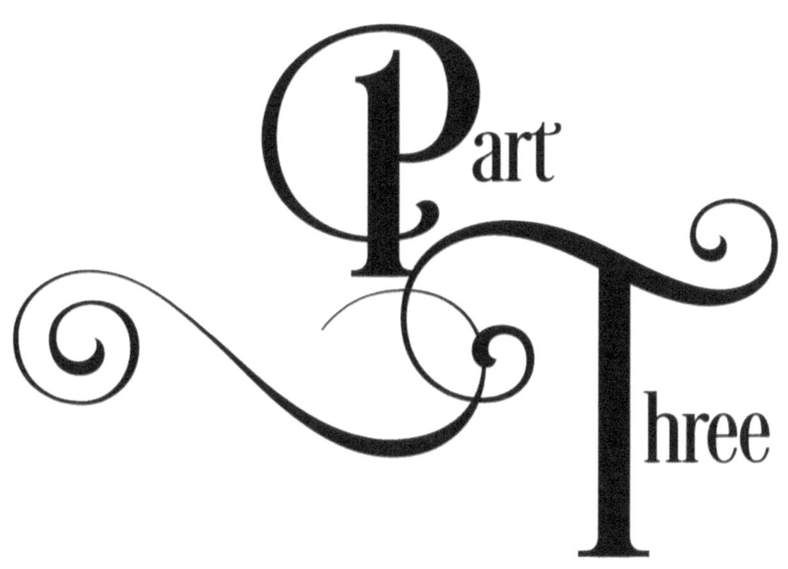
Part Three

CHAPTER FIFTY-SIX

*3*0 December 1928

Damn undercover revenuer is preventing me from moving my shine freely around the property at night. He's costing me money and money equals power. The son of a bitch thought he could hide right under my nose. But I know who he is—Guy Wolfe.

The General has no idea of what is happening. But I do. I know everything that goes on within Twin Springs. Lately, the revenuer's been sniffing around Ruby, giving her roses. The last couple days, the whole place has reeked of the damn flowers. I was just going to run him off but he dared to touch what's mine and now must die. I'll plan a little accident. After all, fire purifies the soul.

Lt. Porter

CHAPTER FIFTY-SEVEN

*J*axon moved to the middle of the dance floor, his arms crossed and feet spread, ready to come to Ava's aid if needed against the old biddy. Across the room, he spotted Logan with his hat dipped low over his face and a rolled up newspaper in his fist. Even with the heavy aroma of flowers, he could smell him coming closer.

Logan halted in front of his Army buddy. "Did you see this crap?" he thundered, before lowering his voice. Smacking the newspaper against his jeans, he paced in a semicircle around Jaxon. "This is bullshit," he hissed. "Complete bullshit."

Watching Ava weave her charms round the Senator's wife from the corner of his eye, Jaxon waived the old bitty's copy of the article at Logan before shoving it into the crook of his back. "We have proof this time and I have security footage of the bastard dragging Ava into the phone booths."

"No shit." Logan halted, pounding the paper against his open palm. "Who is it? Tell me you didn't already contact the Sheriff. I'd like some time alone with him first."

"Wouldn't we all," muttered Jaxon. "Can't see his face from the footage." He considered telling Logan that Ava knew who her attacker was. Perhaps he could help him extract the name out of her. Thinking for a moment, he discounted the idea. He didn't want to break the fragile thread of confidence she had in him. "Do you recognize him from the photo?"

Unrolling the newspaper, Logan studied the picture for a moment. He brought the paper up close to his face and pushed the brim of his baseball cap back to gain better light. "Damn it, no. But I stay pretty far away from the guests. Don't want to scare anyone off."

Wave after wave of guilt washed over Jaxon, drowning him. He gasped for air and for relief from the burden he carried, even for one moment. His voice rough, as if dragged over burning coals, he said, "I'm sorry, Woody." Rubbing his face with his palms, he added, "God, I'm sorry for the pain I've caused you."

Logan's stunned blue eyes clouded then darkened. "What the hell are you talking about?"

The words tumbled from him. "The explosion. Our last mission. Your burns. How I killed every other member of our team that day. How I almost killed you and left you mutilated for life. I'm sorry." He grabbed Logan by the arm. "I'm sorry."

Dumbfounded, Logan stared at his friend's pale face and the agony behind his eyes. "Did you plant that bomb?"

"What?" Jaxon shook his head. "Of course not."

"Did you push us to enter that building?"

Dragging his hands down his face, he answered, "No, but I should've been on the ground with you. I should've stopped you."

"That wasn't your job. Your job was to watch our backs. Lay down fire to cover us, if we needed to bug out quick."

Jaxon shook his head in denial. "I should've known it was a trap. My instincts were shit. I should've known that evil bitch lied."

Little by little, Logan's eyes cleared to a bright sky blue. "You know, I think about that day. A lot. In fact, I relive it almost nightly." He looked away, transporting himself back to the day his life changed. He could almost hear the creaking of the door as he opened it. He clenched his jaw, before taking a deep breath.

Shaking his head, again the fog cleared from his gaze. "Did it ever occur to you that she didn't lie? That she believed the intel she gave us and that's why your instincts were off? You couldn't tell she lied because she didn't. Someone else gave her false information and she passed it on to us as truth."

Shock waves rolled over Jaxon. Stumbling for a moment, he searched his memory and everything she said. She was so sure, and he was positive she was right. Every word out her mouth ringed with truth. "My God, you're right."

Logan thought about his last mission, the pain, the smell of burning flesh all around him. Now a part of him. "You know, Wolfeman, I'm damn glad you weren't in the building. Because if you were, I would've died that day too. And as miserable as this life is, at least it's something. If you didn't get off that rooftop as fast as you did and put the fire out that ate at my body, then dragged me to safety, I would be dead now.

"If you wouldn't have droned the overwhelming enemy force and radioed in for an emergency evac, I'd be dead. You and Doc were a pain in my ass at the hospital, pushing me, forcing me, willing me to live." He looked away, drawing in a cleansing breath. "Perhaps I needed to feel pain to atone for being such a jackass." A self-depreciating chuckle escaped him and their eyes met. "I don't blame you for my burns. I blame the fire, the explosion and the bastards who planted the bomb. That's who I blame."

The creaking became louder in Logan's head, reminding him of that door. The door of choice, that changed his life forever. If he hadn't opened that door. If he'd paused a moment longer. Again, the feeling of something not being right came over him. He looked up. The massive chandelier filling the center of the ceiling swayed ominously from side to side. Years of training took over, and he shouted, "Look out!"

Grabbing Jax up by the back of his t-shirt, he ran. The pain shooting through his leg meant nothing as he pulled Jaxon alongside of him before shoving him clear and diving over top of him to protect his back.

The chandelier fell to the floor. Exploding pieces of crystal and iron shrapnel shot out around them, destroying chairs and flower arrangements with its massive, iron arms.

Screams pierced the air but one voice rang out above the rest. "My daughter's wedding!"

Ava rushed over to Logan and Jaxon, picking her way through the rubble as she went. The men laid inches away from being crushed by one of the massive iron arms. She brushed shards of glass and crystal from each of them. "Are you alright?"

"I will be when Woody stops laying on top of me." Came Jaxon's muffled voice from below. "Are you that desperate for a woman?"

Logan rolled, brushing himself off as he stood. He canted the majority of his weight on his left leg and pushed the weakness of pain away. Aware of the employees and guests surrounding him, he scooped his hat up off the floor, shook it out and shoved it back on his head. "Who's the woman? Had to save your ass. Getting soft and your reflexes are shit."

Turning over onto his back, Jaxon was greeted by Ava's concern filled eyes. Her beautiful face floated above him and her gentle hands roamed his body, searching for injuries. Enjoying her ministrations, he laid back and forced a moan from his mouth. "You're right, Woody. I might need some help." He winked up at Ava. "Perhaps even some special TLC."

With a wirily twist of her lips, she surveyed the cocky grin on Jaxon's face before smacking him on the arm. "You're fine."

Mrs. Whitcomb came over, fanning herself with her hands as the many diamond rings on her fingers sparkled. "What are we going to do? The whole reason my daughter picked Twin Springs was because this room reminded her of the movie *Gone With The Wind*. It's all ruined now!"

"Now, now," tutted Ava. Quoting from *Gone with the Wind* in a heavy southern drawl, she declared "'I've always had a weakness for lost causes once they're really lost.'"

She broke off at Mrs. Whitcomb's glare and searched her mind for a line, a solution, something that would soothe the woman and save the wedding. Surveying the scene, she took in the large chandelier, resembling a dead octopus with all it's legs and arms bent and broken against the floor. "We have another chandelier," she whispered before her voice gained momentum and her body filled with hope. "We have another chandelier, more beautiful and elegant. One that puts that chandelier to shame."

Logan interrupted her, his disfigured brow rising. "What the hell are you talking about. We don't have another chandelier."

Jaxon stood up, dusted himself off and stared at Ava as if she'd lost her mind.

Her smile bright, she waved off Logan's and Jaxon's glares. "It will be perfect for your daughter's wedding. And his father," she jerked her thumb at Logan, "will find it for us. It must be here someplace, Twin Springs never throws anything away."

Stunned, the Senator's wife looked from Ava's face to Logan's and let out a blood curdling scream, drawing stares from everyone in the room. She covered her face with her hands and whispered from between her fingers, "What kind of a monster are you?"

Growling deep in his chest, Logan answered, "The kind of monster that is going to save your ass."

CHAPTER FIFTY-EIGHT

*R*eady and dressed for Kennedy's wedding, a silver evening dress whispered over Ava's skin in old Hollywood luxury. The satin folded and twisted around her torso, molding to her sexy curves and gliding over her hips before bowing at her feet. Crystals shimmered along the swell of her breasts, and the creamy white skin of her arms and neckline was bared. Except for a silver scarf. The gauzy material wrapped around her throat, hiding the evidence of violence, before pouring down her exposed back.

Her mind on the duties at hand, Ava twisted and tied the last of the red roses and white lilies on the wedding arch. She glanced over at Jaxon, June the florist and Diana as they recreated the floral arrangements for the end chairs of the walkway.

As a team, the employees and owners of Twin Springs worked to prepare the Crystal Ballroom for Kennedy's wedding. Logan and Dale, with two other maintenance employees, strained to hoist the newly found chandelier up into the air.

Surprised, her gaze flowed over Logan. His hair was wet from a shower and he had new clothes on. She understood that it wasn't worth arguing with him to not wear one of his ever present band t-shirts and jeans. Especially since his father never deviated from his own blue work shirt, white t-shirt and jeans. Some wars weren't worth fighting. At least Logan's clothes were clean. She watched as the men secured the chandelier in place, adding extra points of contact to ensure this one would never fall.

Once finished, she stood between Logan and his father. Together, they admired the results of the last few hours. The large, broken chandelier and smashed chairs were swept away and replaced. The white platform, backdropped by the line of French doors, dominated the room. Flowers lined the arched window panes above the French doors and along the edges of the stage. A white runner now ran from the stage, down the center isle and up towards the tall doors of the Crystal Ballroom. All awaited the grand entrance of the bride. June flitted around the ballroom, making last minute fixes to her floral arrangements.

With her elbow, she nudged Logan. "Amazing job," she said. "Where did you find the chandelier?"

"Dad found the frame in the crawl space under the breezeway of the west wing of the hotel. The crystals were more of a challenge. I found those in the dead space under the Grand Lobby elevator, packed up in velvet bags and placed in an old shipping trunk."

Tipping her head to the side, she lifted her eyes to meet his. "What made you look there of all places?"

Logan shrugged. "We decided to start low within the hotel and finish with the attics, since employees and maintenance are in and out of those areas more often than the crawl spaces." He shuffled his feet for a moment and his eyes didn't meet hers. "To be honest with you, I used to hide there and pretend those velvet bags were bags of treasure. I didn't put two and two together until I saw the crystals from the broken chandelier scattered all over the floor."

Ava's gaze swept the room. Sparkling white lights and crystals were artfully dispersed within the blooms. The crystals caught the light and cast prisms of color around the room. "Who thought of adding the broken chandelier's crystals to the flower displays? They add a magical feel to the room."

Dale harrumphed and scratched at his gray hair, "Maddy of course."

Smiling to herself, Ava murmured, "Of course. Do you know why the chandelier fell?"

Dale's toothpick snapped between his fingers. He tucked the pieces away and searched the area around him for eavesdroppers. His gentle blue eyes met Ava's. "Someone cut away the supportin' tethers. The weight of the chandelier was held on only by the electric wires. The whole thing could'a easily come down on top of the guests and weddin' party during the ceremony."

Guests began filtering in and filling the seats. They gasped and pointed around the ballroom, speaking to each other in muted tones. The baby grand piano started playing in the background. As more guests arrived and the room filled up, Logan faded into the background and slipped away.

The wedding passed like a dream. The music played, backdropping the approach of the bride. Dripping in crystals and lace, Kennedy performed the time honored stroll with her father towards her awaiting groom.

With each moment, Ava's heart beat faster. She rubbed her suddenly moist palms on the waist of her dress and dreaded taking the stage to sing.

Vows were spoken and the newly married couple walked down the aisle as one. While pictures were snapped of the bridal party at pre-designated settings around Twin Springs, an army of employees in black suits and crisp white shirts treated their guests with hors d'oeuvres. As if by magic, the chairs were dispersed and placed around the circular tables dotting the perimeter of the room. Once the bridal party returned, toasts were made, dinner served and Isabella's elegant seven tier cake cut.

Steadily the hands of time moved forward. Ava's breaths came short and quick in her chest. She placed her hand over her chest and tried to breath. She couldn't seem to fill her lungs with air. Closing her eyes, she steadied herself and purposely breathed in and out to calm her racing heart. The moment approached for the father daughter dance. Noting her cue, Ava stepped up on the stage. Her heart in her throat, she surveyed the audience.

Looking official and in charge in her Executive Chef jacket, Isabella pressed a mike into her sister's cold hand. Concern lining the corners of her eyes, she asked, "Are you sure you want to do this?"

Under the lights, Ava's silver dress shimmered and came alive. But she hesitated. Her eyes, overly bright, darted around the room and she half turned to run. She looked down at the hopeful eyes of the awaiting audience.

Then their energy touched hers and a spark awakened within her, a yearning, a need. Their passion ignited the embers within her soul and warmth spread through her limbs, until she literally sparkled on stage. Lifting her shoulders up and back, she tossed her glossy, jet black hair back with a shake of her head. Ava Fairbanks once again graced center stage. This time, she portrayed a new and exciting leading lady. Ava played the role of herself.

Glittering lights surrounded her and a sultry smile spread across her face, welcoming all into her magical world. She looked down at the bride's fresh, expectant, upturned face, full of future promises and possibilities and winked.

Filling her lungs with air, she pierced the silence with the first note. Through her thick black lashes, she watched the bride flow into her father's waiting arms. Closing her eyes to the outside world, the song and Ava became one, breathed as one. As she sang, AVA, the fake facade the audience had adored, faded away. Replaced by the woman, Ava Fairbanks. A much brighter and brilliant star.

The power of her ballad seeped over the guests, lifting their hearts and souls with the beauty of the melody. Head thrown back, she dug deep and released the final note, holding it until the sound lit the room with its purity. Leisurely, her arms settled to her sides and she looked out over the audience, towards Kennedy and her father. Tears rolled freely down the flawless beauty of the bride's face.

From her peripheral vision, Ava discerned a movement stage left. Fear froze her and time stood still. Ever so slowly, she turned her head and her chin trembled.

For a moment, she saw Ashlee standing there, her hair dripping with water, her lips moving soundlessly and the silver gun held to her temple. Her sight blurred and her legs wobbled. Mere heartbeats felt like hours, until her sight cleared.

Through the lifting mist Jaxon stood at the edge of the stage, handsome in a black tux. Her guy. His golden eyes glowed up at her. A feeling of rightness and love seeped into her body. No composer, song or part could portray the extraordinary depth of her love for Jaxon Wolfe.

The ballroom exploded with applause and Kennedy rushed up onto the stage, enveloping Ava within her excited embrace. "Thank you. I will never forget this. You gave me a beautiful wedding, more than I ever expected or dreamed of. Thank you."

Still on stage, guests approached her one by one. Some blinking back tears but all gushing over her performance. Others, unable to speak, just squeezed her hands and nodded their appreciation. She thanked them all for their kind words and they trickled back to enjoy the wedding festivities, until only her family remained.

Isabella hugged her tight. "Everything's a resounding success. Your singing at the end was magnificent. Two mothers want to move their daughters' upcoming weddings to Twin Springs."

A deep satisfaction filled Ava. The triumph within her spread across her face and she scanned the ballroom, noting the bride's and groom's shining faces and the delight of the parents.

She'd created this magic. She didn't need a director to guide her, a fake backdrop to perform from or lines from someone else's head to be placed in her mouth. Here, she created magic full of love, promise and hope. From which, new beginnings would blossom and grow.

Interrupting her musings, Isabella asked, "How do you feel about planning a wedding for New Year's Eve? I know there isn't much time, but Theo and I have decided not to wait any longer. It's time to make his and Maddy's addition to our family official."

Eyes gleaming with joy, Ava hugged her sister tight. Looking over her blonde head, her eyes met Jaxon's. "I couldn't imagine anyone's wedding that I would rather plan than yours and Theo's."

CHAPTER FIFTY-NINE

The wedding party danced well into the night. In her silver dress, Ava worked the room and ensured every bridal guest enjoyed themself. They continued to gush over her performance and asked if she would always sing for weddings at Twin Springs. She thanked everyone for their warm words, parroting over and over, that the policy on her singings services at Twin Springs was yet to be determined.

With a nod from Ava, Isabella herded the remaining guests into the Grand Lobby. Ava peeled the bride from her groom's arms. She positioned Kennedy in the center of the west balcony high above the awaiting guests.

Female guests, with hopeful visions of their own weddings clouding their gazes, stood arms stretched and vied for prime positions in the Lobby below. Stepping back and allowing the bride her spotlight, flashbulbs lit up the room as the bride's bouquet sailed through the air. A woman squealed with excitement. Kennedy leaned over the balcony, her face aglow with delighted laughter, just as a flash of light captured the moment on film, freezing the bride in time. The Senator's daughter, a perfect picture of white satin and lace, would grace the cover of *Today's Bride Magazine*.

Adjusting the gauzy scarf around her neck, Ava sighed with

relief. The guests mingled and enjoyed the open bar promise at Still Waters Bar & Grill.

Meanwhile, she stood in the middle of the Crystal Ballroom. Her cheeks flushed with color as she surveyed the aftermath of the bride's dream. She did it! She pulled off her greatest performance. Award winning Broadway star Ava Fairbanks premiered as, herself.

She lovingly surveyed the dance floor, muted and scuffed from time, the great white pillars and the crystal chandelier once again presiding in its place of honor. "This is where I belong," she murmured to herself. Standing up a little straighter, she projected her voice and shouted, "This is where I belong!"

Her voice echoing back to her, Ava walked to the middle of the dance floor, cast her arms wide and spun in a circle until her breath came fast within her chest. Her musical laughter filled the air and she lowered herself to the dance floor, lying back, staring up at the beautiful chandelier. She admired the rainbow of colors it cast around the room. The pressure of the day eased from her body. The fragrance of roses floated over her and slowly her lids fluttered closed.

. . .In the distance the low moan of a sax rolled across the Crystal Ballroom's dance floor, washing over her, muting the angry tirade of words the General'd set down earlier and that still rang within Ruby's ears.

As soon as she'd returned from the stables, the Lieutenant was waiting for her, keeping sentry in the Grand Lobby before escorting her directly to the General's office. Her cheeks burned from her father's bellowing voice and harsh reprimands. His voice reverberated off the walls, yelling about her conduct, spending time with the chauffeur, driving around with the chauffeur. The Lieutenant stood in the corner of the room with a sneer on his lips, soaking in her humiliation and taking pleasure in her set down.

Remembering the incident, embarrassment flushed the smooth skin of her neck. Ruby gracefully rose from the white wicker chair she lounged in, her rose scented perfume trailing along behind her. She'd show them. Show them all that they couldn't cage her.

Admiring her reflection within her compact, she touched up the bow of her deep red lips and adjusted the red rose tucked behind her ear. Through the reflection in her compact, she regarded the disapproving, grim glances of the older generation sitting on the fringes and sipping their bland tea. Their mantra of "Lips that touch liquor shall not touch ours," was definitely not Ruby's.

The band in full swing, she snapped the compact closed and snagged a cup of punch. Sipping the punch she'd ordered spiked, her hips rocked and her body kept time to the beat of the music. "Now, this is a Ladies Tea Party."

Sworn to secrecy about how she found the liquor, she slammed back the final drop and spotted her prey. Tapping his felt hat against his leg, Guy appeared to have just rushed into the ballroom. Removing his buff colored duster and draping the jacket over his arm, he leaned back against one of the white pillars. She took in his relaxed frame, looking snappy in his slacks, white shirt and suspenders. She refilled her cup and sauntered towards him, thinking how sexy suspenders had suddenly become.

Stepping close, much closer than was proper, Ruby looked up at Guy from beneath her darkened lashes. "The General pitched a fit about my outing with you." She pouted her lips, running her fingertips along the front of his chest, before laying her palm flat against his beating heart. "I'm ready for my driving lesson."

"I bet you are," Guy murmured, removing the small crystal glass from her hand. Raising it to his nose, he sniffed the punch before taking a drink. "Where did you get the shine from?"

She spun around, the beads on her midnight black gown splaying out around her slender frame and catching the light with her movements. Leaning back against him, she surveyed the fevered pitch of the young ladies dancing around the floor. "What do you care? Besides, you aren't even supposed to be here. This is a Ladies Tea Party."

Canting one hip up, Ruby raised her palms and flicked her fingers to the quickened beat. Her bottom brushed suggestively against him.

Smothering a groan, he reached out to snatch her close.

Twirling away and out of reach, Ruby's lush lips spread into a sexy smile. She raised her index finger and waggled it at him, mouthing the words "no, no," in his direction. The air rang with her laughter and she danced into the mix of women.

Enjoying the frenzied beat, she watched Guy depart the ballroom. Without his presence, the music dimmed around her. Feeling lonely and empty, she searched the blank faces of the elite. Suddenly, the thrill of defying her father seemed tainted and foolish.

Rough fingers bit into her arm. Gasping with pain, Ruby pulled to release the hold and looked up into the Lieutenant's cold blue eyes. He dragged her up against his body and she gagged on the smell of sweat and damp wool.

"Foolish girl," he spat, whispering down into her ear. The crowded room swirled around them and the sticky sweet smell of his breath nauseated her. "The General wants you. But before I deliver you to him, where did you find the moonshine to supply your little tea party?" His fingers tightened. "Have you been snooping where you shouldn't?" With his words, he gave her a little shake.

Digging in her heels, she stared coldly at the Lieutenant. "I don't know why you men care where I found my shine. When you have your own liquor flowing in the Officers Hall."

"Don't futz around with me, Ruby," the Lieutenant hissed. "Who else is asking about the moonshine?" He shook her, spittle spraying her face. "Was it the revenuer? Tell me now!"

Not caring about the guests swarming around the Crystal Ballroom, Ruby gathered a deep breath and used her gift, her voice. She shouted at the top of her lungs, "Take your mitts off me!"...

As if burned, Jaxon released Ava's arm. "Whoa, Ava. I'm sorry. I thought you were sleepwalking."

Ava shook her head and tried to orient herself. The curtain of fog lifted from her eyes. She was still in the Crystal Ballroom but next to the door. "I," she stammered. "I don't know. Don't understand." The decade of the past and present blended before her eyes. "The Lieutenant had my arm. He squeezed it and wouldn't let go. He wanted to know where the moonshine came from."

Smoothing back her hair, Jaxon noted the pallor of her face and the wild glint to her eyes. "You took a hard knock on the head yesterday."

"It's not the knock. It's Ruby." Frustrated, she rubbed her face with her hands, before clenching her hands into fists. "I've had enough. I'll not be anyone's pawn or plaything, damn it." Her voice rose with anger, with determination. "I'm me, Ava Fairbanks. This is my time to shine. You hear me Ruby?"

Her voice vibrated through the room and bounced back at her with a resounding roar. She laced her fingers within Jaxon's, drawing from his strength, before her voice softened. Shaking her head, she addressed the room. "No more using me. No more taking over my body. You don't need to. I'll find you. I promise."

CHAPTER SIXTY

*E*arly the next morning, Jaxon woke with visions a brilliant, circular diamond surrounded with red rubies clustered into the petals of flowers in his mind. He rubbed his eyes with his knuckles and gathered Ava's soft body close within the crook of his shoulder. Their bodies were still intertwined from lovemaking.

He grunted with approval at the deep sleep she enjoyed. What would he do with this beautiful bird? She called to him with her song, her body, her effervescent spirit. When she sang, he peered deep within her and touched her soul with his. When he was with her, she confused the hell out of him but he felt whole. *Right, damn it.*

And the ballad she sang each time they made love…he pulled her closer and enjoyed her soft breasts against his hard body. Her song rose and fell with their lovemaking, marking the time of their journey together. The melody within her snared him, heart, body and soul. It weaved its magic around them. He barely prevented himself from begging like a hungry audience for another song and another second, another minute with her. It had never been this way with any other woman.

Deep down, he realized some people spent their lifetime searching for the connection they shared. Some never found it and some only for a fleeting moment in time. Those who discovered it, needed to grab it with both hands, before it slipped away, stolen by the cruelty of life.

His cellphone on the bedside table buzzed and danced across the polished wood. Reaching out, he snared the phone and raised it to this ear. Mumbling under his breath, "Standby."

Sighing with reluctance, he brushed a kiss across Ava's forehead and untangled himself from their embrace. He pulled on his tan pants and a black t-shirt before slipping out into the hall. "Lee, what do you have?"

His cousin's voice rumbled over the phone. "Sleeping in Jax? Have you completely lost it out there? What is in the water at Twin Springs anyway?"

Jaxon growled deep in his throat, "Shut up, just tell me what you've got."

"Prima donna," Lee grumbled back under his breath. "Maybe I need to get back out in the field and not wait on your every whim back here."

He chuckled under his breath. "You know the phrase, those who can't, teach. Well, in our field, those who can't, run the data. After all, it takes a special breed of man, Lee."

"Kiss my ass," muttered his cousin. "You're special alright."

Listening to Lee grumble, Jaxon strode through the Grand Lobby. He nodded at the guests, noting that some of the wedding party appeared a little green around the gills from last night. Zipping around the corner, he pulled his office door closed, swung his lean body down onto the rolling chair and leaned back. Subconsciously, his eyes filtered through the images on the screens before him. "Is that why you called me? To bitch? I was snuggled up to a warm woman until your call came through. So report or let me get back to her."

"You're truly screwed, Jax. Lost all sense of mission focus."

He thought about his cousin's statement, weighing the validity and consequences of falling in love with Ava Fairbanks, the woman of a million faces. He decided she was worth it. "That's right and I don't give a damn. While you're soaking your hurt feelings about not being out in the field, I need you to buy something for me and have it overnighted out here."

The image he woke to floated through his mind. "I need a ring. Wedding set. Platinum. I'm guessing size 6. I want the engagement ring a simple platinum band with a round two carat diamond. Quality. I want the wedding band to be three rings melded in the back, with rows of small diamonds along the front. Each with a small flower made out of red rubies. Have it so that the flowers curve around the center diamond when the engagement ring is slipped inside of the wedding band. Call in all our favors and get it to me ASAP. Got it?"

Jaxon heard his cousin's chair squeaking as he moved around in it. For once, silence filled the other end of the line. "Jeez, fine Jax. I'll take care of it. If you don't mind, can we veer off your love life and back to the mission at hand? Hope you are ready for the load of shit you'll need to dig out of."

Feeling like a man on top of the world, Jaxon grinned from ear to ear. "Hit me with it."

"Fine," Lee's teeth snapped together with an audible click. "Pull your head out of the damn clouds and listen. Got info on the reporter. You're never going to believe this. Not a man, a woman. Mac Mills is her pen name. She's a friend of Ashlee Hollingsworth. The woman who shot herself in the head on stage next to Ava."

Jaxon swung forward, his boots scrapping off the table before they hit the ground with a thud. "What's her real name?"

"Mackenzie Mills. I'm shooting you a picture of her."

Holding the phone away from his ear, Jaxon stared down into the honey brown eyes of Sheela. Her hair not black but a rich chestnut, falling in waves around her delicate features. The face of a liar and spy.

His nostrils flared and rage pumped through him, picking up steam and rolling into a ball of fire. He stared down at the beautiful face that he'd once thought of as plain. Tamping down the flames for later, he clicked over and returned to the call.

"Mackenzie Mills is one of the Front Desk clerks. She works side by side with Ava on a daily basis."

"Do you think she is the one sabotaging Twin Springs?"

"A possibility." He bit back the anger. "She definitely sabotaged Ava's reputation." He explained what happened in the phone booth.

"No shit. There is more. I tried, sincerely I tried, but JD discovered that I was sniffing around and asking about her past. Shit, you should have seen the firestorm she blew through here when she found out the Geezers had kept a file on her. She had no idea. Our fathers are pissed their secret is out and she wants to know why I wanted the file in the first place."

Jaxon thought of the red head in the portrait and her resemblance to his sister. "I'm not ready for her to know anything about what's going on out here. I don't understand myself how she fits into the puzzle. Keep stalling. Don't let her know it's me that wanted the file. I don't care what lame ass excuse you give her and the Geezers."

"That's too damn bad. She pitched a fit, pulled her knife and I folded like a cheap two dollar bill. I told her it was you. She wants to know why you are investigating her background. Not only that, the Geezer's want to know, too."

"Well, who's the ninety day wonder now, Lee?"

CHAPTER SIXTY-ONE

*A*va mumbled in her sleep. Unconsciously, her naked body reached out beside her for Jaxon's strength and warmth. Still half asleep, her brow furrowed at the loss. Stealthily, the silver smoke rose and engulfed her sleeping form.

. . ."*Am I ready yet?*" *Emma tapped her satin covered toe aching to catch one peek of herself in Ruby's vanity mirror. Wearing her tea gown, she was supposed to be resting before dressing for the New Year's Eve celebration. Not having a lesson in makeup from Ruby.*

"Hold your horses," muttered Ruby. The iridescent bugle beads and sparkling sequins covering her ravishing red dress shimmered as she moved. Her teeth clenched a cigarette holder as she painted her little sister's lips red. "He will think you're the cat's meow when he sees you." She leaned back, puffing on the end of the long black holder, before releasing smoke high into the air above her sister's head.

She spun Emma around on the stool of her dressing table and let her spy herself for the first time. Forgetting about her cigarette, Ruby reveled in her sister's awe struck face and hummed with satisfaction.

Emma twirled about in a flurry of pink satin and lace and hugged Ruby. Neither sister noticed that the cigarette had fallen from the holder and onto the carpet at their feet.

"It's me, but not me," gasped Emma, once again touching her face and gazing at herself.

"That's not all, toots." Ruby brought out a large, square box from her dressing area. From mid-thigh down, the fringe on her dress swayed with her movements and drew the eye down to her gorgeous legs. Opening the lid, she withdrew another dress in flesh colored chiffon from the folds of the tissues.

"Ooh," Emma squealed in response, reaching out to hug the cloud of fabric.

Dancing away with the dress held high in the air, Ruby sternly addressed her sister. "Now do what I tell you. Take this dress into the privy and change. But," she said drawing out the word. "No girdle, no bra and no panties. None of your smalls." Her lips spread into a knowing smile. "This will be a night he'll never forget."

Emma nibbled her bottom lip between her teeth. "Goodness, are you sure? Nothing?"

"Nothing." With one hand on her hip and the long holder up and to the side, she struck a pose. Her sister was such a ninny. A worrier. She brought the cigarette holder to her lips, "Takes a real woman to lead her along the way," she mumbled, taking a long drag for effect before answering her sister.

Ruby dragged on the holder but the nicotine smoke eluded her. She sucked harder, without avail. Thinking that the holder was clogged or something, she abandoned her pose and inspected. Only then did she notice the missing cigarette. Panicked, she scanned the floor, noticing a wisp of smoke and a budding flame emerging from the Persian carpet.

Grabbing a flower vase, she dumped the contents, roses and all to smother the flame.

"Good night nurse," gasped Emma, clutching the dress to her chest. "You must hold that thing right."

Waiving her sister off, Ruby laughed. "Nothing can stop me. You have to take what you want in life. Now go change. You and Jean Claude can live tonight to its fullest. Don't let the General tell you what to do. Live Emma! Live your life," she repeated, pushing her sister to change.

Ruby surveyed herself in the etched mirror. She wound her now *signature, red silk scarf about her neck before holding up a hand mirror to survey the ruby and diamond incrusted head band tucked within her hair. A Christmas gift from her father, she made sure the black ribbons holding it in her hair were tied tight. Her eyes twinkling, she spoke to her reflection, "It's December 31st, New Year's Eve. Tonight, you will sing on stage in the ballroom and dazzle them all. Tonight, you will shine."*

Twirling around in order to survey her emerging sister, Ruby let out a wolf whistle. The pale fabric gave the illusion of nude skin and taunted the imagination. "He won't last the night. You look smashing. Here's the plan. Put in an appearance at the celebration tonight, then escape to meet him. I'll cover for you and waylay anyone from finding you." Holding her away from her, she raised an eyebrow and looked her directly in the eye. "Did you do as I said?" She stood back, watching Emma's body flow freely under the floating dress and realized the answer before her sister said a word.

Covering her reddened cheeks with her hands, Emma protested. "I can't go out like this. I jiggle as I walk. Everyone will know."

The bells of Ruby's laughter rang through the room. "That's the point, dearest. He'll want to strip you down to see for himself. To see if his eyes were telling the truth to his hungry body."

Fiddling with her emerald necklace, Emma exclaimed, "I'm not like you. I'm not brave. I can't."

Releasing an exasperated sigh, she thought for a second before grabbing one of her evening coats from her dressing room. She wrapped her sister within a black satin coat and pulled the red fox trim up against her chin, hiding the possibility of forbidden body movements. Bending, she grasped her by the shoulders and peered deep into her eyes. "Remove the coat before you see him. You are brave Emma. When it matters, you are the bravest girl I know. You can do this." She smiled reassuringly and hugged her sister for encouragement.

From the dressing room, she withdrew another evening coat for herself, in ruby red. Cocooning herself in the panne velvet coat, she covered her own dress, before asking her sister, "Are you ready?"

Emma's green eyes glittered with excitement. "It's so decadent."

"Be brave," admonished Ruby.

Emma released all her pent up dreams within one word, "Yes."

Hand in hand, they rode the private elevator from the Tower to the party waiting below. Within the elevator, Ruby glanced at her reflection in the mirrors inlaid within the paneled walls. Hidden beneath her coat, hundreds of sparkling beads hung from her red dress. Her eyes were coal lined and smoky. Sexy. Her lips and fingers tipped in blood red. Her midnight black hair laid sharp against her jawline, only held back at the temples by her diamond and ruby encrusted headband. The clutch of rubies formed roses at her temple and lounged in a bed of diamond leaves. The opposite side of the headband, she'd embellished with a spectacular, pure white ostrich feather. The plume reached high above her head, almost touching the stars. Her costume was complete.

Turning to tame her greatest conquest, an audience, Ruby exited the elevator. She felt confident and cocky. Each of her steps rocked with a vampish roll of her hips and drew everyone's attention to the sway of her body.

Emma trailed behind and attempted to mimic her older sister's confidence, but failed miserably.

In the Grand Lobby, Ruby paused. There were three different entrances for her to choose from. The Ladies Entrance, the Couples Entrance, and the Men's Entrance off the Officers Hall. She wanted more than anything to strut through the Men's Entrance but she glanced over at Emma. For her, she would play it safe and chose the Ladies Entrance.

The music entwined its way through the dancers and billowed from the ballroom out into the slate floored atrium of the Ladies Retiring Room. The Rockwell sisters glided through the tall doors of the Ladies Entrance to the Crystal Ballroom. "Mingle with the guests," she whispered to her sister. "When I start singing, slip away. Believe me, no one will notice you leaving." Her laughter sparkled like the finest crystals.

Taking her time, Ruby worked one side of the room, greeting guests. Her sister eked around the other side with her eyes downcast and her nervous hands tugging under the evening coat at the fabric of her dress.

Flirting with man after man, Ruby left a trail of broken hearts in her wake while she searched for him. Even though he didn't belong with the cultured masses, she yearned, hoped for him to see her in her finery. She wanted him to hear her sing for the first time on stage and in front of an audience. Keeping an eye on her sister, she noticed Emma blossoming under the attention of the males. Even braving the dance floor a time or two, while clutching at the fur collar. She glanced up at the ticking clock. It was time. Time to give her sister the future she desired, and deserved.

Ruby winked at the man before her, his graying hair, pouching stomach and hunched shoulders. The same man her father wanted her to marry. It was also time for her to start living her dream too. Pressing her punch glass into Widower Henderson's hand, she asked in a low, sultry voice, "Will you hold this for me, dearest?"

She laughed delightedly, when the retired soldier stammered and baulked at her interrupting him mid-sentence of his war story. Without a backward thought, she sashayed away. Her hips kept time to the beat of the jazz song playing in her head and washed out the slow tenor of the waltz flowing through the air.

Moving to the right edge of the stage, she gave the pre-designated wave to the band leader, signaling the band to end the set. The room quieted and all eyes turned. Taking the stage, Ruby didn't fiddle or blush. She shone like the North Star in the nighttime sky.

She noticed the bushy raised eyebrows of her future husband, and allowed a generous sensual smile to spread across her face when the deep whine of the sax pierced the air. She dropped her coat and the lights of the crystal chandelier sparkled off the beads of her dress.

Ignoring the gasp of the crowd, her dark lashes fluttered closed and laid against her creamy white skin. The music sunk into her body, until they swayed as one. Raising her arms out before her, Ruby caressed the audience with her voice, releasing note after note that was trapped within her soul.

The fringe of her dress lapped against her thighs. Her voice low, she embraced the audience, entrancing them and bringing them closer. Until, they pressed against the edge of the stage, hovering and bowing at her feet. Every time she breathed in to release another note, they leaned forward, yearning for more. At last, she released all her bottled up passions and desires in a fury of falsettos, and ended on a high note. She'd stripped herself bare before them with her song, wringing tears from the most hardened souls within the room. She lifted her lashes and surveyed the crowd thundering with applause. Everyone, except her father and future suitor.

The edges of the room gilded gold before her sight. Flashing a brilliant smile to the crowd, she whispered, "Thank you," and exited the stage to her father's fury.

"What the hell do you think you are doing?" his chipped words broke out from behind the smile he presented to the guests. With a hand at Ruby's back, he escorted her away from the lime light and to a solitary corner. "First the shine at the Ladies Tea Party, and now this. Captain Henderson called off."

A smug smile curled her painted lips. "Good," she responded. "Splendid, in fact."

"Splendid?" roared the General, his military metals clanging against each other on the lapel of his black tux before he hushed himself.

She peered past the General's mock uniform sleeve to Everett, her sister's husband. He paced behind her father, a worried expression on his face, tugging at his plaid bowtie. Not dressed for the celebration, his trousers, suspenders, plain shirt and shoes were splattered with drippings of oil paint.

"It's almost time, sir." Everett glanced up to the ticking hands of the clock. "Our discussion will have to wait until tomorrow. Her time is coming."

"Yes, yes." The General waived him off with a flick of his hand. "No place for a husband anyway. Just wait in the Officers Hall like a real man."

Everett's eyes lit up and he pushed his rounded glasses back up to the bridge of his nose, but he turned on his heel without replying.

"Well, it seems as if he might have a backbone after all. I should go and be with my sister."

"Negative." The General glanced around. "I'm sure Emma is with her. Besides, she has her maid there to assist. You're a disgrace. Singing on stage like a common trollop. You, Ruby, are a bad influence. Not only on yourself, but also on your sisters. I'll not have you influencing another generation. It is time for you to marry. Since you have scared away the *men I've picked for you, you'll have to settle for what is left. I think it is time for me to give in to the Lieutenant's request. I'll let him know later tonight that I've accepted his offer of marriage to you. I was going to have him marry Emma but she's too soft. You need someone strong to keep you in line and your head out of the clouds. Perhaps, through him, you'll learn discipline, manners and obedience. I don't want to see you again tonight. In fact, I don't want you to be around your sisters for the rest of the night. You didn't think I'd realize that Emma's painted face, this evening, was due to your tutelage? Ruby Lynn Rockwell, I'm ashamed of you. I'm thankful your mother did not live to see the day her daughter paraded herself on stage." Dismissing her, the General turned to join the guests.*

Ruby looked around the ballroom. The covert glances of younger ladies, the usual disapproving glances from the older generation and the outright blatant stares from the gentlemen guests. The gilded feeling from her performance felt tainted, tarnished, and left a repulsive metallic taste in her mouth. Where she'd once felt joy and sense of belonging, she now felt dirty and foul.

She glimpsed her reflection in the mirrored doors of the Theatre. The sparkling beads hung listlessly from her once vibrant dress. Her eyes were coal lined and smoky, but no longer sexy. They were lost. Her lips and fingers tipped in blood red appeared garish and cheap. The spectacular ostrich feather hung dejected to her shoulder. Tugging the feather free, she tossed it to the ground and watched the guests' feet trotting upon its proud head, until they ripped it to shreds.

Grabbed by the hand, she was pulled from her musings by a handsome man with a pencil mustache and slicked back ebony hair. She forced a laugh and searched for her earlier exuberance. Feeling dejected, she brushed him off with a smile. Song after song flowed through the room and she faded into the background of the crowd.

Later, leaning back against the mirrored doors, she observed the General as he claimed the stage. He waived one beefy hand, while holding a swaddled baby in the crook of his other arm. Ame's quiet husband followed behind, standing back in the General's shadow.

Speaking into the crowd, her father's voice boomed off the walls of the ballroom. He held his newly born grandson up for all the guests to view. "Ladies and gentlemen, may I present my grandson. The newest addition to the Rockwell line."

The General's delight with finally having a male heir was clearly evident. "Let the Champagne flow," he announced.

With those four words, prohibited champagne coursed through the ballroom to celebrate the birth of her sister's male offspring. The unfairness left a bitter taste in Ruby's mouth. "Men with their privileges, make their own rules, live their lives any way they want," she grumbled.

She just wanted a piece of that glory, of that freedom. Looking within herself, she searched for her earlier confidence. Finding a tiny nugget, she cast a sultry smile on her lips and tossed her slender shoulders back. This wouldn't do. She must find a way to prove the General wrong and fulfill her dream.

Turning her back on the spectacle of her father, Ruby walked away from the doors of the Theatre with a gentle sway to her hips. The fringe whispered against her thighs and she searched for her next conquest. Someone to dissuade her father from marrying her to the Lieutenant. Anyone who would take her away from Twin Springs and out into the world. Where she could finally feel free. Her tongue wet her lips and she scanned the room.

There he was, the one who allowed her to be herself. Gilded light filtered the room around him and he leaned nonchalantly against a pillar. His black hair not slicked back and restrained like the rest of the men, but free and curling around his ears.

Guy's eyes sparkled with amusement and he tipped his Champagne glass at her.

Was he mocking her? Did he also think she'd disgraced herself on stage? Fury burned hot within her but her lips curved with a welcoming smile. With a feline grace, she swayed towards him, eyelids dropped, lips parted.

Entranced by her appearance, his jaw slacked and his gaze locked with hers.

She slid her hand up the front of his black tux and laid her palm over the unsteady tattoo of his heart. His hand tipped and they both jumped back when he spilled his drink down between them and onto the shine of his shoes.

Ruby purred, "Having problems holding your liquor, dearest?"

A growl sounded in the back of his throat. His hand snaked out, entwining his fingers into her hair at the base of her neck, and he pulled her lips to his and branded her with his kiss.

Fire filled her belly and reached up to meet his flame. "Meet me in the stables," she whispered against his lips.

Around them, everyone celebrated the birth of the new heir and the coming of the New Year. Their hopes and dreams sparked alive with each sip. . .

Ava woke in the Crystal Ballroom, her arms circled around a pillar and holding its cylinder body tight within her embrace. Three young boys snickered at her as she lustily kissed the pillar. Peeling her lips away, she groaned under her breath and released her hold. She peeked down at her body, thankful that she was not nude as she'd last remembered. Instead, she was dressed in a crimson, skintight slip of a dress, complete with matching pumps and scarf draped around her neck.

Tossing her black hair back, she moved away from the pillar and addressed the gawking boys. "Haven't you ever practiced kissing before?"

Their cheeks flamed and they stared at their feet.

"Pillars are better practice partners than pillows." She winked at them and quickly strode from the room.

The three boys conferred in a tight circle, before nudging one out of their group towards the pillar. Hesitant the boy pushed his blond hair up and out of his eyes. He inched up to the pillar, shooting looks back at his buddies. Pushed onward by their nods, he encircled the towering pillar with his puny adolescent arms and pressed his lips to the cold, painted surface. Only to have his efforts mocked by the howling laughter of his friends ringing in his ears.

CHAPTER SIXTY-TWO

Ava emerged from the Crystal Ballroom, the boys' giggles and hoots ringing out behind her. Planted directly in front of her, holding a newspaper, was Maddy.

Dressed to work at the Front Desk in her black pencil skirt and white collared shirt, Maddy demanded, "Are those boys laughing at you?" her gray eyes flashed like bolts of lightning.

A throaty chuckle escaped Ava's lips. "Honey, the day I can't handle a man, let alone a clutch of boys, is the day I die."

The teenager gave one last look at the door, before holding the newspaper up before Ava. "You have to see this."

"I am done with reviews and with newspapers." The dream fresh in her mind, she rebelled against the unfairness of how Ruby wasn't allowed to follow her dream. This wasn't 1928 and she wasn't Ruby. But Ava Fairbanks and she'd never be a victim again. She wouldn't play any more roles. She would just be herself.

Yesterday, she'd pulled off the wedding of Senator Whitcomb's daughter with dignity and grace. She'd proven to everyone that she was more than just a pretty face. This was a new day. She thought of Jaxon and the possibility of a life with him. Somehow, she'd come to mean as much to him as the names tattooed on his inner arm.

Nothing she loved would be pushed aside ever again. She was not going to abandon anyone. Not Ruby, not Jaxon, not Logan and not even her bird. Twin Springs was their home and no one would chase them away or prevent them from coming home.

Ace deserved to come home to a place where he was safe and appreciated. People didn't understand her bird and even though Theo said no to Ace living in Twin Springs, she'd deal with him. She kissed Maddy on the cheek. "You may toss that garbage in the trash. Even better, use the newspaper to line Ace's cage because he is coming home!"

Clutching the newspaper to her chest, Maddy asked, "Ace is coming home?"

"I'm coming to find you, Ruby," whispered Ava. "The stables, on New Year's Eve, that is the last place I know you went. When I get there, I know you will lead me the rest of the way to find you."

Focusing back on Maddy, she replied. "Yes, Ace is coming home. Then, I'm going to go the stables and find out what happened to Ruby."

CHAPTER SIXTY-THREE

*S*tuffing her laptop and notes into her blue backpack, Mackenzie glanced around the tiny attic room that served as her office while at Twin Springs. A broken wingback chair from the Grand Lobby and an old sewing machine served as her chair and desk. Zipping her backpack closed she left it on top of a box labeled 'Christmas Wreaths' and peered out the window.

Since she'd viewed the footage of Ava being attacked, she'd called in sick to the Front Desk, worked and slept in the same clothes, only leaving the attic room to use the bathroom or grab a bite to eat from Marc or his mother in the kitchens. She kneeled on the window seat and used the meaty part of her hand to rub away the dirt from the large window. Not satisfied, she grabbed the end of the yellowed, lace curtain and wiped at the pane of the rectangular window until she could view the grounds. Finally satisfied, she leaned her head against the cold pane and watched cars working their way down the hill to the circular driveway in front of the hotel.

Somehow, during her time at Twin Springs, she'd fallen in love with the Grand Dame. Not only the warmth of the Grand Lobby at Tea Time, but also the slanted stairways, the webbing of hallways and the people who served her. She'd wronged one of their own and hoped the article published in this morning's paper would right not only that wrong, but many more committed by the Director.

She'd caused pain with her words and hoped her new story was enough to erase the damage. Enough to heal the wounds and enough to begin the process to place Terrence Hollingsworth behind bars. Perhaps then, peace would reach Ava, the other women, her parents and maybe even her sister. She learned a hard lesson at Twin Springs, that being a reporter wasn't about getting the byline, it was about the people entrapped by the story.

She stretched her back muscles to release the fatigue from staying up for forty-eight hours straight. But she'd finished her story. Mackenzie turned, grabbed her backpack and slung it over her shoulder before proceeding towards the door.

Out of habit, she paused at the skinny door, pressing her ear against its aged wood and listening for any rustle of movement. Surprised by the scrapping of feet, she pressed her ear closer and held her breath. In all the time she'd hidden in the attics, researching and writing, never had anyone passed her. This portion of the hotel seemed long forgotten.

Once the shuffling went by her door, she cautiously cracked it open to observe who'd passed. His blond hair barely glinted in the muted glow of the lightbulb. Recognizing him, she gasped and covered her mouth. She let the backpack slide from her shoulder and it dropped soundlessly to the floor. She slipped from the room and trailed him. *Was he looking for her? What made him think to search for her in the attics?*

At the dead end of the hall, he paused and she slipped into the open doorway of another attic room. Her back pressed against the wall, she waited for him to return from the dead end and pass back by her. Controlling her breathing, she listened for his footsteps, the tingling on the back of her neck warning her of a primal danger. When he didn't walk past, she crouched and peeked around the corner. Empty. The hall was empty. "How could that be?"

Perhaps he slipped into one of the other attic rooms. She

glanced back down the hall but the room she'd occupied and her old room directly across the narrow hall were the last rooms. A sound to her left caused her to scuttle backward into the room. She listened as his distinctive tread passed by her door, continued through the hall and down the stairwell. On her hands and knees, she cautiously poked her head back into the hall. He was gone. *But where had he hidden?*

Waiting a moment for safety, she snuck down to the dead end. She examined the cracked and faded white plaster walls. At the end of the hall, hung a large firebox. The rectangular glass and steel box held an ancient ax, with a firehose woven behind. The red paint had faded to a dull orange. Removing the pin from the lock, she opened the glass door.

She removed the axe from its hook and almost dropped it on the ground because of its weight. Lowering the ax to the floor, she leaned it against the wall and felt within the lengths of the aged firehose. Brittle pieces fell to her feet. Not understanding what she was looking for but realizing a story existed, she poked and prodded every area of the firebox.

Not finding anything, she picked the axe up with both hands and, with a grunt, swung the weight of the axe up and back onto its hook. The momentum of the swing caused the hook the ax laid in to click downward.

Silently, the whole box slid inward and took a portion of the wall, the size of one of the skinny doorways, with it. Glancing over her shoulder, she stepped through the opening, into a tiny room and closed the door behind her.

High along the back wall, light from green and cream stain glass windows dimly lit the room. In her mind's eye, she remembered that similar stain glass boxes ran the length of the Lobby. "I must be directly above the General Manager's offices."

A narrow bed slept below the windows, fully made and with clean bedding. Snuggled beside it was an antique cradle, its once blue and white linen now faded and yellowed. To the right, a tall, slender door with a transom above matched the antique doors within the attic corridor. To the left, stood a simple, pine, vanity table, complete with chair, the table heavily laden with a computer screen and stacked papers. A tarnished frame peeked up from behind the paper stack. Plucking it out, she studied the picture.

Obviously from the twenties. Two women, both heavy with child, stood side by side. One woman, her clothes of quality, appeared much further along than the other, judging by the gigantic size of her belly. She bore a striking resemblance to the red headed woman in the portrait from Ava's office. The other woman, in a black maids uniform complete with a little lace cap, and cuffs, smiled happily for the camera. She stood ever so slightly behind and to the right of the red head.

Holding the picture tight within her hands, Mackenzie plopped heavily down on the bed and its springs cried out in protest. She stared forward into the dust covered mirror. Huge in her pale face, her brown gaze reflected back at her from between snapshots of Ava and Isabella taped haphazardly around the oval mirror.

Someone used this room as a place to hide, just like she did with the other attic room. But how did he find out about the room? Contemplating, her gaze dropped to a stack of leather books. Piled high on top of each other, most were held closed with leather cords. Placing the picture frame within the cradle, she reached out and removed the top book, the only one without a string. She opened its aged pages and read, 'Journal Entry. 15 December 1928'.

Engrossed in what she read, at first her mind didn't register the scratching emitting from the secret entrance, but the tingling on the back of her neck warned her.

Her head snapped up as the portion of the wall moved. Tossing the journal back on the top of the pile, she pivoted to the tall door. Swinging her legs over the bed to the other side, she leapt for the exit, pulling it open and slipping out. Slowly, she released the black knob until it latched. Holding her breath, she listened as a man's voice muttered and grew in volume. After a couple moments, she realized how he connected to Twin Springs and her mind raced.

The raging man's voice grew louder and louder. His hatred for Ava spewed forth with each word. Ava's life was in danger. She must warn her. She had to find her before the mad man ranting in the other room did.

Spinning around, she searched for an exit in the square landing. A trifold, wooden door comprising of three tiny panels, each with a dimpled cream window, was the only option. Her panicked fingers curved around a slender black handle and she pulled. With a groan, the old wooden doors folded back upon each other and revealed the black hole of an elevator shaft. Breath held, she pressed the only call button. Looking down into the dark hole, she watched the elevator rise until the doors of a shiny modern elevator opened before her. With a quick glance behind, she saw the man framed in the tall, skinny doorway and gasped.

She slipped through the opening of the elevator's doors and pushed the Lobby button. Her heart thudding in her chest, she stared into blue eyes that, with a blink, changed from surprised to raging mad prior to the elevator doors swiftly closing.

Unseeing, Mackenzie gazed into the mirrored panels of the elevator. How could she be so stupid? She'd missed the biggest story at Twin Springs. Now, because of her short sightedness, caused by her anger and her taste for revenge, people were in danger. Ava was in danger. She exited the elevator on a run and plowed into an unsuspecting Maddy.

"Sheela!" puffed the teen, the breath expelling from her body with the hit. The pile of newspapers she carried scattered on the floor at their feet.

The teenager bent down and began picking up the newspapers, stacking them on her arm.

Righting herself, Mackenzie grasped her by the arm and pulled her upwards. Her fingers bit down hard in her panic. "Where's Ava?"

"Ouch," said Maddy, her brows furrowing. "Ava? She's probably in the stables by now. Have you read this morning's article on her? Everyone needs to read it. Everyone needs to know the truth."

Breaking into a full run, Mackenzie tossed a reply over her shoulder, "Read it? I wrote it." She sped past the Front Desk and out the main doors towards the stables.

"What did you say?" questioned Maddy, a quizzical expression on her face. Shrugging, the teen gathered the rest of the newspapers.

CHAPTER SIXTY-FOUR

Changed into more appropriate wear for her day job, of a black pant suit and white blouse, Ava's determined stride consumed the path below her feet. She'd kept the red scarf to cover her bruises from guests' prying eyes.

Embarrassment crept up her spine as she passed over the spot where Jaxon had found her sleeping in the dirt. Shaking off the feeling, she lifted her gaze to Twin Springs' Aviary. Ace was her main concern now, and bringing him home.

Her steps slowed and she felt as if she was trudging through a deep mud. Glancing down, she marveled at a shimmering silver mist winding a path around her legs and feet. Joined by a second mist of sparkling blue, she watched the mists melding and creeping up her body.

. . . Sitting upon a blanket, layered over a bed of hay, Ruby lounged back against a haystack. Riding high up on her thighs, her shocking red dress glimmered in the moonlight filtering through the large, opened stable doors. Through her eyelashes, she watched Guy. In his black tux, he appeared worlds away from the man hired to be her father's chauffeur.

She couldn't have picked a better man to be her first love. Not only did she enjoy his strong, muscular, sinewy body but, now, he was her only chance for freedom, for pursuing her dream. Plus, he'd caught hold of her heart. He was her trifecta. Strong, independent, free. She loved him. What if he won't take you away from twin Springs? Her mind rebelled, Then, what?

What did it matter? She was ruined not only in the sight of her father but all of society as well. The tips of her fingers felt for the diamond and ruby laden band circling her head. If he didn't take her away with him, she would sell her father's gift to fund her future. Either way, she'd have her dream.

She felt Guy's golden eyes watching her. Lifting the edge of her skirt, the fringe tickled the soft skin on her thighs and she removed a pack of Marlboro cigarettes, along with a box of matches, from their hiding spot under her garter. The heavy foil crinkled as she removed a cigarette and lit the end with a flick of a match. Drawing in on the ivory tipped butt end, Ruby wished for her long holder, so she could set the scene. Instead, she leaned further back, elongating her body before his eyes as she sucked on the tip with her red lips. She patted the blanketed hay beside her, "Come sit. Do you want a ciggy? It's the 'Mild as May' brand. Or is it too feminine for you?"

Spreading himself out beside her, he propped himself up on an elbow. His eyes devoured the long length of her. Removing the cigarette from her fingers, he snubbed it out on a wooden beam. Slowly, he drew her head towards him and replied in a husky voice charged with desire, "You're all I want."

He removed her headband and with a flick of his wrist tossed it behind her. Even with the cigarette smoke lingering in the air, she smelled of roses. Inhaling deeply, he kissed the curve of her neck. Ruby was a rare jewel and her brilliance stunned him. The promises he made to his son echoed in the back recesses of his mind and reminded him that he should track down the flow of moonshine through Twin Springs, but the gut churning hunger to make love to her washed away the call of duty. Peeling away her shimmering dress, Guy paid homage to the magnificent woman before him. He cherished her body with each kiss, each caress. Together they created a melody that mended both of their torn souls and blended them into one.

Guy leaned back and gathered Ruby's nude body in his arms. Looking out at the star lit sky though the large stable doors, duty crashed down upon his shoulders and weighed him down. He pulled the blanket up over her to keep her warm. He didn't want to spoil the moment, but he needed to ask. "Where did you get the shine for your Ladies Tea Party?"

Ruby's laughter rang through the air and she dug around in the hay beside her for the pack of ciggies. Lighting one, she puffed on the end and blew circles of smoke into the air before answering. "You ask me that when Champagne is coursing through the bowels of Twin Springs as we speak. Typical man. Allowing the men to partake but not their sanctimonious women."

"I don't care about the Champagne, Ava. Just the shine."

She leaned up on an elbow, searching his gaze for answers. "Why not? Booze is booze." Then it hit her. His stature. The way he seemed different from the other servants. The way he held himself. The confidence he exuded that attracted her to him like a bee to honey. The revenuer. She'd discovered the undercover revenuer. "You're the revenuer!"

Realizing his moments with her were coming to an end, his shoulders stiffened and, reluctantly, he reached over her. He grabbed his trousers and tugged a black wallet from the back pocket and handed it over to her. "That's me."

The cigarette fell from her fingers and she snatched the flat wallet from his hand. Examining the badge on the outside cover, she ran her thumb along the gold lettering lying in a bed of brilliant blue. 'Bureau Of Prohibition, Agent US Treasury Department'. The inner golden seal shone with the weights of justice and a key. A key to what? she wondered. Making people's lives a living hell?

Guy knew he was damned in her eyes, "But we prefer the term Prohibition Agent."

Nibbling on her bottom lip, she stared into the eyes of the man who was supposed to be her savior, her ticket for escape and for capturing her dream. A foul taste coated her mouth. Her father. As much as she hated the General's hold upon her, he was family. Her blood. "Are you going to arrest my father for the Champagne?" She grasped his arm, her blood red nails piercing his skin. "No, Everett couldn't handle the responsibility of running the hotel. Twin Springs would die. My sisters would lose their home."

For once in her life, she saw past her own wishes and desires to the people around her. She pulled her knees up to her chest, wrapped her arms around her legs and rocked back and forth. "The community," she whispered. "The farms would perish. Oakton's just now budding to life because of the wealth my father and Twin Springs lured to the area." Her eyes filled with tears, not for herself but for others. "You can't arrest my father. It would be the end of everything."

Fascinated, Guy considered the woman beside him. She captivated him, lured him in as no other. Touched his soul. His dead wife was a warm memory in his heart but Ruby burned under his skin and fired his blood. He thirsted for her, couldn't image life without her. "I'm not after your father. Although, he and I will need to have a long talk in the morning. Not just about the booze, but also about you and me."

"You and me," she whispered, hope lifting her spirit. "As in, you and me together, as one?" She held her breath, waiting for his answer.

He tucked a piece of her beautiful hair behind her ear. "Yes, Ruby. Come away with me to DC or back home to my parent's farm. I can't offer you the splendor of Twin Springs but I can offer you a good home, my love and the love of my little boy."

Panic filled her, clamping down on her vocal cords. "You want me be a farmer?" she squeaked. Suddenly, she felt indecent and she pulled a corner of the blanket over her. "I can't be held captive on yet another plot of land. I must sing and act either on Broadway or in one of the talkies. Please, Guy, don't ask me to choose between you and my dream, just like my father. Take me away and live the dream with me."

Sadness clouded his eyes and he stared down at her pleading face. Her lips were kissed bare of their once bright red hue and her darkened makeup was now faded in the moonlight. Stripped of her fake facade, he saw only the aching need below the surface. The craving to capture her dream sparkled from her green eyes. "My son is too young to be toted from stage to stage. What of him?"

Confusion filled her. Then a single tear escaped and spilled over.

Finally, she understood. He carried the responsibility of a child. If she wanted him, and she did, more than even glittering on stage, then she'd have to choose. Why did women always make the greatest sacrifices for love?

She thought about the thrill of the stage and the taste of the audience that she'd discovered for the first time tonight. Singing on stage was now an intoxicating drug in her system and she yearned to feel its glory over and over.

Yet, living her dream without Guy would be empty, unsatisfying and meaningless. Shiny on the outside but with a black hole on the inside that would sap her spirit and leave her unfulfilled. She reached up, drawing his head down to hers until their lips met. Tilting her head, she kissed him deeply. Their tongues met between their two worlds and became one. Drawing back, she held his face between her palms. "I will follow you anywhere."

Love surged through him and he understood that with her anything was possible and within his reach. He rolled over, pulling her over top of him. "We'll figure this out. I promise. I love you and want you happy. We will figure out how to juggle your dream and my son."

Nuzzling her silky neck, he wanted nothing more than to enjoy the moment and again tumble with her into the New Year, but the thoughts of his son and the graveside promise he'd made that must be fulfilled rang out again. His dead wife was innocent and he hadn't kept her safe from the dredges of society. "I must know. Where did you get the moonshine from?"

She lifted up from him and slid over to settle herself beside him. Raising up to support her head with her hand, she leaned on her elbow. "Why? What does it matter where I got the moonshine from?"

"Because, I have to fulfill the promise that brought me to Twin Springs, and to you. I have to find the bootleg operation responsible for killing my wife."

Ruby thought for a moment, torn between protecting those she loved and helping the man she loved. She realized that if she and Guy would have a future together, she must trust him. "Jean Claude, the Head Chef, gave me the moonshine. He said there was a hidden stash, under Twin Springs, that he pilfered it from. But he made me promise to not tell anyone, otherwise the person he'd stolen the moonshine from would find out that he knew about the stash and kill him. He wanted to help me. And, I was kind of," she paused, her cheeks flushed, "using the fact that I knew about his relationship with my sister to prod him into helping me."

Guy leaned back, stunned by her story. "The still is under Twin Springs?" He struggled to grasp the concept before shifting to, "Jean Claude and your sister?" For a moment he was speechless.

Not wanting him to think even less of her, she quickly added, "I wouldn't have told anyone about them. In fact, I helped Emma sort of woo him. I just needed Jean Claude to think I would tell, in order for him to help me."

In the distance, Twin Springs' warning bells rang. Involuntarily, Ruby jumped and grasped the edges of her blanket. "Fire," she whispered, the faint smell of smoke reaching her nostrils. The horses began to snort and shift within their stalls.

Guy scrambled to his feet, gathering his things and quickly dressing. "I've got to help." He leaned down, placing a quick kiss on her open mouth before yanking on his trousers. Out of habit, he slipped his badge back into his pocket. "You stay clear of the fire. Find your sisters and see to their safety while we put out the flames." Using precious seconds, he marked her with a parting kiss. "I love you, Ruby." Sirens called in the distance and he reluctantly released her. He must leave her and protect those in need. Shrugging into his shirt, he took off at a full run.

She stood with the tips of her fingers lingering where his lips touched hers. "He loves me," she whispered. "Someone actually loves me." The moonlight shimmered over her naked curves as she stared after Guy's strong back.

The cold air chilled her skin and the smell of fire jilted her, bringing her back to reality. She needed to hurry. It must be a large fire for the thick smell of smoke to reach the stables. Fearful for her family, she reached down for her sparking red dress and prepared to quickly dress.

"Well, well. What do we have here?" mocked the Lieutenant, his cold

gaze soaking in the sight before him. He tossed a bulging, burlap sack just inside the door. "Another Rockwell sister spreading her legs for the help."

Holding the dress in her hand, Ruby spun around. The beads caught the moonlight and sent tiny beams of light around her. The Lieutenant stood before her, his right eye darkening to ugly purples and blacks. His lips were swollen and bloody. His clothes ripped and dirty. The fire didn't do that to him.

Ruby rose to her full height, her breasts high and proud like the rest of her. "What the Rockwell sisters do is none of your damn business. Why aren't you helping with the fire anyway?" She raised her arms up to slip her dress over her head and down her body.

Letting out an angry bellow, the Lieutenant tackled Ruby and landed hard on top of her. "Help with the fire? Why would I do that?" He cackled and her skin prickled with fear. "I set that fire."

Panic filled her and she gasped for air, only to find the pressure of him pushing down on her chest and fabric filling her mouth. She struggled beneath the Lieutenant's long form, kicking up dirt and straw with her efforts. Her arms were caught up in the dress and the fabric smothered her. Trapped, she felt him lift slightly and fumble with his pants. No, her mind screamed and she struggled, twisting, turning and kicking for her life.

The Lieutenant surged forward, entering her with his hardened manhood. With each thrust he ground out words in her ear. "Bitches, all of you. Ruined my plans. Willing to part your legs for anyone." He thrust with all his might, slamming against her body. "Anyone, but me. I've already killed Emma and her colored lover. You all think that you'll win. Over me? Never!" In one final thrust he arched back and released his evil seed.

Done with her, he rose to his feet. He towered over her battered body, before he pulled up his britches. Scowling down at her, he spat upon her and sneered, "As if I would grant you the honor of being my wife."

Ruby struggled with her dress. She concentrated on one thing—pulling the fabric down over her body and freeing herself. Wetness dripped between her legs and she rose unsteadily to her feet. Pushing her hair back out of her face, she cried inside but her chin clicked upward and she glared at her attacker. Beads and fringe littered the dirt floor at her feet and the stable was now heavy with smoke. Her chest hitched with unreleased sobs but she wouldn't cower, or let him have the satisfaction of knowing how much he'd just stolen from her.

Pushing her shoulders back, she sauntered up to the Lieutenant. With each step, pain shook her legs and stole strength from her. Determined, she continued forward until she stood in front of him. Her hands trembled but she trailed them up the lapel of his wool jacket until they curled around his shoulders.

Shuddering with revulsion, she leaned forward, and pursed her lips as if to speak. The Lieutenant lowered his head, either to capture her lips or listen, she knew not. In one swift movement, she curled her fingers hard into his shoulders, brought her knee up in a swift motion and struck hard at the evil of his manhood.

The Lieutenant crumpled before her.

On trembling legs, Ruby turned and ran. The name of the man she loved burst from her lips, "Guy!"

Hard fingers curled in her hair and stopped her forward momentum. She dug her nails into his arm and screamed for Guy at the top of her lungs, but the fire bells drowned out her feeble attempts.

By her hair, the Lieutenant dragged her out of the stables and towards the smaller building. She clutched at his arm with both hands and her heels kicked at the frozen dirt. Paying her efforts no mind, he shouted at her. "All the same! Every one of you!"

Reaching the porch of the Tack Room, he paused and lifted the canted walkway leading up to the porch, revealing a hole below.

Struggling to loosen his hold, her eyes bulged at the gaping darkness.

Twirling her away from the view, the Lieutenant's hands circled around her throat, pressing in on her vocal cords, causing her to gasp for air. Tightening his grip, he strangled her and chanted over and over with his voice high and shrill, "The song bird will sing no more, no more, the song bird will sing no more, no more."

The world around her darkened and turned black. Ruby felt the life leave her body and realized her dream of performing on stage was insignificant. Nothing compared to what the Lieutenant was steadily robbing her of. A future with Guy.

A new dream began for her. She'd wait for Guy. Even though her body tumbled down into the pitch black hole, her mind was free. She dreamt of when she and Guy would again meet. When her guy would finally join her. Then she'd truly be able to soar free.

Floating high above, she gazed down upon the Lieutenant. His face was twisted with rage and he grunted with satisfaction before wiping his mouth with the back of his hand. Turning, he gasped at a new fire raging within the stables.

It was then, Ruby remembered her errant cigarette, which she'd carelessly dropped into the hay. The horses screamed for their lives and the thick, black smoke blocked the moonlight from above. Amazed, she saw the Lieutenant rush into the stable and emerge with her sparkling headband and a burlap sack.

He dropped the sack down into the tunnel and tossed the headband in after and it bounced off her lifeless body. "I'll be back for those, bitch. The gems will fund a very comfortable life for me, while you rot in hell." He slammed the lid down and cast her into a dark grave.

She watched him adjust himself within his trousers before fastening them. Whistling a tune under his breath, he righted his wool jacket and set off towards the ringing bells of Twin Springs.

Floating above the destruction, Emma joined her. Hand in hand, they observed their loved ones fighting the fire eating at the stables. When the sky opened up above them and the light shone down welcoming them, the sisters' green gazes locked.

The decision was made to remain where they belonged, with their family and with Twin Springs. They must wait, to be found. To be set free. Until then, they'd care for Twin Springs and protect future generations from such evil. Perhaps, one day, they'd walk with their loved ones again. . .

Ava rose from the cold, hardened dirt, tears seeping down her face. She felt raw and her legs trembled underneath her. Sorrow for her ancestor coursed through her body. "I'll find you," she whispered.

Torn between finding Ruby and returning Ace to her office, Ava turned from the Aviary and worked her way back down the path towards Twin Springs' stables. Ruby deserved to be brought back out into the light, to be free, to take the stage once again and shine in heaven. "It's time, Ruby. Time for you to be let out of the dark."

CHAPTER SIXTY-FIVE

At the banging on his door, Jaxon glanced up from his phone call. "Hold a minute, Lee," he said, muting the phone with a quick push of his thumb. "Come in."

Maddy entered the room, her dark curls bouncing in tune with her jubilant walk. She carried a stack of newspapers in her arms and tossed one on the desk in front of him. "Someone is going to read this newspaper."

His golden eyes clouded and he rubbed at the stubble on his chin. "What are you talking about?"

She tapped her toe. "I've been trying to get everyone to read this article on Ava."

Immediately, he hung up on his cousin and snatched the paper from the desk in front of him. "Damn it, another article."

An exasperated sigh escaped Maddy's body. "Finally, someone's paying attention to me. Yes, and you'll not believe what it says. I tried to get Ava to read it but she wants me to stick it in the bottom of her bird's cage."

Thinking of Ava's response, his lips curled into a grin. Quickly, he scanned the paper before him.

The teen sat on the edge of his desk, waiting for him to finish reading. Swinging her feet back and forth, she fiddled with the walkie talkies as impatience filled her slender body. She glanced around the room, rapped her fingers on her black pants, before the stress of waiting boiled up within her and spilled over. She blurted out, without pausing for a breath. "It says that the director of Ava's last play raped or manipulated his lead female actors into having sexual relations with him or he'd destroy their careers."

Abandoning his attempt to read the newspaper himself, he lowered the paper and, instead, listened to Maddy's summary.

"He used his position of power to control the female actors and drummed them out of the business if they fought back. Women are now coming forward to protect Ava. To let the world know she was not responsible for the suicide of Director Hollingsworth's wife. One back stage hand said that Mrs. Hollingsworth killed herself because she was ashamed of hiding her husband's secret all these years and she knew Ava was too strong to be manipulated like the others."

Shifting in his chair, Jaxon looked down at the newspaper and realized the world had wronged Ava. Just like he once did, they only noticed her outer package and not the spectacular woman within. The beautiful human being you glimpsed when she bared her soul through her song.

"There's a picture of the scummy Director on the next page."

He flipped the page and stared down at the pixilated gray and white photo. He didn't need the picture to be in color. He recognized the man and knew he had blond hair and blue eyes. Just like he knew that he stared into the eyes of Ava's attacker and one of the guests at Twin Springs. He leaned back and flicked the photo with his finger. "I've got you, you bastard."

"Got who? What bastard?" questioned the teen.

He raised a brow. "Don't let your brother catch you repeating words you shouldn't."

The teenager harrumphed and rolled her eyes.

Chuckling under his breath, he placed the paper on the desk before him. "Get back to your mission. Make sure a newspaper is delivered to every room within Twin Springs and hand them out directly."

Rising from the edge of his desk, she hugged the stack of papers close to her chest. "What do you think I've been trying to do?"

Of course she's already thought of it, he reminded himself. *She is Maddy after all.* "I know Ava will appreciate it." Guilt filled him, that Ava woke before he returned to her. "By the way, do you know where she is?"

Back on her mission, Maddy answered over her shoulder, "She said something about going to the stables." She shrugged and kept going.

His instincts buzzed and a sick feeling rolled down his spine, chilling him. Ava and the stables, that didn't make much sense. Now, Ava and the Theatre, Crystal Ballroom, or her office, those places clicked for him. Frowning, he squeezed the little ball and leaned forward in his chair to read the article himself. But Maddy's last comment kept sounding off warning signals within his head.

CHAPTER SIXTY-SIX

*E*njoying the full breakfast buffet in the Main Dining Room, Director Hollingsworth looked up from his crepes and into the happy, gray eyes of a teenage girl. His chest swelled within his cream, cable knit sweater and he turned on his most dazzling smile.

She stared at him with a quizzical expression on her face before shrugging and handing him a newspaper, "Here you go, complements of Twin Springs. I hope you enjoy your breakfast."

Automatically taking the paper, he watched her slender form. She gave newspaper, after newspaper, to the dining guests. Lustily, he dug into his crepes and watched the girl's progress through the room, admiring the sway of her hips. "Ripe for the picking," he murmured, shaking open the newspaper with his free hand and scanning the headlines on the front page.

Turning the page, his own face stared back at him and crepes spewed from his lips in shock. Glancing quickly left and right, he hunched and brought the newspaper up and around him, blocking his face from view of the other diners. Fury burned within him as he scanned the article. Reading the byline, he discounted the obviously male name. His hands clenched around the edges and his knuckles whitened. He didn't care what was in print. Whatever name she used, whether Sheela or Mac Mills, he knew the reporter was Mackenzie, his dead wife's friend. He bit out under his breath, "Damn you."

He'd attempted to hunt her down right after the phone booth incident, but she'd disappeared into the bowels of the hotel. He was biding his time, waiting for her to come back to her shift at the Front Desk. Why should he chase her?

Deep down, he couldn't believe a woman would go against his will. Not her and certainly not Ava. It was time to bring them both back under his thumb. *Why not make Mackenzie recant her story and post a gracious, glowing retraction?*

He sipped his coffee with satisfaction. He would control Mackenzie just like he controlled all women. Besides, with Ava at his side and backing him up, no one would deny the storyline he peddled.

A forbidden thought bored a hole into the back of his brain. What if they didn't succumb to his wishes? The Director slammed his cup down on the table. Coffee spilled over the edges and onto the white linen table cloth. His lips twitched and a satisfying idea crossed his mind. He would just have to make them atone for their disobedience and pay for ruining his reputation, destroying his career and his marriage.

The teen rushed over and assisted with his spilt coffee. He slid his sunglasses onto his nose and pulled at the blue collar of his dress shirt poking out above his v-neck sweater. Rising, but keeping his head canted away from her gaze, he asked, "Do you happen to know if Sheela is working the Front Desk today? She's a dear friend of my late wife and I'd like to say goodbye to her before I depart."

Maddy busily mopped at the coffee with a moist towel that Diana rushed up to her with. "I'm not sure if she's working today, but last I knew she was heading to the stables."

Satisfaction hummed in the back of his throat and he tossed a large tip onto the table before heading out towards his prey.

CHAPTER SIXTY-SEVEN

Finished with the newspaper article on Ava, Jaxon leaned back in his chair and mulled over the new information. He stared mindlessly towards the computer screens and reflected back over the sabotaging of Twin Springs and Sheela.

She might be a reporter but it didn't add up that she'd also sabotage the hotel. Didn't the sabotaging start well before she arrived? No, someone was messing with them, and he didn't like it. Images continued to flash on the screens, the Main Dining Room, Front Desk, and then his own face illuminated the screen before switching to the Promenade.

"What the hell?" he muttered. Then it hit him. Someone had placed a camera in the security office, pointed it at him and uploaded it to the feed. "Son of a bitch."

Rage propelled him forward out of the chair and he searched for the camera. A small, black eye stared back at him from under one of the screens. "You're mine," he growled under his breath.

Taking his utility knife from his pocket, he pried the hidden camera from the underside of the screen, rolled it around in his palm and considered his options. "Destroy it?"

That's too easy, his mind answered.

He contemplated different ideas. "Replace it?

Naw, not enough time. Screw with him.

Jaxon nodded his head. Whoever the asshole was wanted him to find the camera, otherwise he wouldn't have connected it to the feed. "Yeah," he spoke to the little lens. "You wanted me to know you were here and that you're one step ahead."

Move it? his inner voice responded.

Satisfaction rolled in his gut. "Why the hell not?" He searched his mind for a place to put it.

Somewhere symbolic, his mind added.

His brain lit up with an idea. *Perfect.* He'd put it in the trash chute from the kitchens. "Exactly where this bastard belongs, in the trash."

Jaxon pocketed the tiny camera and continued to search the room for more tech. With the skill of a pro, he left no stone unturned. Removing each of the security screens, he checked for extra wires, cameras and listening devices. He pulled the drawers from the desk and dumped and sifted through their contents. He opened the walkies for bugs, leaving them in pieces across the desk. He lifted each picture frame connected to the wall behind him, felt around the edges and behind before stacking them on the floor. Scratching at the stubble on his face, his eyes narrowed. "Nothing."

Turning in a circle, he examined the cracker jack box of an office. There was something else within the room. A little prize he missed. He felt it, deep in his gut. He studied the mirror to the left. The oddity of a full length mirror on the wall of a security office struck him. Something was off about it. Not quite centered on the wall, and at an awkward height for anyone to see their entire body within the mirror. His instincts hummed.

Using the tips of his fingers, he felt around the mirror's base and worked his way up to the edges. Half way up on the left side, the sliding movement of his fingers was halted. Pressing his head against the wall, he studied the frame of the mirror. "A latch."

Curling his fingers round the metal, he clicked the latch open and the mirror swung open like a door, revealing a hidden room. "Cool," breathed Jaxon.

Pulling a small, black flashlight from the side pocket of his cargo pants, he stepped over the threshold and into the strangest room. To both his left and right, the walls of another cubby hole room were covered with long, thick wires, tiny knobs, switches and circular gages with their red lines all sleeping on zero. A line of black mouth pieces protruded from the walls. Headphones, hooked to the walls by a thick, gray wire, lay forgotten on a long, wooden shelf under the mouth pieces. Under the shelf, a bench seat ran the length of the room and served as seats. The dust of time covered everything with inches of dirt. If he hazarded a guess, the room appeared to be an old switchboard room for the hotel's telephone operators. "I'll be damned."

Footprints cleared a path through the room to the other side. Across from him was a tall, skinny door, with cobwebs covering a little window above. He opened the door and found a long hallway on his right and another tall door on his left. He entered the hallway. Orienting a map of Twin Springs in his head, he assumed the door on the left opened up into the Presidents Hall. He grasped the knob to pull the door open and the oblong, black knob came off in his hand, the other half of the knob was missing. Pulling his Swiss Army Knife from his leg pocket, he crouched down and used the pliers to grasp the inner workings of the knob. With a twist, he opened the door and revealed the backside of a sheet of drywall. Using his fingertips, he pressed on the drywall. It held firm.

Obviously, someone covered over this portion of the hallway years ago. Turning around, the long hall stretched out before him. The beam of his flashlight was eaten up by the darkness. The long, slender corridor was only a foot or so wider than his shoulders. Concentrating his flashlight on a worn path in the dust, he traversed well over sixty feet to the end of the corridor. In his mind, he mapped out his progress as he moved past Ava's office, Still Water's Bar & Grill, and the length of the Grand Lobby. At the end of the long corridor another tall door greeted him. The knob on this door remained firm in his hand and he pulled it inward, revealing a panel of wood blocking the door. Noticing a hook and a handle, he unlatched a tiny hook and pushed down on the slender handle connected to the wood. Silently, the panel opened into the construction site for the new Confectionary Shop. The paneled wood door supported a portion of the display shelves that ran across the back wall. The room was empty and ready for reconstruction, once Theo gave the word. Pulling back on the handle, he closed and re-latched the panel. "Clever son of a bitch."

Working his way back down the corridor, Jaxon swung the beam of his flashlight from wall to wall, looking for other exits or doorframes. Almost back to the beginning of the hall, his beam bounced off of rack after rack of shelves filled with dusty bottles of liquor. Curious, he removed a couple bottles from the wall and read off the different labels of wines, brandies and Champagne bottles before continuing forward.

On the left, he glimpsed the framed outer molding of another doorway, with its black hinges hanging free without a door. He flickered his flashlight around the frame. The light from the beam pooled at his feet on a tin bucket filled with water and fresh red roses. Amazed he didn't knock it over his first time down the hall, he bent down and felt the water. It was cold, recently placed there.

Placing his flashlight between his teeth, Jaxon felt along the drywall between the doorframe. The drywall was outlined by six inch boards. The beam from his flashlight flickered over a silver coat hook in the middle of the door.

"Strange place to hang a jacket. Unless you use the hook to pull the door closed." His mind hummed with the possibilities.

Feeling along the left edge of the boards, he discovered the rounded top of a metal ball. "A ball latch," he muttered. He pressed hard on the curved surface and released the latch. The door swung open, revealing Ava's office and bounced off Ace's cage. He emerged from the hall to find Logan staring up at the portrait above the fireplace and a long stem rose lying on her desk.

Swiftly Logan turned, arms up, stance ready for a fight. "Holy shit! Where did you come from?" He dropped his fists and rubbed his right hip, pain shooting down his leg from the quick movement. A dirty plaid shirt opened to reveal a black band shirt, screaming the word 'KISS' in white letters with crooked s's and the painted white faces of the band floating above. "Crap, Wolfeman. You took ten years off my life."

His eyes hard, Jaxon's voice held a dangerous thread and he asked, "What are you doing in Ava's office, Woody?"

His face a mutilated mask of resentment, Logan rubbed his leg and growled, "None of your damn business."

"Oh, I think it is my business. Do you have feelings for Ava?"

Logan's one eyebrow furrowed. "Of course I do."

"Tell me," said Jaxon, steadily closing the gap between the two of them. His voice was ultra calm and at odds with the fire burning in his eyes. "Are you the one bringing her flowers? The one sabotaging the hotel and its future success?"

"What are you talking about?" Logan's face flushed with a purplish color. "You come jumping out of a hidden panel in the wall and accuse me of sabotaging the Grand Dame, and a woman that I love as much as my own mother?" He swung at his old teammate. Logan's fist connected with Jaxon's cheek and snapped his head to the side.

Howling with anger, Jaxon lunged. His forward momentum toppled them both over the back of the couch and they crashed into the antique coffee table. With a loud crack the table smashed under their combined weight. Red rage clouding Jaxon's judgment and fists swinging, it took a moment for Logan's words to sink in. *Woody loved Ava. As much as his mom.*

Jackass, his mind chided.

Jaxon paused and Logan's upper cut caught him squarely in the chin, causing his teeth to rattle. Quickly rolling off his fallen comrade, he contemplated Logan's statement. Thoughts flew through his mind like a raging fire. Should he stand aside and foster a relationship between Logan and Ava? After all, his intel mutilated the man before him, ruining any chances of a future with a woman. Ava seemed to see past Logan's scars. *Forget that,* thought Jaxon. *Ava was his.*

Jaxon splayed his hands open before him as Logan scrambled to his feet, "Wait." His gaze brushed over Logan. "You love Ava?"

"Of course I do, asshole. Not that it is any of your damn business." His eyebrow rose. "Awe, I guess Ava found a way past the wall you erected. Leave it to her to breach a man's defenses." He shook his head. "You've got this all wrong. Ava and Isabella are like sisters to me. I'd lay down my life for them, cross fire to protect them. But I sure as hell wouldn't have sex with them."

"Then why do you keep showing up in her office?" Jaxon asked, trying to understand.

Shoving his hands into his pockets of his jeans, Logan shuffled his feet. "It's not Ava," he mumbled. "It's the red head."

His eyes flickered from his buddy to the painting, and back. At a loss for words, he repeated, "The red head?"

"Yeah, all I can think looking up at her is that no woman, that gorgeous, would look twice at an ugly mug like mine."

Brushing the pieces of the table off, he moved over beside his Army buddy. Hands in pockets, both men stood shoulder to shoulder, staring up at the portrait. "Well," said Jaxon dragging out the word, his face devoid of any emotion. "She is dead you know. Worm food, moldering corpse and all. She can't actually see you anyway."

"No shit, Sherlock," shot back Logan. "I can't explain it. But both of us lost everything to fire. I feel a kinship to her."

Plastering a stern look on his face, Jaxon bowed his head and studied the floor. "A kinship, huh?" He attempted to smother his laughter by clearing his throat.

Slugging him in the arm, Logan grumbled, "Kiss my ass, Wolfeman. You have your woman. Leave me to mine."

Rubbing his arm, he smiled good-naturedly at his friend. "I think you've lost it, Woody. Gone completely off the deep end. But there is something I need to tell you." He paused, weighing the consequences of his words. "You know, I have a sister."

Logan groaned under his breath. "Don't go trying to set me up. I already know about your sister. Even though I haven't met her, I'm scared shitless of her. Your stories in the team room gave me nightmares," he mocked. "I wouldn't touch her with a ten foot pole."

Glancing up at the portrait, Jaxon replied. "You might want to rethink that because—"

A loud alarm sounded down the hidden hallway, and filtered into the room. "What the hell is that?" asked Logan.

Identifying the sound at once from the night of the fire on the Promenade, Jaxon raced through the hallway, through the little room and back into his office, Logan nipping at his heels. He examined the flashing lights in the fire alarm box and ran his finger along to identify the area of Twin Springs reporting a fire. "It's the stables. There is a fire in the stables." Mind racing, he whispered, "Ava." His knees weakened with the possibilities. "She's in the stables."

CHAPTER SIXTY-EIGHT

*E*ntering the stables, the smell of hay and manure filled her nostrils. Horse stalls ran down each side of the long building. Row after row of fine horse flesh was on display before her. A creaking sounded above her and she looked up to the loft above but only saw stacks of fresh hay waiting to be dumped down into the awaiting stalls. Tucking her black hair behind her ear, she waved off a fly buzzing around her nose and began to search. Only one thought dominated her mind, *I must find her!*

The swift swoosh of air from behind was her only warning. Taken completely by surprise, she was spun around and pinned against a horses stall. The speckled stallion's chestnut eyes rolled in the white background of his sockets and the horse kicked at the gate that she was pressed against.

With each kick, her head bounced off the metal bars at the top of the wooden stall, but she was held in place by the man's hands at her throat. Those hands tightened and she fought for breath. Pulling and prying at his fingers, she stared up at him as the world blackened around her. Bewildered by how blue his eyes were, her last thought was, *I'll never save her.*

Unable to breathe, the life ebbed from her until her body went limp. Not satisfied, he shook her one last time and squeezed her neck, until he crushed her wind pipe. With little effort, he lifted and tossed her dead body over the gate of the stall, to be trampled beneath the hooves of the frightened beast.

CHAPTER SIXTY-NINE

Director Hollingsworth charged into the stables. "Mackenzie where the hell are you?" he roared. Thundering past each stall, his eyes scanned the area before he skidded to a stop. Blood seeped from underneath one stall door, soaking the hay to a cherry red.

A charred smell filled the air and raised the hair on the back of his neck. Hesitant, he rubbed at the blue collar of his shirt before reaching up and unlatching the stall door. When the horse bolted from within its cell, he scampered back. There, among the blood soaked hay, laid Mackenzie, her bloody body broken and mutilated by hooves.

Hands shaking, the Director withdrew a cigar from his pocket. He fumbled with a matchbook, before ripping off a match. His fingers trembled as he attempted to light the tiny head. Wishing he hadn't lost his gold lighter, he finally ignited the match and lit the end of his cigar without breaking off the butt first. He leaned back against the wooden upright support and puffed, while his mind raced on about what to do.

"My God, what have you done?" Hands clasped over her mouth, Ava stared down at Sheela's mutilated body, then, up to the Director smoking a cigar next to her friend.

Not knowing how to reply, Terrence blinked back at her and his hands dropped to his sides. "I," he stuttered, "I didn't do anything."

Ava couldn't believe his arrogance. The bastard drove his wife to suicide, attacked and tormented her and now he added sweet Sheela to his deranged portfolio of leading women. Reason and fear flew from her thoughts. Rage built up within her and spewed forth. Her green eyes flashed. "Just like you didn't do anything to me in your office? Just like you didn't do anything to me in the phone booths?"

The Director's fingers curled into fists, crushing the cigar and scattering the seeds of the lit sparks at their feet. Snarling, he lunged for Ava. His forward momentum propelled her backward against the opposite stall. The horse pranced away in protest, when Ava's body slammed back against the wooden gate.

He grasped her red scarf, twisting the silky fabric up around his fist until it tightened at her throat. "Me?" He screamed. The blue irises of his eyes were lost in the expanse of white. "It's you women trying to ruin my life. Spouting your lies. Not following direction."

Silently, fire licked a path through the dry hay. Kissing its heat to everything around it. Dark black smoke trailed behind the flames' scalding journey and permeated the air. Smelling danger, the horses neighed within their stalls and called out warnings to each other.

Oblivious to the world around him, Terrence pressed Ava's slender form up tight against the gate with his. Biting out hateful words, he thrust the scarf high up above her head and cut off her air. "Stupid cows, all of you."

The corners of Ava's eyesight darkened. She stared into his florid face, the veins in his neck bulging with wrath. She couldn't let him win. She wanted to live. To live her dream. To create a new life with Jaxon. She wouldn't allow the fear the Director planted within her to grow and fester anymore. This was her home.

Bucking her body against him, she vowed. "I will not die like the other women. I will not die like Ruby!"

He hooted with laughter, spit showering her face. "You will perform the part I cast you in. I own you."

Going against her instincts to tear at the scarf, she grasped the Director's blond head within her hands and gouged his eyes with her thumbs. "I'm not your plaything, your doll to control and manipulate to the scene playing in your head."

For all she was worth, she pressed in on his eyeballs pushing them back into their sockets and ignored the tightening of the fabric at her throat. She choked out the words, "I'm Ava Fairbanks, and I decide my destiny!"

Howling with pain, Terrence released his hold on the scarf and covered his eyes with his hands.

Ava clawed at the fabric, loosening its hold around her neck before casting it aside. Leaning forward, her hands on her knees, she sucked air into her lungs. Her muscles tensed, ready to take flight. Ready to run and hide. But Jaxon's words echoed through her brain. "Fight to the finish. The most committed wins." A part of her was fearful that whatever pain she caused the Director, would return to her tri-fold. In her heart, she loved and trusted Jaxon. Clenching her hands into fists, she brought back her arm and slugged the Director in the throat.

He choked, gasped for air and crashed into her, knocking her into the wooden upright. He stumbled around and back into the stall where Sheela's body laid, feasted upon by flames. The smoke thickening around them, fire bit at the expensive weave of his slacks. Realizing the danger of the fire surrounding him, he scurried backwards and out of the stall. His vision limited by her actions, he bumped into Ava and knocked her to the ground, before running for his life.

Exhilaration filled Ava, seeing him run from her. Scrambling to her feet, she raised her fists and watched the Director. Ready to fight again if necessary.

He paused at the huge stable doors. His gaze blurry from her attack, he glanced back. Blood dripped from his eyes and he sneered. Dragging the towering doors of the stables closed, he locked them with her and the horses inside.

A new fear pounded her chest and she rushed to the gigantic doors. Using all her weight, she attempted to pry the wooden doors apart. Realizing her efforts were ineffective, she leaned back against them and searched for another exit. Coughing, she stared out over the smoke filling the stables and Jaxon's words rang in her head. "Use your voice. Scream, yell, let people know you need help."

Ava's voice rose, rumbling above the whining of the horses and the thundering of their hooves at their gates. Her screams echoed off the walls of the stable and carried down to the two men running her way.

CHAPTER SEVENTY

*B*lack smoke churned from the tin, slanted roofline of the stables. Jaxon realized time was of the essence. He must save Ava, he loved her. He couldn't, no, wouldn't live without her. "No matter what, we have to save her!" he shouted to Logan.

His chest ached from the fear-throbbing pace of his heart that raced to keep time with the pounding of his feet. The heat of the fire reached out to him. Calling for him to hurry. The building before him blurred, converging in his mind with memories of another. The cool, mountain air was suppressed by the arid heat of the desert. Jaxon reached down for his rifle. Feeling only air, confusion wrinkled his forehead and blurred his reasoning. His own voice from the past screamed inside his head, "Double time it, damn it. Your team needs you."

Blood roared in his ears, as a man emerged from the building. For a moment, the man blended with one of his fallen comrades. The shine of the morning sun off his blond hair became the blinding white of fire in his thermal scope. "Roddie?"

Unnoticed by his comrade, fire licked at the bloused pant leg of Roddie's uniform. Horrified, Jaxon watched him closing and barricading the door behind him. As the distance between him and Roddie shortened, flames devoured the camouflaged fabric before engulfing him in a ball of fire. His screams filled the air, joining with the rest of the team in the building. Smoke constricted his throat, as words rushed from his mouth in a harsh command, "Drop and roll, Roddie! Damn it, drop and roll!"

Jaxon felt, rather than saw, Logan collapse to his knees. Skidding to a halt, the Wolfeman stood frozen over his brother-in-arms. In his mind's eye, the right side of Woody's body was eaten alive with the kiss of fire. He fell to his knees and rolled Woody over and over in the dirt. The stench of burning flesh filled his nostrils, gagging him as fate laughed at his desperate attempts to put out the fire consuming his teammate.

Woody's hand grasped him by the arm. The sight of his brother's right hand, the blackened skin pealed back by fire and exposing the bones beneath, was tattooed forever in his mind. Jaxon screamed, "It's my fault, all my fault!"

Woody's lips moved but the roaring in Jaxon's ears muted his words. "Forgive me, Woody."

Flames burst from the building's awnings and stain glass windows. The added oxygen fueled the fire within. Jaxon's instincts told him the visions before him were all wrong. But his instincts were shit. She taught him that. A beautiful face materialized before him, her long blonde hair and cornflower blue eyes floated in his mind. Her brandy wine voice whispered secrets, plans and lies.

Screams rose above the fog, dampening the husky voice from the past and jerking Jaxon back to the present. Another, more sensual face, suspended before his gaze, her eyes clear, light as new grass, her glossy black hair kissing the silky skin of her jawline. The screams of Ava's pure voice drowned out the husky deceptions from the past. Jaxon Wolfe surged to his feet, with only one thought. "Ava!"

CHAPTER SEVENTY-ONE

Quickly, the fire spread through the stables. The flames consumed everything in their path and clawed their way up the walls to feed greedily on the stacks of hay in the loft. Burning pieces of hay fluttered down from above, seeding the floor with new sparks.

Ava spied a fire extinguisher and grabbed it from the wall. She pulled the pin and pressed down on the lever, spreading white foam from side to side. Shouting with triumph, she extinguished one spot, not noticing the fire traveled under the hay and emerged in two others. Working her way down the middle of the stables, she looked down when the extinguisher sputtered in her hands and died. Empty.

The stables were now thick with black smoke and the spreading flames. She threw down the useless extinguisher. Glancing around, she did the only thing she could think of. She grabbed her scarf from the floor and used it to cover her nose and mouth. Making her way through the smoke to each stall, she pulled back the bolts holding the gates closed and released the horses. "Perhaps as the building burns, they can escape."

Frightened horses charged around her and she flattened herself against the wall and slid down to the floor. She kicked out at the hay, so that there was a barrier of dirt around her. The immense heat from the flames stole her breath and the churning smoke choked her. With a resounding crack, the windows lining the roofline of the stables burst and glass showered down upon her head. A blood curdling scream escaped from her throat and shook the rafters.

Finally, she understood. Even though she'd found a man able to peer past the roles she played to the real woman beneath, it didn't matter. Perhaps that was the Grand Dame's greatest secret. Those who tended to her were damned from true love. Permitted to experience love, feel its power and taste its sweetness, for only the briefest moment before it was stripped away by fire or the hand of man.

Singing to herself between coughing fits, Ava dreamed of the life she'd lost with Jaxon. Sipping tea together in the Grand Lobby, her children racing through the attics playing hide and seek, and her creating magical spaces for guests to celebrate the pinnacles of life. Instead, she'd join the General's Gems in the family cemetery.

A speckled horse nudged Ava with his nose, and she rose to wrap her arms around his thick neck. Giving in to the thick smoke, she tied her scarf around the horse's neck and kissed him on the snout. Stroking the horse, she whispered, "Will I haunt Twin Springs with Ruby and sing night after night on the stage of the Theatre? Or, perhaps, you and I will ride through the mountains and we'll be free."

With a whoosh of air, the stable doors opened. Flames, horses and smoke poured from the building. The speckled horse flew from her arms with her red scarf flapping like a banner behind him. Ava looked towards the opening and hoped.

Framed in the doorway, the morning sun at his back, was Jaxon's magnificent body. With his feet spread, he shouted her name.

Beams of burning wood fell from the ceiling around her. Not sure if he was real or just a wish she created, she stumbled forward.

His golden eyes met hers and a growl grew deep in his chest and flowed out, "Always trying to steal the show. Double time it, Ava!"

Her arm covering her nose and mouth, she ran towards him.

Meeting her half way, he scooped her up and carried her from the building. With his body, he shielded her from the falling debris. Free from the building, he didn't stop until they reached Logan. Dropping to his knees, he laid Ava on the ground at his Army buddy's feet, not realizing flames greedily attempted to eat through his black t-shirt, in order to lick at the skin on his back.

Noticing the flames sneaking their way up the back of Jaxon, Logan removed his plaid shirt and beat at the fire. Mission accomplished, he collapsed in a heap. His hands shaking uncontrollably, he held the burnt remnants of his shirt to his chest.

On her hands and knees, Ava filled her lungs with fresh air. With tears streaming paths down the dirt and soot covering her face, she crawled over to Jaxon. She held his face between her palms and peppered his face with kisses. "I did exactly as you taught me," she whispered between kisses. "I screamed, just like you told me. I used my thumbs and my fists. Just like you said. I fought him off but then he locked me in."

He gathered her and drew her onto his lap. "I know. We saw him lock the doors." He glanced over at the burning heap that was once the bastard who attacked her. "He'll never hurt you or any other woman again."

CHAPTER SEVENTY-TWO

Ava surveyed the damage, standing at a distance between the two men she loved most. Jaxon and Logan. Oakton's volunteer fire department quickly responded to the alarm, their hoses watering what remained of the stables to a soggy mess. Only the charred bones of the structure remained.

The horses were rounded up and placed in temporary pens and locked in place. Theo spoke in hushed tones to the Sheriff who kept glancing over at the trio. They looked a mess. Ava, covered in soot, her white blouse now blackened. Jaxon's t-shirt hung from his body, and bandages showed through gaping holes in the back. For once, Logan blended in with his rag-tag clothes.

Reaching out, she laced her fingers with Jaxon's and took comfort in his presence. She leaned her head against his shoulder. "I guess we'll never find her."

"Who?" questioned Logan, relieved to turn away from the carnage caused by the fire. The smoke adhered to his clothes and he knew the dreams would be more vivid tonight.

"Ruby." She filled them in on the vision that Ruby had shared with her. "The Lieutenant dumped her in a tunnel under the tack room of the stables."

After all he'd found earlier, Jaxon didn't know why he was

surprised at the fact there were more hidden tunnels beneath Twin Springs. "Don't worry, we'll dig through the ashes, find the tunnel and Ruby."

Rubbing the portion of his right ear, where it melted into his head, Logan replied, "No you won't."

"Sure we can." Jaxon reached behind Ava and shoved at his shoulder.

"Nope." Logan shook his head. "You can dig in those ashes all you want. You'll never find Ruby if she was dumped under the tack room at Twin Springs in the 1920's."

"Why not?" asked Ava.

"Because in the 1920's the stables were located next to the present day Aviary. The Aviary used to be the tack room for the old stables."

Ava's mouth gaped open. "That's why Ruby always showed me the visions there."

"And why you woke up on the dirt path where the stables used to stand," replied Jaxon thoughtfully.

"I'm going to go find her." Ava turned, ready to rush away, only to be hauled back when Jaxon grabbed her by the hand.

His eyes softened, concerned for her. "Are you sure? You've had an intense day. Let Logan and I find her."

She tugged against his hold and pulled her hand free. "No, it has to be me. I have to find her and bring her out into the light."

Jaxon stared deep into Ava's beautiful green eyes, sensing her determination. "Alright, we'll go together."

The trio trudged along the path towards the Aviary. Rounding the crest of the hill, Ava examined the building where she and Jaxon made love for the first time. How did she not see it before? The slanted walkway, the oak tree, now ancient but still strong, and the tin roof.

She rounded the building, realizing what was once the front porch was screened in and divided into flight cages for the birds. Ava stood before the sloping entrance to the porch and she knew what lay below.

Logan scanned the area. "What are we looking for?"

For a moment, she was unable to speak. Ruby lay at their feet. She'd found her. "Nothing, we're here. She is down there."

"Down where?" asked Jaxon, looking at the solid dirt under his boots.

Ava pointed to the sloped wood of the walkway. She bent down, grasping the ledge and pulled the lid of Ruby's casket up.

"I'll be damned," breathed Logan in awe as he stared down into a dark, gaping hole. "Right here, in plain sight."

"There's a ladder." Ava bent down to crawl in and descend.

Jaxon pulled her back. "Wait, it could be dry rotted." He removed the small flashlight he'd used earlier from his side pocket, and laid down on the ground before the hole to gain a better assessment of the danger. "It looks pretty solid but let me go first."

He lowered his legs down into the hole and carefully worked his way down the ladder, ensuring he had two points of contact in case a piece of the wood gave way. "It's solid." Stepping off, he called up to the others, "Come on down." His flashlight scanned the floor at his feet. Sure enough, the white glow of bones shined in the dirt at the base of the ladder.

"Careful," warned Jaxon. "She's at our feet."

Ava stepped wide off the ladder and shivered, "It's cold down here."

Hearing Jaxon's warning Logan also stepped clear once he descended.

Their eyes adjusting to the dark, Ava bent down and examined what was once Ruby. She couldn't believe the vibrant Ruby was now only bones. Her dreams had rotted away a long time ago. "It is so sad. She'd found her true love. She was willing to give up everything to be with him, but the Lieutenant stole that chance from her."

"And from Guy," added Jaxon, the beam of his flashlight scanning the area.

Logan caught a sparkle from the corner of his eye. Bending

down, he reached into the now shadowed area after the beam of light had moved. He picked up something metal and cold within his hand. "What's this?"

"What?" asked Ava, turning towards him.

Logan held out a band of metal with the shreds of two ribbons dangling from each end.

Unable to believe her eyes, Ava took what Logan found.

Jaxon focused his light down on what she held within her hands.

Her brows furrowed and she turned the headband over and over in her hands. "It's her headband. I don't understand, the Lieutenant was going to come back for this. He needed it to pay for his life away from Twin Springs."

"Something must have happened to prevent him from coming back." Jaxon rubbed the back of his neck. "From what you've told me about him, there is no way he would leave something of that great value behind."

They all stood quietly and Ava said a small prayer for Ruby. She felt like she'd lost a sister.

Jaxon placed his arm around her. "Now that you have found her, let's get you back to Twin Springs. Logan and I will come back with better flashlights, and the authorities. Don't worry, we'll bring her out into the light for you."

Ava laid her hand along Jaxon's cheek. "Thank you," she kissed him soundly and thought she heard a sigh within the tunnel. The headband clasped in one hand, she made her way out of the tunnel with Jaxon and Logan emerging behind her.

Back in the clear mountain air, she walked up to the screened wall of the Aviary and peered in at her feathered friend. Ace's delighted wolf whistle greeted her, bringing a smile to her face as her laughter filled the air. Instantly, he imitated her laughter with his own. She cooed at him through the wire. "It's time for you to come home too, baby."

CHAPTER SEVENTY-THREE

*M*addy tucked her legs under her and splayed the fabric of her sunny blue skirt out around her. She snuggled in between her two sisters, Ava and Isabella, on the couch. "I thought I was going to die, waiting to talk about what happened to Ava and the stables. Somebody had better fill me in on all the details of what took place," the teen demanded. No one in Ava's office was spared from her glares, not even Jaxon and Logan.

Theo shook his head, "We needed to give the Sheriff and the coroner time to finish their investigations. Couldn't have Ava spending time in jail for murder and arson."

"Like I would let that happen," muttered Jaxon.

Crossing her arms, the teenager harrumphed under her breath. "But did we have to wait until after Thanksgiving?" she whined.

Isabella served everyone a cup of tea from the serving cart, except Logan. He stared up at the portrait and she placed his tea on the General's desk for later. She folded her chef's jacket over the arm of the couch and patted the teen reassuringly on the leg. She stretched out her tiny body and relaxed against the couch, comfortable in her skinny black jeans and white tank top. Her thick blonde hair was captured into a ponytail at the back of her head. "Yes,

Thanksgiving is the busiest day of the year for the hotel and the guests come first. The Grand Dame comes first. Besides, we have so much to be thankful for. Ava is safe within her home. Logan and Jaxon were brought back together and we found the last of the General's lost Gems."

A tiny white box burnt a hole in the side pocket of Jaxon's gray tactical pants. Searching for courage, he rubbed his suddenly moist palms down his thighs. He wanted to spend the rest of his life with Ava, but he was a fool and had treated her like crap when they first met. What if she said no?

His panicked gaze searched the room for something, anything to distract himself, until he soldiered up. "I have something to show you Maddy. This is going to knock your socks off." Jaxon distracted himself and Maddy by demonstrating for everyone how to open and close the secret entrance into Ava's office. "From the look of it, the General used this long hall to keep his own private, hidden stash of alcohol. At one time, he might have had a secret entrance in and out of the Presidents Hall."

In a mint green, silk shirt that matched her eyes, and black slacks, Ava gracefully leaned back against the couch. She was stunned by the unfairness of the General's double standards on Ruby. "I can't believe there's another hidden space within Twin Springs."

"It makes sense," replied Jaxon, "The twenties were the decade of hidden stashes, speakeasies and secret rooms."

Ava eyed the empty space where her coffee table had once stood. "Tell me again what happened to my table."

Both Jaxon and Logan mumbled under their breath and refused to meet her eyes.

Having learned how the table was destroyed, Theo laughed at their reaction.

Her gaze pivoting between the men in the room, Maddy asked, "What happened to the table?" At Jaxon's mutinous glare, she mumbled, "No one tells me anything."

Her brother laid his suit jacket over Isabella's and rolled up the sleeves of his white dress shirt to the elbows. "We don't have to. You find everything out yourself." Glancing over at Ava, Theo added, "The coroner found Sheela's remains in the stables. I contacted her parents and they'll be arriving in a couple days. I talked the Sheriff into waiting one more day to take your statement on everything that happened."

Her mouth suddenly dry, Ava licked her lips. "He killed her, you know. The Director. How could there be so much evil within one man? He was smoking when I found him. She laid dead behind him, and he was enjoying a cigar."

"Try not to think about it," said Jaxon, bending down to kiss her on top of the head. "Maddy has something to show you."

In a flash, Maddy pulled a newspaper out from under her, smoothing the wrinkles from it, before handing the paper to Ava.

"Please," said Ava, waiving her off. "I don't think I can take another article on what a wicked woman I am. I prefer not to play that part ever again."

"No, read it." The teen shoved the paper into her hands. "Sheela wrote it. She was the spy at Twin Springs reporting on you."

"Sheela?" whispered Ava, the betrayal cutting her deep. "Reported on me?"

"Yes." Jaxon nodded. "She was a friend of Ashlee Hollingsworth. Her real name is Mackenzie Mills. I think she became caught up in the grief of her friend's suicide at first but, in the end, she made it right by you."

"Exactly," added Maddy. "She cleared your name, exposed the Director and found other women to come forth and add their stories to yours."

Ava shook her head, staring up at Ruby. "And she was murdered for her efforts."

"Since we are clearing the air," Jaxon took deep a breath and addressed the room. "I wronged all of you by coming to Twin Springs under false pretenses."

Ava opened her mouth to reply but Jaxon held his hand up,

silencing her. "I spoke with the insurance company. They're releasing the funds for your claims. And, if you will have me, I'd like to remain at Twin Springs as Security Manager. I'll do a better job. I swear. As you told me, your old Security Manager, Niles, started the sabotage. It seems that Director Hollingsworth or Sheela carried on the sabotage after he died. I can't find any other explanation. Perhaps both caused the havoc, making it appear orchestrated."

"I'm just glad it is all over, and my family is once again safe." Theo reached out and shook Jaxon's hand. "As I said before, you're perfect for the position."

"Thanks." Jaxon rubbed his damp palms on his pants. He tapped the tip of his fingers against the box in his side pocket. "In fact, I'd like to help Twin Springs gain momentum towards financial solvency. I know a reclusive artist, a famous one." He paused for dramatic effect. "The artist, DiWolf. I talked DiWolf into an art show and public appearance here at Twin Springs. Patrons will finally meet the famous artist."

Maddy squealed with delight. "That sounds wonderful! I've never met an artist before."

Theo spoke up, "I've seen DiWolf's works in acrylic. Powerful."

Prying his eyes away from the portrait, Logan chipped in, "I have one of DiWolf's pen and ink's. Dropped a month of my hazardous duty pay on it."

"I forgot about that." Jaxon's golden gaze twinkled at his buddy.

"That sounds wonderful. We appreciate your help." Theo sobered and addressed Ava. "I need to let you know that the coroner was unable to give us the cause of Ruby's death. With only bones left, strangulation was difficult to confirm. There were a lot of broken bones and any of them could be contributed to a fall."

Ace squawked within his cage, happily chewing on apple slices. He trilled a whistle and sang out a jazz tune.

Shivering, Isabella rubbed her arms. "That gives me the heebie-jeebies."

Ava hushed the parrot. "It doesn't matter what the report says. I know how she died. It was terrible and she didn't deserve it. No one does."

Her fingertips brushed against the fading bruises on her throat. Shaking her head to clear it, she added, "Once the coroner releases Ruby, we can bury her along with her sisters. Finally, the Rockwell sisters will be back together. It's too bad she can't be buried with Guy but, I understand that he might be buried with his first wife."

Jaxon rubbed Ava's shoulders. "I asked my cousin to research this. His wife was laid to rest with her parents at a cemetery in DC. He was buried on his family's farm, here in Virginia."

Isabella squeezed Theo's hand. "Do you think your family would mind if we moved him here to be with Ruby?"

"I already asked." Jaxon shook his head. "They want him to be with Ruby, the woman he loved."

Averting his eyes from the painting, Logan asked, "How did it go? Filling your family in on their history here at Twin Springs."

Tapping the side of his leg, Jaxon took his time replying. "Well, according to my cousin, it caused one hell of a ruckus."

"I'm sure it did," added Logan. Coming forward he handed a rectangular cardboard box, the size of a shoe box, over to Theo. "After Dad and I lit up that portion of tunnel with lights, we found the cracks in the walls littered with these little papers. Once we realized what the papers were, we took pictures of the area and documented each paper and where it was found."

Frowning in confusion, Theo opened the box. Within were a mass of tiny little papers. Drawing one out he read in broken English. "George, I be in free Pittsburg, Harriet." Paper after paper, repeated different names and the locations where they could be found. Some in broken English and many in a woman's flowing script. Handing the aged scraps around, he looked up to Logan. "What are they?"

"Oh Theo, don't you know?" Maddy wiped away tears with the back of her hand and sniffled hard. "They're notes to loved ones, telling them where they will be. Where they can be found in the free North."

Logan spoke up. "We found the original use of the tunnels below Twin Springs. They were used as part of the Underground Railroad to help slaves escape to the northern free states. Someone helped those who couldn't write to leave notes for their loved ones, who'd follow behind. It makes sense that your ancestor, the Executive Chef of Twin Springs, knew about the tunnels. As a black man, his ancestors probably assisted those slaves in their journey and passed the location of the tunnels down from generation to generation. Somehow, the Lieutenant found out about the tunnels and used them to transport illegal liquor."

Holding a slip of paper in her hand, Isabella asked, "Who do you think the woman was helping them? She obviously had a high born education. Her penmanship and grammar are impeccable."

Logan shrugged, "Probably one of the women of Twin Springs."

"That would make her your ancestor," piped up Maddy.

"Maybe," he said, gazing up at the portrait. "In all likelihood, we'll never know."

"May I see Ruby's headband?"

Ava passed Maddy the jeweled headband. The freshly cleaned diamonds and rubies caught the light and cast dancing beams around the room. "It's beautiful. What are you going to do with it?"

"We could sell it to pay for all the repairs for Twin Springs," stated Theo dryly.

All three women gasped.

"You'll not sell it," admonished Isabella, her green eyes sparking in the light.

"I was thinking," replied Logan. "What if we carve out a space in the bottom of the new Tower for a museum of Twin Springs. We could finally record the timeline of the Grand Dame. We could have a section highlighting the letters found in the tunnels that document Twin Springs' role in the Underground Railroad."

"And a section on the General and his Gems," added Maddy.

Listening to them talk, the ring his cousin had expressed out to him burned a hole in Jaxon's pocket. Thinking of Ruby and the slaves torn from their families and the ones they loved, he wondered why he worried about asking Ava to marry him. It didn't take courage to ask her to be his wife. He would need courage after they were married, trying to keep up with her. "Talking about diamonds," he said, moving forward before Ava. He glanced over to Maddy, addressing her first. "I understand it's a tradition to do this in front of you." He bent, coming down on one knee in front of Ava. Taking both of her delicate hands within his, he swallowed, trying to remove the lump in his throat, and rolled his shoulders. Feeling foolish in front of the other men, he declared. "Ava, I love you."

Once again the women in the room gasped in unison. Isabella covered her mouth and Maddy squealed, jumping in her seat.

Theo hushed the room, "Let the man do what he needs to do."

Taking a deep breath, Jaxon searched Ava's gorgeous green eyes and removed a small, square box from his pocket. By some stroke of luck, he'd found a soulmate in Ava. A drop dead, gorgeous soulmate with a heart of gold and the voice of an angel. Somehow he'd convince her that he was worthy of her love. "Like I was saying, I love you. More than words can say. Hell," he stopped at the slip of his tongue. "I mean, I wish I had a script to give you the fancy words you deserve. All I have is the love burning deep within my soul for you."

He opened the lid of the white box and a brilliant diamond winked at Ava, surrounded by ruby flowers. He now understood that not all beautiful women were the same. "If I promise to never call you beautiful, will you marry me?"

All eyes pivoted towards Ava. A sultry smile spread across her full lips. "Hell yeah, I will." She cupped Jaxon by the back of his neck and burned her lips to his. At the end of their kiss, she whispered against his lips. "I love you more than life, Wolfeman."

The group exploded into a round of applause. Tears and hugs shared between the women and slaps on the back by the men.

Maddy clapped her hands and bounced up and down on the couch, admiring Ava's engagement ring. "Will you go back to acting? Now that the Director is gone and you are going to be married."

Ava watched Jaxon and Logan shaking hands. Somehow she'd found a man not fooled by the roles she played and able to see past her beauty to the real woman beneath. She shook her head. "I might sing on stage but I'll never play any other role but myself."

A ruckus in the Grand Lobby interrupted the celebration. Jaxon heard two burly voices booming beyond the doors. "Crap," he muttered. "The Geezers arrived."

"The Geezers?" parroted Ava.

He grasped her hand within his. "Yeah, the Geezers are my dad and uncle."

A loud woman's voice hushed the two men beyond the doors.

Jaxon glanced over to Logan. "It sounds like they brought my sister too." He watched as Logan's good eye widened and he rushed to slip out the secret panel within the back wall before the double doors to Ava's office exploded with Jaxon's family.

Happy to have everyone together, Ava looked up at Ruby in the portrait. "Guy will be home soon," she whispered under her breath. So immersed in her thoughts of Ruby, and a future with Logan, she didn't pay attention to the ruckus around her. The smell of roses filled the air. Her family was safe within the Grand Dame's loving arms.

Ace squawked above the booming voices, "Get the fuck out."

CHAPTER SEVENTY-FOUR

2 9 November 2018

Even the smart and talented AVA, doesn't have a clue that I've been hiding in Twin Springs. The whole time. After the reporter discovered my secret place, I had to kill her. She would've spoiled my surprise. When Hollingsworth showed up at the stables, he almost caught me strangling Sheela. No, I guess her name was Mackenzie. It doesn't matter.

In the end, it worked out perfectly. Everyone thinks the Director killed the reporter. When Ava appeared and was caught in the fire, I laughed at the irony. I didn't care if Hollingsworth burned down the stables, and killed himself. But the idiot allowed Ava to escape.

Standing in the crowd along the perimeter of the stable, I enjoyed watching the destruction caused by the fire. The way the flames consumed everything in its path. The anger of it. The power of it. That's how I will finish them. With my friend, fire.

Through the panel, I hear them celebrating in the General's office. Even my sweet Izzy thinks they've won. But I'm patient and have time at my disposal. I'll wait until they lower their defenses before I destroy them all. They'll pay for the pain their family inflicted upon mine. Just like my ancestor killed the General's Gems, one by one. I'll destroy them, one by one. They'll atone for their actions with their lives.

Niles Porter

HELLO, MY BOOK-LOVING FRIEND, THANK YOU.

Dear Reader,

I hope you were swept away by Ava and Jaxon's love story—two souls bound by dreams, danger, and a past that left scars.

Their journey through the shadows of Twin Springs continues the legend of the Three Gems… and the secrets that refuse to sleep.

Don't miss the final chapter in the trilogy: **Book Three,** *Haunted by Amethyst.*

Want early access to my newest mysteries, short stories, and behind-the-scenes inspiration? Subscribe to my newsletter and become part of my reader circle, where I spill the tea about ghosts, grit, and the heartbeats behind every story. My subscribers always get sneak peeks before anyone else!

If you love books, laughter, and a dash of chaos, join my **Book-Loving Friends** Facebook group. It's where readers and I share favorite reads, twisty mysteries, and plenty of fun during live chats and giveaways. The tea's always hot—and there's always a chair waiting for you.

If Ava and Jaxon's story touched your heart or kept you turning pages late into the night, I'd love to hear what you thought.

Even a few words in a review can help other readers discover *Sleepwalking with Ruby* and the world of *Twin Springs.*

☞ **Scan the QR code** for all the links in one spot — my reader circle, the Book-Loving Friends Facebook group, review page, and more. One scan and you're in.

Turn the page for a special sneak peek of **Haunted by Amethyst**, the final chapter of *The Mystery of the Three Gems*.

I can't wait for you to see how it all ends… and how love still finds its light, even in the darkest places.

I'll keep the kettle warm until next time—

Love,
   ~ Dee

One scan and we will be Book-Loving friends.

Haunted by Amethyst

THE MYSTERY OF
THE THREE GEMS, BOOK THREE
A TWIN SPRINGS TRILOGY

DEE ARMSTRONG

CHAPTER ONE

Dear junal

Momys dead. izzys dad says we r a famly.

the twin springs famly he says izzy and ava hav to play wif me. Today we got fire flys. trapt them in a jar. izzys eyes glowd like the fire flys and my tumy fel warm and hapy i eat a fire flys and it roll and play in my tumy

izzy make me fel good and hapy. i luv her. i want her to luv me to. i want to be dis happy forevr to play wif izzy forevr she maks me glow to

niles

CHAPTER TWO

For her eighth birthday, Diamond didn't wish for a pony, a Nintendo Gameboy or even to find out who her father was. She wished for one thing—to kill the Woman. But the Woman was already dead.

Diamond plodded a path towards Happy Springs Motel and avoided the worst parts of the cracked, uneven sidewalk, but stomped in each puddle of water. Rain soaked her long braids and the soggy paper bag of groceries she carried dwarfed her. She ignored the roar of the cars that passed her on Virginia's US Route 1 as she squeezed the bag closer to her flat chest. The red strands of her bangs blurred her vision and she blew them out of her way. "Couldn't even get one lousy wish," she grumbled.

A quick wipe across her face with the back of her hand only paused the raindrops that dripped from the brim of her hoodie and down her nose. She dug into her back pocket for the oversized green key ring to hotel room 115. Home, at least for today.

Resentment churned in her stomach. She scrunched her freckle covered nose and her eyes stung with unshed tears. She sniffled, rapidly blinked and shunned the weakness. Pushing hard on the door, she fumbled with the key. The rain swelled door wouldn't budge. She muttered under her breath, "Stupid hotel. Stupid door. Stupid wish."

Shoving her small shoulder into the door, she pushed with all her weight. With a groan, the door released, and she stumbled forward. The toe of her tennis shoe snagged on the crooked threshold and she fell heavily, scraping her knee through the already gaping hole in her jeans. She flattened the mountain of cellophane bags and a tall, lean jug of milk tumbled from the ripped sack. A giggle escaped her lips. "I'm okay, Mom. The Ramen Noodles saved me."

No response.

Her heart picked up its pace and thudded hard in her chest. She scrambled to her feet. A quiver of fear laced her voice, "Mom?"

Her panicked gaze searched the room. Sucking in a great breath of air, she prepared herself for what she might find. Raindrops, stale cigarette and pot smoke combined with the smell of lavender filled her nostrils. Immediately, she understood why her mother sat frozen on the bed, hugging her pajama clad legs with her head averted towards the wall. The Woman was here.

From the corner of her eye, she caught a glimpse of scraggily, long gray hair before the Woman's black and white form faded into the wallpaper. With a swoosh of air, Diamond released the breath she'd been holding. Relief flooded her limbs. Her mother was okay. Until the next time the Woman came.

Bending down, she filled her arms with the little square noodle bags and dumped them between mounds of half melted candles on the out of date wooden dresser. "Hey Mom! Got some grub." In the dimly lit room, her voice was overly bright and loud.

On the corner of the old dresser, a half full jug of milk laid in a bed of melted ice cubes. She dragged the milk out, twisted off the lid and sniffed. Wrinkling her nose, she replaced the lid and dropped the jug into a small, open trash can. Hooking her fingers through the handle of the new milk, she plopped it in the bucket. "Don't worry. I'll get more ice."

She tossed her wet hoodie on top of a small heap of clothes in the corner. Her gaze lingered on the TV and she longed to drown out the morning with an episode of Full House. Instead, she walked over to her mom, her purple Sketchers squishing with each step. Brushing aside the little bottles of pills that helped her mom get through her days and nights, she crawled up on the bed and snuggled beside her. Her mom was old. Almost thirty. Reaching up, she stroked her mother's once vibrant red hair back from her high forehead. Her mother felt cold to the touch. She had for years. Diamond assumed that was how the walking dead felt. Cold.

Her mother clutched her hand within her frigid grasp.

Diamond stroked her mother's bone thin fingers and then linked hands. The blue veins were easily visible through her sheer, pale skin. Like an opal, once blazing with color but now faded. "Whoever named you, must've had a magic eight ball or something. Opal fits you." *Unlike my stupid name.*

She stared down at her dirty jeans, faded to a light blue with holes and frayed bottoms. She owned two pairs of jeans from the Salvation Army, three t-shirts, plus her rocking Sketchers and a stupid pair of ugly, bright yellow rain boots that her mother had insisted she needed. Tossing one of her long, wet braids back over her shoulder, she brooded. "I'm not rich or shiny. Diamond's a stupid name."

Opal shifted on the bed and paper crinkled under her. Her voice cracked. "You're strong. Brilliant. Perfect name."

The crinkling sound drew Diamond's gaze. She tugged a piece of lined paper out from under her mom's butt and studied the huge brick building that her mom had sketched.

The building was long with arms stretching out to each side. A tall tower grew out of its body like a long neck with a shiny, bald head at the top. She snagged the pencil from behind her mother's ear and with quick, talented fingers, rounded off the top of the tower and drew in the face of a clock. "Right here, this is where the clock goes." She flipped the pencil around and scrubbed the eraser across the paper. "The columns aren't round. They're arched in curves like this." She glanced up and searched her mom's face for approval.

Opal's washed out green eyes filled with moisture until a single tear slipped down over the protruding bones of her cheeks.

Diamond caught the tear before it dropped and blinked up at her mom. They both had green eyes and red hair, but they couldn't have been more different. Her brows furrowed. *Why can't she fight? Fight the sadness for me?*

Quickly, she crumpled up the paper, the tear and the pencil together. She wanted to absorb her mom's pain and squeezed the small bundle until the sound of the pencil breaking popped within the silence. "Just a stupid building. Stupid. We can draw anything we want." She dipped her head and swallowed hard to press back tears. "How about the mountains? You love drawing mountains."

The scent of lavender flooded the dingy room. Opal stiffened and turned back towards the wall. "Why don't you go play? Grab something from the vending machines. Use the money from the dresser." With each word, her voice broke, as if it was difficult for her to pull the sounds through her clogged throat. "I just need time. Then we can draw."

Diamond couldn't see the Woman. Yet. But she smelled her. Felt her. Knew in her belly that she was coming. She grasped her mom's hand the best she could with her two small ones. "It's okay. I'll stay with you."

Her chin dipped to her chest and Opal shook her head. "Take your time. Light some candles and crack the window before you go."

Fury beat within her heart. She realized her mother was trying to wash out the smell of lavender, just like she tried to wash out everything else in her life. *Why couldn't she just tell the Woman to go away?*

She stomped over to her hoodie, pulled it over her head and struggled with the wet fabric. Her head popped out and she heard her mom furiously whispering. Dragging the rest of the hoodie down her front, she watched her talking to thin air. The lavender stench thickened within the room and gagged her with its overbearing weight.

Reaching over the dresser, she pushed the curtains aside and tugged the window wide open, not caring if the rain came in and ruined the ugly dresser. One by one, she lit her mother's candles and their various fragrances combated the reeking lavender scent.

She pretended not to notice the Woman taking full form. The hem of a long, ratty dress filled in with grays and fluttered without the help of a breeze. Bit by bit, the long length of her body and the rest of the tent like dress appeared and filled in. Her charcoal colored hair clung to her ashen face and cascaded around her shoulders. Only her glowing silver eyes and dark gray lips penetrated the mass of hair that covered her face. Leaning down, her lips brushed Opal's ear, and she urgently whispered.

Opal shook. She popped one of the bottle's lids and sprinkled her palm with the little pills before she tossed them in her mouth and swallowed them with a flick of her head.

Rubbing a piece of the broken pencil against her jeans, Diamond hesitated. "Mom, I'll get something later. Let's watch a show. I'll make you beef ramen. Your favorite. We might even have some hot sauce left. I can spice it up for you." Her heart beat faster and the Woman glowed in different shades of gray just like a character from an old TV show. "Please, let me stay with you."

Again, the Woman leaned down and whispered. Her mom slouched beneath the blankets and covered her head. It didn't matter. The Woman continued to speak.

Her voice muffled, Opal yelled from beneath her blankets. "Fine! I'll tell her. Wear your rain boots Diamond."

She studied her favorite shoes, not wanting to be parted from their pretty purple and white design for even a minute. "But, Mom," she whined.

"Do as I say." Her mother's voice slurred as the pills took hold. "Wear the damn boots."

Glaring at the Woman, Diamond kicked off her wet shoes. She shoved her feet into the stupid yellow boots and her bare skin skidded against the rubber insides. The boots came high on her knees and she felt like a complete reject. Turning back towards the dresser, she removed the striped birthday candle that she'd snuck out of the store and relit it on one of the candles. She closed her eyes and whispered, "I wish I could kill the Woman. I wish I could kill the Woman. I wish."

She blew hard, opened her eyes and looked back at the bed.

The Woman stroked the mound of blankets covering her mom.

Her heart felt like a heavy stone in her chest. She rammed cash, along with the green room key, the broken pencil and her mother's drawing, into her boot. Grabbing the door handle, she tugged hard to free the door. "Stupid wish," she muttered.

Rain dribbling from the overhang above, Diamond sat on the cement next to a vending machine with a bag of Cheetos and chugged down her second Pepsi. The heat and the soft hum from the back of the machine soothed her frazzled nerves. She licked her orange fingers before wiping them down the front of her hoodie. Her favorite meal, Cheetos and Pepsi. Tossing another Cheeto into her mouth, she sipped a little Pepsi and enjoyed the feeling of the pop snapping against the Cheeto until it became a soggy mess within her mouth. She munched it down and chased the Cheeto with another slug of Pepsi.

She scowled down at the stupid yellow boots. Reaching into her right boot, she pulled out the piece of notebook paper and smoothed it out on the cement between her spread legs.

Leaning forward, she added mountains to the background, a curved driveway and a pool off in the distance. Her quick strokes didn't hesitate. She'd dreamed about this building every night of her life.

Shading in the glint of the sun off the rows of tiny double

windows that ran the length of the roof line across each arm of the building, she scarcely registered the smoke that tickled her nose. It wasn't until the wailing fire trucks screeched to a stop in front of the motel that she glanced up. She watched the firemen in their heavy coats. Her lids grew heavy from the warmth of the vending machine as they dragged long hoses from their trucks. Disinterested, she focused back on her drawing and hummed in tune to the vending machine.

Gradually, the Woman took form next to the soda machine. Dull as the world outside the hidden spot.

Diamond's small body tingled, warning of her approach. Her heart picked up and beat faster and faster. Her hands shook as she shoved the paper and pencil back into her boot. Once the Woman had fully formed, she understood and clambered to her feet. Awkward in the big rain boots, she raced from her hiding spot.

A fireman scooped her up before she charged head first into the gaping hole, blackened with smoke, that was once room 115. Over his shoulder, she noticed the owner of the dump pointing towards her and speaking to a young woman in a cobalt blue rain jacket.

The stranger popped open a golden yellow umbrella that looked like the sun shining. In high heeled shoes, she purposely picked her way across the parking lot, stepping over the spider web of hoses and mud puddles. She tapped the shoulder of the fireman, opened a folded piece of leather and showed a card to him. "Social Services. I'll take her from you."

Placed on the blacktop, Diamond's legs trembled beneath her.

The stranger bent down and the hem of her skirt trailed in a mud puddle. "I'm Miss Dodd. I'm here to take care of you." Her eyes were the color of a clear blue sky and swept Diamond up and down. "Nice boots. I should've worn mine. It's always good to be prepared." Her smile was prettier than any Diamond had seen. "What's your name?"

"Where's my mom?" she sniffled, guessing the answer but wanting the stranger to say it. Needing to be told what she feared.

Miss Dodd's eyes clouded and she gazed over her head towards the hotel room. "What's your name sweetie?"

"Diamond," she replied, wiping her nose with the back of her hand.

"What a beautiful name," she murmured in a soft voice. "What's your last name sweetie?"

She listened to the rain tapping on the top of the umbrella and watched as tiny drops flowed down the outside and dripped around them. Her throat thickened. Tears escaped from the corner of her eyes and blended in with the rain on her face. "Don't have one. It's just Diamond." Her voice careened high, until it was unrecognizable, even to herself. "I want Mommy."

Secluded in another world under the golden umbrella with Miss Dodd, she learned that her mother had finally escaped her pain. Diamond's birthday wish had finally come true. She'd killed a woman. Just the wrong one. Now, she was all alone in the world.

Alone with the Woman.

CHAPTER THREE

Shoving another Cheeto into her mouth, JD Wolfe chased it with a swig of Pepsi. Her midnight black SUV blended into the darkened street. Raising her binoculars, she studied the exterior of a row of dilapidated townhouses and focused in on the end unit with its peeling, mud brown paint. Blood red sheets blocked her view through the upper two windows. The light, trying to escape from the upstairs rooms, cast an eerie glow onto the sidewalk below. Behind those windows, there was a ten-year-old girl. A little girl scared for her life.

Last week, on a brisk Tuesday afternoon, little Harmony Scott had walked home from school. She was counting the days until Thanksgiving break, like any other kid her age. But Harmony never reached the safety of her home, and quickly became one of JD's lost children.

Today, while other families gave thanks around a table and were oblivious to the outside world, Harmony's family spent it on their knees begging for their daughter's safe return. Fishing in her tall, black leather boots, JD tugged out a small, spiral notebook.

She unwound the faded gray rubber band that strapped down its pages, flipped past the drawings she'd made from snippets of her dreams, to a penciled portrait.

She considered the sketch that she'd rendered using eyewitness accounts. A young man, early twenties, Caucasian. From outward appearances, he looked like a nice guy. The witnesses had said that he was incredibly thin with a clean-shaven face, short cropped, dark brown hair and an easy smile. Surveillance cameras from a gas station had shown him wearing clean clothes, a tucked in checkered button up shirt, dark waist coat, and dark dress pants. Witnesses had assumed that the young man was the girl's father or uncle at least. But the collar of his shirt had blown open in the wind and eyewitnesses swore tattoos of faces covered his neck. Tattoos of what had seemed to be kids' faces.

She didn't understand the so-called adults. She spoke to the face in her sketch. "If your tattoos had seemed odd, why didn't the witnesses say or do anything? Why did they allow you to take Harmony by the hand and walk with her around the corner?" She shook her head and glared down at the sketch, "But those odd tattoos, that's how I finally tracked you down, asshole. Found you right here at 'Looser Lane' in Alexandria, Virginia."

Lost and endangered children were her specialty. She not only understood how children thought, she understood the evil that preyed on them. Parents called White Wolfe Investigations and requested JD Wolfe's services when their child had disappeared and the system had failed them. Most parents assumed she was a man. But in the end, they didn't care. They wanted their loved ones back. She didn't know how the parents knew to call her, but they did. When asked how they came by her name, through tears and strained faces, they only replied, a friend of a friend.

As word spread, police detectives had begun calling and requesting a meet with Invastigator JD Wolfe. In back alleys and coffee shops, they'd slipped her the case files of a child they couldn't find. Once she'd recovered the lost child, she gave the officer all the credit, preferring to keep her name out of the newspapers. She had one condition, however, that her oldest and only true, female friend, Miss Dodd, who since her marriage went by Mrs. Malloy, processed the children and ensured their safety.

That was how she and Rodriguez had truly started working together. He'd slipped her a tan case file with pictures of three little boys. She tried not to think about her first police case with Rodriguez and the boys that she'd found too late. The emotional devastation of that case and the press afterwards had proved Rodriguez was trustworthy. The one and only cop she'd ever come close to calling a friend.

Slipping the notebook back into its hiding place, she once again raised the binoculars. The sheets within one room fluttered and brightened, as if spot lights had hit them from within. Frowning, she froze and searched the red glow for clues. Her heart picked up a beat and she tossed the binoculars onto the passenger seat and dug under candy wrappers and empty Cheeto bags for her cell phone. Realizing it was in her back pocket, she snagged it and texted Mrs. Malloy, who's number was still under her maiden name of Dodd.

Her thumb tapped out a quick message. "Got a bad feeling. Need you now. What's your ETA?"

The dimmed screen flashed, "Twenty min, I-95 backed up."

Her gaze flickered up to the sheet covered windows. Twenty minutes was too long. A lot could happen to a little girl in a lot less time.

Her phone vibrated. Impatient, she glanced down at the text, "Did you call Rodriguez?"

"Of course, I did," she muttered under her breath and pressed speed dial on her phone. Rodriguez picked up on the first ring. "Where the hell are you?" she spit into the phone. She could barely hear Rodriguez over the sirens screaming in the background.

"On my way. A semi-truck jackknifed on 95. Having a hell of a time getting around drivers that don't know to keep off the shoulder during a traffic jam."

The sticky sweet scent of lavender filled her vehicle and her nose wrinkled up at the offending scent. The sick feeling of dread that she'd felt earlier dropped into the pit of her stomach and gnawed at the lining. She realized little Harmony's time was almost up. "Shit, shit, shit," she muttered under her breath before taking a deep breath in and steeling herself. An ice-cold thread entered her tone. "Gotta go, Rodriguez. Gotta go now."

He understood. "I'll call for back up. And let them know there's a friendly on scene."

"Get here as fast as you can. So I don't have to deal with the boys in blue." She hung up and refused to glance over at the Woman, but through her peripheral vision she saw that her transparent form now sat in the passenger seat.

She removed a hair tie from around the gear shift and secured her long pony tail in a knot on the top of her head, so the length of her red hair couldn't be used as a weapon against her. She replaced the notebook in her right boot, and verified her knife was accessible in her left. She drew the knife out and slid it back into its hidden sheath to make sure it wouldn't catch if she needed to wield its power. Leaning forward, she removed a Glock 42 from the holster in the small of her back. With a push of her thumb, the magazine popped out and landed in her palm. She checked the number of bullets before snapping it back into the well and raking the slide back to send a round into the chamber.

Her trigger finger lying on the side of the barrel, she laid the weapon on her thigh, cocked and ready. For a precious moment, her finger tapped the metal that was warm from her body's heat. Would the Woman ever leave her alone? Or would she drive her crazy, just as she had her mother? She continued to just show up and butt into her business. "Couldn't stay the hell away could you?"

"*No,*" the Woman whispered, but her voice ricocheted within JD's brain. From experience, she knew that only she could hear the ghost's cultured tones. Time to face facts—she'd never have a day without the ghost yelling in her head.

She knew there was no way to block her out, ignore her or push her away. She just had to deal with her. Anyway, the most import thing in her world right now was getting one little girl out of the townhouse alive. There was never anyone there to save JD. She knew how it felt to be helpless and without choices. Bottom line, the kid needed her more than she hated the Woman's presence. "Harmony's in danger?" she asked, but she already knew the answer.

The Woman nodded, and her glowing gray hair lit up the air around her.

The brighter she glowed, the more urgent JD knew little Harmony Scott's situation was. "Stay in the god damn car and let me handle it."

Behind the tangled screen of her hair, her face was drawn and there was a sad smile on her charcoal colored lips, but she nodded.

JD's gaze flickered up and down the street, before she eased her car door open and soundlessly latched it. In her black leather jacket and matching jeans, she faded into the darkness. Keeping her eyes on the windows for movement, she quickly crossed the street, the moonlight guiding her steps. Searching for a point of entry, she circled the townhouse. Her soft soled leather boots slipped sideways on slick ground. *Virginia weather,* she sneered. *Snow in the morning that melts into a muddy mess by afternoon and freezes into ice overnight.*

The rear windows of the townhouse were high and out of reach. The back stoop sunk sideways into the icy, uneven ground. A ripped screen door hung from the back door and flapped in the cold wind. The lower panel of the wooden door had been knocked out as a makeshift doggy door. Heavy construction plastic sucked in and out of the hole like a chest breathing. Because of the massive size of the opening, her gaze searched for an enormous beast. She hoped that she wouldn't have to give away the element of surprise by shooting a charging mutt.

Across the yard, she spotted the owner of the doggie door. A sad excuse for a dog lay chained to a tree by a thick, muddy silver chain. Skin and bones, the once huge Great Dane lay sideways on the frozen ground. His belly was painfully bloated into a large ball. The heavy chain collar was ingrained into the skin around his neck. His white fur, spotted with black, glowed in the moonlight, though matted and caked with mud, along with a suspicious darker substance. *Blood.*

Either not willing or unable, the dog didn't raise his head, only stared at her with flickering light blue eyes, so human it pained her. A low, pitiful whine rolled across the yard and reached her ears. The moon slipped behind a cloud and darkened the world between them. She raised a finger and pressed it to her lips. "I'll be back for you," she whispered, before crawling through the hole in the bottom of the door.

CHAPTER FOUR

*E*ntering a world of filth, JD plastered her spine back against a lower kitchen cabinet. Her Glock at the ready, she crouched momentarily in place and allowed for her eyes to adjust to the darkened room. The green glow of numbers from the stove emitted just enough light for her to survey the situation. It was four am kitchen time and the floor moved with hundreds of cockroaches, but no humans. Sliding her back up along the paneled cabinet, a roach crawled a path down her shoulder. *Disgusting boogers*, she thought, with a flick of her finger.

Reaching behind her, she carefully jiggled the knob of the door that she'd gained access to the house through. She unlocked it, allowing for a quick exit if needed. Not taking her gaze off the only other entrance to the room, she slid her hand up the door and searched for any latches that would prevent her and Harmony from getting away. Satisfied, her gaze continued to sweep the room. Sink filled with dirty dishes, half the cabinet doors missing, take-out boxes piled high on a small silver and teal Formica table, along with two aluminum and vinyl chairs in a mustard yellow. And, of course, an army of bugs searching the filth for their next meal.

She softened her knees into a ready stance. One hand palming the other, she held her weapon close to her body, ready. She stepped forward and cockroaches crunched beneath her boots. The sound rebounded off the walls. She paused, holding her breath deep in her chest. She listened for one heartbeat, then two. Satisfied she couldn't be heard, she purposely crunched her way across the kitchen and down a narrow, darkened hall. On her journey, she cleared a small bathroom, only finding more filth and crawling bugs before the short hall opened up into a living space.

Mounds of trash were piled throughout the small living room. The back of a long, putrid green couch almost touched both ends of the room, facing a huge flat screen television and the front door. Softly stepping over clothes and through rotting food containers, she mentally thanked her trusty boots for protecting her as she approached the couch. She was unsure if someone slept on the ugly sofa and she knew that she needed to clear the room or she'd end up trapping herself upstairs. Her forward momentum halted as she contemplated which side of the couch to move towards. If she picked the wrong side, a big enough man could sling her over the back of it. Then, she'd be in a world of hurt. And she wouldn't be doing herself or Harmony any good. *A damn crap shoot.*

Quietly as possible in the mounds of trash, she made her way to the foot of the couch that she considered would have the least favorite view of the massive television. She steadied her hands, held her breath and rounded the couch. She expelled her breath in a soft swoosh of air when only little critters faced her. Shifting her attention to the open stairway, she squeezed around the couch and moved cautiously across the room. She released the lock on the front door and left the door ajar. Before she turned away, the wind moved the door ever so slightly. She reconsidered and eased the door closed but unlocked.

In somewhat of a crouched stance, she padded her way up the dirt brown, shag carpeted stairs. Quickly, she cleared another bathroom. Then, she hesitated, considering her options. From the layout of the windows visible from the street, she figured the top floor held two rooms, both of which had light illuminating from beneath the doors. Pick the wrong room and her element of surprise turned to shit. Scenarios raced through her brain and she decided on the far-right room. The one where the light behind the sheets had brightened unnaturally. Decision made, she moved determinedly forward towards her goal.

Suddenly, the Woman materialized and blocked the hallway. Unable to stop her forward momentum, she charged right through the Woman's transparent form. Fury exploded through her. What if she got ghost dust in her mouth? *Damn it!*

She raised her arm to wipe the offending concept off her tongue with the back of the sleeve of her leather jacket. Her arm froze only inches from her mouth, realizing she didn't know what filth was on her clothes from her journey through the house.

Pursing her lips, she wished that she could burn the ghost with the heat of her anger. But no, she wouldn't wish a fiery death on anyone, not even the Woman.

Raising her hands, palms up, the Woman shrugged. Glowing in her long ratty gown, she appeared right at home in the filth.

Calming herself with a breath, she silently mouthed, "What?"

Urgently, she pointed a gray finger towards the room she'd just prevented JD from entering.

Shaking her head, she mouthed, "No, shit." She turned and proceeded down the hall with her gun ready.

Again, the Woman appeared in front of her, hands raised and moving frantically in front of her semi-transparent form.

Completely giving up on her fighting stance, her weapon hung limply in her right hand. She pushed at damping the anger burning within her. "What?" she hissed.

Raising a finger to her lips, the Woman actually shook her head at JD. Through the charcoal colored strands of hair flowing down in front of her face, she gave JD a pointed look and tapped her bare foot on the carpeted hallway.

Her left hand squeezing into a tight fist, she wanted to scream at the Woman, jump up and down with her arms flapping and perhaps even shoot her. But Harmony needed her more. So, she calmed herself, readied her weapon and waited for the Woman to move.

A satisfied smile spread across the Woman's face and she nodded at JD like a proud mama.

Gritting her teeth, she stared heavenward before focusing back on the Woman's light gray eyes. "Gotta go." Soundlessly, her lips formed the words.

Brows furrowing over serious eyes, the Woman nodded and held up two fingers while pointing to the door with her other hand.

She nodded and mouthed, "Harmony." She flicked up her index finger, "Bad guy," and her middle finger joined, "Two."

Vehemently shaking her head, her monochrome curls fell around her face and she glowed even brighter in the hall. She held up three fingers. The word *three* rocketed from the Woman and through JD's brain.

Wincing with pain, her eyes flickered from the Woman to the door. "Three. *Shit,*" she whispered. "Two bad guys and Harmony. One guy, I could handle. Two, dicey." She hesitated, wanting to save the little girl. But, if things went to crap, then she might lose her.

The Woman's eyes widened and she glowed brighter, the brightest JD had ever seen. Her transparent form flew down and hall and she pointed at the door. Her gaze was frantic and intense.

JD realized it was now or never. "Time to go," she muttered.

Steadily, she moved towards the door. Her muscles tightened, and her gaze fixed on the target before her. Without hesitation, she pressed her lips together and traveled through the Woman's ghostly form before swiftly raising her boot and planting a hard push kick next to the door knob. The thin paneled door crumpled back against the interior wall and she entered, weapon ready.

Startled shouts bounced off the walls of the well-lit room. Taken by surprise, the occupants froze, dumbfounded by her presence.

Bright cylinder stage lights, supported by tripods, blinded her for a moment. From the brilliance of the lights, two black dots filled her vision and partially blocked her view of the room, and its inhabitants. She blinked rapidly and attempted to recover her full vision, losing valuable seconds.

Her gaze swept the room. She distinguished within the fuzzy dark dots a huge, older black man that was clad only in boxers with a large gut protruding over his elastic waist band. His jaw flapped open and closed and he stood sentry by a professional movie camera, complete with sound bar. Thick black wires lined the floor and traveled from the film equipment to a computer and wall plugs. Not pausing her forward momentum, she side kicked the large man back into the jumble of lights and cords and her gaze continued sweeping for Harmony.

In the middle of the room, stood a brass, four poster bed draped with a gauzy pink canopy and white satin bedding. In a demur, white cotton nightgown, that only just covered her bare bottom, perched little Harmony. Her slender arms were wrapped tightly around her bent legs, and the top of her forehead scrapped her bare knees.

Still as a statue, a skeleton of a man kneeled before the little girl. His pale, naked skin was luminescent under the bright lights. With his white cock proudly raised, his scrawny form was covered from chin to belly button with the tattooed faces of children. Boys, girls, black, white and brown were inked on his body for eternity.

JD's piercing gaze bounced from him back to Harmony. Her hair was pulled back from her face by a bright pink bow and curled into blonde ringlets that bounced with her sobs. She sat frozen in place, hugging her knees and JD's mind shifted to a time she never visited in her past. To a crappy hotel, where her mom had sat frozen on a bed, hugging her knees. Only one thought rebounded through her mind and scratched deep grooves through her consciousness. *No more lost children.*

Her roar filled the room and she brought justice in the form of a swift round kick that slammed hard into the base of the skeleton man's skull. He crumpled in a heap, knocked out cold.

Turning, she pivoted her weapon to the other man left in the room. Having regained his feet, the man held his hands up in front of his face, the fat under his chin jiggling with his movements. "Don't shoot."

"On the floor!" she yelled. Anger raged through her veins. "Face down. Now!" She leveled her weapon towards the man's crotch. "Or I shoot your dick off." She wanted more than anything to pull the trigger.

Amidst broken bulbs and wires, he dropped face first on the floor, his bald head reflecting the remaining lights in the small bedroom.

"Lace your fingers behind your head. Now!" Cautiously, she approached. Grinding her boot down on his face, she held him in place. She holstered her weapon in the small of her back, removed a zip tie from her back pocket and reached down to secure the man's hands.

Suddenly, the man's thick hand snaked out, grabbing her heel and jerking her foot high.

She was propelled backward and landed hard on her back. The holstered gun slammed into her spine and the back of her head hit the dirty carpet, rattling her teeth. The force of her fall expelled the air from her lungs.

Moving extraordinarily fast for his massive size, the fat man was on top of her, grappling for the gun behind her back. His huge belly nailed her to the floor. Raring up, she caught him with a swift elbow to the jaw, before slamming her palm into the soft underside of his nose. Blood spurted and instantly covered both of them.

The fat man howled in pain and stanched the flow of blood with his hands.

She reached down, withdrew the knife from her boot and sliced the man's side.

Recoiling as if burned, he pulled back. Knowing it was now or never, she surged her hips upward and over, flipping him over. Now, she straddled his massive stomach. Crawling up the gigantic bastard, she pinned one of his wrists to the floor with her knee and positioned her other shin on the side of his neck where his carotid artery pumped oxygen to this brain. Pressing her leg down with all her weight, she cut off the blood flow. Her knife at the ready, she watched until the bastard's eyes fluttered closed and he no longer moved beneath her. She slapped him on the back of his bald head. "Have a good nap, asshole."

Breathing heavily and covered in blood, she rolled the fat bastard over and secured his hands and ankles with zip ties. Gaining her feet, she wobbled for a moment from the rush of blood to her head. Sighing deeply, she walked forward and secured the skeleton man and tossed him on top of his partner before turning to Harmony.

For a moment, JD just sat on the edge of the frilly bed. Leaning forward, she propped her elbows on her legs and allowed her hands to dangle while she calmed her breathing. Harmony was still crying into her knees and JD envisioned her mom. She couldn't help her mom, but she could help this little girl. "Harmony."

The girl stiffened and sniffled.

She rubbed her tired eyes with her knuckles and shifted more towards the little girl. "Harmony, I'm sorry there're bad people in this world. But right now, you're safe. I won't let them hurt you."

The girl raised her head. A thick foundation coated her skin that was shades darker than her china doll complexion. Florescent pink lip gloss was lacquered to her lips. Heavy electric blue eyeshadow weighted down her lids and her once child-like eyes brimmed now with grown-up tears. Stained with black eyeliner, tears dribbled over, running thick tracks down her still chubby cheeks and dripping off her chin.

JD lifted her hand and wiped some of the eyeliner away with the pad of her thumb. "Did they put this makeup on you?"

She nodded, her hair springing around her.

Snorting and twisting her features into a funny face, she declared, "Well, they suck at it."

A giggle escaped Harmony's lips. She studied the stranger

before her, judging her and weighing her trustfulness. Her chin trembled, then she launched herself at JD. Wrapping her skinny arms around her neck she sobbed hard into her shoulder.

She hugged the little girl tight and let her cry. Brushing the curls on the back of her head, she wished she could erase everything the girl had endured. Once her tears settled down into hitching breaths, she asked, "Do you want to help me take out the trash?"

Harmony lifted her head and confusion filled her gaze. "Trash?"

Thumbing her nose at the two men piled on top of each other, she raised a brow and considered the little girl. The choice she made now would determine her future course. Would she remain cowered on the bed and allow the past to rule her future? Or would she take action and set her own destiny. She waited. Only Harmony could decide her path.

Stiffening, the young girl considered the two men. Tremors shook her body and her chest hitched with her suppressed emotions. Turning back to JD, her painted lips squished into a thin line. "Take out the trash."

A proud smile spread across her face and she hugged Harmony tight. She too had experienced the powerless feeling of being a child at the mercy of an adult. "That's your first step in taking your power back. You just showed how strong you are. Resilient. You're going to be just fine."

Intensely, Harmony gazed up into JD's eye. "Do you think so?"

"I don't think so." She removed her leather jacket and helped Harmony weave her arms within the warmth. "I know so."

Off the floor, JD snatched up and shook out a pair of jeans the little girl's size. She handed them to her before grabbing a pair of purple and white sneakers. "Cute shoes," she said with a wink.

A tear slipped from the corner of Harmony's eye. "My mom and I bought them."

Crouching down before the girl, JD leveled her gaze, "I know people who will take care of you. Get you back to your parents.

They're on their way. Let's take out the trash until they arrive. You get dressed and I'll take care of the fat bastard. Then we will pull the skeleton down together."

Looking at the two men trussed up on the floor, she nodded. "He does look like a skeleton. An ugly, mean skeleton."

JD did just as she promised. After taking care of the fat bastard, together they dragged the skeleton through the filthy house and out the back door, depositing them in the snow beside the dog. Sirens wailing in the distance, they released the dog and used the heavy chain to wrap the two men to the tree.

Later, JD sat in the front seat of her SUV. She watched the boys in blue, Rodriguez and Mrs. Malloy handling the situation. Noisy neighbors shivered in the cold, unwilling to miss any of the excitement so they could gossip. She waved to Harmony. Bundled up in a blanket and sitting in the back of an Ambulance, the girl's blue eyes stared at her. Little Harmony was lucky—she had parents at home anxiously waiting for her. Some didn't.

JD's childhood path had been different. She never knew her father. Her mother, well, she'd killed her when she left candles lit in their motel room and the window open. The cheap curtains had caught on fire and set the whole motel room ablaze.

For three years, she'd lived within the system, moving from group home to group home. She understood the law of the land. Only the strong survived. If it weren't for Mrs. Malloy sending prospective families to the orphanage, she never would've found a real home and a real family.

She'd be a statistic just like the girl before her. She knew in her gut that she'd be a fatal statistic if Milton Wolfe hadn't come to the home searching for a little girl for his wife and a sister for his son, Jaxon. They'd brought her into their pack, given her their last name, and had protected and loved her. It was then Diamond had become Justyne Diamond Wolfe.

Through the family company, White Wolfe Investigations, she'd found her life calling. Tracking down and helping as many children as she could. Giving them the justice they deserved. The job paid decently, but it wasn't about the money. She stashed away every penny so that she could one day give the other kids what she found with the Wolfe's. A home, a true home. A place where lost souls would have a chance to heal and gain their power back.

A whine from the back seat of her car caused her to reach out and turn up the heat. Not too much heat, too fast. The dog's frozen body needed to adjust gradually to the changes in temperature. She and Rodriguez had a hell of time getting the huge mutt into her car. "What am I going to do with you now?" she asked the dog, studying him from her rear-view mirror.

Gradually, the Woman materialized in the back seat and filled the car with lavender. Settling in, she sat with the dog's head in what would've been her lap, but was just empty air.

Hoping to gain relief from the awful smell, JD cracked a window. The phone in her boot buzzed and she dug it out. "Hey, Jax. What's up?" she murmured absentmindedly. The sun rose above the townhouses, warming the earth with its rays. The neighbors faded way, either going to work or losing interest in all the early morning excitement.

"Hi, JD. Heard you found the boy and were already on a new case. Got a minute?"

She inched the window down a little more and turned up the heat to compensate for the cold air rushing in. "Just painting my nails. What do you want?"

Her brother's deep voice hummed across the line. "Well, as you probably know I'm working an insurance fraud case in the Blue Ridge Mountains of Virginia."

She snickered under her breath. "Yeah, Lee said you screwed it up. Scuttlebutt is you need a woman to finish the job. Not like you Jax. Getting lax in your old age? Lax Jax. That's what the Geezers will call you." She could almost hear Jaxon grinding his teeth over the phone before continuing. She bit her lip to keep from laughing at his obvious discomfort. "Lee wanted to send me in but we got the call to find little Harmony."

"Is that the case you're on? Did you find her?"

A smile spread across JD's face as wide as the freckles peppering her nose and cheeks. "Yes, Mrs. Malloy and Rodriguez assure me that she'll be back with her family by lunch time. Harmony Scott might have missed Thanksgiving, but she'll have Christmas."

"You're amazing. There isn't a better tracker in the States. Hell, probably in the world. Don't know how you do it, but I'm glad you do."

Jaxon's pride flowed over the phone, warming her. A part of her enjoyed his praise but she pushed away the weakness. Glancing up to her rear-view mirror again, her light green gaze clashed with the Woman's gray one before bouncing away and focusing in on the dwindling crowd. "Don't go getting all misty on me," irritation laced her voice. "What the hell do you want Lax Jax?"

He stuttered.

She frowned and rubbed the back of her neck where the muscles had relaxed and released the tension of her hunt. "Spit it out."

"I'm going to ask a woman to marry me," his breath whooshed in her ear. "There, are you happy? Couldn't let me just say it in my own time."

Listening to her brother grumble across the phone, she felt like a piece of her was being ripped away. Of course, she knew he'd one day marry but the thought of losing him hurt. "No shit," she whispered. "Do the Geezers know?"

"God, I hope not. Look, can you come out?"

"Don't know what to do with a woman, huh? Perhaps Lee can help you out. I'll dial him right now. We can conference call. Get you fixed right up. If we can't help you, then," she paused for drama, "we'll have to go to the Geezers."

Her brother's voice was low and deep and promised repercussions. "My dear, sweet sister—screw you."

Busting into laughter, she pounded her palm on the steering wheel and wiped the moisture away from her eyes with the back of her hand. "Isn't that the problem, Lax Jax? You're lacking in that department."

An ominous growl came through the phone, causing her to laugh harder. "Stop the bullshit. I need you."

Instantly, she straightened, and the laughter faded from her lips. Her brother never needed her. Never. All business, she replied, "Okay. Whatever you need."

A long, drawn out breath escaped him. "The woman I want to marry owns the hotel I was sent to investigate. It's all on the up and up. They aren't filing fraudulent claims. But the damage that was done to the hotel has created a financial burden. Bookings are down, and until the insurance money comes through, the hotel needs to draw in more guests and the revenue they bring. I was hoping you would—," he paused.

She waited for him to continue, but silence stretched between them. "I would what?"

"It would be a huge boon to the hotel for the artist DiWolf to display her works for the first time at my fiancée's hotel. The first ever meet and greet with the reclusive artist."

Revulsion rolled down her spine. She felt exposed when connected to the raw feelings that she'd inked onto paper with her art. Each piece, a glimpse into soul. Into the dreams that haunted her. It was easier just to let others handle the sales of the pieces she dared to part with. "Are you crazy? A meet and greet? You want me to parade around, shake hands and actually talk with people over four feet? Do you want me to wear a damn dress too?"

Her brother backtracked. "No. Okay. It's a lot to ask. Maybe not a meet and greet. How about just displaying your artwork? Please, Diamond."

JD brooded. Thought about her brother's request. He never called her Diamond. She looked over the scene before her and Harmony waved goodbye from the ambulance. She returned the little girl's wave with a little two finger salute. She wanted more than anything to help lost children like her.

Perhaps her artwork was the way. Perhaps it was time to turn her back on the past and use her artwork to help others. Others, who unlike Harmony, didn't have a family waiting at home to love them. *Damn it. If I'm going to deal with strangers, then I might as well go all the way and hold an auction to finance my dream of opening a good home for children in need. Anyway, adults are just tall children. Aren't they?*

Silence stretched over the phone until Jaxon spoke. Defeat laced his subdued voice. "Don't worry about it. But I still need you to come out. There's a painting here you must see. No one will need to know you're DiWolf."

Ignoring her brother's comment, her thoughts ran full steam ahead. She could do it. *Slap some palms, smile for a camera. That kind of shit.* "I'll do it. A meet and greet. Plus, I'll auction off some pieces. Ten percent of the proceeds go back to the hotel."

He sputtered over the phone, "You don't have to—"

A long, low whine emitted from the back and she stopped listening and glanced up. In her rear-view mirror, the Woman stroked the dog's matted fur and began swaying as she hummed a song within JD's head. Furrowing her brow, she glared at the ghost, who returned her look with a bright smile. Snarling, she mumbled, "Gotta go," and hung up on her brother mid-sentence.

Putting her car in gear, she absentmindedly waved to Rodriguez and Mrs. Malloy. As they became pin pricks in the distance, the Woman also faded from sight, confirming what she knew in her heart. She'd never marry and have children. Kids were for other women. Women who didn't see and talk to ghosts. Women who couldn't pass the insanity gene on to their children for them to be tormented. She'd never do that to her child.

She'd endured years of being tormented and teased because others couldn't see the Woman she talked to. The system had tried to help by sending her to their psychiatrists with all the fancy letters following their name. But nothing could help her. Not the therapy, not the drugs they prescribed and not the hypnosis. She rubbed her temple where they'd placed the leads of their torture machine. Sure as hell not the shock treatments.

She'd been committed to the loony bin for six months, before she was dragged out by Mrs. Malloy and placed in the orphanage. During that half year, she'd learned a hard lesson. If you don't want to be strapped down, drugged, and have experiments done on you, then don't let people know you see and talk to a ghost. But Mrs. Malloy and the Wolfes had saved her. From then on, she'd learned to keep her mouth shut, her boots on and her weapons ready.

CHAPTER FIVE

Unlike the families celebrating Thanksgiving at Twin Springs Hotel and Spa, Logan Oakes didn't spend the day stuffing his face with turkey and all the trimmings. He was holed up in his hooch. The parachute material was a sorry excuse of a shelter. Barely kept the cold away. Nevertheless, he couldn't stand the thought of being trapped in a building. Like his team.

What if fire snuck up on him? Again. Or worse, trapped him in a building?

In his mind's eye, he pictured Amethyst Fairbanks' portrait. Her beautiful, green eyes, full of kindness. Red hair framed her sweet face and made her skin appear milky white. Pure. "I'm pitiful," he groaned. Drawn to a dead woman like a moth to a flame. "Perhaps it's because she also experienced the wrath of fire before she died."

Like her, a sea of flames had extinguished any chance of love. He'd never experience it for a day, an hour or even a second. Not like the passion his friends enjoyed.

He continued talking to himself, anything to keep sleep away. The flashbacks away. "How quickly love grew between Isabella and Theo. Between Ava and Jaxon."

First hand, he'd witnessed a love powerful enough that it

enabled a man to traverse freezing water or run into a burning building to save his soul mate. "It's humbling." His lips curved into a slight smile. "They deserve it."

Still, a searing pain for the loss of something he'd never felt and would never experience, pierced him. Willingly, his battered body absorbed the additional agony as he pushed buds deep into his ears and flicked his music on loud in a futile attempt to mute the ringing in his brain and drown out the memories. "Better to live in a tent than to fail my friends again. Besides, animals belong in the woods."

He chuckled and mocked himself. "I fooled myself," he stared into the dark. "Thought I could walk among the living." However, living in the human world was too painful and fate had proved him wrong. "Face it asshole," he condemned himself, "no one will let you forget how disgusting you look. You're unfit for human eyes."

He rubbed the beard on the left side of his face, the untouched side. "At least with my beard hiding the man I once was, no one will question what I've become. An animal. The beast fire forged.

"Half man, half beast, no one wants you."

Pulling his poncho tighter over his head, Logan attempted to ignore the biting cold and meld with his music. The ringing in his ears had abated but the cold had seeped deep into his bones. "Too damn cold for November," he grumbled and blared his music even louder.

"What does it matter if I freeze to death? During the day, the world can't stand the sight of me. At night, I can't stand the thought of my sleep being infiltrated by the memories of what turned me into a monster." He lay there, staring into the dark, ignoring the wind penetrating the tent and fighting the sleep attempting to overcome his resolve to stay awake.

"Don't close your eyes. Don't fall asleep." He stretched and found a sharp rock beneath him. Ground his back into the rock. Pain renewed his strength. "Stay awake. Otherwise the dead will come."

Will play out behind his lids. He'd be back with the ghosts of his team or watching Director Hollingsworth stumble from the barn, his body engulfed by flames, his death screams filling the air until the only thing that remained was white silence and burned flesh. "Screw that."

However, memories of smoldering death had plagued him way before the Director's fiery end. It was that memory that hunted him. The one where the putrid stench of burning flesh wasn't only his own, but that of those he loved. Respected. That was the dream he feared.

Pushing back against the heaviness of his lids, he pulled his eyes wide. "Maybe if I hold sleep at bay long enough, then when exhaustion finally over takes me the dream won't register. My brain will be too exhausted to remember it." He blinked to help the dryness. "Maybe."

Little by little, his lids lowered, and his body slumped. A deep slumber filled his body, eased the tension from his muscles, weakened him and left him vulnerable to the deep recesses of his brain. Shuffling in his sleep, he fought the inevitable and the nightmare overtook him. . .

. . .Normally the dry desert air stifled Sergeant First Class Logan Oakes but, after eighteen different missions in the sandbox, he'd learned to ignore it. Today the air lay eerily quiet.

Through his night vision goggles, the world around him was cast into shades of green. He adjusted his stance and raised the tip of his M-4 rifle up, ready. Long barrel today. Just in case he needed to take out a shooter on a roofline.

He scanned the flat roofed, ugly gray building to his left, then the hulled-out hospital that his fellow Americans had built on his right. No movement. He never understood why the locals had stripped the hospital bare of anything of value after the allies had left, but they did. Down to the pipes and electrical wiring.

Something was wrong. He checked the muted face of his watch. He felt it. All was quiet, too quiet. Rolling his shoulders, he attempted to push off the feeling. Quiet was also good, though. Get in, grab the head of a new terrorist cell plus his right-hand man and get out before the city woke for morning prayers. That was the plan.

The rest of his team had already entered the squatty building and he was covering their six. In his mind, he followed his team through the building and waited for confirmation that they'd connected with Tango one and Tango two. Taking them alive was the mission. Plus any intel. Still, his headset was silent.

Had the cell bugged out? Maybe it was bad intel. Naw, Wolfeman had verified it. If Wolfeman said the intel was good, it was spot on. He was never wrong. His instincts had saved their asses more than a few times. He resisted the urge to glance up at Wolfeman's sniper perch in the upper right window of the hospital and give him away.

Logan checked the target pack on his wrist. The area photo showed a picture of the two story building. Each side color coded. They'd entered through the green side, as planned. Still, something didn't sit right. His headset was unusually quiet. "Sixty seconds till exfil," he murmured into his throat mic.

No reply.

Like a dog with a prize T-bone, the bad feeling sunk its sharp teeth into his bones and chewed relentlessly. He paused at the door, studied the area and searched for something. He didn't know what.

Suddenly, his headset went nuts. A jumble of voices sounded off. The whole team was sounding off over each other and chopping the line into unintelligible gibberish. A shout reached out from within the belly of the building. Then another. The bad feeling sunk its teeth in and ripped at his bones, no longer a suspicion but fact. His team needed him.

Ready and willing to sprint inside and join the fight to defend his brothers, he jerked the door open. A creaking sound to his left distracted him. Immediately, his head turned to confront the added threat. Across his headset the code word "Avalanche" was shouted. BOMB. Too late.

The sand trembled beneath his boots before a whoosh of air wrapped an invisible fist around his body and dragged him inside the open doorway. Just as quickly, the blast of air expelled him, spitting a rolling ball of flames over his body and propelling him back twenty feet through the air.

Screaming pierced the air. Horrible screams. Death screams. Engulfed within a terrible heat, he staggered to his feet. He must help his brothers. Through a fiery glowing haze, he observed one, then two of his brothers spilling from the building, now an inferno from hell. An inferno ate at their camo uniforms and illuminated the horror melting on their faces. The gut wrenching screams continued to puncture the air and combined with the screams of his brothers-in-arms, branding his brain with their agony.

Collapsing onto his knees, Logan rolled in the tan dirt and pebbles. Feverishly, he attempted to kill the flames that licked at his right side. Rising to his hands and knees, he inched forward. The smell of burning flesh smothered him as he crawled. Dirt caked the smoldering wounds on his body. Smoke scorched his lungs. A single mantra tattooed a mission within him, "Regain my fighting position. Aid my brothers. Get everyone home alive."...

Logan rolled over in his poncho. He'd made it through another night. "Damn it."

Rubbing his fists against his eyes, he attempted to grind away at the memory filled dream. He laid back and stared unseeingly at the top of his tent, blinded to the fact that the snow from the previous night had partially collapsed his hooch.

Even though the nightmare was no longer reality, a foul taste coated his mouth. The flavors of a banked fire, smoke and burned flesh mixed with great loss and failure. His dry tongue rolled around within his mouth in a vain attempt to dispel the nauseating combination.

He smacked his lips, swallowed hard and thought about his last mission with his Special Forces team. It wasn't until after the mission, when he laid in the hospital, wrapped in loose gauze bandages, and reported a haphazard bedside debriefing that he'd realized the screams filling the desert air that day were not only his brothers, but his own.

Cold air penetrated the tent and seeped into his bones. He welcomed the freezing temperatures. It banked the fire, cooled his heated memories and froze the pain of his failures, past and present. As usual, the dream had increased the constant ringing within his brain. He massaged his right ear, where it melted into his skull. He didn't try to fool himself. He understood why he'd pitched his tent in Virginia's Blue Ridge Mountains during the dead of winter. "I'm a worthless piece of shit."

The snapping of the tent's door being thrust back didn't register through the heavy metal music that blared in his ears. The flash of late morning light, shining through the olive-green parachute material of his poncho, brought him on high alert and tensed his muscles. Before he could react, hands grasped his ankles and dragged him out of his make shift tent, poncho and all. He threw off the binds of the material and his muscles tensed when his mind commanded his body spring up into a fighting stance. Partially upright, pain seared through his hip. His leg crumpled beneath him and he collapsed backward. Unable to pull himself up out of his muddy position, Logan raised his fists and prepared himself for the beating that would follow when he lost the fight.

ACKNOWLEDGMENTS

As with everything in life, nothing worth having is created in a vacuum.

I would like to acknowledge the superstars in my life. They're my balcony people. The ones who believed in me when my own faith faltered. The ones who supported me with my dream of writing.

First and foremost, I would like to thank God for giving me such a great hunger to create.

My father, who when I told him that I wanted to write novels, treated me as if I was already a successful published author.

My mother, who gave me the love of reading and checks every page for errors that I've missed.

My husband, who has supported me unconditionally, pushes me for excellence and threatens to send me to the "cabin" if I'm allowing the silly stuff to derail my writing dream. (Once, I rented a cabin to write in for a week. I was so lonely that I came home after one day.)

My daughter, Kasie, who kept the light lit in the window and rejected the naysayers. One of my greatest cheerleaders.

My daughter, Lacey, my voracious reader. She read every version and spread the word on my books. Another one of my greatest cheerleaders!

My son, Kody, who stuns me with his imagination and his natural storytelling. One day, my son, you too will write, and the world will be better for it.

My Developmental Editor, Tessa Shapcott. She pushed me to

write the best stories possible and, with her British whit, challenged me and allowed me to grow while lifting my spirits.

Copy Editor Shannon Eversoll, who fine-tunes everything to a professional shine. Checking all those P's and Q's.

This book wouldn't have been the same without each and every one of you.

I have been truly blessed.

-Dee

ABOUT THE AUTHOR

Dee Armstrong writes thrillers and romantic suspense with a paranormal twist — stories that squeeze the heart, rattle the nerves, and still leave room for love, laughter, and sass. She pits tough heroines against bad guys you'll love to hate — with twists that keep the pages flying and endings that fight for hope.

A former U.S. Air Force Russian linguist and three-time Taekwondo Black Belt National Sparring Champion, Dee believes the vulnerable should be protected and justice must be fierce—because the past never stays buried, and the truth never sleeps.

When she's not writing about danger and desire, Dee is chasing after her littles, sipping tea on the porch, and plotting against the weeds in her garden.

Find her at www.DeeArmstrong.com or @DeeArmstrongAuthor for sneak peeks, behind-the-scenes chaos, and stories that leave a fingerprint on your heart.

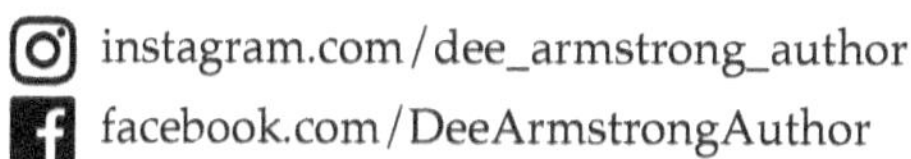

www.ingramcontent.com/pod-product-compliance
Lightning Source LLC
Chambersburg PA
CBHW031613180726
48284CB00005B/1523